"Thank you." Wolf [...] [...]
assist her departure. "[...] [...]
your father finds you mi[...] [...] e
a *real* strong suspicion, Miss Malone, that your father hasn't
the slightest idea you are here. Nor does your mother."

"And to inform you," she continued as if he hadn't said a
word, "that whenever you've a mind to ask me to marry you,
the answer shall be yes."

"Wha . . . what?" Wolf swept around the chair in front of
her and bent at the knee. He studied her face, disbelieving
what he'd heard. Her eyes held not a hint of mockery. The
heady scent of roses filled his nostrils again—and that alluring scent that was hers alone. This was a hell of a time
to let her plump, moist mouth distract him. "Leave, Miss
Malone."

She sat steadfast and resolute. Unblinking.

Perhaps she was daft after all. The dull thud in his head
returned with a vengeance. "What the hell are you up to?
Are you trying to get me killed?"

Also by Kathleen Bittner Roth

Celine

Published by Kensington Publishing Corporation

Alanna

Kathleen Bittner Roth

ZEBRA BOOKS
KENSINGTON PUBLISHING CORP.
http://www.kensingtonbooks.com

ZEBRA BOOKS are published by

Kensington Publishing Corp.
119 West 40th Street
New York, NY 10018

All Kensington titles, imprints and distributed lines are available at special quantity discounts for bulk purchases for sales promotion, premiums, fund-raising, educational or institutional use.

Special book excerpts or customized printings can also be created to fit specific needs. For details, write or phone the office of the Kensington Special Sales Manager. Attn: Special Sales Department. Kensington Publishing Corp., 119 West 40th Street, New York, NY 10018. Phone: 1-800-221-2647.

Zebra Books and the Z logo Reg. U.S. Pat. & TM Off.

First Printing: November 2014
ISBN-13: 978-1-4201-3530-5
ISBN-10: 1-4201-3530-9

First Electronic Edition: November 2014
eISBN-13: 978-1-4201-3531-2
eISBN-10: 1-4201-3531-7

10 9 8 7 6 5 4 3 2 1

Printed in the United States of America

To my mother, Glenda McGillivray Bittner.
You shared your love of the written word with me,
and then you encouraged me to become a writer.
I wish you were still here
so I could share my stories with you.

Prologue

Boston—Christmas night, 1830

From an upper-story window, the six-year-old boy watched a lone figure scurry from the mansion and vanish into a swirling vortex of snow. A lump caught in his throat. He swallowed hard, fighting the dread pounding through his veins.

Mrs. Guthrie was the last of the servants to leave the five-story brick manse, gone off to spend what remained of Christmas with her family. A shudder racked the boy's body at the idea of spending the night alone in his room. Dejected, he turned and made his way toward his bed, glancing none too bravely at a doorway alive with shadows.

A soft thud echoed from below.

He froze.

His thoughts scattered as he strained to hear past the sudden pounding in his ears.

Another thud.

Unholy fear shot him down the dark corridor and into his parents' room. His mother lay propped against a mass of soft pillows with a book in her lap, firelight casting a soft glow over her smile.

"Mummy!" He clambered onto the four-poster with breathless little grunts.

His mother slid an arm around him and pulled him into her warmth. "Is that old tree thumping against the house again, dear?"

He snuggled tight against her. "Uh-huh."

She brushed her cheek across the top of his head. "Your father will see to its removal when he returns from England, sweetheart. Would you like me to read you to sleep?"

"Uh-huh." He slid an arm around her middle and cuddled closer. The familiar, safe scent of Mum mingling with the fragrance of fresh linens soon beckoned him into the lazy space between sleep and consciousness. He lay without thought now, wrapped in warm blankets and the security of gentle arms.

A sound, like the shattering of glass, broke the silence. His mother's stiffened body threw him wide-awake.

"Mummy?"

"Shh!"

Muffled noises swept through the house. A distinct shift took place, as though the very currents of air around them wailed in violation.

Hot terror gripped his heart. "Oh, Mummy, that's not the tree—"

Her fingers pressed hard against his mouth. "Not a word." Bundling a blanket around him, she snatched him off the bed and stuffed him underneath it. "There you go, up against the wall." She kissed him, covered his face, and then crawled back onto the bed.

He whimpered.

"No!" she whispered. "Whatever occurs, do not move or make a sound until I tell you it is safe. No one will see you in the shadows if you lie perfectly still."

Fingers trembling, he managed a slit in the folds of the

blanket. Across the room, a full-length mirror tilted at an angle cast a dim reflection of his mother through smoky glass, her eyes round and darting about the room.

When the door swung wide, she shifted on the bed, the creaking loud in the boy's ears. Polished black shoes and the lower half of a man's pant legs appeared. The boy crammed a corner of the blanket into his mouth to keep from crying out.

"You!" his mother gasped.

The door slammed and the boy gritted his teeth against a shivering that threatened to take hold of his body. A hard click of heels on the wood floor, and the back of a thick-necked man with black hair materialized in the mirror. He moved to the bed.

Mute cries exploded in the boy's head. *Mummy!*

"Well, well, well." The man stood before her, the tips of his shoes under the bed, his words a harsh rasp. "I don't have to tell you no one will come to your aid now, do I? You know what I came for."

Pressed deep against the pillows, the boy's mother held the covers tight against her chest. "You'll not find what you seek in this house."

"And where will I, madam?"

When she failed to respond, his hand cracked hard against the side of her face. "Cease your foolishness!"

The boy stuffed more of the blanket into his mouth.

The man bolted from beside the bed. Snarling and cursing, he flung open drawers and wardrobes, the contents spilling onto the floor in great heaps. He moved back to the bed and knelt. Heavy grunts—so close—shot a new wave of panic through the boy. He squeezed his eyes shut and held his breath until his lungs burned. He nearly wept as his bladder betrayed him and emptied its contents into the blanket. Would the man be able to smell the wool now dripping with hot urine?

A soft knock sounded at the door. The man rose and moved toward the noise. The boy's eyes shot open. The mirrored image evaporated, leaving only shoes and pant legs visible once again. Another set of shoes appeared at the open door. A muffled argument flared and then faded. The door slammed shut and the man returned to the bed.

"You are making me quite angry now, madam," he bellowed. "If I have to force you to talk, things will become quite unpleasant for you." The man's reflection in the mirror wavered as he leaned over the bed and dug his squat hands into her arms.

"Please," she whimpered.

A strangled sound gurgled from the man's throat. He hit her again. Blood smeared the side of her mouth.

Oh, Mummy. How could he help her? He should stop this. But cowardly fear kept the boy plastered to the wall.

The man struck her once more, then planted his knee on the bed and dug into her throat. He shook her like a rag doll, violent animal sounds whistling through his teeth. At last he released her, tossed her against the pillows, and left the room, closing the door behind him.

The terrified boy huddled beneath the bed, his gaze fixed on the reflection of his mum's unmoving figure. One of her arms dangled over the edge of the mattress. She had not told him to move yet, nor to speak, but he spied one of her ear bobs lying on the floor. With a trembling hand, he snatched up the bauble and buried it in the folds of the blanket.

The door swung open again. The man's shoes and pant legs appeared once more and moved to the bed. He searched for something before bending to the floor again. "Damn it!" His hand brushed along the floorboards, sweeping danger- ously close. The bed gave and creaked as he lifted himself upright. He ripped the remaining earring from her ear, and then made his exit.

Afraid to call out lest the bad man return, the boy huddled beneath the bed, staring at his sleeping mother's reflection while the blazing fire dwindled to ash and the room chilled. After awhile, he came to the devastating realization that calling out would do no good. Tears streaked his cheeks, but the horror of it all, and fear of the man's return, held him fast to the wall.

Two servants found the boy and his dead mother the next morning. Terrified of the murderer, they secretly transported him to the countryside to await his father's return. Lonely and grief-stricken, the boy clutched to his heart the one tangible thing he had left by which to remember his mother— the gold and garnet earring.

Days turned into months, and months into years, but his father never came.

Chapter One

San Francisco—1854—Twenty-four years later

"Tell me something, Wolf. How long do you intend to track down everyone else's problems before you decide to find whoever it was that murdered your mother?"

A ghost-cold finger ran up Wolf's spine at the serious edge to the feminine voice floating across the table, snapping him out of his torpor. He shifted in his seat, glanced about the elegant dining room of the hotel Dianah's family owned, and realized silence hadn't pervaded the space after all. In fact, the air around him buzzed with conversation, the hard edges softened by the mellow notes emanating from a piano set in a far corner.

After drinking steadily for two days, Wolf had turned to sipping water these past few hours. Nonetheless, his mouth went dry. Years of living on horseback while he tracked lost people had left him with a fatigue that could no longer be abated. He'd been on the trail for weeks with Trevor Andrews, searching for his fiancée, who'd been snatched by Indians, and then spent the winter bringing the woman safely to San Francisco. The thought of climbing on his horse in the morning and heading back home to Missouri left him about as excited as he would be to eat a plank of wood.

How many predators would he fight before he made a fatal mistake? How many more times would he turn his bounty over to someone who paid him well, only to find himself alone once he rode off? And how many more goddamn months or years before he simply dropped from the saddle and didn't bother getting up?

"Well?" The prompt came from Cameron Andrews, Trevor's cousin and co-owner of the lucrative Andrews Shipping Company Limited, who sat next to Dianah.

Cameron's serious tone unsettled Wolf nearly as much as Dianah's questions. They were the only two friends he had left now that Trevor and Celine had married and sailed off to China. And these two weren't friends very long in the making. "Go ahead, Dianah. Speak your piece, because I have nothing to say."

Cameron lifted a forkful of chocolate cake to his lips. "Ever the diplomat, aren't you?"

Wolf shoved his plate aside and regarded both Cameron and Dianah. Cameron spoke with an odd mix of French Creole Southern drawl and British accent—the former from his roots in the French Quarter, the latter from a Cambridge education. As for Dianah, her Southern accent would likely remain thick as honey, no matter how long she lived in San Francisco.

She reached over the table and gently touched the garnet earring in Wolf's ear. "Does your search have anything to do with why you wear this?"

"Don't recall." Irritation hardened the edge of his already set jaw.

When he didn't say anything else, Cameron spoke. "There are three kinds of memory, Wolf—good, bad, and convenient. Since we're your friends, a convenient memory seems unnecessary."

"You just got boring." Wolf liked his life kept private. Very private. "But that's what I get for making friends who meddle in my affairs."

Cameron threw him a vexed look. "Meddle in your affairs? For God's sake, we don't even know your last name. We know so little of you and yet, after what you did for my cousin and his wife, we have given you our trust and loyalty. The least you can do is offer something in return. You intend to leave tomorrow, and we don't know when or if we'll see you again. I don't call that sporting."

Cameron's words cut through Wolf's chest like an arrow piercing a dove's breast. "You know the earring belonged to my mother and that someone murdered her. What the hell else do you need to know?"

"As much as will lighten your heart." Dianah lifted a silk fan to her face and blinked her green cat eyes at him. After an interminably long silence, she sighed and lowered the fan. "When you return to Missouri, either figure out who killed your mother, or remove that ear bob and bury it with her."

She reached over and covered his hand with hers. "You simply cannot wander around in the middle of nowhere without purpose forever. You're a prisoner of your own life choices, and it's wearing on you."

Wolf set his jaw again.

"And don't try masking your feelings with anger," she said. "I won't have it."

He'd never talked about his mother to anyone. Not once. He didn't know if he could get the words out. He slumped back in his chair and fingered the rim of his glass. "The murder didn't take place anywhere near Missouri." He cleared his throat, embarrassed by the way his voice broke.

Dianah gasped, while Cameron's brows knit together. "Then where?" he said.

To hell with just water. Wolf filled his glass with sherry. "Boston. It happened in Boston."

Cameron and Dianah shot curious glances at one another. "Boston?" Dianah asked. "You . . . you're not originally from Missouri?"

"Did I ever say I was?"

Cameron leaned over the table. "You never say much of anything, so how the devil were we to know you came from elsewhere? You've always referred to St. Joseph as your home. Not to mention, that's where my cousin located you. I have a ship leaving for Boston in two days. You could be on it. It's a clipper, the fastest-sailing vessel in the world. You'd be there in no time."

Christ, not on the water. Never again on the water. Wolf hedged. "I can ride back on my roan until I get to St. Joe, where I can hook up with a train heading east."

"Aha!" Cameron punctuated the air with his fork. "I've seen that look on a man's face before. You, *mon frère*, detest sailing." He dived back into his dessert with gusto. "But sail you must."

Wolf downed the sherry in one gulp and reached for a refill. "You pompous ass." He studied Cameron and Dianah for a long while. A realization that they were both right settled deep in his bones—it was time to resolve this once and for all. Past time. At the finality of his decision, a sudden shift in mood overcame him. He leaned back in his chair, lifting the front legs off the floor. "You've got a boat sailing in two days, you say?"

Cameron's eyebrow spiked. "Repeat after me. *Ship*. Never utter the word boat aboard one of my fine crafts or you'll be tossed overboard by the captain himself."

Dianah reached into a hidden pocket in her gown and stretched her closed fist over the table toward Wolf. "I was hoping you'd say yes. Hold out your hand."

Wolf slipped his hand under hers. A small golden hoop and a gold chain fell into his cupped palm. "What's this?"

"One of a pair of earrings I had as a child, and a chain on

which to carry the one in your ear. Even though it's been over twenty years, if whoever murdered your mother is still alive, he might recognize that earring you wear." She reached out and touched the garnet at his lobe.

He gave a jerk of his head.

"I know this is sacred to you, but wearing it could place you in jeopardy. It would behoove you to keep it under your clothing."

She shoved the golden hoop and chain his way. "This can stand as a symbol for your mother's."

Cameron reached over to inspect the earring. "Maybe you should forget a replacement altogether. Besides, this thing is too small for your elephant ear. *Merde*."

"Oh, hush." Dianah slapped at Cameron's fingers with her fan. She reached to remove the garnet earring from Wolf's lobe.

A cold, hard pain shot through him. He grasped her hand and slowly lowered it to the table. "I'll think on it."

Dianah's eyes widened a fraction. "All right." She wriggled her fingers free. "They're yours should you decide to take my advice."

Cameron grinned. "That hoop's so small, you'd look like an underpaid pirate."

Dianah waved Cameron off with her fan. "Cameron's going daft from drinking too much liquor."

Cameron stopped eating, his gaze directed to the door. "Don't all ogle at once, but would you look at the beauty who just walked in?"

Dianah inclined her head to the door. "That would be Mr. and Mrs. Malone and their daughter, Alanna. They are guests here at the hotel, so pray, be civil."

With a slow turn of his head, Wolf caught sight of the family in question.

The maitre d'hôtel escorted the tall, portly man and his

equally thick-waisted wife past them to a table, their noses in the air. In between the two floated their daughter.

"That lovely frock would be from Paris," Dianah murmured.

Cameron snorted. "He's not looking at the dress, Dianah. I doubt he could even name the color if his life depended on it."

The young woman wore a white gown emblazoned with large, navy flowers outlined in shimmering beads. But the bold design wasn't all that caused her to stand out in the room. The raven-haired beauty would have caused every head to turn no matter what her clothing. She was taller than her mother, and much more slender, and there was something strangely elusive about her that caused Wolf's blood to heat.

As the trio passed, so close Wolf caught the faint scent of cinnabar and roses, the girl turned her head and stared boldly at him, her cool demeanor at odds with the fire in her eyes. And then her lips parted, as if she needed more air. A punch of lust hit Wolf's groin.

Cameron leaned over the table. "She certainly cast a rather brazen glance your way, old boy."

Wolf checked an urge to shift about in the suddenly uncomfortable chair. He shrugged. "She has striking eyes."

Dianah lifted a finely arched brow. "In case you haven't looked in the mirror lately, you have the very same *striking* blue eyes."

Cameron sniggered. "I do believe he's fishing for a compliment, Dianah. What say you?"

Wolf moaned and leaned forward on his elbows, clutching the stem of his glass. "Since the human eye isn't found in too damn many colors, that leaves you about as clever as a preacher in a whorehouse." He drank his sherry in one guzzle, set his glass on the table with a thud, and leaned back in his chair. "Color's not what makes eyes remarkable. It's what's behind them that does. Maybe that's why yours have such a dull cast to them."

Dianah laughed softly as she tipped the bottle of spirits into Wolf's glass once again.

"No," Cameron said. "Although my eyes are indeed a decidedly clear, intelligent amber, *monsieur*, yours are of a different ilk. And they match Miss Malone's."

Wolf snorted. "*Amber*? Your eyes have a definite shade of bullshit to them, *mon sewer*. Comes from being filled with it." He shot Dianah a quick glance. "Sorry. This friend of yours drives me to the brink. Made me forget my good manners."

"Good manners?" Cameron was at the ready, but Dianah splayed her fingers across his chest, stopping him. "Wolf, the blue of your eyes is edged in black that makes them stand out against the whites, just like Miss Malone's. I know, I've seen her up close." The increased flicking of Dianah's fan gave away her cat-and-mouse game. "And by the way, she now studies you rather shamelessly."

He fought an intense urge to glance over Cameron's shoulder and across the room to the table holding the very intriguing Miss Malone.

Cameron eyed Wolf's untouched plate. "Do you intend to eat that?" Not bothering to wait for a response, he slid the plate his way. "You can forget about getting within ten feet of her." He raised a hand, stopping Wolf before he could make a snide retort. "Don't bother. Did you see the way her parents marched in here like a couple of gendarmes with their daughter stuffed between them?"

"Who said I was interested?" Wolf shot back.

Cameron smirked. "Your thinly veiled admiration, old boy. Would you like a surgeon called in to have your eyeballs set back in place?"

Dianah's velvet laughter bubbled over. "I'm willing to

wager that because of her parents, you could not get close enough to Miss Malone to so much as speak her name."

"Not interested." Wolf quit fighting the urge—he glanced across the room. Alanna Malone's sharp blue eyes struck the distance between them like summer lightning. But oddly, her exquisite face held no expression whatsoever. Caught squarely off guard again, Wolf raised the glass of sherry to his lips and watched her over the rim until she looked away.

"Care to wager?" Cameron was at it again.

"No."

"Ah, a man of so many words. Well, you would have lost." Cameron turned to Dianah. "I'll bet that chain hanging from her father's vest pocket doesn't hold a timepiece at all. Said pocket hides a key to a chastity belt. And one guess who's wearing the belt."

"I don't believe so, Cameron." Dianah tapped him on the shoulder with her folded fan. "If anyone carries a key to a chastity belt, it would be the mother."

Wolf shook his head and retreated from the conversation.

Mock seriousness knitted Cameron's brows together. "How so?"

"The mother has taken note of her daughter's reaction to Wolf." Dianah leaned discreetly over the table, whispering wickedly. "A woman knows that certain look. Believe me, the mother is the one who would carry the key to the belt, not the father."

Wolf rolled his eyes. "Jeezus. Together, you two form one demented brain. All of this in thirty seconds of someone's passing by?"

"Oh, it hasn't been just thirty seconds." Dianah fanned her face again until only her cat eyes appeared above the starched folds. "They were here when you wandered in two days ago."

Cameron set down his fork. "Miss Malone couldn't possibly have recognized him as the same man. Look at him now. Good Lord, he looks completely different. Almost humanlike."

Dianah tilted her head and with a sly grin, appraised Wolf. "I think women find you deliciously appealing. By the way, Miss Malone is still focused entirely on you. I think she knows you're the same man."

"Mind like a steel trap, this tracker of lost people," Cameron responded.

Wolf ignored Cameron. "You're picking at me, Dianah. Why?"

"Sweetheart, other than seducing women on the run, you fight intimacy with everyone you encounter. Why, that horse of yours is the only living creature you have for company for months on end and have you bothered to give it a name? I swear if I hear that beast referred to as *the roan* one more time, I'll shoot it."

"So why are you picking at me?" Wolf studied her now with a calm intensity, his voice smooth but insistent.

"I suppose I'm trying to make you think about a few things before you leave us. I sense a shift taking place in your life, and I sincerely hope the change will include opening up to the idea of loving someone."

"What makes you think something like that would be good for me?" Wolf managed his words without inflection.

"Because, dear one, we *all* need the balm of love. Love is what keeps us at peace. It heals our wounded souls, and Lord knows, yours is in need of a good healing."

Wolf's thoughts returned to the captivating young woman sitting across the room. As he glanced over her father's shoulder, the raven-haired woman met Wolf's gaze once again. His body wasted no time imagining nothing between the two of them but bare skin.

* * *

At the sight of him sitting very still in his chair, boldly staring at her, a buzz raced along Alanna's skin, then slipped inside and warmed her. There was pure sin in his startling blue eyes. The moment hung suspended between them, and then expanded as his feral gaze held hers, until finally, she tucked a smile into one corner of her mouth and looked at her plate. That her mother was aware of the silent communion between her daughter and this stranger held little significance.

Stranger? Not to Alanna. He went by the name of Wolf, and he was a legend in these parts. No one knew much about him other than that he roamed the West as a relentless tracker of lost persons. She'd seen him enter the hotel two days before wearing dusty buckskins and a gun belt slung low on lean hips. His disheveled hair grazed his fringed shirt and a full beard obscured his face. There appeared to be not an ounce of fat on his broad-shouldered frame. Hard to recognize that man as being the same person who now sat across the room dressed in tailored clothing that rivaled any worn in London or Paris. Sun-streaked hair, clubbed at his nape with a black ribbon, shone tawny gold beneath the gas-lit chandeliers. Clean-shaven now, his chiseled face could pass for a work of art.

Two days ago hadn't been the first time she'd seen him. A few months prior, he'd charged into the elegant Morgan Hotel after weeks on the trail, dragging a woman by the hand and cradling a rosy-cheeked babe in one arm. A fascinating man, he'd captivated Alanna on the spot. Or had she merely fallen for the romantic notion that he'd made a daring rescue of the woman by his side? She'd heard that the woman had been captured by Indians and ended up giving birth to a son while surrounded by wolves. That today the woman had married the boy's father . . . the man being none other than the wealthy part-owner of the shipping company her own father used to transport his goods.

"Stop staring," her mother spat. "Not only are you being utterly rude, but have you forgotten you are soon to be married?"

Oh, wouldn't she like to forget that unfortunate fact. "I'd rather slit my wrists with a butter knife than marry Jonathan."

Her mother's jaw twitched and her lips thinned. "Don't start that again, Alanna, or I'll have your father correct your manners."

Alanna settled her mouth into a faux smile. "My father who sits here and ignores us entirely?" She leaned over and patted her father's plump hand. "Isn't that right, Father?"

He glanced up from the folded newspaper beside his plate, fork in midair. "Huh? Oh. Yes. Yes. Correct. Correct." He went back to reading and eating.

She pursed her lips against a real smile. "See, Mother? Not an inkling."

She glanced up, just as Wolf stood, dropped his serviette on the table, and turned on his heel. He moved toward the exit with a fluid grace, his muscled hips rolling seductively, his long legs stretching out in a slow, purposeful glide. Something less than virtuous heated Alanna's insides. Oh, why did a man like him have to live in this part of the world and not in hers?

As if he'd heard her thoughts, he paused at the doorway and made a swift turn of his shoulders. He settled a blue-fire gaze on her, scorching every nerve in her body.

Her mother gasped. "Ignore that awful man at once!"

Alanna paid her mother no heed.

"*Mr. Malone*," her mother hissed. "Would you *please* rid yourself of that dratted newspaper and have a word with your daughter about indecently gawking at a perfect stranger?"

Her father glanced up. Wolf had disappeared. "What does it matter? We're gone in two days." He turned to Alanna. "And I *have* heard every word, Alanna Mary Malone." The soft Irish lilt infusing his words thickened, revealing his repressed anger. "There *will* be a wedding and that's all there is to it. You so much as breathe in a way that ruins our chances of entering the upper ranks of society and you will lose everything you hold dear."

She straightened her spine against his ire. "Well, since I don't give a fig about finances and material things, that wouldn't be much of a loss, now, would it, Father?"

"Watch your tongue. You know quite well what I mean, so do not pretend otherwise."

Alanna wiped all expression from her face, but beneath the table, her hands twisted her serviette as if it were her fiancé's neck. "I have yet to walk down the aisle with the man you sold my soul to, so do beware."

Chapter Two

Wolf widened his stance against the roll of the ship and leaned his weight on hands spread flat against either side of the cabin's porthole. He stared out at San Francisco's coastline, little more than a gray brushstroke dividing sunny skies from the calm blue sea. As he struggled to keep his mind off whatever lurked in the watery depths below, nausea bit at his gut.

"Drowning must be one helluva way to die."

Thompson, the ship's captain, grunted. "No one shanghaied you aboard, my friend. You could've ridden that horse of yours all the way to Boston if you'd a mind to." He took a slurp of steaming tea. "Of course, its legs would've been worn to nubbins by then."

Wolf's stomach lurched again. Had he turned green yet?

Thompson took another noisy swig of the oolong. "You might want to keep your eye on the horizon. It tends to fend off seasickness." He emptied his wide-bottomed cup with a long swallow, set it on the table with a *clink*, and stroked his graying beard. "And force yourself to think of something pleasurable. It'll keep your mind off your stomach."

Wolf snorted. "Something that gives me pleasure? Hell, dry land would do the deed."

Thompson chuckled.

Wolf let go a ragged breath. Find something—anything—to focus on. The memory of the woman who'd strolled past him in the dining room two nights earlier hit him so hard, he could just about smell the faint scent of cinnabar and roses that had trailed behind her. A shot of desire went through him. *Alanna Malone.* Even her name hung about him like sultry air on a hot day.

A gentle roll of the ship and a quick twist of his stomach ended Wolf's brief distraction. He heaved a sigh. "May as well get started. Don't want to end up hanging over the rail the whole damn trip."

Thompson glanced up from the tea leaves he pondered at the bottom of his cup. "Get started?"

Wolf turned and took measured steps to the steamer trunk that stood next to the bunk and flipped it open. His old buckskins lay on top. What was he thinking, packing the blasted things? He emptied the trunk onto the bed and stuffed the worn leather pants and fringed shirt back into the flat bottom. Whatever the future held, he hoped it wouldn't mean going back to riding the West, and searching for people as lost as he felt.

He repacked his new, fashionably tailored clothing into the steamer atop the buckskins. Thompson studied every move he made. Even though the captain had been good enough to share his quarters on the merchant ship, Wolf could think of nothing better than being alone. Eyeing the small carpetbag he'd left out of the trunk, he emptied the contents onto the bed, counted out ginger tea sewn in little silk packets, a number of small gray pebbles, and several narrow strips of cloth.

Thompson made his way over to the bunk, lifted one of the bags, sniffed, and grunted. "What's all this for?"

"It's supposed to hold seasickness at bay." Wolf rolled up the sleeves of his shirt and strapped the small hematite stones to the insides of his wrists with a couple of bands of cloth. "If this works, like that little Chinaman back in San Francisco said, I won't have to spend this god-awful trip heaving my guts out in a bucket."

Thompson chuckled and headed out the door. "Sounds like someone sold you a load of crap, my friend. You'd better hope for some decent weather until we hit Cape Horn."

Two mornings out, the winds changed. By afternoon, the seas turned black and began to buck. Shortly thereafter, a squall hit with so much fury, Wolf's blood ran cold.

While a mate stood spread-legged and bellowed orders for all hands to take their places, shrieking winds swept the ship's bow and turned small whitecaps into violent waves that crashed down on the clipper. Two foremast hands, with only their heels on the footropes and their bellies to the yardarm, hung in space, grappling for a topsail.

All hands on deck worked with ropes tied around their waists, tethered to the ship for safety. Thompson ordered Wolf lashed to his bunk lest a wave beat the door down and wash him out to sea. Goddamn, he hated sailing.

The sweeping gale howled through three terrifying nights.

There'd been barely a quiver to his stomach though, and he remained clearheaded. After awhile, he wondered if he'd simply outgrown seasickness, or if the items from the depths of his carpetbag were doing the trick. Either way, he was far from comfortable.

At least he wasn't hanging his head in a bucket.

An odd mix of anguish and bewilderment struck him—along with a bleak remembrance of something he'd experienced when he was eight years old. Back then, the couple who'd acted as his guardians after his mother's death had ordered him into a similar craft. Without explanation, they had unceremoniously turned him over to a stranger in the dead of night. Wordlessly, the man had rowed Wolf toward an ominous-looking ship floating in the gray waters of New York Harbor.

When Wolf had turned around to try to catch sight of his guardians, they had vanished. Forlorn, and overwhelmed with a sense that he would never see them again, he stared dry-eyed at the ship looming in the harbor, anger settling deeper in his bones.

"Liverpool," was all the man had mumbled when he'd lashed Wolf to a berth. A terrible nausea that never abated had plagued him the entire trip, causing him to wonder if he might perish. There were times he'd been certain the only thing keeping him alive was a vision of his father waiting at the docks.

But when Wolf had arrived in Liverpool, gaunt and filthy, his father had been nowhere around. Instead, he'd been met by yet another stranger, one who'd offered no explanations, only silence and a set of fresh clothing to replace the vomit-soaked garments he'd worn throughout the trip before they set off to . . . to *where*? He couldn't remember.

"Christ Almighty!" Wolf sat up, shoved a hand through his hair, and eyed the liquor cabinet.

The door crashed open, and the captain rushed in. He grabbed a towel and swiped at his bearded face and hair. "I got some pretty sick people aboard, and if you think anything in your bag might help them, I'd like you to offer it up and tell me what to do."

"I'll do it."

Thompson shook his head. "I'll handle this. Can't risk having you washed overboard."

Nonetheless, Wolf untied the rope lashing him to the bunk and went about freeing the carpetbag. "How many are down?"

"Four."

Setting his feet apart for balance, Wolf dug through the

bag's contents and produced eight smooth, gray stones. He showed Thompson how they should be tied against wrists. Next, he wrapped several packets of ginger tea in another piece of gauze and shoved it inside the captain's slicker. "Get that tea wet and it'll be useless."

Thompson turned on his heel and started through the narrow door. Mischief coursed through Wolf's blood. He plopped on the bed, and crossed his arms behind his head. "And you can kiss my royal butt for the rest of this godforsaken trip if that so-called *worthless crap* gets your crew up and running."

By the fourth day, the storm receded. Boredom settled in on Wolf. No longer was he concerned with what might prowl beneath the ship or whether or not he'd survive seasickness. He decided to take a little tour of the deck. He was unleashing himself from the bunk when the captain returned for more ginger tea. "The stuff doesn't reproduce itself, you know. Have you got a plan for when we round Cape Horn if you use everything now?"

Thompson ignored him. "Give me five bags. The others are in decent shape now, but one of the women is still sick."

"Huh?" Wolf paused at the captain's words, the rope held in midair. "Women? What the hell are you doing with females in your crew?"

Thompson shot him a curious glance. "Crew? Where did you get that fool idea?"

"Correct me if I am wrong, oh captain of mine, but isn't this a commercial ship? I thought I was the only passenger aboard—and that's only because of my friendship with the Andrews cousins who own the damn thing. If I'd known there was any spare room aboard, do you think I'd bunk in your quarters?" Wolf dug into his bag again. "How many passengers are there?"

"Four." Thompson's voice grated with fatigue. "The ship's cargo belongs to them. Expensive goods. The old man sails with it most times, but this time around it's a family of three and a lady's maid, I've had the daughter aboard with him before. She's a good sailor, but the old man usually sickens for a day or two at the start." Thompson shook his head. "Never like this, though. Then the three women went down. Seems the storm did the damage before they had a chance to get their sea legs. I got concerned when they weren't getting any better."

He headed for the door and glanced at Wolf. "Best if you don't venture outside until I give you the all clear, but you'll be safe wandering around in here. Careful about lighting anything that might catch fire, though. Old Neptune still has a bit of pitching about to do."

"Jeezus." Wolf exaggerated his exhale. "I'm about to go addle-brained in here."

Thompson paused in the doorway, leaned over, and tapped on the beveled glass doors that encased a small library of leather-bound books. "You might want to scout around in here for something to keep you occupied." He stopped outside the door and ducked his head back in. "The old man considers you to be his lifesaver, by the way. He wants to meet you, so I invited them all to dine with the captain and his *guest* once the sea allows."

"Damn." Wolf rolled his eyes. "Real live people. Can hardly wait."

Thompson failed to stifle his amusement. "You might want to use your idle time brushing up on your manners. And clean up your English. It'll give you a chance to get some practice in before you land in Boston. Seeing as how that's where this family hails from, you might want to take my advice real serious-like."

"Kiss my royal—"

"Uh, uh, uh." The captain shook his head and disappeared.

* * *

On the fifth evening following the storm, Wolf removed his mother's gold and garnet earring from his right lobe for the first time since an old gypsy had placed it there on his seventeenth birthday. Over the years, he'd gotten so used to it that he never gave it much thought, paid no attention to the curious looks. But when he rolled it around in his hand like this, when the light caught the beveled edges of the stone, jagged memories flooded in, images filled with as much fire as the blood-red stone he held. Twenty-four years since he'd cowered under his mother's bed in horror while a stranger wrenched the life from her with his bare hands.

A shaft of pain lanced his heart.

Blowing out a heavy breath, he slid the earring onto the gold chain, turned it backward, and tucked it under his shirt. He guessed there were certain kinds of memories buried so deep in a person's bones, no amount of time leached out the hurt.

He picked up the small golden hoop Dianah had given him and slipped it on. Odd, the act seemed an egregious betrayal of his mother's memory. But his friends were right—whoever murdered her could still be in Boston and might have the earring's mate. That is, if the bastard was still alive after all this time.

He heard the captain enter and begin ordering servants about. Fragrant aromas reached Wolf, and his stomach growled. He checked his stock tie in the mirror, buttoned his fitted gold brocade vest, and slipped into his jacket. Smoothing a hand over his clubbed hair, he stepped from behind the wall that separated the bathing chamber from the rest of the cabin.

"Are those Saratoga chips?" With a new lightness to his step, he sauntered across the room and surveyed the table already filled with an array of food. "Ain't this a fancy spread?" He popped an olive into his mouth and eyed Thompson's dog, which was curled in a ball under the table. After tossing a chip to the hound, he grabbed a fistful for himself. "Still warm. Didn't know you carried fresh potatoes on board."

"Carrots and potatoes are good keepers. You'll be sick of them soon enough."

Wolf paused, glanced again at the dog sprawled on its side under the table, and turned to Thompson with a frown. "I just noticed something peculiar. Your dog has a load of male parts hidden under that pile of fur."

"Am I supposed to be impressed by your late, but brilliant, observation?"

Wolf bent down and regarded the scruffy hound again. "But *his* name is *Julia.*"

Thompson unlocked a door to a hidden liquor cabinet. "My daughter was only three when she named him. If you don't tell him otherwise, he'll never know the moniker's not fitting. Plain whiskey or something fancier?"

Wolf chuckled and tossed another chip under the table. "Whiskey." He straightened and regarded Thompson. He was as tall as Wolf, big-boned, but slender. Wolf liked him. An easygoing man, the captain possessed a dry wit that played off Wolf's crusty sense of humor. And since he hailed from Boston, perhaps he might prove helpful once they arrived. "What are these women like who'll be here tonight?"

Thompson pulled the stopper off the whiskey decanter. "Nothing you'd be interested in."

Wolf's back stiffened at the captain's curt reply. "I took you for a broad-minded sort, but here you are judging me— or your other passengers, I'm not sure which. For your information, I recently discovered yet another reason why I'm not fit for life at sea, besides my definite dislike for whatever swims around down there."

Thompson handed a whiskey to Wolf. "Oh, do tell."

"Plain and simple. I enjoy the company of women—of all ages. They don't irritate me like men can."

"All ages? I thought you only went for young barmaids of loose persuasion. No attachments."

"That, too, but given the choice while aboard ship, I'd definitely prefer the company of an elderly woman over a young one."

"Why is that?"

Wolf shrugged. "An older woman would likely have some good conversation to offer, while a young one could turn into a powder keg if things turned sour." He grinned and lifted his glass to a portrait of the captain and his wife, three daughters, and gray-haired mother. "Here's to women. They manage to slip into old age a little softer than we men."

Thompson took a swig of his drink and exhaled with a satisfied smile. "A little softer? What makes them any different from us besides the obvious?"

Wolf wiggled his glass, signaling a refill. "Women take their experiences into their hearts and never forget. But men? They take their experiences into their heads and can never remember. Turns them into grumpy old farts."

Thompson shook his head and bit off a grin. "And here I thought you hadn't a philosophical bone in—"

A knock sounded on the stateroom door.

"Our guests," Thompson announced.

The galley boy tugged at the bottom of his formal white jacket and hurried to the door.

Alanna Malone stepped across the threshold.

Wolf sucked in a quick breath. *Goddamn!*

Both of them froze for a brief moment and stared at one another in a tableau of utter astonishment.

Her recovery was so swift that, as she rebounded, her body's movement continued outward in a fluid, graceful turn of a shoulder to the door. The jerk of her head became a regal pivot toward her mother. Her hand stopped its protective journey to her throat and swept forward to assist her mother through the entry.

Wolf fought a grin. Well, hadn't life just gotten a helluva lot more interesting?

Chapter Three

Alanna blinked in surprise. *Wolf.* She caught hold of her shock and remembered what she'd been taught: *Let your enemy see nothing but stoicism.*

Enemy?

This man was no adversary. But oh, if things went her way, he could become something far more powerful and formidable.

Her mother huffed and puffed, propelling her wide girth through the door. With Father right behind them, mumbling as always, the distraction gave Alanna an opportunity to scrutinize Wolf.

She took in a slow, quiet breath and exhaled so softly a feather would not have fluttered. With the eye of a master, she took in every detail of the man who'd haunted the corners of her mind since that last night in the hotel. She snapped back to the present when she realized Wolf regarded her with a steady gaze. He'd paused for a brief moment when they'd caught sight of one another, and she'd swear a shock of recognition had washed over him. But then his countenance had shifted, and he'd stepped forward with graceful nonchalance, his features unreadable. Despite his aloofness, she was certain he remembered her.

She swallowed—discreetly. Lord, up close he was even more splendid. And those eyes. Thick, gilded lashes swept over magnetic blue eyes in a slow and lazy consideration of her. He could pass for a fallen god.

For a brief moment, something primal shimmered in all that blue. She didn't flinch, nor did she look away. Getting caught staring at him wasn't worth a second thought. One corner of her mouth begged to curl. She let it.

He lifted a brow.

And then his eyes danced.

Ah, good. The man had a humorous side. Nonetheless, rapier-sharp steel flashed beneath the amusement.

At the sight of Wolf, her mother stopped in her tracks and stared, slack-jawed. With a dip of his head, he turned to her. Her mouth clamped shut in a thin line. Her startled gaze flicked from the captain to Wolf and back again as she fought to recover her composure. Her spine stiffened and the air around her turned glacier cold.

Wolf's mouth relaxed into something resembling the beginning of a smile, and with total calm, he appeared not to recognize her. Alanna bit her lip to keep from grinning like a miner who'd struck gold. This was rich, so very rich—and just what her belligerent mother deserved for the way she'd lit into Alanna back at the hotel. *Hurrah!*

Her father nudged her mother, mumbled something unintelligible, and sidestepped both of them, his arm extended. "Captain Thompson, ah, there you are, there you are. So good to be here. So good to be here." He pumped Thompson's hand with a meaty paw, his booming voice laden with anticipation.

Not bothering to wait for Thompson's reply, he bounded over to Wolf and forced Wolf's arm up and down while he slapped him on the shoulder with gusto. "So this is the one. Yes, yes. Nice to meet you. Nice to meet you, Mr. Wolf."

Something subtle altered in Wolf's demeanor. Wolf was

not his last name, but rather his only name, she'd been told. So why hadn't he corrected her father? Despite Wolf's reputation as the best tracker in the Territory, she'd also heard he could be lethal if crossed. Perhaps her brusque parents would do well not to show him their arrogance.

Both men were tall, but Alanna's father was wider of frame, robust, and fleshy, and appeared somewhat larger than Wolf—but only in girth. There was a curious vitality in Wolf, the source of which escaped her. But as she observed the two men together, the answer struck her—Wolf burned with a raw, feral power that sprang from beyond the physical—a quality her father did not possess.

The finesse her mother used to deter Wolf from touching Alanna's hand when the two were introduced actually impressed her, the action was so deft. The way her mother leaned her large frame between them while she patronized the captain was exceptionally subtle, as if she were completely unaware that she blocked Wolf from her daughter.

A surge of mischief shot right through those magnificent eyes of his.

When he strolled over to the table and casually pulled out the chair next to the captain, where her father should have sat, Alanna wanted to laugh. Captain Thompson lowered his head and suppressed a grin. Wolf's action forced her father to sit at the opposite end of the table from the captain, which left her mother in a dilemma—whether she placed Alanna across from Wolf, or next to him, he would have easy access to her. However, if her mother switched places with Alanna, she would refuse the place of honor to the left of the captain. The fusspot would never commit a social blunder of that magnitude.

With a small *humph,* her mother placed Alanna directly across from Wolf. Amusement tickled Alanna's senses.

Let the games begin.

* * *

Wolf spoke first when they were seated. He turned to Mr. Malone. "So, was the fourth person in your party to take ill a servant?"

Malone's grin split his face in two like a precise line carved straight across his features. "Very astute, Mr. Wolf. Very astute." He heaped more mashed potatoes onto his plate.

Wolf made certain his manners were impeccable, his demeanor calm, but beneath his composed exterior snaked raw emotion. It took all his discipline to withhold the foremost question in his mind—since the Malones hailed from Boston, had they known his parents? Before the ship arrived at its destination, they'd tell him what he wanted to know.

Don't reveal yourself, Cameron had warned. *The elite of this young country is made up of a rather small group of families—one never knows who is related to whom. With no royalty in America, wealth replaces throne and scepter. There are those who took precarious risks to earn their lofty positions. Take note.* Wolf hadn't required Cameron's advice. He intended to remain anonymous as he located his mother's killer.

Malone stretched his arm over Wolf's plate until the sleeves of his coat and shirt inched back enough to reveal a stone still strapped to his wrist. "Just in case. Just in case." His eyes were mere slits, caused by the width of his potato-flecked grin. His smile traveled nowhere near his eyes.

Mrs. Malone's lips thinned. "Are you from Boston, Mr. Wolf?" She attempted nonchalance, but regarded her plate as if something far grander than a hunk of chicken and a blob of potatoes lay before her. She made tight stabs at her food before she deposited it into a mouth that grew more disapproving by the moment.

Wolf took his time to respond. "Yes and no. I was born in

Boston, but my parents relocated to St. Joseph, Missouri, when I was an infant," he lied.

Mrs. Malone's nose wrinkled in distaste. "Why would anyone want to settle *there?*" She jerked at Malone's sharp exhale.

As if he had all the time in the world, Wolf set his fork on his plate, and gave her his full attention. "I never got a chance to ask them, Mrs. Malone. They left me an orphan when I was six."

Her cheeks pinkened and her mouth clamped so tight it was a wonder any utensil could be wedged past her lips.

He'd accomplished what he wanted—she was unnerved by the way he studied people as though he had all day. "Oh, well . . . ahem. Poor thing. Do you have any living relatives in Boston?"

"I never said my parents were deceased, Mrs. Malone. I only said I was an orphan. It happens to a great many nowadays, as you are likely aware. I don't consider having been orphaned anything extraordinary." He'd restrict his lies to his parents only—less chance he'd slip up. "And no, I have no one in Boston. I travel there on business."

He sat with his eyes fixed on her and calmly answered questions she obviously didn't care to ask in the first place. Judging by the set of her mouth, she was keenly aware he'd deliberately hung her out to dry. A nerve quivered up one side of her squat neck. She squared her shoulders. By the sudden shift in her demeanor, he figured she was about to join in his game.

"Well then, how did you manage to turn yourself out so *nicely,* Mr. Wolf?"

Touché. The woman must have had a great deal of practice in the art of belittling.

A slow, easy grin broke loose. "I do all right for myself, Mrs. Malone. Nothing quite as dignified or grand as your husband here. They say one has a tendency to be attracted to whatever one knows. That's why so many farmers beget farmers, lawyers produce lawyers, that kind of thing. And since I didn't know what my father did, I suppose I was attracted to what I knew best."

His focus remained steady on the crass woman. "I spent a lot of time trying to run my parents down, and found so many other things along the way that I got pretty good at tracking lost people and goods. At least that's what my clients tell me about the same time they're complaining about my fees. People like your husband are the sort who usually hire me." He paused, savoring his next words. "Or women such as yourself."

Confusion mapped dour lines on her face. "Oh, for heaven's sake, whatever would a woman such as *myself* do with the services of the likes of *you*?"

"Why, Mrs. Malone." The words rolled off his tongue as sweetly as hers had earlier. "To find, shall we say, the secondary lifestyles of wealthy husbands? You know—mistresses, second families, bastard children, and the like."

A small gasp escaped her lips.

Wolf shrugged nonchalantly, and turned to Malone. "Does your work require much travel away from your family?"

Alanna laughed, a soft, throaty purr that shot right through Wolf. She lifted a slender eyebrow and glanced his way before turning back to her mother. Up 'til now he'd wondered if she possessed a voice at all.

Thompson jumped into the conversation, informed Wolf that Malone was a merchant who dealt in diverse business ventures—textiles, railroads, diamond mines in Africa, and Chinese imports. It wasn't long before the subject drifted elsewhere. When the captain shot a scowl at Wolf, he only raised his brows in amusement.

As the patter of conversation continued, Wolf shifted his attention across the table, to a place he'd purposely avoided until now. Alanna sat before him, her bold gaze steady on him. Damn, but the woman was unreadable—like a book with blank pages. Well, he'd make certain that situation didn't last long—he'd have the whole trip to fill each page— one by one.

The view across the table could not have been more pleasant. He drank her in while slow heat simmered his blood. A wealth of raven curls piled atop her pretty head revealed the slender column of her neck—one he wouldn't mind settling his mouth on. A jolt ran through him and tugged at his groin. He regarded the silk rose at her low neckline. The delicate pink petals brushed against her skin with the rise and fall of each breath—a breath that, if he wasn't mistaken, had quickened.

He'd observed back at the hotel, and again this evening, that although there was a deep, feminine curve to a waist that flared out to well-shaped hips, her shoulders seemed much stronger than those of other women, her posture more erect, arms slender but firm. Strangely, Wolf was reminded of the sleek ballet dancers in a troupe that had passed through St. Joe, and of the bodies of the young, fit braves out on the prairie. She sat before him like a goddess come to life.

He boldly etched her features in his mind, scrutinized her for clues to her nature. When he reached her blue eyes, they met and caught his, held him immobile. A tremor shot through him. Time stood still while he studied her. He leaned back in his chair, stretched his legs under the table, and imagined doing God-knew-what to her. One leg bumped into the captain's dog. He brushed a foot back and forth against the hound's fur.

With a start, he realized it was no longer fur he rubbed against, but smooth flesh covered in a silk stocking.

The twitch of Alanna's mouth told him he had not been mistaken. He stilled his leg, realized she had dispensed with her slippers and that her feet ran through Julia's thick coat as well. She continued what she was about with eyes gone wide in false innocence, a silent message that she did not intend to cease her actions.

Ah, the filling of a once-empty page.

He left his leg in place. Rather than being purely sexual, the effect of her foot brushing against him also soothed. An urge to drag her across the table and into his arms beset him. Christ, he had to diffuse the situation—the old lady had a bead on him.

He picked up a Saratoga chip and deliberately handed it under the table to Julia. "Lucky dog." He grinned when he came up empty-handed.

"Did you say something, Mr. Wolf?" the girl's mother snapped. Her high-pitched tone grated on him. He snuffed the urge to tell her to hush.

"I noticed your daughter has your lovely skin and hair and her father's unique blue eyes." And lips so full and lush, he could bury his mouth in hers for a week and never come up for air. He shifted his attention from daughter to mother, and was equally bold in how he observed the matriarch.

Mrs. Malone shifted about in her chair, her chin lifting. "Unique eyes?"

"Yes, the thin dark ring around the blue is fascinating."

Her grim slit of a mouth grew even grimmer. "Since they are like yours, I can only deduce that you seek a compliment, Mr. Wolf."

With a small tilt of his head, he gathered his calm and responded. "On the contrary, ma'am. I am always intrigued by the interesting meld of hereditary features in offspring. Forgive me if you think me bold, but I only meant to amuse myself." A casual smile creased the corners of his mouth, but he had done what he'd intended with his rebellious ways—he'd destroyed the woman's confrontational manner by turning her own tactics against her.

Malone scowled at his wife as if he wasn't sure what had just transpired. When the irritation on her face dissolved into a properly submissive look, he returned to his dinner.

Wolf decided now was as good a time as any to slip in a serious question. "Have you lived in Boston long, Mrs. Malone?"

"Several years," Malone answered for her.

Damn, that wasn't the response Wolf was after. He could wait. When the pause in conversation lasted a beat longer than was comfortable, Mrs. Malone lifted her chin. "I'll have you know that despite being first-generation residents, we are well-set in Boston society, Mr. Wolf."

She smirked at Alanna. "Especially since our daughter is now affianced to Mr. Jonathan Hemenway, the third. He happens to be the eldest son of Mr. Jonathan Hemenway, the second."

"Do tell." The name didn't mean a damn thing to Wolf, but it meant something to the braggart by the way she tossed it on the table like the ace of spades.

Thompson cocked a brow at Wolf. Obviously the name held meaning for everyone but him. Mischief danced a jig through his veins. He could always trump the silly woman's card and rile her a bit more. Why not? He'd never met anyone so discourteous who should have known better. "I'm afraid I am not familiar with the Hemenway name."

He let his deliberate pause ride until Mrs. Malone was about to open her mouth and set him straight. "Oh, yes," he interjected. "Aren't they the family who distills illegal blended whiskey?"

She dropped her fork. No, one could say she actually tossed it on the table.

Thompson jumped into the fray. "I've saved a surprise for a clear evening." He stood and left the table. "Wolf, help me out here, will you? Malone, come see this."

Wolf made his way over to where the captain stood, and

helped him retrieve a long, heavy black case from behind a wall panel. Malone edged in. The women craned their necks. Thompson opened the case to reveal a magnificent telescope lying in pieces on black velvet.

"Oh, my, my, my," Malone exclaimed. "Wherever did you get the likes of that, Captain?"

"Had it special made." Thompson stood, hands on his hips, and shook his head back and forth. "For the life of me though, I can't figure out how to put it all together. What about you, Wolf?"

He shrugged. "I can try."

Malone and Thompson stepped to the bar while Wolf sat on the floor, cross-legged and with his back to the room. He began to assemble the telescope with little effort.

"Do you know much about astronomy?" Thompson queried.

"A little," Wolf responded. "But not like you, I expect. You're the sailor, not I."

Thompson signaled to the Malones. "You may as well adjourn to the foredeck and relax under the stars. Wolf and I will join you after we get this thing together."

When the Malones were out of earshot, Wolf spoke up. "When *Wolf and I* get this thing together? Jeezus, I don't see your busy little fingers at work."

Thompson sat next to Wolf with a grunt. "You sure gave the old lady conniptions. Have you two met before?"

Wolf shrugged and kept at his task. "The Malones were in the Morgan Hotel dining room the same time our mutual friend Cameron was there. You know how he is when it comes to pretty women. Especially after he's had a few drinks. Guess it didn't sit well with Miss Malone's overprotective mother."

"And you are innocent, of course."

"But of course." Wolf grinned. "Now it's my turn to interrogate you." He paused with his hands in his lap for a moment. "What the hell's wrong with that daughter of theirs, anyway?"

Thompson's brows perched over his eyes in a hooded frown. "What do you mean?"

Wolf picked up a piece of the telescope, slapped it in place and screwed it into the shaft. "She's a strange one, isn't she?"

"Not as I've noticed." A barely discernible twitch at the corner of Thompson's mouth belied his dry monotone.

"Have you ever heard her speak?"

"I've heard her speak."

Wolf nodded toward another piece of the telescope. "Hand that one over. Then she's not a mute?"

"Now, if she spoke, how can she be mute? Uh, uh, uh," Thompson put in when profanity formed on Wolf's lips.

Thompson smirked. "Good God, what a catch she would be for the likes of you—beautiful, wealthy, and silent." He flicked an imaginary speck of lint from his lapel. "Perfect match. You two would have exactly the same thing to say to each other—nothing."

"I wasn't about to ask for her hand, for God's sake. I was only making conversation. As if I'd have anything to do with that bizarre family. With the way her father has a habit of saying everything twice, and her mother's *genteel* way of doing the talking for her, I guess Miss Alanna Malone, of the *oh, so verrry important* Boston Malones, can't squeeze a word in edgewise. Oh, and don't forget, she is formally affianced to that *verrry* important Hemenway chap of the *verrry* important Hemenways—whoever the hell they are."

Thompson chuckled. "Now there's the biggest mismatch of the season. With the Malones being Irish Catholic, their daughter is their only ticket into Boston's upper echelons, so they're forcing the marriage. However, I doubt Miss Malone has any intention of meekly doing her parents' bidding. And she speaks when she's of a mind to, by the way. I've known her since she was a child. You might not want to underestimate her."

Wolf attached the last piece to the telescope. "Whatever the hell that's supposed to mean. Toss me the lenses, damn it."

Thompson handed Wolf a small round container. "By the way, may I commend you on your impeccable manners and *eloquent* use of the English language this evening, *Mr. Wolf.*"

Wolf shot a wicked sneer at Thompson. "Kiss my ass."

"Back to your infernal cursing? Are you afraid that if you stopped peppering your sentences with profanity, you'd end up with the vocabulary of a four-year-old?"

Wolf grinned. "You don't want me to answer that, do you?"

"By the way, my good man, if I met you for the first time tonight, I would never suspect your gentlemanly deportment to be anything less than a natural part of you. Care to elaborate?"

Wolf's guard went up. "So? I'm not the first person in the world to fake good manners."

"Ah, but tell me, Wolf, how does a man with a decidedly fractured use of the English language, who has spent his adult life roaming the West alone on horseback, suddenly *fake* perfect diction and manners the way you did over dinner? Not to mention that your vocabulary increased by leaps and bounds."

Wolf merely grunted.

Thompson sat back and studied Wolf for a long moment. "I noticed something else rather curious about you during Trevor and Celine's wedding reception."

"What's that?"

"After a good many drinks, you seemed to let your guard down. When you and the Andrews cousins parried with one another using numerous accents, a thick Scottish brogue fell off your tongue as if you'd been born to it. What was that about?"

Wolf scrambled to his feet and rubbed the small of his back. He whistled for Julia, grabbed a handful of butter mints, and sauntered out the door with the telescope in hand. "Bring the tripod, will you, oh captain of mine."

When he reached the foredeck, most of the crew was gathered about in anticipation of the captain's new toy. Others were scattered around the aft deck, enjoying the evening with its clear skies, calm sea, and balmy breezes. The Malones awaited the entertainment in chairs the deck hands had placed in a semicircle.

To no one's surprise, Malone was the first to take hold of the contraption, like a spoiled child. "Well, would you look at that? What a sight, what a sight. I feel the sky is right down around me. Well, I never. Oh, would you see here. "

He riddled Wolf with questions. Fortunately, he was able to answer them all. Not much time passed before everyone figured out he knew more about the stars than the average person. While Malone peered through the telescope's lens, Wolf told tales of the mysteries of the heavens.

After Malone had hogged the telescope for what seemed an eternity, he eventually gave over his hold on it to his wife. Wolf turned to her, but Mrs. Malone stretched out her hand to Thompson. "Captain, would you be so kind?"

"Of course." He escorted her the short distance to the telescope. After a brief moment of twisting the adjustments about, he turned to Wolf, held up his palms in a helpless gesture, and stepped aside. "You're going to have to help me out here."

Mrs. Malone stiffened. Wolf moved in close and placed a hand ever so gently at the small of her back, guiding her to the telescope's lens. Since this brash woman had given him a set-down at every turn, he intended to make certain she experienced him in the same way her daughter was about to—and that she could do nothing to stop him without appearing the fool.

His provocative actions with the mother became deliberate, yet so subtle she could not have been certain whether they were intended. His cheek purposely brushed hers while he instructed her on how to peer through the telescope; he made certain his voice dropped to a husky murmur so his words were lost to the others amidst Malone's chatter. When he touched her shoulders, or nudged her head in a different direction with the tips of his fingers, he had to fight a grin at the way she stiffened beneath his touch.

And then, it was her precious daughter's turn.

Wolf took a step back. "Any questions before your daughter has a go, Mrs. Malone?" Even in the moonlight, she visibly paled. Her hand dropped away from the telescope and she swept it along the length of her shawl as if to wipe away perspiration.

"Your turn, Alanna," Malone called out.

Wolf tilted his head a bit and gave Alanna a half smile.

Mrs. Malone's mouth worked like a fish out of water. To deny her daughter a turn at viewing the stars through such a magnificent instrument would be unthinkable. What could she say—that *Mr. Wolf* stood too close? That he spoke in far too sensuous a voice? That he touched her shoulders, the small of her back much too intimately? Surely such a reaction on her part would cause Malone and Thompson to think she'd gone daft since they sat barely ten feet away—and she would risk offending the captain by refusing his offer.

Wolf turned to Alanna, gave a nod, and gestured for her to join him. "Come, Miss Malone, I'll show you what your mother just experienced."

He choked back laughter at Mrs. Malone's distressed face when she plopped down in the chair beside her husband and folded her arms over her overly large bosom. If eyes could shoot bullets, Wolf would be a dead man.

* * *

When Wolf laid his hand on the small of Alanna's back, her skin heated right through the layers of fabric. Deftly, he guided her to the telescope and stood next to her, his one hand still in place while he adjusted the lens with the other. When he spoke, the husky, velvet currents in his voice ran over her skin like a caress. His breath warmed her cheek, and the scent of mint lingered in the air around them. Well, at least one of them remembered to breathe.

"Damn the brazen man," Wolf purred as he adjusted the telescope's lens.

His words tickled her ear and sent a shudder running through her before it settled low in her stomach. She leaned forward and set her eye to the lens. "What do you mean?" She managed to sound calm despite the quickening blood pounding in her ears. He stepped a shade closer, until her shoulder fairly nestled in the curve of his arm. The palpable heat of him surrounded her.

"Those are likely your mother's thoughts about now, Miss Malone."

His words feathering her skin sent every nerve in her body vibrating. He would be right, of course—Alanna was well aware of what he'd been up to with her mother, and knew full well why. The scamp.

He readjusted his hand at the curve of her back in a way so subtle no one else would be aware. She only had to step away and that would be the end of what was going on between them. Instead, she leaned slightly into him.

His fingers pressed ever so gently into her back in response, and he chuckled lightly. Her heartbeat stuttered at the way his warmth branded her. With all the self-discipline she could muster, she forced her attention back on the stars. There could have been two or ten thousand—she could not tell for all the fireworks bursting in her head. She forced aloofness to surround her. "And Mother would think this utter nonsense because?"

His sweet breath grazed her ear again. "Nonsense? Hardly. She curses such a man as me who influences her daughter. And since she stood in the very spot where you now stand, endured similar physical contact, she knows exactly why she curses me."

What a delightful evening this had turned out to be. Oh, but wasn't Wolf the wicked one to taunt her mother in such a devilish way. Well, Mother deserved even worse for her disgusting treatment of him. "And why is that, *Mr. Wolf*?"

His breath fanned her cheek now, his voice so softly intense she fought a desire to turn her head and touch her mouth to his. "Because your fiancé holds not a speck of the fire your mother glimpsed in me, and in her eyes, that makes me dangerous."

With a subtle shift of his body, he drew even closer. If she turned her head a hair—only a hair—their lips would meet. Oh, God, she could barely stand, her knees were so weak. "And how could you possibly know of what you speak?"

His mouth brushed her cheek, his voice a husky rasp. "Because the kind of fire your mother sees in me, Alanna Malone? You'd best think twice before you decide to play with it."

Chapter Four

Looking about as forlorn as any dog could manage, Julia sat in front of the closed door of the captain's quarters, his head turned toward Wolf in quiet desperation.

Wolf hustled to the door. "All right, all right, I'm coming. Say something when you need out, damn it. Don't just sit there expecting a body to read your mind."

The dog slid through the opening of the door, and hightailed it toward the back of the ship.

"Jeezus, if I had to piss that bad, I sure as hell wouldn't sit in front of the door waiting for someone to open it."

"Guess that's the difference between a wild wolf and a civilized dog," Thompson replied, still bent over his ship's charts. "A wolf would lift its leg anywhere."

"Clever." Wolf ran his fingers through his tousled mop with one hand, and swiped the other over a plate beside the captain. He yawned, popped the filched roll into his mouth, and strode to his steamer trunk, where he pulled out a pair of black, knee-high boots.

"Hungry?" Thompson queried.

"Close enough to noon, may as well wait." Wolf stuffed his shirt into his trousers. "Thought we could take a walk on deck, so you can show me around."

"Can't right now."

"How long you going to sit stoop-shouldered over those damn maps, anyway? You've been at it since dawn."

"Doesn't have a thing to do with my charts. This is Miss Malone's exercise period. And how would you have a clue as to how long I've been out of bed?"

"Miss Malone's *what?*" Wolf hobbled over to the table with one boot on, the other in his hand. "We aren't allowed on deck because she—are you playing me?"

Thompson dropped his pencil and sat upright, rubbing at the small of his back. "No males allowed on deck during Miss Malone's scheduled time. Only enough crew to keep the ship moving." He lifted the teacup to his mouth, took a swig, and checked the clock on the wall. "Should be clear in another fifteen minutes."

Wolf leaned over the table until he was eye level with his roommate. "Tell me, Captain Thompson, of the oh-so-high-and-mighty Andrews Shipping Company Limited. Is this to be a daily event, or is this someone's little whim today?"

"Oh, there are no whims when it comes to Miss Malone. Hers is a daily schedule you can count on—except during extremely foul weather. She is quite a disciplined young lady."

Wolf cocked his head to one side. "Would you mind filling in a few minor details? Does this mean whenever one of the three women aboard decides to sun herself, we are all supposed to run for cover? Or is it only when Miss Malone decides to saunter about on her own?"

He hiked over to a porthole and caught a glimpse of the blue sky. Rebellion fired his blood. He'd be damned if anyone would pen him in. "Son of a bitch." He struggled into his other boot.

Thompson's chuckle sounded like little more than a grunt. "Back to your normal speech, I see. You'll find the women about the deck fairly often. What I'm talking about is a certain private time for Miss Malone. She's pretty energetic for a woman. Doesn't like being cooped up in a cabin."

"And I do?"

Thompson ignored him. "She's been sailing aboard my ships going on thirteen years now. Started when she was ten. So did her exercise periods. Don't see any reason to put a stop to them just because there's a stubborn mule aboard."

Wolf stomped his heel into his other boot. "Who is she to be taking over an entire ship anytime she damn well pleases?"

Thompson leaned forward. "Have you forgotten there is a thousand tons of cargo in the hold, and every bit of it belongs to her father?"

"So what?"

"He fills a ship a month, that's 'so what.' If it weren't for people like him, there might not be an oh-so-high-and-mighty Andrews Shipping Company Limited. Guess I can afford to acquiesce to someone else's forty-five-minute schedule every now and again."

Wolf grabbed his jacket. "And during the day's prime hours, while the rest of us all sit around with our thumbs up our—"

Thompson raised his hand. "Come now, Wolf. You have twenty-three and one-quarter hours of every day when you don't have to be concerned about who is, or who is not, on deck. Of course"—he shrugged his shoulders—"I could move the time period to an hour earlier, when you're sure to be asleep—"

"Kiss my you know what, and whose stupid idea was this anyway? Hers or her *genteel* papa's?" He shoved his arms into his jacket, and headed out the door.

Five minutes later, he shot back into the room. Julia scooted in behind him. "No one's out there."

Thompson smirked as he toasted him with his tea. "I know.

I figured you'd pull the stunt you just did, so I lied about the time by a good twenty minutes."

Alanna stood at the fore of the ship and marveled at its sleekness—all gleaming brass and polished wood. A rush of power coursed through her veins as the ship fairly flew across the surface of the smooth water. What a perfect day for sailing. No matter how many times she traveled by sea, the sight of yards of white canvas billowing against a blue sky still left her in awe.

Leaning over the rail, she watched the figurehead dance at the ship's bow—a white and gilt goddess, her carved gossamer robes flowing about her sylphlike body, her outstretched arms pointing the way. Legend had it that the figureheads adorning ships knew every dolphin. And when they swam alongside the ship, the figureheads called each of them by name. A wave arced in the sunlight, casting a shimmering rainbow upon the waters.

"Alanna, you get back here before you fall overboard!" Her mother's screech swooped through the air like a squawking seagull.

Humph. If Mother only knew what the exercise period entailed, she'd faint dead away. Thank heavens Father had seen to that situation years ago. Straightening, Alanna made her way to where her mother and the tiny Asian maid sat with lounge chairs pulled together, sewing colorful glass beads onto a length of fabric. Busy work. Certainly nothing Alanna was interested in. Separating her chair from theirs, she stretched out in the shade of the cabins with an open book in her lap and feigned a nap to avoid her mother's nattering.

Movement caught her peripheral vision. Wolf and Thompson strolled from the opposite side of the ship into full view, their backs to the women. A sharp thrill rushed through her. Wolf appeared relaxed as he walked alongside the captain. Each step he took was fluid and graceful, and when the two halted at the bow, he planted his booted feet apart to steady himself. She smiled. He'd gained his sea legs. He stood tall and straight, like a towering spruce, his finely tailored clothing accenting his broad shoulders. His hair was tied at his nape, revealing the clean, chiseled cut of his profile.

Judging by a few words floating in the breeze, the captain was giving Wolf a detailed tour of the ship. She studied him through eyes hidden by lashes she closed discreetly whenever her mother turned her way. The men headed toward them.

Her mother grunted her disapproval.

Acting as detached and aloof as she could manage, Alanna drank in Wolf's every movement, burned his image into her memory. Even from such a distance, she could feel the power that coiled within him. As he and the captain conversed, the sound of Wolf's voice reached her, sending one delightful tremor after another through her.

"Well, would you look who's on deck?" Thompson left Wolf's side and stepped over to the women.

Alanna raised her head. Wolf stood directly in front of her. He just stood there, devilishly handsome with those compelling blue eyes and a vague smile as intimate as a soft kiss.

Her cheeks flushed at being thrown off guard. The heat in them heightened when he bent at the waist, gently lifted her hand from her lap, and let his warm mouth touch her bent knuckles. Only she could have heard the soft chuckle in his throat as his mouth opened a sliver and he nipped her skin. An electrifying shudder shot up her arm. Her lungs froze.

Heedless flirt!

She inclined her head and desperately searched for some form of balance while she pretended not to have been cognizant of his bold gesture. Heat emanated from his body, and a current moved out of his fingertips and into hers before he released her hand. She managed a slow, imperceptible exhale, centering herself. She thought she had regained control, but when she looked up once again, the smoldering flame in his eyes startled her. Why, he was taunting everyone, not just her, by getting away with what he just did. Damn his boldness!

Her mother strained to peer around the captain who had—could it be?—planted himself most strategically between the two women. He leaned over her mother in animated conversation until finally, she grew so perplexed in her straining to try to catch a glimpse of what might be going on between *that* man and her daughter, she lost her balance. Beads and crystals scattered across the deck, shimmering in the sun as they rolled about.

"Oooh, nooo!" her mother squealed.

Both the captain and Wolf dove in hot pursuit of the baubles while the little maid scurried behind the men.

Alanna bit her tongue to keep from laughing outright. She remained seated while her mother heaved herself off the chair and stood ramrod straight, her cheeks flaming. Sailors joined in, shouting at one another and chasing the beads and glittering crystals, more for sport than out of courtesy. Wolf and the captain were making a game of the melee as well.

And what could her mother do about it? Alanna sat back in her chair, her hands folded calmly in her lap, glowing with pure amusement. She'd needed a little spice added to her day.

Her mother openly seethed, her mouth a white slit. Wolf was the first to return to where she stood. With one hand cupped under hers, he rained a measure of beads into her plump palm, and then bent his head to examine them, poking gently about in the small mound with one finger. Alanna remembered the clean scent of his hair, the firmness of his fingers, and she moved to stand. Her mother's lips retracted even further and she shot Alanna a glowering warning not to become involved.

Alanna sat back down, amused by the spectacle.

"These are very pretty, Mrs. Malone." Wolf gave her mother a devastating grin. "I promise we'll not let a one slip overboard. May I ask what you intend them for?"

Her mother sputtered. No matter what Wolf did to offend, she had yet to find reason to object without appearing the fool. Alanna knew her mother well enough to know that as far as she was concerned, this brash man would be faulted for the entire incident—although by now Alanna was pretty certain her mother was becoming mightily confused as to what actually *had* transpired.

The others—the captain, crew, and servant—hovered around her mother with what they'd managed to retrieve. Alanna gathered the bead bag from the chair and stood, held it in midair, and waited for her mother to notice.

Her mother snatched the pouch from Alanna, and after dropping her supply into it, she held it open for everyone to make their deposits. Wolf returned to the hunt while most of the crew dispersed.

By the time he returned, her mother had gathered her things in a great huff and made motions to leave. He stretched his closed fist out to her, but she turned her back to him, and with a flip of her head, said to Alanna, "Come. Enough of this folly."

Wolf ignored her mother's rude gesture, and turned to Alanna, his face filled with a sudden—and secret—expression.

Her heart thudded. She stood to leave.

Wolf appraised her from head to toe. "You look . . . ah . . . invigorated. Your exercise period must do wonders for you."

The lusty mischief in his eyes compounded the quickening in her belly. When she'd spied him back in San Francisco, something had shot right through her, but it hadn't been a sexual thing at the time. It had been a kind of power in him that mesmerized her. When had things changed?

She still saw him as perfect for what she needed, but now something else tugged at her. She wanted him in a far different way. She'd like to reach over and lick the side of his face and taste him. She fought an urge to set her mouth to his and draw from him—she didn't know what.

In silence, she turned on her heel and left him before he realized what he did to her insides.

Wolf sat alone in the stateroom, his legs stretched out, his booted feet parked on the upper edge of the darkened fireplace's coal scuttle. A beveled glass half filled with whiskey rested on a table beside him, along with a small bag that had once held ginger tea. He amused himself with the contents—a cache of beads and sequins he'd inherited from the rollicking sport on deck. He pored over them with the captain's magnifying glass, lost amid the fascinating optical illusions, rich textures, brilliant colors, and amplified surfaces, when a sharp rap sounded on the stateroom door.

"Do they have woodpeckers this far out to sea?" he hollered, and checked the time. Too soon for Thompson to return from meeting with the Malones. "Door's not locked. Come on in." He went back to studying the beads.

Another harsh knock and irritation bloomed. He set the magnifying glass aside and reached for the small bag, but the pounding continued. "Christ Almighty!" He threw the pouch aside and made for the door, still clutching the beads.

"Mrs. Malone?" He stepped aside as the portly woman marched past him. She halted in the center of the room, her back to him, and leaned on the parasol she'd used to hammer on the door, her chin shoved so high, her back arched.

"Do come in," he remarked, unable to resist a bit of a

bow. Closing the door with purposeful calm, he stepped over to the woman and made certain his manner was easy, non-threatening. "Care for a chair, something to drink?"

"I won't be staying." Her voice was shrill, her eyes hard as pebbles.

He strolled back to the fireplace and leaned his shoulder into its high, carved mantel, forcing her to turn his way. He tilted his head and made certain his lashes shadowed the distrust in his eyes. "You have something you would like to say to me before you get back to the meeting with the captain and your husband?"

The woman's chest expanded with the intake of her mighty breath. "I want you to stay away from my daughter."

"Not a problem." He waited. No change in stance, no change of expression.

"You heard me, Mr. Wolf." With the raising of her voice, she took an aggressive step forward, her knuckles white where she gripped her parasol.

Could any woman appear more ridiculous? She reminded him of a giant bumblebee in her outlandish black and yellow sideways-striped frock and matching hat. The companion parasol—her stinger—she'd treated as a lance. In some strange way, compassion for the blustering woman rolled through him. While her every movement, every word, was intended to reject, bully and threaten, he saw her belliger-ence only as a great weakness.

He spoke softly, in a slow, deliberate tone. "You are afraid of me, Mrs. Malone. How is that? I have been more than courteous to you and your family. I have barely spoken to your daughter. To be truthful, I doubt she would recognize me in the street should we meet after this sailing." Now, wasn't that a lie?

He leaned forward, as if to step away from the fireplace. She jumped back.

He returned to leaning his shoulder against the mantel and folded his arms over his chest to give her more space. "What's gone on to cause you to feel so threatened by me?"

The woman turned her back to him, crossed over to a porthole, and stared out. She stood as far from him as possible without leaving the room entirely.

"My daughter is engaged to be married. To a wonderful family . . . er . . . man. We do not want your interference."

"You do not have my interference, madam."

What seemed an interminably long period of silence followed, but in fact, only seconds had passed, according to the mantel clock's soft ticking. "What makes you think I am interfering with your daughter's life?"

She turned to face him. He caught the slight quivering of the hem of her garment. Once again, he could sense the onset of a maddening confusion within her. And he knew why. He'd made certain she could not pinpoint some *one* thing, *anything* to toss in his face.

Her lips moved briefly before she sputtered. "Surely, if you hadn't practically saved our lives with your treatment for seasickness, Mr. Malone would be on my side in a flash. He would see you for the man you truly are."

Wolf should have been amused, but shards of ice formed in his gut. "And what kind of man am I?"

"You . . . you . . . you are not fit for my daughter."

Despite his growing disgust, he couldn't help himself. "You do not know me, or my circumstances. By what measure have you come to judge me so harshly?"

"By . . . by your very own words, Mr. Wolf. You told us you were a small child when your parents abandoned you in despicable Missouri."

"And?"

"*And?*" Mrs. Malone's flaming cheeks and drawn mouth told Wolf she had moved past any shred of courtesy she might extend him. "You are nothing more than an adult street urchin."

"A what?" Not only had his gut grown stone-cold, his heart had joined in.

"A . . . a ragamuffin. And a border ruffian at that," she sputtered.

This time his heart felt a sharp stab of pain. "Mrs. Malone," he began slowly, deliberately. "Not everyone raised in Missouri is an uncivilized border ruffian. I can assure you there are people residing there who are as sophisticated, as wealthy, and as philanthropic as the best in Boston. But are you actually telling me that if your daughter fell in love with a wealthy, self-made man who just happened to have spent a childhood fending for himself, that he would not be fit for her?"

"Are you a wealthy, self-made man, Mr. Wolf?"

"I wouldn't call myself *wealthy*, but—"

"Well, there you are." She made a move to exit. "Once a street urchin, always a no-good."

A couple of long strides, and he stood in front of her, blocking her exit. She came to an abrupt halt to keep from running into him. A flicker of fear shot through the coldness in her eyes.

"A few questions, Mrs. Malone, and then I'll see you out."

The woman's jaw slackened. Nonetheless, she boldly lifted her chin and met his hard gaze straight on.

"As you wish." Any attempt to sound strong and forceful failed—her voice wavered.

His words emanated from deep within his chest, barely above a murmur, as he kept his emotions contained. "If you were ever to come across a ragamuffin, would you give him warm clothing on a cold winter's night?"

Mrs. Malone's hand lurched to her throat.

"And if a street urchin were ever to invade your home

looking for food, would you have him arrested? Shot? Or would you see his roguishness as redeemable, and set yourself to give him the guidance he never received in his youth?"

The tip of her tongue darted out to wet her lips, and she looked over his shoulder to the door, as if she was about to force her escape.

"Perhaps," he continued, "our conversation should take a different direction here. Perhaps, I should be telling *you* to advise your daughter to stay away from *me*."

She gasped.

He moved to help the woman out the door, his hand held gently against her elbow. "One more thing, Mrs. Malone."

She turned back and paused in the doorway, confusion written all over her face.

He winked. "We might want to keep this little clandestine meeting to ourselves."

She exhaled with a *whoosh* and nodded.

"And let's keep one other secret, shall we?"

"What . . . what's that?" she stammered.

Waywardness engulfed him until it tilted the corners of his mouth. "Perhaps what you perceived to be a problem did not actually exist. But perhaps you managed to create one in the wake of your own fears."

Her eyes rounded, and her pudgy, ring-encrusted fingers crept to the base of her throat.

He leaned casually against the doorjamb, crossed his arms over his chest, one closed fist still filled with beads. "Because, you see, warning me to stay away from anything"—his voice came low and mischievous—"even so much as a piece of apple pie, is like waving a red cape in front of this street urchin's bullheaded face. Good day, madam."

He shut the door after the woman was well out of sight, and whistled lightly as he sauntered over to the table where he'd left the ginger tea bag. His thoughts ran curious now as to what the dinner hour might hold.

As he reached for the bag, his hand brushed against the whiskey glass, sending it shattering against the coal grate. "Ah, hell."

He deposited the beads into the bag, and then bent to clean up the broken glass glittering under the sun's rays streaming through the porthole. An idea seized him. He paused with his hand in midair and studied a shard of the thick, beveled glass through the shaft of light. Turning it to one angle, then another, his idea took full form. He grinned. "Well, thank you, Mrs. Bumblebee, for your ill-mannered visit."

Chapter Five

"Forgot to give this to you last night." Malone dumped a silver card case in front of Wolf just as the galley boy was about to set a dinner plate before him. With a deft sweep of the galley boy's arm, the plate came to rest in front of Malone instead.

The server continued his duties without missing a beat. Wolf nodded at him. "I'm impressed."

"Thank you," Malone responded without looking up, busy oversalting his potatoes. "It's for coming to my family's aid during the storm."

Thompson lowered his head and shoved his fork into his mouth. Wolf grinned, picked up the case and studied the ornate engraving. The galley boy slid another filled plate silently into place under Wolf's hands.

He set the case aside. "Silversmiths are renowned in the Orient, are they not?"

While Malone erupted into a lengthy dissertation regarding the finely crafted goods coming from that part of the world, Wolf picked up his fork and ate. A nod now and then was all he needed to enjoy his meal.

Eventually, his attention drifted to Alanna. He stared boldly into her cool, blue eyes and decided her silent observation reminded him of some of the Chinese men he'd befriended back in San Francisco. She was no longer a blank page. Slowly, but surely, the pages were filling in—the slowness of the soul's writing only added to her intrigue.

A subdued Mrs. Malone kept herself engaged in quiet conversation with Thompson. Stung by her own stinger? He doubted he would ever be able to think of her as anything other than Mrs. Bumblebee again. Her gown tonight wasn't bad, but the load of jewelry attached to any available appendage—wrists, neck, ears, clothing—astonished him. A wonder she could lift her fork. Christ, what godawful taste that woman possessed. So, she'd given up some of her fight, had she? Here he'd sharpened his wits the entire afternoon, had come to dinner fully armed. At least the odd family kept the damnable trip from boring him to death.

He turned his gaze on Alanna again. Wouldn't there be an uproar if he leaned over the table and kissed those plump, moist lips?

Her brow arched.

He arched one of his right back. "I recollect that you have a fiancé, Miss Malone. Would it be rude of me to ask you if you've set the wedding date?" His eyes drank her in, paused where the lace of her dress separated and cast shadows about the base of her neck. The pulse at the soft hollow of her throat beat like the breast of a hummingbird. If he set his mouth right there . . .

Her eyes danced with a vivid light. "No date has been set." Her silken voice floated through the air and landed on his ears like a soft breeze.

He wanted to laugh aloud for the sheer pleasure of her presence. "Why, Miss Malone, and here I was beginning to think you'd never fully recovered from your bout with seasickness, you were so quiet. If that had been the case, well then, I would have had to return your father's gift. I'm pleased you finally accepted my offer to ease your illness."

Alanna appraised him with a keen eye. "You seem to have some curious information. What makes you think I refused help in the beginning?"

He leaned back in his chair. "Pretty easy figuring. Your father normally becomes ill at the outset of a trip, and since you've sailed with him since your childhood and are not prone to taking ill while on the seas, I suspect you tried to overcome it on your own."

Malone's head bobbed up and down, and he shook a finger at Alanna, who appeared slightly amused. "You have our stubborn daughter pegged, Mr. Wolf."

"Oh, it's not so much stubbornness," Mrs. Malone piped in. "She thinks she can control anything and everything with that mind of hers." She gave a sidelong glance at her husband. "And you know exactly how she came to be that way, Mr. Malone."

"Blame me, will you?" Malone shoved more potatoes into his mouth.

Alanna laughed softly.

One corner of Wolf's mouth kicked up. "It's nice to see you can laugh at yourself."

"To do otherwise would be a sign of false pride," Alanna responded.

There was something decidedly different about her self-possession. He couldn't figure it out, but it made his pulse jump. "Isn't stubbornness pride, as well?"

She tilted her glass of sherry and turned it around with both hands, gazing into its liquid depths. The beginning of a secret smile tipped the corners of her mouth. Slowly, as she spoke, she lifted the glass to her lips, her eyes rising to meet Wolf's. "Everything has its opposite, *Wolf*. Stubbornness is merely patience turned upside down."

A heart-stopping emotion Wolf could not put into words raced through him. His lips parted to assist his suddenly shallow breathing. For a brief moment, he was no longer aware of his body. Nor was he aware of the room, or anyone else in it.

"Miss Malone." He took a breath past the tightness in his chest. "Even if everything has its opposite, wouldn't stubbornness still be false pride?"

"Then what of patience?" She ran the tip of her finger slowly around the edge of the wineglass.

Stop that! His head buzzed and his groin tightened at the slow, circular movement of her supple finger. "Mmm, isn't patience something connected with our spirit nature?"

"Oh." Alanna looked Wolf squarely in the eye, lifted her finger from the edge of the glass and licked its tip. "The man doth read."

Mrs. Malone broke the spell with her shrill voice. "See how she makes her own rules?"

So, her mother had missed nothing.

With a hard scowl at Wolf, Mrs. Malone turned toward Thompson. "Keeps me on edge, the girl does."

Thompson nodded. "Since I've known her." When he winked at Mrs. Malone, his was a face filled with mirth. Her mother's was the opposite.

"Do you plan to remain in Boston, Mr. Wolf?" Malone asked while slurping his sherry.

"No, only tending to some business, then back to St. Joe. Are you and Mrs. Malone originally from Ireland?"

"We are Scots-Irish, sir!" Malone's defensive bellow brought even Julia's head up to knock against Wolf's leg.

He appraised the man's livid response with cool detachment. "Sorry, I would never intentionally—"

"Quite all right, quite all right." Malone waved his fork in the air, and then brought it down to use it as a pointer for emphasis. "There's a big difference, you know. We are not those poor Irish Catholic immigrants. We came with a good deal of wealth, and before the deluge of Ireland's poor—"

"And we are no longer Catholic. We are *Unitarian*," Mrs. Malone put in with a firm nod to her head.

Malone flashed her a blazing look. She hushed.

Wolf clearly understood Malone's circumstances. Not only was the man fighting to fit in to Boston society, the belligerent oaf most likely had not fit in while in Ireland either, no matter his financial worth. How the hell had these two managed to raise someone as enigmatic as Alanna?

"We came here long ago," Malone went on. "1830 to be exact. Right before Christmas."

A jolt ran through Wolf. *Holy God—1830. The same year my mother was killed.* "You came directly to Boston?" He shifted his gaze to his sherry, not wanting Alanna to read him.

Mrs. Malone chimed in, suddenly eager to talk. "Heavens, yes. What a trip. And me heavy with child. As much with child as a woman could ever be. Across the choppy Atlantic we came."

In only a moment, the energy in the room had shifted, and the Malones unconsciously slipped into old speech patterns. The sudden pounding of blood in Wolf's ears, the cotton in his throat, nearly undid him.

Old feelings burst to the surface in a blur of red rage. An urgency to rush the conversation, and garner all the information he could, grated at him. He shot a nervous glance at Thompson, whose demeanor appeared guarded.

Wolf turned his attention back on Mrs. Malone. "Tell me about your experience." He swallowed the lump in his throat and spoke quietly. "I can't comprehend risking a trip across the sea with you in a tender state. Whatever prompted such an action, if I may be so bold?"

Malone answered for her, his chest puffed. "We wanted our child born in America, we did. And that was our Alanna here. Born on baby Jesus's birthday, she was. Well, on the eve of it. That's why we named her Mary."

Wolf's eyes shot up from his glass, straight to Alanna's. His mind screamed. *That was the night before his mother was murdered!*

He fought his churning gut. He swallowed his sherry, forced himself to breathe deeply and gain a modicum of control. He turned directly to his adversary. "I'm sorry if I appear rude, Mrs. Malone. As I said, your sailing the Atlantic in such a delicate condition and in the middle of winter . . . well, I'm astonished. Did you know anyone in Boston to help you get settled, help you with your newborn?" *Damn it, did you know my parents?*

"Oh, getting help was no problem. There were so many out there who needed work. But no, Mr. Wolf, we knew no one. And didn't for a long while, because of what happened. I would have given my right arm to move back to Ireland then and there. But Mr. Malone refused."

A chill snaked down Wolf's spine. "What do you mean? What happened?"

Malone rapped his knuckles on the table and scowled at his wife. "Oh, now you'll be leaving that morose stuff alone for once. We were enjoying ourselves, we were."

"Well, he *asked*." Mrs. Malone's volume, as well as her back, went up. "It would be rude of me to ignore him."

Wolf was too close to learning something—he couldn't allow her to stop chattering. He switched from sherry to whiskey. The burn of it down his throat seemed somehow more comforting. "Now you've piqued my curiosity. Tell you what, why don't you finish your story, and afterward, we'll turn your husband loose on the telescope again."

Mrs. Malone tucked a wayward lock of hair behind her ear. "We had barely moved our things into a home we'd purchased sight unseen, when our Alanna came into the world. The very next night—Christmas, mind you—a woman was horribly murdered." Her eyes widened and her voice grew secretive. "Not two hundred yards from our front door."

The rush of blood to Wolf's head nearly deafened him. He willed his body and mind into silence. "Was she murdered in the street, then?"

"No, no." Mrs. Malone waved her hand about. "She was murdered right in her own home." There was no stopping the woman now. She rattled on like a train without a brakeman.

The long-familiar story that had stalked the corridors of Wolf's lonely heart prowled once more. The band of pain encircling his chest nearly defeated his calm, but he had to get whatever information he could. "What of the woman's husband?"

"Oh, poor thing." Mrs. Malone pulled a handkerchief from her sleeve and dabbed at the corner of one eye. "We moved to another home soon after, but I'm told he returned to Boston a couple of months later. To nothing. *Ab-so-lute-ly* nothing. Can you imagine? Well, I wanted to leave America, I tell you. I was so young, and I was lonely for my family back in Ireland. Not to mention I was so very frightened. Why, Mr. Malone wouldn't allow me out the front door for the longest time. He hired men to guard our home."

"As did every other husband who could afford to do so," Malone put in.

His wife waved her hand again, her breath coming in great heaves. "He was afraid whoever took the boy would come after our baby. I tell you, there wasn't a house with a small child in it that wasn't guarded day and night. We had a special guardian for Alanna. He's still with her to this day. Back in Boston, that is."

Wolf concentrated harder on the whiskey in his glass. "Was there any speculation as to what happened to the child?"

"At first, everyone thought the boy was placed in hiding for his own protection," Mrs. Malone answered. "There was a rumor amongst the servants that he might have seen who murdered his mother. However, his father returned in mid-February, but the boy never did."

Wolf's gut churned like the sea beneath the ship. His father had come back after all?

Mrs. Malone continued. "Everyone pretty much guessed after awhile that the boy had been done in. Either that, or taken and sold to those awful Turks as a slave boy."

"Oh, Mother." Alanna's voice was calm, but her attention remained riveted on Wolf.

He downed his whiskey.

"Well, those kinds of things *do* happen." Her mother shook her finger in her daughter's face. "And don't you forget it." She finished her thought with her chin in the air. "My daughter thinks nothing could *ever* happen to *her*. Thinks she's invincible."

Wolf shrugged and tried to appear nonchalant. "Perhaps the boy joined his father later, after everything quieted down."

"I don't think so," Malone said. "Too much time had passed before the father arrived. His neighbors told me the man lived and breathed for his family, and that for nearly two years after the murder, they watched as he went back and forth to work. Nowhere else, mind you."

A new kind of misery taunted Wolf—his father had remained at the house for two damn years without coming for his only child. "Did he ever remarry?"

"Oh no, *tch*, *tch*. They said he kept a light on in the boy's bedroom window, in case he found his way home. Gossips said he finally gave up on ever seeing his son again, sold the house, and moved on."

Sadness flooded Wolf, and then bile rose in his throat. He fought to keep his voice clear. "Did anyone ever hear what became of the man?"

"Somebody said he went off and joined the Royal Troops, the Brits you know. Went to India and got himself killed over there."

Christ! Thunder roared through Wolf. A sharp pain sliced his temples.

Mrs. Malone sighed. "I saw his wife the day before the murder. Right out my own window, I did. Prettiest thing you could ever lay eyes on, and just as sweet as could be, so they tell me. Oh, she had the loveliest hair, all chestnut and shiny. Her child seemed a dear thing, as well. He had a mop of blond hair that puffed up like a dandelion gone to seed."

Mrs. Malone fanned herself with the handkerchief, not looking at anyone or anything in particular. "Strangest thing happened about that mother's beautiful hair."

Good God, what else? "Her hair?" Wolf's voice would soon betray him if this conversation continued. But he had to know. He had to.

Her eyes rolled dramatically. "Someone chopped it all off some time after the murder, and before the funeral. They said she had it all when they found her, but after she was laid out in the parlor for the viewing, the servants got up the next morning, and there she was with her hair all hacked to within an inch of her head. Neat little piles of it placed all over the house. Even in the servants' quarters. No one knew how anyone got in without waking the staff. Frightened the help half to death. They all ran off except for one couple who waited for the man of the house to return. Soon as he did, they left too."

Wolf heaved a sigh and rubbed at his forehead.

"Oh, dear. I've upset you, haven't I?" Mrs. Malone's hand made a feeble gesture to reach across the table before she thought otherwise and snatched it back. "Men don't usually get so upset. But . . . but then, you *were* orphaned, after all. Oh, my."

"It's all right, Mrs. Malone." He managed a feeble smile. "I just don't take well to any harm coming to women or children, that's all. Never have been able to figure out what would go on inside a man's head to cause him to do such terrible things."

He stood, took in a deep breath, and spoke as he exhaled. "If you'll excuse me, I'll get the telescope for Mr. Malone."

"Let me check the sky before you do that." Thompson was at the door before he finished speaking and stuck his head out. "As I figured, not a star to be seen." He returned to stand behind his chair. "It's just as well. Ladies and gentlemen, this weary captain needs to be sharp as a penny nail tomorrow, so I beg to be excused."

When the Malones departed, Thompson locked the door, and strode over to where Wolf sat in front of the fireplace, his feet on the grate, his arms resting on his lifted knees, and his head buried in the folds of his sleeves.

"Take your feet off the fireplace, son, so I can light a fire. We need to talk."

When Wolf finally raised his head, Thompson's brows furrowed even deeper. "That little boy with his hair like dandelions gone to seed?"

"Yeah?"

"That boy was you, wasn't it?"

Chapter Six

Wolf rolled out of his bunk and into his trousers in one fluid motion. After a night of too much whiskey, his tongue was coated, his mouth dry. A furious pounding in his head served him well—it kept thought at bay. He'd had enough of dealing with feelings and thinking to last a while.

The only thing on his mind this morning was that Julia had not returned after he'd been let out, and Thompson hadn't come back from a meeting with the Malones. Wolf had propped the door open with a chair so he wouldn't have to get up again, but still, no dog. Despite clear skies, the crisp air blowing through the open door sent a shiver down his bare arms. They must have sailed into cooler waters during the night.

"Damn, Julia. Who thought you'd be so much trouble?" He eased into his boots and shirt, and yanked on a sweater. Shoving his fingers through his tangled hair, he headed out the door.

When he didn't find Julia at the back of the ship, and the helmsman said he hadn't seen the dog in quite a while, his mood worsened. He made his way toward the stairs leading to the lower deck, where Thompson held his meetings with the Malones.

He spied the lady's maid, Hsui Lin. She stood with one hand on her thin hip, the other protecting her eyes from the sun's hard sparkle. She stared upward, at something in the rigging. Beside her, fast asleep, lay the scoundrel dog.

Wolf's gaze tracked hers into the mass of billowing sails. "Holy mother of God." Shielding his eyes, he moved forward, positioning himself for a better view.

There was Alanna, at least twenty feet up the mainmast, scampering up its one-hundred-forty-foot spire like a monkey on a vine. Barefoot and clad in sailor's jeans, she also wore what appeared to be a man's shirt, rolled at the sleeves. A single braid hugged the back of her head and trailed down the middle of her back to her waist.

Where the hell was the crew? Suddenly, it dawned on him. *Miss Malone's exercise period.* He dropped his hand from his eyes and turned in a slow circle. The deck was as empty as a ghost ship.

He moved into the shade of the boatswain's cabin to cut the sun's harsh glare. He leaned into the wall, folded his arms over his chest, and watched, fascinated.

Here was an arena in which Alanna played with obvious familiarity. Long, lithe legs stretched through the air as she reached out, hooked her toes in the ropes, and deftly drew them to her. Up she went, at times using only the sheer strength of her arms. Gracefully, she lifted her body to hang in midair like a trapeze artist, timed the wind's blustery forces against the ropes and white canvas sheeting, and made a leap. She paused, and stared off at the horizon, clearly lost in her own sensory world, a look of sheer bliss on her striking features. The sun created a dazzling nimbus around her. Arching her body, she set her face to the wind, and closed her eyes, as if she'd left the outer world behind.

There had to be music flowing through her head, judging by the way she glided upward with the elegance of someone who followed a captivating rhythm. Watching this wild beauty nearly undid Wolf. At first, the simple rush of adrenaline at her intrepid risk had been strangely intoxicating. But then her suppleness when she wrapped only a leg and arm around a rope or sheet, the rest of her stretched out to the wind, sparked unholy images in his head—visions of playful, sensuous tussling amid sheets of an entirely different kind.

The breeze whipped around her, pasted her shirt and trousers against her slender body like a second skin. She closed her eyes again, and let the wind kiss her face. Wouldn't he like to do that?

An erotic tremor shot through him that would have knocked him over if he hadn't been leaning against the cabin wall. He blew out a hot breath. A buzzing in his ears replaced the headache. The tightness in his groin grew painful. Too damn long without a woman.

Already, she was so high up the mainmast that soon she would be visible as little more than a small, doll-like figure. Surely she didn't intend to make her way to the top? Sailors fell to their deaths on ropes like these. Yet she seemed to be completely at home on them. Her father allowed this?

So caught up was he in the magic of it all, he failed to sense the approach of another until Malone's hand whistled past his ear and slammed hard against the wall. The *thunk* reverberated in Wolf's ear, snapping him to his senses.

Still leaning his head against the wall, his arms still crossed at the chest, he turned and stared into Malone's menacing eyes.

"I meant to miss, boy!" The man's sour breath passed over Wolf. Rage filled every line and crease of Malone's face. Veins bulged purple at his neck and temples. He nodded furiously as he spoke in low, menacing tones. "With that look on your face, I'm surprised you don't have your hands down your drawers right now, yanking on your tally-whacker."

Wolf never so much as blinked. Slowly, he turned his

head toward the man's meaty hand, which was still firmly planted on the wall next to Wolf's face. Then, just as slowly, he eased one knee up until his fingers touched the knife in his boot, while he let his head drift back to face Malone.

Not a muscle flickered in Wolf, but the fury boiling beneath the surface begged for release. "Now that would be a waste of time, wouldn't it? What with all that saltpeter Thompson dumps in our food." Despite his anger, Wolf's voice sounded easy, without tension. He paused, let his message sink in. "Or have you been married too long, or grown too old to notice?"

Malone kept his hard eyes leveled on him. So, he wasn't giving in, either.

"Not everybody's out to bed your daughter, Malone. Not unless this is a game your independent little Alanna plays. Is she used to making her own rules in that department, as well? Acting the aggressor, like she does on the ropes up there?" He nodded upward, his eyes still on the other man, narrowed now, and hardened. "Come the wedding night, she just might disappoint that highfalutin fiancé of hers."

Malone reached for Wolf's throat. Wolf yanked the knife from his boot and flashed the flat side of the blade between them, stopping Malone's hand in midair. Surprise flickered in the man's eyes.

"It was the growl in your throat that gave you away." Wolf tapped the point of his knife on the man's chin. "You shouldn't make noise before you strike. It'll give you away every time."

Wolf's knife disappeared back inside his boot as quickly as it had surfaced. Malone's stunned gaze followed the action. He pointed to where his daughter still scrambled about the rigging. "That little girl of mine has been guarded and protected from the likes of you since she was two days old. She's been raised and schooled to fit in with the best."

A vein pumped in Malone's temple, then disappeared into gray hair beginning to curl from the film of perspiration covering his face. "If you think I'm going to start letting her near someone like you at this point in her life, you've got a lot to learn."

Wolf lifted his hand to his chin, rubbed the stubble. "Guess I neglected to shave."

"Don't mock me, boy!"

Wolf cocked his head toward the galley. "See that twelve-year-old peeking out the galley window? Now, there's a boy. A *galley* boy, to be exact, Mr. Malone. To you, I am *Mr. Wolf,* no matter where you attempt to place me in society's ranks."

Malone opened his mouth to speak, but Wolf shook his head. "Hear me out and you might rest a little easier with regard to your *precious* daughter."

Malone stepped back and eyed Wolf warily.

"She wouldn't interest me. Oh, it has nothing to do with her, or her outrageous behavior. I find both quite appealing, as a matter of fact. You see, it's this way—anyone wanting to court your *little* Alanna will have to deal with her entire family. With you in the picture, Malone, you can rest easy that not only am I not interested in your daughter's hand, I wouldn't begin to be interested in compromising her position, or her honor, while she and her *upstanding* family are aboard this ship."

Malone's face took on the hue of cooked beets. "Why, you . . ."

Wolf raised his hand. "With your tedious self in the picture, you'd have a helluva time marrying her off to some European nobleman, like the wealthy tend to do here in America. But then, you probably already figured that out." He went back to resting his head against the wall, his arms crossed over his chest. "I'm pretty sure I understand why you're so eager to marry your daughter into an upstanding family in Boston. Must be they need their coffers refilled in exchange for assuring you a place among them."

Malone eased away. "Her name is *Miss Malone* to you,

Mr. Wolf. Don't you ever let me catch you calling her Alanna. And if I find you so much as ogling my daughter again, let alone even thinking of pointing your tallywhacker her way, you'll find yourself overboard, using your cock to troll for sharks." With that, he trudged toward the door leading below deck.

Wolf waited until Malone reached for the door's handle and then slid the knife out of his boot again. In one swift and powerful movement, he let go. It whizzed past Malone's ear and pierced the doorjamb, the sharp point plunging into the wood, the hilt quivering. Julia lifted his head, ears pricked.

Malone jumped back. "You goddamn fool! You could've missed and hit me."

Wolf strode to the door. "You're right." He pulled the hunting knife from its mooring. "I did miss my target, didn't I?" He rubbed his thumb across the notch the knife made in the wood, directly beneath the head of a brass screw. "Must be the wind, or else I don't have the sea legs I thought I had." He sliced another new line into the wood, directly above the screw's head. "I meant to hit there."

He turned, and whistled for the dog. "Come on, Julia. Better get you back to the stateroom before Malone here cuts your little tallywhacker off and uses it for fish bait."

Wolf was curled up on the bunk, his hands shoved between his knees, still fighting a hangover and replaying scenes in his head of Alanna in the rigging, when Thompson entered the stateroom for lunch.

"Malone wants you flogged for disobeying orders," the captain said dryly.

Wolf snuggled his head deeper into the pillow, his eyes closed. "Yeah? Well, I want him flogged, too. He wants to cut my tallywhacker off. Julia's as well." When he got no response, he winged an eye open.

Thompson stood in front of him, a smirk on his face. "Hungry?"

"Unh-uh. I might consider a bath though. Would that be too much to ask?"

"Under the circumstances, I think we can manage."

Wolf blew out an exaggerated sigh, and rose on one elbow. He pitched the hair out of his eyes and rubbed his forehead. "Now, that might be worth getting up for. I decided after that go-around with Malone, and chasing Julia to hell and back with this splitting skull of mine, that today's probably a good day to lie low. Nothing's about to fix me up but time."

He groaned as he swung himself into an upright position. "Jeezus. What the hell kind of shit do you pass off as whiskey, anyway?"

"With the quantity you consumed, I doubt quality matters. Got some soup coming in. When the boy gets here, I'll order up a bath. It'd be best if you put about as much water inside of you today as you soak in. That much liquor in a body dries out the veins."

"You sound like it's the first time I had too much to drink. Next thing, you'll be calling me boy, like someone else I know." He slid off the bed, rubbed the sharp pain at his temple, and eyed Thompson's serious expression. "What? You look like I filleted the man."

"Guess we should discuss the knife. Only reason for anyone to carry one aboard my ship is if they use it for work-related tasks."

"Been meaning to discuss that very subject with you. I need something to do." Wolf gave up, flopped back on the bunk, and stared at the blue sky through the porthole. "I can't sit around on my butt the rest of the trip. I'll be ready for Bedlam when we dock if I don't have something to keep me busy."

"Been wondering when you'd ask." At the muffled noise outside the door, Thompson opened it. The galley boy trudged through, carrying a heavy iron pot filled with an aromatic broth.

Despite his headache, Wolf's stomach growled. "God, that smells good. I changed my mind about being hungry." He blew a hank of hair off his forehead. "Hey, Charlie."

Charlie mimicked Wolf's action and grinned back with teeth still too large for his face. "Hullo, sir."

"Did you go and kill a chicken on account of my little whiskey headache?" Wolf teased.

Charlie giggled. "The captain here ordered the soup early on, sir. Said like as not you'd need a bucket of it, so Cook obliged. Got enough for the whole crew, so they's sittin' in a right good mood."

The galley probably ran rife with juicy gossip about what had transpired between Wolf and Malone. Since the boy had been the only crew member who'd caught the confrontation, he was no doubt the center of attention, and eager to take back anything he could to maintain his status.

"Got a deal to make with you, Charlie," Wolf said.

The boy scurried to the side of the bed. "Sir?"

"Got some spare wood?"

"Wood, sir? Ain't none to spare. I uses it to start Cook's coals in the morning."

"Just a small piece, maybe eight, ten inches at the most, and yea around?" Wolf formed a circle by touching his thumb and forefinger together. "There's some whittling I want to do."

Charlie's face fell, and his shoulders slumped. "I'd be in a heap of trouble, sir." His nervous gaze flicked to Thompson, who stood at the stove with his back turned.

Wolf heaved himself off the bed and strolled over beside Thompson. He ladled soup into a bowl, and padded back to the table. "If you can find me a little wood to whittle on, son, when the captain's gone, I'll let you in on what *really* happened on deck." He winked.

Thompson turned. "See to Wolf's bathwater, and bring a piece of wood."

Charlie's face lit up and he scurried from the stateroom.

Thompson shook his head at Wolf. "Don't know what you're up to, but if it'll keep you out of trouble—" He headed for the table, a cup of tea in one hand, a steaming bowl of soup in the other.

"Told you, I need to stay busy."

Thompson pulled a chair up to the table. "You might be useful after all."

"How's that?"

"You good with numbers?"

"Some."

"We've found a difference in the bills of lading. There's supposed to be over a thousand tons of cargo in the hold. But the paperwork shows about a five-hundred-pound difference. Doesn't sound like much next to the total, but it's all silver, artwork, inlaid tables, carvings, and the like. Expensive stuff. Maybe you can help figure it out."

"Could they have shortchanged you back in Whampoa?"

"No. We work with a man named Honquoa. You'll not find a more honest man in all of China. Even has an American ship named after him."

Wolf scratched his head. "Could it have happened on the docks in San Francisco?"

Thompson stuffed a piece of bread into his mouth. "Maybe we're not missing anything at all. Maybe something's just wrong with the paperwork. Can't figure it out."

"Is the stuff insured?"

Thompson nodded.

"Maybe Malone stole it himself, or had it stolen. Sells it

in San Francisco, collects the insurance when he gets to Boston, and ends up with a pocket full of change."

Thompson glanced up from his soup. "I've never known him to cheat on anything. You two may not see eye to eye, but he's honest as far as I've ever known. He takes extreme care with regard to his image in Boston, as well."

"Well, he has lying eyes," Wolf said dryly. "I know. I was up *real* close today."

"Get over it. I had a hard discussion with Malone regarding his actions. I reminded him that in order to round the Horn, it's going to take everyone working together, and you two had better meet somewhere in the middle."

"Did you remind the son of a bitch that I hold the ginger tea in case he gets seasick again?"

"I did."

Wolf shoved his empty bowl aside and leaned back in his chair. "The Malones sure are a strange lot, don't you think?"

Thompson finished his soup, and reached for his cup of tea. "What do you consider strange?"

"For one thing, how the hell many ships leave Boston with a woman hanging off the ropes?"

Thompson shrugged. "How many leave port with a male dog named Julia?"

Chapter Seven

Fresh from his bath, Wolf sat before a warm fire, his bare feet buried in Julia's fur, as he carved on a piece of wood. A pot of the captain's good Formosa oolong and a ship's flat-bottomed mug sat to his right.

Already, he'd bored a hole through the wood's center. Fractured pieces of the broken whiskey glass he'd salvaged lay on a piece of cloth. Every so often, he sifted through the shards, picked up a piece and held it to the wood, then resumed his intently focused carving.

Julia's head came up and he gave a short whine. "You lazy good-for-nothing." Wolf rubbed his foot atop the dog's head. "I was the one drinking last night, not you."

The door opened behind him. A chill wind hit his back. Julia stiffened, but when the door shut with a thud, cutting off the cold air, the dog flopped back down.

A scent of roses invaded Wolf's nostrils. *Oh, Christ.*

Alanna boldly pulled a chair up next to him. Without a word, she sat at an angle facing him, her knees grazing his thigh, her eyes filled with dignity and purpose. She wore a high-necked, long-sleeved dress the color of her eyes, and a small matching hat over hair drawn back in a tight bun.

"Another Malone visitation?" Wolf closed his eyes briefly,

attempting to control his temper—and whatever the hell else shot through him like a bolt of lightning. He shook his head. "Oh, no. Not another Malone for me today, thank you."

He tossed his knife on the table, shoved his chair back, and stood. "I'll see you to the door."

Alanna gripped the sides of her chair like a stubborn child.

Wolf sucked in his breath and fought for patience. "In case you haven't noticed, I resent your intrusion into my quiet afternoon. I'm sure you can find something better to do with your time."

"I came to apologize on my father's behalf. I—"

"Thank you." Wolf moved to the back of her chair to assist her departure. "Now please excuse yourself before your father finds you missing and blames me, because I have a *real* strong suspicion, Miss Malone, that your father hasn't the slightest idea you are here. Nor does your mother."

"And to inform you," she continued as if he hadn't said a word, "that whenever you've a mind to ask me to marry you, the answer shall be yes."

"Wha . . . what?" Wolf swept around the chair in front of her and bent at the knee. He studied her face, disbelieving what he'd heard. Her eyes held not a hint of mockery. The heady scent of roses filled his nostrils again—and that alluring scent that was hers alone. This was a hell of a time to let her plump, moist mouth distract him. "Leave, Miss Malone."

She sat steadfast and resolute. Unblinking.

Perhaps she was daft after all. The dull thud in his head returned with a vengeance. "What the hell are you up to? Are you trying to get me killed?"

"It was very wrong, what my father did and said to you today. I feel uncomfortable about what transpired."

"Then you just might have a small inkling, ma'am, as to how incredibly uncomfortable I am feeling at this particular moment. Maybe you can manage a little compassion and remove yourself with great haste." The bridled anger in his harsh whisper was fast accelerating into scalding fury.

She threw her head back in stubborn defiance. "Before you lose your temper—"

"Alanna Malone, it's too late. I have *already* lost my temper! Now then, you spoiled little snippet, leave and take your insane ideas with you or I will carry you out and dump you on the other side of the door. *That*, Miss Malone, *will* drive me into even further rage, because I do not condone manhandling women."

"I will not leave until—"

He decided to try another tack and scare the hell out of her. He leaned closer. "Are you trying to seduce me?"

"No."

Her daring gaze reminded him of the night he'd first laid eyes on her back in San Francisco. In a flash, Wolf slipped back into his chair and scraped it closer to hers until the corners touched. He reached his arm across her lap, rested the palm of his hand on the far edge of her chair, and leaned into it for support. His other hand rested on the back of her chair. If anyone walked in, he was a dead man.

He was so close he could feel her breath falling on his mouth, could smell a trace of chamomile soap beneath the soft scent of roses.

She blinked and, cool as an ice princess, stared back at him.

An unwelcome heat flashed through him. He cast it aside by drawing on his anger once again. If he had to scare the wits out of her, so be it. If she was indeed insane, then he would soon learn that, as well. Either way, he had to get her the hell out of the stateroom—and fast.

"I think I have this whole thing figured out." He studied her through half-closed lids. The lush curve of her mouth as her lips parted sent a wild throbbing through his groin.

"Thompson told me he's met your fiancé and that he is a homely man. Dull. Always sniffing and wiping at his nose." He arched a brow and let the devil play at the corners of his mouth. "Wealthy as sin, though."

Alanna simply gazed at him without expression.

"I wonder, Miss Malone. Do you figure this is your last chance to savor a few wicked delights before settling down to monotony?"

When she still failed to make a move, he drew his hand slowly across her lap, then boldly rested it on her knee. His fingers warmed from her heat.

She ignored his blatant act. "I'll never marry that swine."

"So, you want me to save you, do you?" His mouth drew closer to hers. "Am I your last hope before the ship docks?"

"Oh, do grow up."

Wolf was caught off guard by the sudden vibrancy of her voice. "No, Alanna Malone, *you* grow up."

He leaned further forward, his voice deceptively calm. "Do you have any clue what you are asking for by coming into a man's quarters like this? Do you have any idea what could happen to you if it were someone besides me?"

"Why don't you tell me?" she said with easy defiance.

That did it.

Without warning, his hand flew off her knee, under the hem of her skirt, and up her leg. He gripped the top of her bare thigh.

Surprise shot through him. "Christ. Where are your drawers?"

"I don't wear any."

"That is scandalous!"

"Only to one with a hand up my dress." Her eyes were languid pools of blue calm.

Try as he might, Wolf couldn't suppress the amusement that washed through him. But his hand was still immobilized on her smooth, naked skin. The heat of her melded into his palm and his heart thumped erratically. God, the tips of his fingers were entwined in soft curls.

"God forbid there should be a strong wind." He was unable to suppress his humor, yet his body filled with a familiar ache.

"I would probably wear them then, but only as necessary."

"Are you—"

"Yes," she answered.

"How can you—"

"Know what you were about to say?"

He nodded.

"You are very readable now, Wolf. Your eyes are filled with many questions." She blinked slowly, deliberately. "You were going to ask me if I am virginal. The answer is that I do not care to so much as kiss a man who sniffles all the time, let alone yearn to have him bed me. I don't know how to kiss, by the way. You'll have to teach me."

"And are you wanting that from me now?" When had he leaned closer? One hand rested on the back of her neck, while the other was still suspended on her hot thigh. He caught the faint scent of chamomile again.

"I don't think so." She spoke without guile, yet a smoky flame smoldered in her eyes.

"For the life of me, Alanna, I can't figure you out."

He didn't know what to make of his emotions now—they were a strange mix. He'd never had anything to do with a woman like her—he'd spent his life living in hotels, befriending barmaids. And he had a goal to accomplish. He had to find his mother's killer. The last thing he needed was this impossible situation.

Now tell that to his body.

* * *

The calm demeanor Alanna struggled to achieve warred against the hammering of her heart. Silence pervaded the room as she studied him. "You have hungry eyes," she finally responded. "And a rebel heart."

"Aren't you afraid then?"

"No. But you are."

"How's that?" Humor still touched his mouth, but there was a hint of dark, delicious sin in his eyes.

She steeled her mind against any thought that might weaken her resolution or allow her thin veneer of strength to crack. She knew without doubt that he was what she needed. She just had to convince him without giving away her secret. "Because wielding force in an aggressive manner is just another form of fear. And fear is the result of a lack of a sense of power."

Wolf studied her, his eyes hot and hungry. And then he leaned over and brushed his lips lightly against her cheek. Her pulse jumped. The moment hung between them like some magnetic force. It was plain he wanted more, but he wouldn't take it. But then, she already knew that about him or she wouldn't have come.

He released his grip on her thigh, as if reluctantly, but the heat of his touch remained. His hand slid down her leg and out from under her dress. He brushed her skirt into place and returned to leaning against the back of his chair.

Alanna's gaze roamed his face. His nostrils flared. "You have caught my scent, sir."

He laughed. "Your *what*?"

"My scent. The part of me that mixes with you. Something you cannot deny."

"What do you want, Alanna?" He scanned her face. She swore his lips were softer now, even lusher.

"You want me, don't you?" she murmured.

He sucked in a breath between his teeth. "Once again, I

am finding it hard to believe this conversation. You need to leave."

"You say you want me to leave, yet you are fighting the urge to keep me with you."

"And?" Humor suddenly crinkled the corners of his eyes.

"And you are quite taken with me, sir."

"Well, what of you, Alanna Malone?" He leaned forward. "Have you caught my scent, also?" A smile tipped the corners of his mouth.

Her heart thumped in her throat. "Long ago." Her answer was nearly a part of her exhale, it came so soft.

They sat in silence—so close she could feel his breath fall rhythmically on her mouth. He closed his eyes and let his lips barely touch hers, for a brief moment only.

He withdrew, just enough to look into her eyes. "Am I your knight in shining armor, then?" he asked mockingly.

"Yes."

"But I might not fit the bill." He reached up and lightly tucked an errant curl behind her ear.

The heat in his eyes warmed her in places that were better left untouched at present. She took in a shallow breath, which was all she could manage. "Oh, your armor has dents, make no mistake. I don't consider you to be perfect. On the contrary."

"And do the dents in my armor offend thee, fair maiden?" There was a thickness to his voice now.

But she was dead serious. Her bold stare never left his. "Oh, I would not want a knight with no dents. It means he has never been to battle, never fought for his honor, the things he believes in, or for sheer survival. Without the dents, sir, I would not trust my knight to be fully human."

"And what if your almighty knight fixed the dents? Or got new armor?" Those gilded lashes swept low as his gaze slid from her eyes to her mouth and back again.

Something hot shimmered in her blood. "A good knight would keep his armor. Repair it, but never entirely smooth it out." Her words grew heavy in her throat. "That would be an impossible task. And I would not want a knight who insisted on having new armor, the surface always shining and clean. He would only be living for who he thinks he might be, or for what others in the world desire him to be."

Wolf regarded her for the longest while, his body communicating a language even she, in her innocence, could understand. "I think, Wolf, now is the time for me to take my leave."

"Why do you call me Wolf, and not Mr. Wolf?"

His words, little more than a murmur, collected in the pit of her belly. "Because that's your name, *Wolf.*" She mocked him. "*Wolf. Just plain Wolf.*"

"Where did you hear that?" His voice grew deliciously rough.

She stared at his mouth, mesmerized by its sensuous curves. "In the hotel in San Francisco."

"Well, then." The air shifted, as if a sultry breeze had blown in. His gaze filled with a spectrum of emotions. He leaned forward, his lashes lowering. "Tell me to stop, Alanna Malone, because I can't seem to help myself."

The sharp intake of her own breath echoed in her ears. She closed her eyes.

His hands cupped her face. "Sweet Christ," he uttered as his mouth, warm and soft, gently covered hers.

She parted her lips to breathe, and the kiss deepened. He tasted of mint and tea, and when his tongue touched hers, every nerve in her body came to life. A shudder ran through her. The most intense pleasure she had ever known gripped her heart—she'd been lonely and never known it.

He pulled away, his chest heaving. "You need to leave."

She stood, nodding. Wrapping her arms around herself, she walked to the door and flung it open.

"Alanna?"

"Yes." She stepped outside and turned to him.

"You don't ride sidesaddle. You ride like a man, don't you?"

She laughed at his absurd way of defusing what had just occurred. Relieved, she cocked her head. "I beg your pardon?"

A lighthearted grin curved his lips. "The muscles in your legs are evenly matched." He leaned a shoulder against the doorframe. "Oh, one other thing."

"What?"

"That little dagger strapped on the outside of your left leg is a little too high. Not an easy reach. Even with your skirts up, it could cost you precious time."

She folded her arms over her chest. "It's not a dagger, it's a *sgian dubh*."

"Well, I'll be damned." Mischief threaded through his words. "How is it you know what a *sgian dubh* is? Or is it the Scots part of that Scots-Irish blood of yours?"

She turned and tossed her words over her shoulder. "And how would you, a border ruffian from the middle of nowhere, know about a particular knife worn inside the stocking of a Highlander in full dress kilt?"

Chapter Eight

Wolf sat before the fire tearing pages from the daily journal he kept, and tossing them one by one onto the flames when Thompson returned. The captain, his usual cup in hand, pulled up a chair beside Wolf. "Care to share the dull mood?"

Wolf shot Thompson a glance, and resumed tearing the paper into strips and tossing them into the flames. Guilt seeped through his gut again.

With a loud slurp of tea, Thompson leaned back, stretched his legs, and heaved a tired sigh. "I hope your foul mood isn't about Malone. You can't be sailing the waters of Cape Stiff feeling melancholy. Not when you're apt to spend a good deal of time strapped to your bunk."

"It's not about Malone." Hell, no place on board to be alone.

"Better to clear the air, son."

Wolf tossed what remained of the ledger on the floor beside him and pinched the bridge of his nose. "I did something today I'm having trouble living with."

Thompson remained silent.

Wolf shrugged. "Not sure I know how to go about correcting things."

"You mean the knife?"

"No." Wolf kept his gaze fixed on the flames charring the paper he'd tossed in. "I mean I accosted one of your passengers today, and it's not sitting well on my conscience."

Thompson cocked a brow.

Wolf heaved a sigh. How the hell did he go about saying what needed to be said? "While you were meeting with the Malones, their daughter came to call."

Now it was Thompson's turn to keep his eyes fixed on the fire. "What happened?"

"I'm not sure if I really know. She invited herself in here, but when I tried to help her right back out, she wouldn't budge. Sat there muttering something . . . some crazy fool things." He didn't know why, but for some odd reason, he didn't want to divulge the part about her suggesting marriage.

"And?"

"After the battle I had with her father this morning, I sure as hell wasn't in a mood to go another round if he found her in my stateroom. I finally got mad and shoved my hand up her dress to scare her off."

Tea spewed back into Thompson's cup. "You . . . you what?" He leaned forward, bent to look at Wolf's face. "You're serious, aren't you?"

"Would I make this up?"

Thompson set his cup on the floor. "And she let you?"

Wolf frowned when he saw a look of amusement mixed with incredulity on Thompson's face. "*Let* me? Damn it, Thompson, she didn't have a choice. I had one arm behind her, and the other crossed in front of her. She had no place to go."

Thompson leaned back, his look of amused surprise turning to one of undisguised humor. "She must like you," he said with a little chuckle and a shake of his head. "Tell me more."

"*Like* me? God Almighty, Thompson. Don't try to tell me if you spent the morning threatening me and warning me to stay away from your daughter, and I sat here tonight telling you I spent the afternoon with my hand shoved up her dress so far I could steal her necklace, that all you'd have to say is, *she must like you.*" Wolf grabbed his journal, tore the rest of the written pages out, and tossed them all into the fire. "What the hell's wrong with you, anyway?"

Thompson slid his body down so his head rested against the chair's back and grinned. "What you did wasn't right, I'll grant you. If it were any one of my daughters, I'd probably have you thrown overboard. But Alanna?" Thompson's lips trembled. He leaned on an elbow and covered his mouth with one hand. A chuckle slipped out. "Forgive me, Wolf. I'm so tired, I suppose I'm slaphappy." And then he broke into a hearty laugh. "I wish I could've been a mouse in the corner."

Wolf's frustration turned to boiling anger. "You can be such a horse's ass."

Thompson finally contained himself. "Ease up on yourself. There was nothing you could have done to hold Alanna down if she didn't want to be there. She can yell and scream and raise the biggest hissy fit a female ever made, if she's of a mind to. Although, come to think of it, I haven't seen her do that in many a year."

Wolf shoved a hand through his hair. "I sure as hell didn't figure your reaction right at all, so I guess it's best if we put a halt to this conversation." He pulled an envelope from between the pages of his ledger and handed it to Thompson. "Would you deliver this apology to Alanna in secret?"

Thompson slipped the envelope into his jacket pocket. "I'll see she gets it tomorrow, first off."

He sat back and stroked his beard as he studied Wolf. "You've had some pretty rough treatment from her parents, by the way. I think you've handled it well. I do hope you're man enough to admit to yourself that rejection hurts." Thompson measured his words. "Especially when it comes from the parents of someone you're attracted to."

Before Wolf could speak, Thompson raised a hand and continued. "And after what you've told me just now, and what you said the first night they came to dinner, when you claimed you'd rather have any elderly woman aboard for feminine company than a powder keg of a young one? Well, it makes sense that you ignored her all evening, because she's one helluva powder keg."

A gale hit the next day, welcoming them to the Horn.

Mates bellowed for all hands. Topmen scrambled up the rigging, furiously gathering canvas as the storm blasted the clipper with all the lethal wrath she had in her.

Thompson ordered upper yards lowered to take the strain off the mast as the storm plunged the tips of the ship's yardarms below the sea's boiling surface. Passengers were ordered to their bunks to tie down—crew members lashed themselves to the rails and masts to keep from being washed overboard by the waist-deep waves pounding the deck.

All night long, the clipper lurched and heaved as the mighty surf exploded all around her. The torrent of rain and hail mingled with the roar of the waves until Wolf thought his eardrums would burst. He vowed this would be his only trip through such a hideous place.

The next day a blizzard struck.

The passengers saw little of one another over the next thirteen days as the ship repeatedly tacked back and forth over the same route in the screaming winds—a desperate attempt to gain miles through the icy rains or blasting snow-storms that pelted the ship.

When the storm finally abated, and they headed toward

the Atlantic and the Eastern Seaboard, Wolf stayed busy and kept to himself. Oftentimes, he was able to find work mending sails or ropes and checking the inventory that lasted throughout the dinner hour.

The few times he could not avoid the gathering, he joined them, but offered little in the way of conversation, or eye contact with the other passengers. Alanna continued to observe him with the same calm, but made no further attempt to meet with him.

During her exercise periods, Wolf made sure he worked below. But there were times he assisted the crew on deck when she, and her mother, or Hsui Lin were there. She watched him then.

Always.

And he knew it.

He detested that Thompson was right about his attraction to her. He also resented his feelings, resented the urge to speak to her, or even to think about her. Most of all, he resented her constant intrusion upon his dreams.

He worked diligently with Thompson and the crew. The men came to respect him for his willingness to do whatever it took to get the job done. Any job. In time, Wolf was able to make sense of the bills of lading. There wasn't anything wrong with them. Cargo was missing.

Among the crew, Wolf could not find one that he could come close to suspecting. By the time they neared Boston, Thompson had no recourse but to sadly point his finger at Malone. That, he would do after authorities were called aboard.

Wolf and Thompson kept their decision to themselves. No one would have guessed there was anything wrong, especially at the captain's dinner their last night. The Malones were punctual, as usual, but tonight, the women came dressed in their finest.

Wolf squelched his bright flare of desire when Alanna entered the stateroom. She wore a cream-colored dress of a soft fabric, which hugged the curves that had grown increasingly sensuous to him. Over her dress, she had on a short beaded jacket—the very beads that had spilled across the deck.

Wolf flashed a wicked grin at Thompson.

"We used every last bead we had, not a one left over," Mrs. Malone announced when both the captain and Wolf complimented her on her handicraft.

"How long do you plan to remain in Boston?" Malone asked Wolf.

His lips thinned. "Only as long as business requires." *Not to worry, you won't see my face again, you sorry bastard.*

"Will you be returning to San Francisco, or Missouri?" Mrs. Malone chimed in.

"Missouri." Wolf had no idea where he would go after he solved his mother's murder. A sudden emptiness at the idea threatened his mood. He glanced across the table, and nearly winced. Alanna was so without guile—a breath of fresh air never to be taken again after the morrow.

Abruptly, he excused himself. The others at the table ceased their discourse. He returned with two small packages, and a third that was cylindrical and approximately ten inches long.

He handed one of the small packages to Malone. "For you. The remainder of my ginger tea and wrist bands."

Mr. Malone's grin widened. His head bobbed up and down.

He turned. "For you, Mrs. Malone. A bag of beads, the remainder of those I'd collected the day they scattered all over the deck." Wolf grinned at her with overstated innocence she could do nothing about.

Thompson chuckled.

Mrs. Malone regarded Wolf, not much differently from

the way she had the day she'd refused his find. "Thank you.
I . . . I appreciate your kindness." Pink splotches marked her
cheeks.

Wolf reached across the table and deposited the round
package in front of Alanna. "And this is for you, Alanna
Malone," he said softly.

Mrs. Malone's gaze darted from Wolf to her husband,
who sat quietly waiting for his daughter to open her gift.
He didn't so much as flinch at Wolf calling her by the name
he'd forbidden Wolf to use.

Alanna picked up the object, and unwrapped the cloth
surrounding it. "Oh," she whispered. Lifting it, she turned
the carved cylinder in her hand, inspecting the way Wolf had
fitted the broken pieces of beveled glass into the front, and
on each side and bottom, in small slits carved into the wood.
At the center of one end of the cylinder rested a small vial
Wolf had appropriated from the ship's medicine chest and
filled with oil. Beads and sequins glistened and floated in
the clear liquid, some of the very ones Mrs. Malone had
turned down the day they had scattered across the deck.

"What the devil is that?" Mr. Malone demanded.

Alanna lifted it to one eye and pointed it at the chandelier
hanging over the table. "It's a kaleidoscope." Her voice was
soft as a whisper when she laid the piece of wood down and
bent her head over it. Silence permeated the room as she ran
her fingers, feather soft, over her gift, as though she were
lost in her own world. "Thank you."

She raised her head and looked into Wolf's eyes. With a
blink, a tear splashed down her cheek. She made no attempt
to wipe it away or to hide it. "I shall keep this with me,
always."

Wolf's heart thundered.

"Let me see that." Malone snatched the object up in his
plump hand, and played with it until her mother begged for
a turn.

Wolf was surprised at the Malones' lack of objection to Alanna's response. It was as though an invisible power held their tongues. Perhaps it was because it was their last night aboard ship that they chose to ignore the way Wolf looked at her; or perhaps it was because he'd presented the gift to their daughter openly.

The Malones pleaded fatigue shortly after dessert and left for their bunks.

Wolf and Thompson spent their final evening in front of the fire. They were sipping whiskey and chuckling over events when a knock sounded at the door. Before either man could stand, Alanna entered the room and marched over to the two. She handed the captain an envelope.

"This is for you." She turned to the fireplace, her back to them.

"What is it?" Thompson queried.

Uncomfortable, Wolf rose to excuse himself.

"No. Don't leave. This concerns you, as well." Her back went a little straighter, her head a bit higher. "My father knows I am here, but he does not know why. And I beg you not to address this issue with him, Captain."

Thompson's face was a sudden display of fatherly concern. "Good God, what is it?" He started to rise once more.

"Please, sit, sir. I won't be staying long. In that envelope is all the money for the missing cargo. I stole it."

Wolf flew out of his chair and moved across the room, far enough away to gather his wits—and to observe her. He sensed she wasn't lying. She still acted calm and reserved, but he saw great pain etched in her face.

Thompson reached for her.

She retreated.

Wolf stared at her, torn between wanting to rush to her side and an odd sense of having been betrayed.

"It was my running-away money. My last hope before I

returned to Boston." She flashed a pained glance at Wolf, then back at Thompson.

Direct and forthright, she continued. "I hired certain men, not aboard this ship, to help me while we were in San Francisco. As you well know, Captain, I have sailed with my father for a long while, and helped him in his business. Enough so that I thought I could get away with it."

Wolf came forward, stood directly in front of her. Her eyes held his penetrating gaze. "Why would you have to steal from your own father? Surely, if you wanted money to run . . . to do whatever, you must have jewelry—"

"I have nothing of my own. My father owns everything, controls everything—and everyone. All I hear is 'this will all be yours one day, Alanna,' until I could spit."

Pain shadowed her features like a cloud passing over the sun. "Oh, I can have whatever I want, do whatever I care to do, as long as it goes on his account or passes under his nose."

She flashed a glance at Thompson, her eyes filled with hot, angry tears, her voice filled with repulsion. "But marriage to someone I cannot stomach for even five minutes? I will not do that."

She turned back to Wolf. "But what I have done is not right. This was no way to gain my freedom. Nor was coercing or manipulating anyone else." Her eyes narrowed at Wolf. "That is something I would never do."

Wolf nodded silently.

She turned to leave. "Do what you must, Captain, even if it means informing my father."

Wolf stepped in front of her and caught her at the shoulders. "But what will he do?"

She shrugged her shoulders free. "Oh, you mustn't worry about my father hurting his precious daughter. At least not physically, if that's what has you concerned. Obviously, you did not hear me clearly. Father will simply find other ways of controlling me. The captain has been around my family long enough to know my father can be extremely clever when it comes to drawing a circle around someone from which there is no escape."

"Keep the money, Alanna." Thompson's voice sounded weary.

"I cannot. We've been friends too long, and I know you would only replace it with your own." She smiled through a shimmer of tears.

She walked over to the captain. "See me to my cabin, will you please?" She slipped her arm through his.

"Good evening, Wolf," she said, and looked directly at him one last time.

He shook his head, amazed by her steady demeanor.

"Good evening, Miss Malone," he murmured. An odd stirring rolled through his gut at her calm manner—and at her imminent departure.

He was still by the fire when Thompson returned. They sat quietly for a time.

Finally, Thompson spoke. "You know what I think?"

"What?"

"I think you're going to miss her a helluva lot."

The last thing Wolf needed was a discussion of the woman who'd just left his life. "Don't start." He grabbed a glass of whiskey and stomped out of the cabin.

Chapter Nine

Boston—Late October

A hollow ache in Wolf's gut overrode his hunger. Who the hell cared about food—or anything else, for that matter? What a disgusting three weeks he'd put in, with today being the lowest point. Not bothering to don anything more than trousers, he lay on his bed in the Tremont House Hotel, watching a crack in the ceiling seem to lengthen in nightfall's deepening shadows.

The more he dug into the past, the more obscure became the mystery surrounding his mother's death. He'd finagled his way into the dank chambers of Boston's newspaper archives this morning. The only things he'd found surrounding the date of his mother's death were neatly clipped empty spaces in yellowed newspapers. Forays into the local cemeteries proved futile as well. A search through the hall of records produced nothing with regard to his parents. Furthermore, he couldn't even locate a record of his own birth.

It was as though his family had never existed.

His reception at police headquarters this afternoon had been even more of a riddle. What the hell was *that* about? He'd been greeted with stern consternation by a seasoned watch commander who'd disappeared briefly after Wolf had inquired about the murder. He'd returned alongside a growling, saggy-jowled superior enveloped in an aura of menace. The man had demanded to know who Wolf was, and why he was inquiring about a murder more than twenty years old.

They'd situated him in a moldy-smelling room in the belly of the building. Despite the officer's vulgar coughing, he'd failed to cover the sounds of a key grating in the old lock. Wolf had promptly vacated the premises by way of a small, high window he'd forced open with his hunting knife.

Misery clouded any expectations of finding his mother's killer. In the short span of three lonely weeks, Wolf felt as though he'd lost the final vestiges of his childhood. The emptiness of the man he'd become, and where his aimless life had led him invaded the fortress he'd built around himself. Had there ever been much of anything to his life after all?

How long he'd lain in his bed, he couldn't tell. In any event, the day disappeared altogether and the frequency of voices along the hallway diminished. This meant most of the guests had departed, either for the hotel's dining room or into the crisp night air to one of Boston's renowned restaurants.

A tree limb scraped against the window, its shadows scurrying across the ceiling like spiders on the run. His skin crawled. With a laborious sigh, he kicked his feet to the floor and padded barefoot to the window. Pressing his palms to each side of the window casing, he watched the branch grate and thump against the pane. Tomorrow he'd change rooms. He yanked the drapes tightly together, moved to the gas wall sconce across from the bed, and lit the flame.

A knock sounded on the door.

He checked the clock on the wall—twenty minutes past eight. "Aw, Christ."

This was the second night in a row he'd failed to appear at the Thompson home for dinner. Why the hell had he agreed to go? It must have been the youngest Thompson child's winsome, gap-toothed smile that had done it.

Guilt replaced dejection. He headed for the door, hoping Thompson hadn't brought the child with him—*another* of the man's promises if Wolf failed to show. After such a dismal day, he doubted he could handle the mercurial emotions of a six-year-old.

He opened the door and swallowed a gasp.

There stood Alanna Malone, chin up and back stiff. Behind her hovered a hulk of an Asian man. He was tall— and ageless. His black, riveting eyes sparked deep into Wolf's, seeming to pierce his very existence. A flash of lightning shot through him. He swore it had come straight from the man's eyes.

Very few people were capable of disturbing Wolf's demeanor of indifference, but this man did. And so did the woman standing before him. His memory hadn't played tricks on him—if anything, she was even lovelier than he remembered.

"Invite us in, please." Alanna breezed past him.

"Yes, ma'am." Wolf caught her scent as she passed. He suppressed a smile, shook his head in amused surrender, and stepped aside for the stranger.

An aura of inherent wisdom hovered about this enigmatic man who entered without a word. An almost intimidating power enveloped him, yet one without any residue of threat.

Intriguing.

Wolf shut the door and moved toward the center of the room where Alanna stood. Had the temperature in the room gone up or was it *her* firing his blood? Thompson had been right that last night aboard ship—Wolf had missed the hell out of her.

The strange man stepped across the room, paused in front of the wall sconce, and crossed his arms over his chest. His actions reminded Wolf of how he himself settled in to observe a situation. The light shining from behind the man created a nimbus around him that made it virtually impossible to make out his features—a trick Wolf often used.

He turned his full attention to Alanna. Did the man's presence add a certain propriety to her being in Wolf's room? Was that the reason for her boldness? He didn't know—and he damn well didn't care. New life bloomed in him, vanquishing the low mood that had gripped him over the past weeks. He wanted to tease Alanna once again, to reach out and touch her hair, run a finger lightly down her cheek.

Hell, he wanted to kiss her.

Instead, he fisted his hands on his hips. One corner of his mouth inched upward. "How did you know where to find me?"

"You disappointed Little Mary when you failed to show for dinner, and the Thompsons are concerned about you." She set a purple reticule on the bed and fiddled with it. "Wolf, meet my guardian, Old Chinese." She didn't look up as she spoke. Instead, she began lining long shiny needles in rows and laying out small gray pieces of something Wolf could not discern. Old Chinese stepped forward.

"Whoa!" Wolf reached for his shirt. "I saw enough of that torture going on back in San Francisco's Chinatown to know it won't be happening to me anytime soon."

"Don't bother putting that on," Alanna said matter-of-factly. "There are circles under your eyes and you're strung tight as a drum. These will relax you and it is hardly torture."

"Oh, no. Unh-uh." Wolf backed away, shaking his head. "If you think this guardian of yours is about to shove needles in me, think again. And I hope you're not of a mind to hold me down, because it would take an army."

This time Old Chinese flashed a broad grin, exposing a set of crooked, very white teeth. "You are perceptive, sir. And you carry a good sense of humor."

A shaft of surprise ran through Wolf. The man spoke with

a flawless Oxford accent, his resonant voice filled with deep authority. Where the hell did he come from?

Alanna continued laying out the needles.

Wolf jerked his head toward Old Chinese. "I will not allow anyone to stick those nasty-looking needles in me."

He took Alanna by the shoulders and turned her to face him. Chamomile soap, roses . . . and her personal scent hit his nostrils. The muscles in his groin clenched. "No," he said softly.

Her eyes narrowed. "Why not?"

An incredulous laugh escaped Wolf's lips. "Because this is insanity, that's why not."

"Are you afraid of a few needles?"

No, he was afraid he couldn't keep his hands off her. "I haven't laid eyes on you since the ship docked some three weeks ago, and suddenly here you are, knocking on my door with a stranger at your side, and announcing with no explanation whatsoever, that you and Old Chinese here would very much like to puncture various parts of my anatomy. And you actually expect me to comply?"

"Yes."

A spark of humor creased the old man's face.

"Ah, Alanna, darlin'." Wolf's hand came off her shoulder and under her chin, tilting it upward. "Your diplomacy stinks."

Old Chinese grinned and tapped his hard biceps. "I am to hold you down. Miss Malone will stick you."

Wolf dropped his hold on Alanna and stood assessing the two for a long while. While each of them was a powerful presence in their own right, together they seemed to form a third, even more commanding energy. They said little to one another, yet they moved in unison. She appeared to have a stronger and more vital connection to Old Chinese than to her parents.

"Let me guess. This man has been your guardian since you were—"

"Born," Old Chinese interjected.

Wolf took his time studying the man. "Pardon my ignorance, but you happen to be about the least likely candidate I'd ever figure to be looking after the Malones' daughter. Care to elaborate?"

Old Chinese moved to the bed and perused what lay atop it. "I met Malone on the docks in China several years prior to Miss Malone's birth. He hired me to guard valuable goods meant for transport." He took up a needle, and holding it to the light, squinted at its tip. "There was a murder that took place not two blocks from where Miss Malone was born. A child went missing, which set families on edge. Since I am trained in a particular martial art, I was assigned to protect her. Suffice it to say that not only did her self-centered parents have no time for her, they were incapable of rearing such an intelligent, headstrong girl, so the duty fell upon my shoulders. As it turned out, my role in her life has served us all rather well."

A chill ran through Wolf at the mention of his mother's murder. "But why are you still guarding her when she's a grown woman?"

From behind him, Wolf heard a soft, feminine ripple of laughter.

Old Chinese set down the needle and picked up another, holding that one to the light as well. "Since Miss Malone has no intention of marrying the man chosen for her, she could pose a threat to her parents' only chance of being accepted into the upper echelons of Boston society. It's no longer a matter of guarding Miss Malone from harm so much as keeping her out of mischief until the wedding."

Wolf turned to Alanna, who sat in the chair with a lazy grin. "Now, that I can easily understand."

Setting down the last of the needles, Old Chinese swept his hand toward the bed. "I am the perfect solution for selfish, prideful parents. Now, if you please."

A wayward thought slid to the surface of Wolf's mind. "Alanna, what were you doing at the Thompsons'? You didn't just happen in on them at the dinner hour, did you?"

"Of course not. I wouldn't think of dropping in on someone unannounced—" She stopped speaking when she realized what she'd said.

Mischief coursed through Wolf again. God, he'd missed that, as well.

The Asian bent over the bed and completed what Alanna had begun. To mask a grin?

This time it was her turn to place her hands on her hips. "I was invited. I visit often—have done so for years. And did I know you had been invited as well? Most assuredly."

Wolf lifted a brow. She'd always been able to throw him with her detached honesty.

"I was very much looking forward to seeing you again, Wolf. And since the captain told me your business matters have you at odds with yourself, I thought perhaps, if I . . . we—" She nodded toward Old Chinese. "If there was anything we could do to help, we would."

Wolf's hand slipped to the chain holding the backward garnet earring. Alanna's eyes had been leveled there the entire time she'd spoken. She couldn't know of his true purpose in Boston—Thompson would never have told her. He slipped the necklace off, made his way to the dresser, and deposited it in the top drawer.

Old Chinese studied him with an intensity that made the very air in the room swell. Wolf could feel the power in the man surge, as if the life force within him increased to envelop Wolf.

"I'm not the one who does the sticking, by the way," Alanna said. "That's Old Chinese's wicked sense of humor."

Wolf chuckled. "What a pair the two of you make." No wonder she was so very different from any woman he'd ever met. He turned to Old Chinese. "You raised her while her parents busied themselves trying to gain a foothold in society?"

"Mother never had any patience with me," Alanna responded. "And Father? Well, he would have preferred a son."

Wolf walked over to the bed and lay back on the stack of pillows. He crossed his hands behind his head and appraised Alanna from toe to head, and back again—drank her in like a man in the desert stumbling upon an oasis. Sometime in the last few minutes, his dark mood had evaporated like lake mist under a warming sun.

Alanna stepped back. "My friend here has wonderful hands. He can massage the tension from you, with or without the needles. Now that I know you've been under a great deal of pressure, I'm pleased I followed my instincts and came to you."

"Why do you have to be so damn honest, Alanna? Makes me feel like a rat."

"Let Old Chinese work on you," she said. "If you don't care for what he does, he'll stop and we'll leave you be."

Leave him? That was the last thing he wanted. He threw his hands in the air. "All right, I surrender." He turned to Old Chinese. "Do whatever you wish, but if I so much as raise my pinkie, you stop. Got that?"

"Got that," the man answered, his face creased with pleasure.

Wolf held his palms upward. "Where do you want me, and how?"

Old Chinese waved his hand back and forth across the bed, indicating Wolf should lie sideways. "It would be best if you disrobed."

Wolf leaped from the bed, his hands on the first button of his trousers. "Sure enough. And what does Miss Malone do while I strip naked?"

She pointed to the towel rack by the nightstand. "Miss

Malone closes her eyes while you wrap that bath towel around your derriere, you arrogant boor."

Wolf, filled with devilish curiosity as to how far he could go with his insolence, started on the buttons.

Alanna sat in a chair, folded her hands in her lap, and shut her eyes.

He dropped his trousers to the floor in a heap and sauntered across the room wearing nothing but a wicked smile. Whatever the hell her behavior while with Old Chinese, it was substantially different from what was acceptable in staid Boston.

"You aren't the only one who doesn't wear drawers, Alanna. Or are you tonight, what with this freezing weather?" *Explain that little remark to your guardian.* "Back or front?" he asked and flopped on the bed.

"Arse down, please," Old Chinese responded and laid a towel across Wolf's pelvis.

Wolf snorted and closed his eyes.

For the next two hours he floated in and out of himself as the Asian worked. Incense filled the room. Fragrant creams were massaged into his skin with strong hands that varied the degree of pressure and heat, seeming to increase their warmth at the points where Wolf's muscles were most tender. Long, thread-thin needles were inserted into various parts of his body—ears, hips, inside his calves—releasing flashes of childhood memories in Wolf's head. The intensity and clarity of his visions surprised him, yet they did nothing to dampen his peaceful mood.

By the time Old Chinese completed the session, Wolf lay on the bed feeling more at ease than he could recall. Gone was his belligerence, the lack of caring, the sense of isolation.

Alanna still sat in the chair with her lids shut. Now, though, she appeared softer, less determined. Wolf viewed her in an entirely different light.

He climbed off the bed, slid into his trousers and fastened them. "You can open your eyes now."

She stood. "Captain Thompson said your business undertaking has been delayed and you'll have to depend on him and others to complete it. Old Chinese lives deep in the countryside on a farm belonging to my father. He'd like to have you as his guest for however long it takes to complete your business. Would you accept his offer?"

Wolf made his way to the window, where he parted the drapes and stared out at the night. "And have your father stumble across me? No thanks."

"My father rarely visits the farm. He likes the idea of owning a great deal of land, but doesn't care for country life." Alanna flashed a slicing, cynical smile. "He's too busy being a *tycoon*."

Wolf grunted. "Don't tell me. Your father turned the place over to Old Chinese, but every time he comes to call, it's in better shape than the time before? Smart man."

"I have worked diligently for Miss Malone's family," Old Chinese said. "In exchange, I have free run of the family farm. I consider it my duty, not to Miss Malone's father, but to the land I live on, to give back more than what I take. I am quite comfortable with the arrangement."

"And what of you, Alanna?" Wolf drank her in. He could sense that she and Old Chinese wouldn't be staying much longer. Already he was aware of the briefness of their visit.

"What about me?"

"Would you come visit me on the farm?" His lips pursed in a small smirk, his voice teased, but he veiled his eyes from hers.

"Yes, of course. I visit there often. I would like that."

Immense relief washed through him. He'd grown damn weary of living alone in hotels.

Alanna glanced at Old Chinese, sending a silent message.

The man collected the contents of the reticule, drew the strings together, and disappeared from the room in a flash.

Wolf stood transfixed as moments passed and Old Chinese failed to return. "Is he standing outside the door with his ear pinned to it, or did your guardian actually leave you alone with me?"

Something ancient shifted in Wolf.

He moved toward her. "Or was that odd look you sent across the room your signal to send him on his way? Are you his little ward, or his employer?"

Without a word, Alanna stood and made her way to the window. She separated the drapes and looked down at the street.

"Aren't you concerned you'll be recognized coming and going from a hotel?" he asked.

"Old Chinese will see to it that I am not."

"How so?"

She didn't respond.

Wolf felt compulsively drawn to her side. He looked down and saw a hulking figure standing in the shadows. "How the hell did he get down there so fast?"

Alanna remained silent.

Against his will, Wolf brought his hand up and touched her shoulder. He let his finger trace lightly down her arm, the side of her hand. A shiver raced across her flesh as his hand closed ever so gently over hers. His heart gave a jolt.

Like gunpowder set alight, his blood exploded. He closed his eyes, steeled himself against the heady emotion. If he didn't do something at once, his loneliness would take him beyond mere thoughts of what he wanted to do to her.

He gritted his teeth and stepped back from her. It took all the strength he possessed. "What are you doing alone in a man's hotel room?" His voice came as a harsh growl. "For God's sake, this is worse for you than aboard ship. Leave."

Alanna turned around. "You're right. I must go, but not

for the reason you think." Nonetheless, she stood in one place.

Wolf returned to the bed. He flopped on his back, his head against the pillows. Had he actually seen her eyes fill with desire? An incredible feeling of tenderness, and a craving to express it, overcame him.

He observed her through half-closed lids. Where he'd once thought her strange, he now found her fascinating. He was attracted to her unconventional personality, to the way she strained old codes of behavior and still managed to maintain her dignity. He also found her self-control enticing, a discipline that conveyed a sense of complete security.

It was this very restraint that Wolf wanted to challenge. Perhaps her strength of will masked underlying passion. A hell of an ache gripped his groin. He spread an arm out and patted the space beside him. "Come lie beside me." His voice grew husky. "For only a moment, Alanna. Let me hold you before you leave."

Alanna steeled herself. "I cannot do that."

Wolf was far tenderer than he'd care to have anyone know. And everything about him right now was a full expression of that terrible tenderness threatening to vanquish her self-control. Dear God. To lose herself in him before he felt safe enough to share his heart would destroy what she desperately wanted. She had no choice—she had to set strong boundaries.

Nonetheless, she was inexplicably drawn forward, only able to halt her approach when she reached the end of the bed. Her hands gripped the brass foot rail. He regarded her with eyes that seemed to bare her very soul. A slow-moving heat rippled through her, pooled in her belly.

Sensuousness coalesced with the mischief in Wolf's smile as he snuggled his head a little deeper into the pillow. "You must be an enigma to Boston's society. Too bad you are owned by your father—such ownership precludes autonomy."

They stared at one another for an eternity—he, spread out like a banquet; she with her knuckles white from gripping the bed's foot rail.

"Take your hair down for me, Alanna."

His husky words blazed through her veins, sent her heart pounding erratically, and whipped wicked pleasure through her thighs. "No."

"Are you afraid of me, Alanna, or just plain cold?"

"I am not cold." Her fingers gripped the brass railing tighter, the metal heating beneath her hands. He was so near, she absorbed his ruggedness, his vital power. Blood hammered in her ears. "I have great passion, Wolf. So great, I feel as though I cannot take in a deep breath, as though I might lose myself entirely."

His expression changed. He rose on one elbow. Startling blue eyes pierced the distance between them. The tip of his tongue swept his bottom lip, leaving it moist. "I'll say it again—take your hair down for me." Raw with emotion, his voice came as a bare whisper.

"No."

"Tell me why not."

"Because I doubt I would be able to control myself thereafter." Her answer came clear and determined, but with a hint of beseeching.

"Because your hair is down, you could not control yourself?" Fire raged in his eyes.

"Why do *you* want my hair down?" Her chin rose in defiance. "Tell me what setting my hair free will do for *you?*" She watched a tremor pass through him.

His nostrils flared. "Would it be so terrible if taking your hair down did the same thing to both of us? Would it be so terrible to share such sweet feelings?"

"Sweet?" She cleared her throat as his eyes roved slowly

over her body. "I'm afraid such feelings, as you are well aware, are beyond sweet." Her resolute strength turned to excruciating longing. "I cannot . . . I feel as though I would lose myself entirely, and . . . and you are not at that place yet."

His head tilted quizzically. "What *place*?"

"I want you to fall off the ends of the earth in love with me. That's the place of which I speak—the one place where I am willing to lose myself in you." Head spinning, she let go of the brass bed rail as though it burned her flesh. "It would be a slow death to do otherwise."

"How long have you felt this way?" Wolf was still on one elbow, regarding her with blue fire.

"Since I first laid eyes on you. Back in the hotel in San Francisco."

"Over one little dinner? You stared at me and my friends throughout one meal, and you came to these conclusions?"

"Before then, Wolf. The first time you stayed at the Morgan Hotel."

Wolf leaned back into his pillow, studying her with a new and curious intensity.

"You don't remember me, but when I saw you in the hotel that first time, wearing buckskins and a scruffy beard, I saw through the dirt, as if I were seeing you through a special lens. I knew you would be back. I knew the second time, in the dining room when you were clean-shaven and formally dressed, that it was you."

She turned to leave, but paused with her hand on the door-knob. "You love to touch the flesh of a woman, don't you?" Her voice had grown thick with emotion. "But you're afraid to go much beyond that. Something tells me you shield yourself from the fear that every relationship ends sooner or later—through death, or through someone's leaving. It's a part of the human condition. You know it is as much a natural part of a relationship as breathing is a natural part of staying alive, yet the idea frightens you. And so you avoid getting caught up with anyone. But here I am."

His lips parted in surprise, and his face paled. Quickly, he put on a smile that set her on edge.

"That's it, isn't it, Wolf? You're afraid of someone leaving you."

He shook his head slightly, but she suspected it was less in denial than in consideration of what she'd said.

She opened the door. "Once you are no longer afraid, then it will be easy for you to fall off the ends of the earth for someone." Alanna nodded to the space beside him. "Then, when you ask, that's right where I'll be. Forever."

Softly, she closed the door behind her, pulled the hood of her cloak over her head, and hurried to the servants' stairs.

Chapter Ten

One week later

Wolf leaned against the coupe rockaway in the silver dawn, its door hanging open as he tried to coax Little Mary, Thompson's youngest, and Alanna's namesake, out of the carriage. Off in the distance, the captain hollered for Julia. The dog's rambunctious yipping told Wolf there'd be no rescue from this sticky situation anytime soon.

Little Mary's round eyes lit Wolf's world when they filled with joy, but let tears fall, and his heart broke faster than he could figure out how to help her.

She brushed at her wet cheeks and busied herself by pushing rows of white eyelet ruffles into place beneath her red coat. "Will you be marrying Miss Malone right off when we get there?"

"Wha . . . what?" Wolf straightened away from the carriage.

"I said—"

"I heard you, sweetheart." Where the hell did she get that insane idea? He pressed his forehead against the cold metal of the carriage. No wonder she insisted on stowing away—and wearing that fancy dress—she thought she was going to a wedding! He doubted he'd ever get used to the uninhibited spontaneity of this winsome chatterbox. Alanna Mary Thompson, or Little Mary, as they called her, had a bad habit of eavesdropping, only to skew the information she culled.

Still, he adored her. "Sweetheart," he began while collecting his thoughts. "Where did you get the idea we were going to a wedding today?"

"From you." She grinned, exposing the gap where she'd lost her front teeth.

"Me?"

"Yeth." Her pink tongue poked through the gap. "You thaid you'd like to marry me, but you'd be a very old man by the time I'm grown, tho you'd have to find another Mary."

"Whoa, wait. That I did say, but your father and I are attending a business meeting, not a wedding." He took a step back, scanning the area for Thompson. Where the hell was he?

"Watch out for Julia!" Little Mary giggled uproariously as the dog bounded around the corner of the carriage and climbed all over Wolf. He swore under his breath at the muddy paw prints all over his fur-lined broadcloth coat.

Thompson trotted up. "Princess, if you'll see Julia inside for Papa, when I return, I'll take you both on a fancy carriage ride about town."

"Can we stop at the thweet shop?"

"Of course."

Little Mary's face lit up. She scrambled out of the carriage and raced for the house without a backward glance. Her mother waved and closed the door behind girl and dog.

"That's all it took?" Wolf climbed onto the front seat of the rockaway.

Thompson grinned. "Care to take the first leg?"

Wolf grabbed the reins and with a flick of his wrist, set the two Morgans in motion down the drive and onto the street.

"Sorry about your coat," Thompson said.

"The worst of the whole business was I couldn't curse at the damn dog with your daughter's ears out like an elephant's."

Thompson laughed. "Maybe that's a good thing."

"Don't think so." Wolf picked at a clump of mud clinging to his coat. "Holding anything in tends to curdle a man's insides over the long haul."

"Leave the dirt alone," Thompson cautioned. "It'll brush right off when it's dry."

Wolf scowled. "I'm not ignorant. How the hell do you think I kept my buckskins clean?"

"You call those rags clean? What a relief you packed them away."

Wolf ignored him. "Did you know your daughter thought she was going to Miss Malone's wedding, and I was the groom?" He shot a scowl at Thompson's chuckle. "I am not that man."

"Perhaps you could be."

"You seem to ignore the fact that I would make a piss-poor husband for the likes of anyone. Not interested."

"Well, she's interested in you."

Wolf jostled the reins, half to speed the horses and half to hide his jolt of embarrassment. "Like hell. Women of her class don't marry because they like someone. They marry for convenience. And don't go reminding me about your Martha—again. Besides, it usually helps if the feeling's mutual."

"I'd wager it is. You're plenty sensitive to have noticed Alanna is attracted to you."

"I'm not sensitive enough to know crap." Wolf handed the reins to Thompson, shoved his arms across his chest, and stared out at the skeletal trees that arced against the sky's bleak backdrop.

"Sure, you are. Look what you just did."

"What the hell did I just do?"

"You did two things," Thompson replied. "One, you handed me the reins, which tells me you know that what affects you affects the horses. And two, you slipped back into your old attitude and crude manner of speaking. Seems to me, that's where you hide out."

Wolf continued to stare out at nothing. He should have stayed in the West. He should have kept riding his goddamn horse all over nowhere.

He could use a shot of whiskey. Good whiskey.

They were out of the city and into the countryside when Wolf spoke again. "You happened to have had decent work when you and Martha met. What the hell am I supposed to do, throw a woman on the back of my horse, buy some old nag, and line my kids up on its swayback according to height? Ride around the prairie for the rest of our goddamn lives?"

"Is that what's stopping you, son?"

Wolf went back to staring out at nothing, no longer sure what all bothered him of late. "I'm here to find out who killed my mother and then I am going back to St. Joe. Understood?"

"Aye, aye."

Alanna climbed out of the tub and grabbed a towel. A puddle formed around her feet on the hard wooden floor of Old Chinese's bathing area.

Take your hair down for me, Alanna.

Wolf's passion-filled words vibrated through her, as fresh as the night he'd spoken them. It happened again—an involuntary quickening, something no amount of discipline seemed to discourage of late. The tips of her breasts hardened. Liquid heat pooled in her belly.

She wondered dispassionately what it was about her that he found attractive. Her skin was a shade too dark. Well, blame the sun. And according to her mother, her lips were completely unfashionable as well. As if Alanna cared what society dictated with regard to anything, let alone the shape of a person's mouth. Thank goodness her long, skinny legs had finally filled out. Nonetheless, her mother still had the annoying habit of bruising her thighs when she pinched them in passing and complaining of their wretchedness. And in her mother's eyes, Alanna's full breasts were hopeless. A man would surely be reminded of a cow if he were ever to see such a ghastly sight, her mother had repeatedly told her.

Suddenly, something pricked her senses. Her head snapped up. She focused on the windows at the front of the building.

He was on his way to her.

She could feel it in her bones.

Barefoot, Alanna padded across the room to where her starched clothing lay. She dressed slowly, meticulously, in her white garb, and then fitted a black sash twice around her waist so the ends tied in front. Next, she smoothed her hair and braided it, left the single braid to trail down the middle of her back.

When she sensed Wolf was close enough, she stepped directly in front of the window and peered down the long driveway. A black speck, no bigger than a fly, appeared in the distance.

It was time to begin her other preparations. Silently, she slipped from the window, sat with her legs crossed and her eyes closed. In her mind, she entered the fire of the dragon.

The thin sun that briefly appeared never did manage to lend any warmth to the crisp air. The low, gray sky reminded Wolf of a tilled field turned upside down, ready for the planting. He breathed deep of the fresh, cold air, and exhaled a cloud of mist.

After a long silence, Thompson spoke. "I've been thinking."

Wolf grunted. "Life gets real dangerous when you go and do things like that."

"If you're as easy with women as you are with a horse—"

"Told you it gets real dangerous when you think."

"I was thinking about that graphic picture you created of an old nag's back lined with ragamuffins." Thompson grinned. "Somehow I doubt you'd ever let anything like that come about. You strike me as a man who would see to his children's needs, no matter what the cost. I see the way you are around my girls. You must not do too badly for yourself financially, either."

Wolf shrugged. "I do all right. Sure as hell not like you, though. Christ, you gave me some kind of song and dance back when we sailed the Horn about how your poor little Martha, coming from noble British stock, married down. In case you haven't noticed, that house you live in is a mansion. And the trappings inside don't come cheap, either. No wonder your kind are referred to as merchant princes. If your wife married down, I'd hate to see your idea of wealth."

Thompson slowed the horses and made a turn onto a long drive. "I don't think a woman like Alanna gives a hoot about material things."

Wolf grunted. "You're in a rut with this conversation."

"Well, I do have somewhere to go with it if you'd allow me to finish. I sure am curious as to what happened to your parents' wealth."

A cloud of misery settled in Wolf's heart. "What in God's name is going on? It's as though my past fell off the face of the earth. It had to have taken a good deal of money to live in that area of Boston. Do you suppose my father died penniless? Did those years after my mother died break him financially?"

"It happens," Thompson answered. "But what if he transferred everything to England before he left for India? Is England where he was from originally?"

"Don't remember." Wolf tapped his temple. "But ever since that Chinaman stuck those damn needles in me, I've been having odd dreams that make me recall things here and there. Guess England's next on my agenda, since that's where I was shipped off to school. I can remember the name of the place now. Yesterday, I sent off a letter of inquiry. There had to have been some kind of monetary arrangement for my education and personal needs. That could be a lead."

Thompson scratched his head. "When I return to town, I can instruct your detectives to begin an investigation of European financial institutions as well."

Wolf nodded. "May as well. The agency will likely have to hire extra men to handle it all. I'll send a letter of authorization along with you." He heaved a sigh. "Oh, hell. Here I am, supposedly the crème de la crème of trackers, and all I'm doing is holing up on some farm and hiring other people to do the work."

"You *are* the best," Thompson replied. "But you're too close to the matter to make objective decisions. Even men of medicine don't try to operate on themselves. But you already know that or you wouldn't be on the road with me today."

They cleared a small knoll and an expansive mansion loomed before them. The brick home sprawled across a gently rolling hill nestled in a grove of tall, graceful trees, the stark branches like great masses of veins exposed against the cold, gray flesh of the sky.

"Well, hell, Thompson, now *that* monstrosity resembles a farmhouse about as much as that house of yours looks like a rundown sea shanty." The corners of Wolf's mouth twisted into a cynical grin. "I should have known when we started up this fancy drive that carries on for God knows *how* long, we wouldn't find some farmer pointing the way to Old Chinese with a pitchfork." He swallowed another curse and turned forward, settling down to observe his surroundings.

Granite statues of fauns and nymphs stood guard over a frozen ghost of a garden that extended to a haze of woods fronted by a pale ribbon of water. Gnarled vines in deep hibernation created arbors over carved paths jutting from the main house.

Wolf counted three floors to the red brick manse, its entire front graced by huge columns covering a walkway and porte cochere.

He wondered when Alanna planned to visit.

Surprise snagged him when Thompson drove past the house and continued down the tree-lined lane over a small hill. He headed in the direction of a glossy white stable with a massive rust-colored barn set to the rear.

A rush of excitement flooded Wolf at the sight of white-painted fences, frozen pastureland and a herd of horses, their heads to the ground and nibbling on brown grass.

Memories tumbled into Wolf's head—from the bustle of San Francisco's gold rush and its harbor clogged with tall-masted clipper ships, to the nightmarish Horn's howling winds battering against the door of his cramped quarters. Then on to staid Boston—yet another confining space stuffed with neatly compressed rows of fashionable brick and granite town houses.

Freedom.

He breathed deeply of the fresh air. How much he'd missed the wide-open spaces, and the feel of his loins hugging horse and saddle. Bewilderment banished his smile as Thompson failed to stop at the stables.

"Stables?" Wolf queried.

"Sure are. The best you'll ever find. Same with the horses inside."

Something was oddly out of place. Except for the horses and a few pigs roaming loose, the place seemed peculiarly devoid of life. Old Chinese couldn't possibly reside out here entirely alone. Could he? Despite the eerie silence, Wolf felt a thousand eyes peering at him from the safety of dank woods and through windows harboring darkened rooms.

His skin chilled.

At last, Thompson brought the carriage to a halt at the doors of the barn, a dull red hulk of a rectangle with a deep pitch to its shingled roof. Only two sides of the massive building were exposed. The remaining two sides butted against a high, deep berm. The barn held the look of a fortress.

"Home," Thompson announced and placed the reins in his lap. He glanced upward to a stack of paned windows fronting the barn.

Wolf followed suit and spied a shadowed figure at the window. "Home?" He looked at Thompson. "Aw, no. Don't tell me Old Chinese lives in the barn for Chri . . . in the barn?"

"Sure does." Thompson smiled. "After spending half your life sleeping under the stars, I think you might like it."

Wolf rolled his eyes.

Broad, rough-hewn double doors, managed by two slender Asian males, grated open in front of the waiting horses. Slight smiles, understated nods, and warm looks of recognition directed toward Thompson elicited his small nod in return.

"Guess the old man's not alone after all." Wolf sprang from the carriage, deftly missing the mud and thin sheets of iced-over puddles. He glanced around, committed his surroundings to memory as he waited for Thompson's directive.

The ground floor of the barn housed both horses and carriages. So what the hell was the building that looked like a stable? A pristine white vis-a-vis and a shiny black, horse-drawn sleigh stood glistening at the ready. There were Belgian draft horses, the color of glimmering gold, with luxurious hair as white as snow feathering down from knees to enormous hooves. The passive beasts watched calmly as everyone strode by.

Wolf trailed the group. As they entered the tack room with its array of gleaming saddlery and rich smell of polished leather, Wolf turned in a slow circle, trying to take it all in. His senses came alive to the familiar scents of horse and hay.

"You will have ample opportunity to choose as you please among all that is here," one of his escorts told him with great courtesy.

A hidden door, fitted discreetly into the wall at the rear of the tack room, opened to reveal a plain, but well-built, staircase leading to the upper levels of the barn. Incense. The same scent he'd encountered that night in his hotel room filled his nostrils. Old Chinese stood in wait at the head of the stairs. A shock wave set every nerve in Wolf's body tingling when he saw who stood beside the old man.

Alanna!

A familiar rush coursed through Wolf.

Gone was the Occidental attire—for both Alanna and Old Chinese. He wore a formal, brocade silk robe, indigo in color with what looked like a coat of arms embroidered in white on the sleeve. Beneath the open robe, Wolf spied a white uniform of some sort tied at the waist with a purple sash edged in black. Cloth slippers, fitted tight to the foot and split between the first two toes, adorned the man's feet.

Alanna wore a similar type of robe with what appeared to be a simple wide skirt beneath. As Wolf climbed the stairs, he saw that the white garment was split up the center like loose trousers. Her unadorned cotton clothing was tied at the waist with a black sash. She stood barefoot.

The two Asians entering the room behind the group gave crisp bows to Old Chinese, removed their slippers, and disappeared silently into the room.

After greeting Old Chinese in the same manner as Thompson and the men before him, Wolf stepped in front of Alanna, blood roaring in his ears.

No matter that she'd fully prepared herself in the manner in which she'd been trained, a startling current raced through

Alanna's veins at the sight of Wolf. His lips twitched, as if he might be biting them in order to suppress a wicked grin. Without a flicker of distraction, his smoldering gaze clung to hers as he lifted her hand and pressed a warm mouth to her flesh. A quiver ran up her arm.

A chuckle left his throat, so soft it sounded like held breath escaping. Ever the scamp, this one. He'd intended for her to hear it. He let go of her hand and unbuttoned his overcoat. His flashing eyes still boldly locked onto hers, he shrugged the wrap from his shoulders and into the hands of an attendant.

As Wolf's gaze drifted to the erratic pulse thrumming in the hollow of Alanna's neck, she struggled to swallow. Without a word, he turned and, following Thompson's lead, removed his boots and strolled into the room behind the captain.

It felt as though Wolf had embraced her and surrounded her with his warmth, only to leave her at the mercy of a cold draft. Head buzzing, she turned to Old Chinese, awash in bewilderment.

Amusement danced across his countenance. "You forgot to breathe."

Chapter Eleven

Old Chinese's manner had not altered since the night in Wolf's hotel room. Yet here, in his domain, he was clearly in charge.

"My dojo," Old Chinese said with a proud nod. "*Do* means *The Way*, and *jo* means *the place*. Dojo is where The Way is studied."

Wolf raised an eyebrow. What the devil was "The Way"?

Old Chinese's eyes glittered like black diamonds. "My dojo is a place for *Budo*, the art of keeping peace."

"Yeah, like my trusty knife manages to keep the peace." Wolf scanned the high walls of the cavernous space, where an array of formidable weaponry hung. He'd seen some of those lethal tools in action in San Francisco—a man could lose his head with a precise stroke of an innocent-looking pole. What the hell kind of place was this? And Alanna spent time here? What of her parents?

The old man swept the room with his hand. "The true mastering of these instruments is to become so well-trained that one rises above any need to use them."

"You don't say."

A fire blazed in a round iron container in the center of the room, sending a thin wisp of smoke exiting through a ventilation shaft in the high ceiling. Except for two gold and black lacquered chairs flanking a small table in one corner, the room was bereft of furniture. In some strange way, the place still gave Wolf a sense of comfort.

The other side of the large room suddenly hummed with men, all dressed in white, carrying food and drink. Where the devil had they come from? Wheat-colored woven mats were being set in a long, wide line across one end of the floor. Polished wooden plates were placed atop the mats, chopsticks were laid across the dishes.

A young man approached, carrying a bright-red lacquered tray filled with mugs. He handed one to Old Chinese, another to Wolf.

Old Chinese solemnly lifted his drink. "To you and your new home. May we serve you well."

Wolf raised his mug and then took a long swallow. The cool, aromatic ale raced down his throat and settled nicely in his stomach.

"Come, I must show you my proudest possession." Old Chinese escorted Wolf to a back corner of the room and toward a series of ornate screens.

Stepping behind the screens, Wolf chuckled. There stood an elaborate claw-footed tub, large enough for a man his size. Pipes jutted in and out of the walls. "I'll be damned."

Old Chinese beamed. "There is a cistern on the roof and a woodstove beneath it. I get hot water."

God, imagine stretching out in something like this. He could barely fit his ass in that small tub back in the hotel. "Do you ever share? The tub, I mean . . . alone . . . not together?" A quick image of Alanna flashed through his head. He raised the mug to his lips, hoping to hell Old Chinese couldn't read minds.

He nodded, and studied Wolf for a long moment. Something shifted in Old Chinese. "Tonight, we celebrate your arrival with a fine ceremonial banquet." He took a sip of his drink. "Tomorrow we shall begin your work."

For whatever reason, the subtle change in Old Chinese set Wolf on edge. He already knew he'd need to keep himself busy out here. The sight of those horses had him thinking, but what was running through the old man's head? "My work?"

"If you wish to discover who murdered your mother, you must first discover yourself and your misplaced memories."

Shit! The very air around Wolf shuddered and then closed in on him. Old habits—surveying the quickest exits, closing himself off to the people around him, mentally checking weapons hidden on his person—took second place to the buzzing in his brain and what felt like an iron band gripping his chest. He took a slow drink of ale while he regained control. "Thompson told you why I came to Boston, didn't he? Did he tell Alanna, as well?" Where the hell were those two anyway?

"He only told her that your business venture was going badly and he was concerned about you. You have much work to do, Wolf, and I am here to see it done."

Wolf stood in silence, aware of the beehive of activity beyond the screen, but not listening to it. He swallowed the rest of the ale and wiped his mouth with the back of his hand. "That acupuncture was your idea, wasn't it?" A muscle twitched alongside his jaw. "Don't bother answering what we both know. Whose idea was it to talk me into coming out here?"

"Miss Malone has her own reasons for wanting you here. You now know mine. You appear to be a sensible man when you set your stubborn pride aside. Given a little time, you'll see there is no other way to achieve your goal."

"So you fancy yourself my savior now, do you? You've got a hell of a way of asking me whether or not I'm interested, you son of a bitch."

Old Chinese chuckled. Even his laughter exuded a kind of mystery, as if he held the answer to some great, cosmic joke.

Wolf set his empty mug on the floor and stalked off, giving no heed to the men on the other side of the room, who were still preparing the celebration. He headed to the large window at the front. At least there he could look out at some open space.

To Wolf's surprise, men dotted the landscape. Some led horses in from pasture, others herded pigs into a pen, while still others scurried toward the barn carrying more platters and vessels. Wolf was amazed to see some of them walking about barefoot on the frozen ground. Others wore sandals, held to their feet by single black straps. All wore the same white uniform as those inside. None wore overcoats. What the hell was Alanna doing among all these men? Nothing made sense.

A small group was assembled beneath an immense leafless tree atop a wheat-colored knoll. The men performed exercises of some sort—long, smooth stretches of their legs, supple kicks in slow, controlled movements. Masterful hands thrusting forward and back in rhythmic maneuvers filled with grace and power.

Even from where he stood, the energy sent a quiver down Wolf's spine. Jeezus, these were finely honed masters of a killing art. They could defend themselves in ways so foreign to Western man that a bullet seemed meager self-defense in comparison.

Was Alanna as well-trained?

A tall, broad-shouldered man, quite distinct from the others, approached the group. He stood separate from them, observing. While the others all wore black sashes tied around their waist, this man's white robe was held together by a belt of fiery red. He was taller than Wolf, his hair cropped short, the color of coal, and it clung to his head in a halo of tight curls. He was definitely not Asian.

Wolf studied the scene before him while he listened to the hum of activity behind him. Old Chinese was right—Wolf couldn't seem to get any further on his own. And if those goddamned acupuncture sessions opened a curtain to his mind, then he'd agree to them. Maybe along the way, he'd learn a little of what these trained assassins knew.

Old Chinese appeared beside him. Wolf didn't so much as flinch. He'd have to get used to people knowing as much as he did—or more—about silently stealing up on people. A servant slid another tray filled with ale in front of him.

Wolf grabbed a mug and nodded toward the stately brick house. "Obviously you find this barn more comfortable than the main house, but why?"

"That dwelling is for my students. I am their teacher. I could not allow them to live here and I there," the Asian answered blandly.

Wolf glanced at Old Chinese. "Students? What goes on here?"

Old Chinese shoved a hand into each side of his large sleeves. "Blacks in the South are not the only ones bound by slavery in this country."

Wolf regarded Old Chinese, wary once more. It was plain that youth had long since cycled through the man—and the grounds of middle age had long been tilled and planted as well. Yet, here stood a vigorous, ageless man, his body held taut by as much sinew and muscle as any one of the students.

Wolf drained his mug, only to have it refilled with the powerful ale—by Alanna. Where had she come from? She stood formally erect, and with the same calm poise and confident set to her shoulders, the same bold assuredness flowing from her eyes as from her teacher's.

So this explained her unusual behavior aboard ship, including her climbing the masts with ease. He remembered that day aboard ship when she'd scampered up the ship's ratlines and mizzens, and stretched her limber legs to catch a rope between her toes.

A slow smile tipped the corners of his mouth. Even in the same garb as the others, her fine hips were still sensuous. He could easily pick her out amongst the others. He touched his mug to hers, every nerve in his body alive with an erotic flame.

Old Chinese turned on his heel and left. Standing alone with Wolf, Alanna didn't seem so bold. Had she merely used her training, unknown to outsiders, as a mask? The way he used his surliness to gain a formidable reputation?

An urge to step closer, to smell her, to taste her, nearly overwhelmed him. He assessed her face frankly, and then slowly, and with purpose, regarded the pulse throbbing wildly at her throat. He leaned to her ear. "Oh, what you do to me."

She turned her face from him but not before he saw her lips part. "Ah, you want me too, don't you, Alanna? Right now. Right here."

The column of her throat rippled with a hard swallow.

He longed to bend and kiss that mouth set in stunned bewilderment. "Your stoic detachment doesn't quite hold things together when a hungry heart beats wild, does it? What happens now that we are thrown together, Alanna? Did Old Chinese instruct you on how to handle this—the battle of all battles?"

Alanna stood mute, his words flowing over her skin as smooth as warm honey. Her chest and head pulsed as though they were about to burst from the dizzying pressure. Heat, smoldering through her veins, threatened to engulf her.

He was right.

She wanted him.

The last thing she'd ever expected was that such potent feelings could overwhelm a person. Or that they could be laced with pain.

In the end, what did she really want of him? What would happen if she were to awaken on the morrow and find him gone? Never to return? Even standing before her, he was obviously a restless soul. Something inside her turned over, the sensation so jagged as to threaten her composure. Somehow, while she'd been self-righteously convincing herself that Wolf would want this life—would want her—reality had snuck in and settled in the pit of her stomach like a coiled snake. She shifted on her feet and gathered her self-possession around her like a cloak. From across the room, Old Chinese studied her through keen eyes. She turned from his steady gaze. The man never missed a thing.

A cacophony of music filled the room, tossing her back into the moment. Wolf winced at the harsh sound. A minstrel sat on bales of hay draped in bright red silk and plucked at an instrument with an extended neck, square box, and three strings, similar to a guitar.

"Such music has a distinct purpose."

Wolf smirked. "You could've fooled me."

So, he was back to his old, bantering self, was he? She took a sip of ale to wet her dry mouth. "The notes being played are elaborately linked to mathematical equations."

"Too bad they don't make a decent sound."

"You have to listen beyond your Occidental ear, Wolf. Each note, as discordant as it may sound, corresponds directly to the energy flowing through one's physical body. Depending on how the notes are put together, they can soothe, set one to battle, open intelligence, aid in the power of healing, and so on."

"Sounds like you recited that right out of a book. Got it written down somewhere?"

"When one learns the ancient secrets of harnessing such a powerful energy, the old arts that were once taught clandestinely can be mastered by anyone willing to learn."

"Lesson finished." Wolf flashed a lazy grin filled with sultry promise and went back to watching the musician.

While he appeared to be paying more attention to the minstrel's playing than to her, she knew better. Although he hadn't responded to her comments much, he'd listened to her intently. And now he was trying to figure out what effects the music had on him. He was smarter than he wanted people to believe.

She pursed her lips to suppress a wicked smile. "Do you like our music, sir?"

Wolf rocked back on his heels. "If a cat got up and sang, I would not know which sounded better."

A giggle erupted from Alanna. Wolf turned to her. He caught her scent. She was too damn close for him to control himself. Slowly, he ran the tip of his finger around the thick edge of his mug, mocking her behavior their first evening at dinner aboard ship. Lifting his finger to his lips, he licked the tip. "Oh, the lady doth laugh."

He chucked her under the chin before sauntering off to where Thompson stood. Wolf spoke through his teeth. "Thompson, you cunning bastard."

Thompson had his eye on the generous platters of food being laid on the mats. "How so?"

"You know damn well what I mean. That night aboard ship when I told you I'd shoved my hand up Alanna's dress, trying to scare her off. 'She let you? Oh, then she must like you,'" Wolf mimicked. "Christ, I'm fortunate to still possess my hand, considering what she's capable of."

Thompson snorted. "Told you she must like you." A gong sounded from somewhere in the building. Thompson gestured toward the food, on which a throng was descending like ants at a picnic. "Sit to the right of Old Chinese."

"Same as Western manners or is there a hidden reason for my placement?"

"By tradition, guests, who might be enemies as well, keep their weakest side to the host, while the host keeps his side of greater strength to his guest. Oh, and approach your place from the left. That's protocol, also."

"What *place*? It's a goddamn mat on the floor."

"Shh," Thompson replied. "You could lose your head for offending your host."

"Ah, bullshit. And just where do you intend to sit?"

"Any place I choose. You're the honored guest, so you're the only one with any particular designation tonight."

"Then you'd better sit across from me so I can follow along with whatever you do. I had dinner with the Dakotas once. An invitation by demand, shall we say. Thought I was going to be their next trophy when I didn't know enough to—"

Wolf spied Alanna standing close to the tall, curly-haired man that Wolf had seen in the courtyard. "You go on. I've got someone I need to bring to dinner."

He strode boldly across the room to Alanna, hooked a finger in her belt, and tugged her toward the mats. "Time for celebratin', darlin'."

She stiffened. "What do you think you are doing?"

Wolf chuckled. "Don't even think about stopping me with your high kicks and deadly punches. You'll only look the fool insulting your honored guest." The air fairly vibrated with his wild mischief.

"What brought that on?" Her countenance was suddenly passive and remote. More training?

Ignoring her comment, Wolf halted at the right of Old

Chinese. With his fingers still hooked in Alanna's belt, he sat, taking her with him—all the while nonchalantly assessing the food laid across the mats.

Thompson crossed his long legs in front of him and picked something round and brown off a tray. Wolf's stomach turned. "Tell me those aren't snails."

Old Chinese shoved a jug of rice wine in front of him. "A few glasses of this and anything will look appetizing."

Wolf grabbed a piece of chicken instead—at least he hoped it was fowl of the barnyard variety—and proceeded to enjoy the evening, including a stunning demonstration of *Kendo*, the powerful art of the sword. Long after the presentation concluded, the air still crackled with the energy of the display. He still hadn't figured out what trained warriors were doing in Boston's countryside.

Alanna rose and filed past what was, by now, a room full of noisy men filled with rice wine. She glanced back at Wolf, a half smile on her face, the smooth sway of her hips tightening the muscles of his own. She'd drunk as much rice wine as any of them and was headed for Old Chinese's magnificent water closet appointed with all the latest conveniences, thanks to a clever windmill and gravitational water flow system. Where would she go off to sleep when the night ended? Surely, she wasn't housed with all these men? Was she? What did her parents say? Surely . . .

Wolf turned back to Old Chinese. "Alanna tells me most of your teachings and the weaponry is of Japanese origin, yet you are called Old Chinese. Why is that?"

When Wolf's question went unanswered, he let out an exasperated breath. "I guess I'll get the answer when you're good and ready to tell me, so I'll ask you something else— how do you manage all this with Alanna's overprotective parents?"

Old Chinese tossed a chicken bone he'd picked clean onto a growing pile and licked his fingers. "Manage what?"

"You know what I mean. Alanna's parents don't let her sneeze without reaching for a handkerchief. How is it they allow her out here, ot all places'?"

"Of all places? Do you not find my home to your liking?" Old Chinese refilled Wolf's glass and slurped from his own. "I am pleased you like my rice wine."

"You didn't answer my question. It's obvious Alanna knows her way around here, so she's no stranger. How is it her parents condone her coming here?"

Wolf made a point to look up and down the long line of noisy males. He paused to stare pointedly at Curly—the sobriquet he'd given the tall, curly-haired Westerner, who had yet to take his eyes off the staircase Alanna had climbed.

With a deliberate turn of his head, Curly stared at Wolf with stoic calm.

Wolf threw his head back and downed the rice wine. He thumped the empty glass on the table and returned his attention to Old Chinese. "I'll get right to the point. Hers is not ladylike behavior, nor is tonight a social-climbing endeavor that would snare her parents a place on Boston's social register. And dare I mention the fact that she is the only woman surrounded by at least thirty men?"

He held his mug out for another refill from the urn Old Chinese controlled. "When it comes to those incredibly *charming* parents of hers, not a bit of this fits."

"Oh? And how does this not fit?"

"Oh, for God's sake. Her father nearly keeled over with me aboard ship. And that was with her mother breathing down my neck at every turn."

"Ah." Old Chinese shook his finger at Wolf. "But *these men* are not *you*." He bent forward and went nose to nose with Wolf. "When there is no mutual connection, there is no *thought* of mutual connection."

Wolf took a long swallow of wine and wiped his mouth with the back of his hand. "I can see why the Malones would want their daughter out here so she can't sabotage her own wedding, but she's obviously been training with you for years. That's another thing I don't get."

Old Chinese picked up another leg of cooked fowl and gnawed on it. "Alanna's father wanted her to learn a little of the martial arts in order to protect herself, and her mother was told Alanna's training would ease the pain of childbirth, which had been a near tragic endeavor for Mrs. Malone. I taught her father what he knows of the arts, well before his daughter's birth. He was a lazy student, but with Alanna, I found an intelligent apprentice, one who long ago was able to discern the deeper aspects of Budo; it is much more than a way of beating someone senseless. Her pending marriage is the only fly in the ointment of the plans I have for her."

He wiggled the half-eaten drumstick at Wolf. "An added benefit is that teaching Alanna out here keeps her secluded and well away from men like yourself, another of the Malones' concerns."

"Such as myself? But what of all these men?"

Old Chinese went to work on the chicken. "The Malones don't know I have any students other than Winston over there."

"Sweet Jesus!" Wolf shot a glance at Winston, the tall, curly-haired man, who was busy splitting his time between observing Wolf's every move and eyeing the staircase. "What about him? Has he been with you long?"

"Since he was two."

Wolf scowled. "And her parents have trusted him and you alone with their daughter all these years?" Something definitely didn't add up.

A shroud of mystery suddenly engulfed the old man's countenance. "Her personal safety has been seen to."

Alanna returned and sat beside Wolf. He reached up and brushed a loose tendril from a corner of her weary-looking eyes and tucked it behind her ear. He let his hand slide, feather-soft, down her back.

Winston studied them with an unwavering gaze.

"Sleepy?" Wolf's husky voice skittered along Alanna's spine, as effortlessly as his fingers slid down her arm. "I much prefer sitting next to you to sitting across, as I did for so long aboard ship."

Despite fatigue, her body responded to his tender touch, to the sound of his voice. By mid-evening, she had already given up trying to subdue her involuntary reactions to him. When he was sitting so close, every nuance, every flutter of his gilded lashes made her breath catch, while his occasional touch jolted her and sent tremors through her. Early on, she'd become aware that although he talked with the others, his attention was focused mostly upon her.

Throughout the entire evening, he refilled her wineglass, and when his fingers brushed against hers, the effect was like a flame to a powder keg. He leaned over to whisper questions, and his soft lips lightly touched her ear—*Sweet Heaven*.

Without preamble, Old Chinese stood. Thompson sent a silent signal to Wolf that he should also rise and incline his head to Old Chinese. The older man bowed and walked away.

The students quickly gathered plates and platters, stacked the mats in a neat pile and exited in silence. Only Wolf and Thompson remained.

Where the hell had Alanna gone?

Wolf's mood sank. He surveyed the room. Someone had made a bed on a thick mat. For Old Chinese? Oil lamps had either been extinguished or turned to their lowest settings. The room was spotless, the fire pit aglow.

A hushed, almost reverent quality pervaded the barn's interior. Thompson unhooked a lantern from a nail on the wall. "You're to remain here with Old Chinese. I'll see you in the morning." He exited down the stairs, as quietly as had the others.

Silently, Wolf slipped over to the window. A glimmer of lanterns evaporated into the night. Had Alanna gone with them? Oddly tangled sensations fragmented Wolf's thinking. He turned from the window wondering, *What next?*

Alanna emerged from behind the gilded Oriental screen that hid the bathing tub. She carried a rolled mat and blankets balanced across her arms. Wolf's head roared with new blood and his mood lightened. He started forward to assist, but she ignored him and dumped everything in a heap beside the fire pit.

When she disappeared behind the screen once more, Wolf's eyes narrowed as he squinted through the shadows. Confounded, he waited.

In a few moments Alanna reappeared, dressed in a flannel sleeping gown, her hair still in a braid. She carried another armful of blankets and, never looking his way, made her bed not ten feet from where Old Chinese lay facing the wall and snoring.

"And a good night to you, too," Wolf muttered, his mood falling once again. Damned if he knew the protocol. He turned and made his way over to the fire pit, where the other bedroll lay, some thirty feet from Old Chinese and Alanna. He glanced one last time through the shadowed room to the darkened corner where she lay.

He felt suddenly and utterly alone.

Removing his jacket and stock tie, Wolf loosened his hair and went to crawl beneath the covers, fully clothed. With a flare of rebellion, he disrobed and climbed in nude.

He lay there, staring up at the firelight's faint shadow play. Thinking. Feeling. And taking long, slow, deep gulps of air to try to quiet the mounting tension of his driving needs. Her presence was so thick in the air, she might as well have curled up right beside him. He was unnerved by an insane desire to simply get up, walk over to where she lay, and drag her to his bed.

The whole of the evening, with her sitting next to him, had seemed so right—so natural. It was as though she had always been beside him. It must be the time spent together on that confining ship that made him feel so.

Visions of her father, his fist to the wall, veins at his temple bulging with rage, filled Wolf's head. And then there was her mother, Mrs. Bumblebee, shaking her parasol at him. Their eyes of stone and ice contrasted with visions of his relatively comfortable life before sailing—San Francisco with its noisy streets and busy wharf; St. Joseph and the barmaid he'd left behind with her sweet infatuation. Life had been a helluva lot easier before he'd boarded that damnable ship.

What in God's name was he doing here—and why?

Chapter Twelve

"Get up, you bag of bones!" Old Chinese, chipper as a morning warbler, kicked at Wolf's ribs.

Wolf rolled away from the wicked jabs and squinted at the thin winter light sifting through the window. Somewhere, a rooster crowed. "What the hell time is it?"

A mass of hair tumbled about his throbbing head. He moved to rise on his haunches, only to spy Alanna's toes mere inches away. "Christ Almighty." He flopped back onto his naked stomach, bunched the covers around his hips and glared at Old Chinese, who appeared every bit as fresh as he sounded.

He picked up Wolf's clothing and examined the shirt cuffs and inside jacket pocket. "Why do you have your initial embroidered all over everything? Is it so you can remember who you are after a night like the one you just had?" He puffed up his chest and laughed until his eyes crinkled shut.

A crisp white something landed next to Wolf with a soft *plop*. On closer inspection, he recognized the uniform everyone wore, only with a white belt.

"This is called a *gi*." Old Chinese tossed Wolf's clothing in a heap out of reach. "More comfortable when you work."

Alanna calmly dragged one of the only two chairs in the room to Wolf's pallet and sat sipping from a steaming cup. She was also garbed in crisp white and acted as perky as Old Chinese.

Wolf decided the wisp of a smile playing about her mouth was because she knew his head was giving him fits. He could kiss that smirk right off those lips in less than a minute. Despite his pounding temples, lascivious thoughts skittered through him and landed in his groin.

She raised a brow, as if she knew what had just occurred.

He bent a knee to try to relieve the sudden discomfort. "All right, I give up. You two had as much to drink last night as I did, so what's your secret?"

"Ha!" Old Chinese gave a hearty laugh. "You must learn to drink our ceremonial rice wine with expanded *ki*."

Wolf rubbed his hand over his face and blew a hank of hair off his cheek. He had to piss. He was naked. And Alanna sat not three feet from him. "I'm not in the mood for one of your goddamn lessons. Get out of here so I can dress."

Old Chinese picked up a skinny pot from the edge of the fire pit, poured steaming liquid into a mug, and handed it to Wolf. "Ki is what keeps your heart beating and your lungs bellowing. I would suggest you learn how to use the energy to your advantage."

The acrid odor of the liquid in the cup gripped Wolf's sinuses like a whiff of hot vinegar. "What's this, the devil's brew?"

Old Chinese sniggered. "Don't ask. Drink. Then take a walk in the cold air. Perhaps then you will gain enough in-centive to learn about ki."

Alanna left without a word, giving Wolf the privacy he desperately needed.

Within the hour, his head cleared and his energy returned to normal. The drink had worked magic. But Old Chinese was right; its foul smell and taste were motivation enough to learn whatever it took to steer clear of the disgusting stuff again.

To Wolf's irritation, when it came time for the first lesson, the ever-silent Winston climbed the stairs with Alanna. They carried a full-length cheval mirror.

"You will be taught *kenseido*," Old Chinese announced. "It is a Japanese martial art form combining the external elements of karate and kung fu with the internal qualities of aikido and jujitsu."

Wolf snorted. "I know hand-to-hand fighting intimately. Learned it from the Arapaho."

Old Chinese ignored the mockery. "Alanna and Winston will be your teachers as well as your partners. Step to the mirror and choose your first partner, please."

Wolf assessed the two standing before him. Alanna— female, slender, and shorter than Wolf. Winston—male, taller, and broader in the shoulder. "Is there a trick to this?"

When Old Chinese didn't answer, Wolf chose Winston.

Old Chinese nodded his approval. "Stand side by side and observe one another through the mirror. What is it you see that is the same between you?"

Wolf grew wary. Choosing the obvious could prove mighty embarrassing. He studied Winston's reflection. "We're both males?" He stiffened, ready to wince at a scolding—or laughter.

"Good!" Old Chinese clapped his hands.

Curious as to Alanna's reaction, Wolf ventured a glance in the mirror at her.

"No!" Old Chinese yelled. "Focus on Winston."

Wolf's heart pumped out old rebellion. He didn't have to put up with this bullshit. He could always inform the son of a bitch he was going back to Boston with Thompson.

Cynicism got the best of him. He couldn't resist naming similar body parts such as arms, legs, and mouth. To his surprise, Old Chinese responded with zeal. Winston grinned at one of Wolf's more colorful descriptions of the male anatomy.

He lifted a brow. "Whoa, Winston has a sense of humor. Who would've thought?"

"Exactly—who would've *thought*?" Old Chinese sprang to his feet. "You are figuring out who Winston really is. Once a person learns of the similar and dissimilar aspects of the core of another, he has no enemy."

Old Chinese paced the floor, his eyes glittering like diamonds on midnight velvet. He rattled on for a good thirty minutes. The powerful energy he exuded and the nonstop information mesmerized Wolf.

Finally, Old Chinese plopped down on the floor. "Tell me what you see that is different between the two of you."

"I think we have different personalities."

"Now change your sentence from 'I think' to 'I feel.'"

Another trick? Wolf rolled his eyes and started over. "I *feel* that we have different personalities."

A new set of emotions—somehow more intimate—flowed through Wolf.

Damn!

His cheeks heated, and he stepped away from the mirror. The mere shifting from one word to another had filled him with a sense of vulnerability. Whatever edged into his awareness just then, whatever flowed through his feelings rather than his thoughts, seemed to change the very air in the room as well. Hell, when was the last time he'd referred to anything or anyone using that word?

A faint smile flickered past Old Chinese's mouth.

Wolf fisted his hands on his hips and sucked in air. "What was that? Is this the ki you speak of?"

Old Chinese gave a small nod, as if in deference. "Already, you have learned much."

"I didn't learn anything, it just happened. I wouldn't know how to do it again. Or would I?"

"You struck a balance between thinking and feeling. Your ability to distinguish between the two allowed you to transcend two opposite worlds for a moment." The smile played at the corners of the old man's mouth again. "You have done such on your own before, in various ways."

Wolf shrugged. "Up to a point, I suppose. I can feel something in a room shift whenever I end up in a precarious position. That's when my instincts take over."

Old Chinese nodded. "Also when you make love to a woman. Especially when you reach your climax—that's when you are able to suspend all thinking, and just feel sensation. You are good at that particular method of getting in touch with your feeling nature."

A buzz shot through Wolf. "Christ Almighty! It's one thing to talk like that in front of Winston. But Alanna—"

Old Chinese ignored Wolf's protest. "Feminine energy is gentle nurturing—that is your feeling nature."

An overwhelming urge to check Alanna's reaction gnawed at Wolf. God, get this over with.

"Male energy is when you take action." Old Chinese grinned, making Wolf want to squirm once again. "You gain ultimate power over an enemy when you use your feelings first to seek out his weakness and then take aggressive, male action afterward."

Wolf crossed his arms over his chest, and stepped back. "I get the idea."

A husky chuckle came from Winston's throat.

Wolf glared at him. "You think this is funny? You son of a bitch."

Winston merely cocked a brow, chuckled again, and fell silent.

"Now then," Old Chinese continued. "Look in the mirror and using the feeling word, ask Winston to do something for you."

Wolf stepped back to the mirror. He damn well knew

what he'd like to say to the man. Instead, he peered at Winston's reflection and chose something simple. "I feel like having a drink of water."

Winston trotted over to the jug in the corner and returned with a full glass. Wolf emptied the contents. "Thank you."

Winston nodded and turned back to the mirror.

Wolf could no longer keep the frustration from his voice. "So what's the almighty lesson here?"

Old Chinese moved behind the men and shoved his face between them. "Winston has been deaf since infancy."

"Huh?" Wolf spun to face Winston.

Winston's black eyes sparked with fresh humor.

"He reads your lips," Old Chinese said. "He feels vibrations through the floor and in the air. He can hear better with his other senses than you can with your two good ears. Winston is my best student, and if you are wise, you would make him your ally."

Wolf heaved a sigh. "Damn. I'm sorry."

"No need to be," Winston said in an odd, off-key voice.

"Now, then." Old Chinese clapped his hands together and sat again. "It is Alanna's turn in the mirror."

As Winston stepped aside, Wolf decided Old Chinese's quick changes of pace and constant assaults on his emotions were important parts of the lesson.

While Alanna and Winston switched places, Wolf became acutely aware of yet another shift in the room. Seeing that Alanna and Winston exuded two different kinds of energy came easy for Wolf. However, standing beside her, looking in the mirror at their side-by-side reflections, and at the likeness of their blue eyes rimmed in black, jolted him.

Blood hammered in his ears at this new perspective. The powerful vision had a disquieting effect on Alanna as well— her cheeks flushed a dusky rose.

"Now then," Old Chinese began again. "Alanna, tell me what is different between the two of you."

Both Alanna and Wolf shot fast glances in the mirror, surprised that Old Chinese addressed her and not Wolf. The color in her cheeks flared. Old Chinese sat calmly in position, his legs crossed, staring into the mirror.

Alanna's eyes locked with Wolf's. He let the smile working the corners of his mouth fill with the promise of delicious sin.

Her chin lifted. "I feel he has the manners of an ass."

Wolf let out a bark of laughter.

Old Chinese clapped his hands in delight.

Wolf tilted his head at Alanna. "Ever heard the word 'subtle'?"

"No!" Old Chinese yelled.

Wolf turned back to the mirror. "Don't forget, my turn is next," he said through his teeth.

"No!" Old Chinese scolded him again.

Wolf smirked. He knew that was coming, but teasing her was worth getting his butt chewed out.

"I *feel* he is uncaring of another's feelings," Alanna went on. "I *feel* he does not know how to care about anything or anyone other than himself. I *feel* he wouldn't recognize his best interests if they were snakes crawling up his legs."

Wolf's brow shot up at her unexpected answers. He swallowed a curt reply. Old Chinese sat calmly observing him through the mirror, but the depth of the man's obsidian eyes shot right into Wolf's soul. Chills ran the length of his spine. What the hell was the old man trying to teach him? He wondered what time it was; he was growing weary of the odd lessons. Thompson intended to return to Boston before noon—with Alanna in tow.

"It's barely nine o'clock," Winston said and walked off.

Old Chinese clapped his hands together. "Time for tea."

Instead of joining them, Wolf slipped below to the horses. Ten minutes alone with the beasts and he regained some of his composure.

When they resumed the lessons, Old Chinese called on Alanna once again.

"Time for Alanna Malone's lesson again?" Wolf murmured when he got close enough. She stood facing him, motionless, as though ice water ran through her veins.

Old Chinese clapped his hands together. "Move closer, you two, until you can feel one another's subtle body energy. Stay fixed on the eyes. They are the windows to the soul. Focus deep, and they will tell you in four seconds what is going on inside the person and what he or she is about to do. Every four seconds, move closer."

Every nerve in Wolf's body jumped to the surface of his skin. He broke position and walked away. Thrusting his hands on his hips, he stared at the floor. "What the hell is 'subtle body energy'?"

When Old Chinese failed to respond, Wolf threw his hands in the air. "I give up—I'll figure it out on my own. And what the hell does any of this have to do with solving my . . . with solving my business problems?"

"You shall soon see," Old Chinese said quietly.

Wolf took his position in front of Alanna again and stared into her cold eyes. He counted the four seconds in his head and moved closer, a little at a time. The energy around them suddenly shifted, as though he'd slipped into denser, warmer air. The hair on his arms rose and his lips tingled. He paused and shot a glance at Old Chinese, who gave a small nod.

Concentrating, he inched closer.

An involuntary desire to sweep her into his arms flooded him. Sweet Lord, they were working, not loving. He stopped his movements and felt her presence run through him. *Her scent.* There was far more to this than catching the enticing fragrance of a woman and wanting to take her to bed. Nonetheless, the flame that lit his loins refused to die.

He stepped away from her and turned his back to the others. "This did *not* happen when Winston and I stood here." Such arousal was only supposed to happen when he wanted it to—in private. He took a couple more steps away from her and glued his eyes to the floor, feeling pathetically vulnerable. "Let's move on to another lesson."

"Fine," Old Chinese said, surprising Wolf with his acquiescence. "We shall have one more lesson today. Tomorrow you will learn how to outrun pain."

Wolf grinned. "Now there's a lesson."

"So, Wolf, let's finish for today. Lunge for your partner's waist with the intention of attacking her. Pay careful attention to her movements."

Attack her? "Why?"

"Because it's your last lesson of the day, that's why."

Wolf stepped forward.

"Stop." Old Chinese grunted. "You move like some frightened kitten afraid of a mouse. Move with all the force and power you have. Attack!"

Wolf turned on his heel. "I can't do this."

Old Chinese scowled. "Why not?"

"She's a woman."

"Would you hesitate even if the woman was trained to kill and intended to?"

A memory of his mother being battered flashed through Wolf's mind and shot through his heart. "I . . . I can't."

Old Chinese looked down his nose. "Are you afraid?"

Anger boiled, wiping out the memory of his mother. "It's not in me to attack a woman, goddamn it!"

He didn't know where Alanna came from. He only saw the flash of her hand as she struck his gut, knocking the wind out of him, and sending his senses reeling.

A hard smack of her foot followed and sent him flying across the room to land on the hard floor with a resounding thud. He lay where he fell, his shoulder pasted to the wood, unable to breathe. He tried to gather his sense of feeling, of direction.

He heard his own groan as he rolled onto his hands and

knees, gasping. His hair, knocked from its tie at his nape, tumbled about his face. Ten men on a rowdy night in St. Joseph couldn't have done as much damage.

But worse than the physical hurt was the utter sense of betrayal, of feeling cast out, of being made a complete fool. He staggered to his feet, still bent over, his hands clutching his gut, his ragged heaving for air the only sound in the silent room.

Slowly, he straightened. He remained still, hands on hips, face to the ceiling, until his breath flowed freely. Then he turned and headed for Alanna.

Gone was Wolf's bewitching warmth and humor. The lethal blaze in his eyes pierced the distance between them, stunning Alanna. Fire and ice flashed imperious warning as he halted within inches of her.

"Don't you *ever* try that again."

A shudder slithered down her spine.

With a sneer, he turned and stalked to the room where his trunk full of clothing was stored.

Alanna turned to Old Chinese and met his accusing eyes. He stood inches from her, his head held rigid. "If you want to truly destroy an enemy, you do not kill him." His carefully spoken words came low and guttural. "I have taught you this, have I not?"

Alanna nodded.

Old Chinese regarded her with contempt. "Instead, you remove his power. You demean him. You destroy all that he stands for within himself, and then you leave him to walk the earth in misery for the rest of his days."

His voice was now of a deeper, more powerful timbre. "Why is it, Alanna Malone, that I invited a guest into my dojo and you, one of my finest students, turned on him? Treated him as the enemy?"

Alanna's mouth dropped open.

"You fool. You shame me."

Bewilderment dizzied her. "But he . . . he was afraid to act on your orders. You did that to me once, when I was afraid."

"He was not fearful." Old Chinese's deep voice rattled through her. "He displayed his virtue."

Alanna's cheeks grew hotter. She waited, for he had not dismissed her. A door slammed behind her, followed by loud footsteps. She turned as Wolf strode past her and on to Old Chinese without a glance her way.

Gone was the gi. Wolf was sheathed in buckskins and wore an old pair of boots. He carried a heavy jacket. His demeanor was one of self-containment and resolute strength.

He faced Old Chinese. "And as for you, you can kiss my royal ass, you sorry little prick!" He strode past Alanna and Winston without a word, and disappeared down the stairs.

"What are you going to do about *that*?" Alanna demanded when Wolf was out of earshot.

"Do about what?" Old Chinese turned to her, his voice flat, hard.

Winston inclined his head to Old Chinese and backed out of the room.

She grew confused. "He can't speak to a sensei like that." Had Old Chinese turned on her?

"I am not his sensei," he growled. "Wolf has not chosen me. I chose him." His eyes narrowed dangerously. "And he is right, Alanna. You had better *never* do that again. But you wouldn't get the chance to repeat the act if you wanted to, so why do I waste words?"

Alanna sucked in her breath. "He's leaving?" Tears filled her eyes.

"No. He will not leave. But you will never have a second chance to offend him because Wolf has something you do not yet possess—something that will not allow you to repeat your mistake."

Alanna's heart, taking on the burden of more confusion,

wrenched in her chest. She opened her mouth to speak, but he shook his head.

"You have studied hard all these years. But that is all you have ever done. It is easy to be a student. You can only learn whether or not you are truly a master out there." Old Chinese pointed to the window. "On your own, not here in my dojo."

"But—"

Old Chinese raised his hand. "You have lived a very soft life. One filled with every convenience and comfort the world has to offer; you have never had to give a thought to expense. Wolf has not lived such a life as yours. He has learned to survive without so much as a single coin to call his own, let alone the knowledge of where one might come from. While you dressed in the finest clothing money could buy, with a servant to close every delicate button for you, Wolf was alone, searching for food to fill his hungry belly, content with enough clothing and shelter to keep from freezing. He has faced death and survived. You have yet to face life. You haven't even proven whether you can survive your own stupidity."

How could Old Chinese know all this about Wolf? From Thompson? Hot tears cascaded over her cheeks. "I don't—"

"Do you honestly think you impressed Wolf with that aggressive male act you performed? Do you think he admires your expertise? Do you think he is awed by your disrespect and insensitivity?"

Alanna's hand slid to her throat. She didn't think she could manage to stand much longer.

Old Chinese's eyes narrowed. "Wolf has lived and breathed Budo without knowing it."

"How can you say that?" she sputtered. "He openly curses. He is rebellious. He flagrantly does whatever he chooses without a care for anyone else. And . . . and he is not virtuous."

"Not virtuous? How do you figure that? Because *you* invited *his* hand up your dress?"

"I should never have told you about that incident." His words smarted worse than a bee's sting. "And as far as his lack of virtue is concerned, I base it on what I heard you tell him today regarding his intimacy with other women."

"And he became your enemy because of that?"

Alanna's confused emotions rolled through her like waves on a beach, swallowing reason.

"You reacted to your own fears of inadequacy, Alanna. There is a word for the emotion that prodded you into acting the way you did—it's called jealousy."

Old Chinese raised a hand, halting her words once again. "And don't speak. I've grown weary of listening to you. Kenseido is the only place where you allowed yourself to go into the depths of your own senses. And then Wolf came along. He opened up a whole new world for you—of sensuality, of ecstasy. This new world frightens you, does it not?"

Alanna's eyes found the floor in front of her toes. "I don't think I want to experience ecstasy with a man who has experienced it with so many others."

"Ha!" Old Chinese strode away, but then he paused and turned. "Your little world was shaken to its core today, wasn't it? From the very first time you laid eyes on Wolf, you felt superior, as if you possessed a secret knowledge he did not. And your intention to amaze and impress him today was punctured like an inflated balloon when you found out you are not superior after all. Good. You needed that mighty lesson."

More tears scalded Alanna's flaming cheeks. The crumbling of her confidence was the greatest pain she had ever endured.

"What makes you think Wolf has experienced true ecstasy with a woman?" he demanded.

She swiped tears from her eyes and tried to see through her tangled, wet lashes.

"There is a vast difference between experiencing something sensual with a woman and experiencing ecstasy. The latter means to surrender completely," he said. "Which is something Wolf has never allowed, because in order to do so, he would have to go to a level of intimacy that threatens his very life blood."

"I don't understand. You told him that he'd achieved the female energy with women when he . . . that—"

"Hush!" Old Chinese scolded. "His having a go with a near stranger is not an intimate act at all. That kind of sex has energy, but it is low-grade. Bedding women like that has been just enough to keep him going, to keep his spirit from suffocating from loneliness. Why would you deny him the touch of a female under such circumstances, little fool?"

Alanna began to pace. "How can you say such a thing? Having the kind of intimacy he's experienced . . . with other women . . . in his bed—"

Old Chinese crossed his arms over his chest. "That's not intimacy. Wolf is far more likely to take off his clothes in front of a stranger than he would be willing to let down his defenses with someone he loves."

Alanna didn't care that her tears wouldn't cease. Her shoulders rose in a gesture of question. She thought she saw compassion leak through Old Chinese's harsh regard. She hoped so.

He studied her before he spoke. "Our friend is ill at ease with human contact. It is difficult for him to be intimate— he has too much to lose."

"But why?"

"Because—" His voice softened. "He has suffered a great loss. And whatever his loss was, it was profound and still vivid. If you will get out of your own way and watch him closely, you will see for yourself what I know to be true. Today I was beginning the slow process of taking him back to where he needs to be, to help him heal, to learn to trust again."

Her chin trembled. "And I destroyed all that?"

"There are two lessons you had better learn, Alanna. One

of them is that he hasn't given you the power to destroy him. The other is the trust you destroyed by kicking him across the room when he allowed himself to be fully vulnerable to you."

Old Chinese walked to the window and peered for a long while into the woods. "If you *ever* expect a man to truly love you, then you had better learn there is only one woman in the world he will ever want to show his soft underbelly to, and that is a woman he can trust." Old Chinese whirled, seizing her gaze with his. "And by God, Alanna, if a man is willing to be vulnerable to you, to trust you enough to show his underbelly to you, then you had better *never* go at it with a sword!"

Alanna caught her breath. Devastation was fast consuming her. All the years of study, all the levels she had worked so hard to reach, and he was telling her she knew nothing.

"You said he has something that I do not possess." Her words quivered in her throat. "What would that be?"

"He has a sense of humor. You have none. That, Miss Alanna Mary Malone, is another of his virtues. Humor helps him survive."

She winced as Old Chinese continued. "You heard the man call me a derogatory term on his way out the door. He has made a connection with me—with this place." His hand swept the room. "If he never intended to return, he'd have left without a word and never looked back."

Alanna's hands shot to her mouth, covering her gasp. She threw her arms around Old Chinese and hugged him tight, her cheek to his chest. She laughed and sobbed simultaneously.

"Wolf is in the woods," he whispered. "Go before the Thompson carriage is ready for you."

A raw wind bit at Wolf's cheeks. He leaned his back into a tree and gathered its energy the way the Dakota had taught him. He moved into a place of nothingness. No thought. No action. Just the simple act of watching puffs of mist escape his lips.

Brown grass. Stark trees. There was a kind of nothingness to the fall season that made it special in its own way—nothing to obstruct his thinking—nothing to stand in his way. Soon, this blank landscape would give way to an entirely new world—one blanketed in white. He liked the way snow insulated the earth from noise.

He still had not dared to go beneath the surface of himself, to examine his feelings for Alanna. He couldn't even go deep enough to try to figure out the why of things. What he did know was that in spite of what had happened, there remained an inescapable, underlying gentleness in his feelings toward her.

A crush of leaves—a roar in the silent wood—resounded in his ears. How did he know it was her? Was it the length of her stride? The soft crunch beneath her feet—too heavy for a child, too light for a man? Or was it that he seemed to be able to feel her presence no matter what?

The rough bark dug harshly against the back of his head. Somehow, its jagged hardness soothed him. He could sense her. He knew what the look on her face would be. And he knew she observed him, watched his unmoving stance.

Suddenly, he wanted her to come to him. More than he wanted to breathe, he desired her presence. Yet, he wondered why the wisest part of him would send such an unproductive message. He thought of leaving before she could reach him, but he could not bring himself to move. A wild shaft of pain tore through him, but it did not obliterate his wanting her.

The crisp rustle of dry leaves ceased behind him. He remained unmoving, silent.

* * *

Alanna wished the incessant roaring of blood in her ears would stop. He had to have heard her approach, yet he was as still as the tree he leaned against.

Her heart pounded in her breast, and breathing grew more difficult. An insistent rush through her body urged her to walk up to him, to slide her arms around his waist and put her cheek to his chest. She hoped she'd figured him right, that his silence was a signal that approaching would be acceptable. And she prayed her voice would not fail her.

"I'm sorry, Wolf." She hung back, waiting. When he failed to respond, she repeated herself. "I'm so very, very sorry."

"What a cold word sorry is," he said without moving. "People say it as a matter of course, whether they mean it or not." The smoke of his breath evaporated in the air.

Captured by the wind, his voice wound around the trees, haunting in its timbre. It was as if the icy wind punished her by carrying his words through the woods for all of nature to hear before releasing them to her. She wanted to run. She took in a breath of cold air. Icy needles pierced her lungs.

He shifted his body against the tree. "What you don't know, Alanna, is that after my mother's . . . after my parents abandoned me, I was given no answers, no explanation as to why I had no mother, no father, no home, no hope. All I ever heard were the words 'I'm sorry' spouted over and over by caretakers. 'I am so sorry for you,' they repeated until I never wanted to hear those empty words again."

"Oh, Wolf." Alanna stepped forward and winced at the loud snap of dry leaves. She walked around him and paused. One look at him and she stepped back with a soft gasp. What she saw was not what she had expected. Kindness infused his countenance. Such vulnerability. Such gentleness. Heart-stopping tenderness flowed from his powerful gaze. And the warm softness about his mouth nearly brought her to tears. It was as if his spoken words had come from another world.

In one strong, fluid movement, Wolf reached out, caught her at the waist, and swung her effortlessly around to him.

She let out another small gasp.

He brought her to a halt and leaned her against the tree. He caged her with one hand against the ragged bark, while the other held her at the small of her back. He brought his face down to hers, so close the heat of his breath fell against her eyelids. "What am I to do with you?" he murmured.

His very essence seemed to seep through his pores and permeate her as she drank him in. He kissed the top of her head, ever so lightly. "There's a wonderful poise about you, Alanna. One that draws me to you like a fly to a spider's web." His lips brushed over her brow.

"Am I the poisonous kind of spider, Wolf?"

"No."

Closing her eyes, she got caught up in his magnetic presence. Her body quickened with the burden of desperate longing. She couldn't help it—she pressed against his hardness, all the while trying to will away a feeling of insatiable hunger. Such resolve proved futile.

His hand made soft, soothing, rhythmic circles. He pulled her gently closer to him and moaned. He held her tighter, pressed between the tree and him. His gentle massage sent currents of desire spiraling through her, making her senses reel.

His lips trailed down, brushing feather soft against the lobe of her ear. His hand continued to pull her into him until she, too, moaned softly.

"Stop me, Alanna."

"I cannot," she sighed into his chest. She pulled him still closer. "Lord, but I need you."

Wolf pulled back and gazed into her eyes. Heat blasted through her body. Her breath labored. "Alanna," was all he said before his mouth—sweet, full, and cool—found hers. He coaxed her lips open with his tongue, eased it inside.

Her breasts and belly arched against him. She moaned.

His thighs shifted between her knees and he cupped her hips, drew her against his male hardness with one hand and roamed her body with the other until he found her breast. Her heart hammered against fingers that caressed and kneaded. Her body shuddered.

"Alanna!" Thompson's voice echoed through the woods, shattering the moment.

Wolf lifted his mouth from hers. "You've been saved." He smiled, but his voice was still husky, his breathing heavy.

He planted a hard kiss on her lips. Her senses reeled once again.

"Must you leave?" he whispered.

She nodded. "My father's birthday is in little more than a week, and then the busy holidays follow. These three months are my parents' favorite time of the year to be seen. Father would definitely come looking for me if I failed to show."

"The holidays—I forgot." His eyes held a fleeting shaft of pain.

Would he suffer at her leaving, as well? With a start, she realized he had more than likely spent many holidays alone. "You have a family here, Wolf. These are good people. Winston is loyal. Old Chinese is fatherly, given the chance."

He only nodded.

"I meant it when I said I needed you," she whispered.

He tucked a stray hair behind her ear, ran a knuckle down her cheek, and held it under her chin. "What happened to us in the classroom this morning?"

There was no need to respond. They both knew.

"Alanna!" Thompson's insistent call echoed through the woods.

"I have to go."

Wolf brushed his lips against hers and then gave her a gentle push. "Don't forget to come back, darlin'."

* * *

He returned to leaning against the tree, his thoughts in a tangle. Why the hell had he gone and said something so foolish? Alanna Malone was the last woman he'd consider touching again. He liked his neck attached to his body just fine. A memory of her scent cleaved a sweet path through his mind. Christ, he'd been without a woman too long; that was what had his thoughts in a muddle. He intended to be long gone before she returned. St. Joe, and the little barmaid who took care of his lusty needs, suddenly sounded damn good. Once his mother's murder was solved, getting his sorry ass out of Massachusetts and headed west couldn't happen fast enough.

He remained where he stood until his feet felt near to freezing, and then he made his way back to the barn. But he didn't climb the stairs. Instead, he went to the horses. He combed each one until their coats took on an even glossier sheen, and until he was so exhausted he could barely make it up the stairs to fall into bed.

And fall into his dreams.

There was a pond, a lovely pond, with a pair of white swans floating gracefully about. And then he was being rocked in the arms of someone who smelled sweet, and spoke in a soft, Scottish brogue. But then the dream turned ugly and he was stuffed under a bed. Mist filled the room, and through the mist he could make out a mirror. In the mirror, a figure moved about in the mist and shadows.

Wolf awoke, thrashing about in a pool of sweat.

Chapter Thirteen

Late November

What began as simple curiosity and a way to cope with boredom soon became vital to Wolf. Despite the wear and tear on his body, he attacked the lessons Old Chinese administered with a relentless fury. Under Old Chinese's direction, Wolf and Winston sparred daily, with Wolf being pounded to the floor more times than he cared to count. Each night, he fell into bed drained of thought or feeling.

Then there were the acupuncture sessions that amplified his dreams. Little by little, the smoke in the mirror evaporated and the man stalking his nightmares began to take shape.

Most mornings vivid memories of Alanna floated in that obscure space between sleep and wakefulness. They also managed to hang around all day—if not at the forefront, then at the periphery of his mind. The taste of her mouth, the satin of her skin—everything about her seemed more than a recollection. Barely a month had passed since that day in the woods, but it seemed more like a year. Missing her forced him to come to terms with his fear of relationships, his fear of having his heart torn out again.

Wolf rolled over and shook another memory of her from his head. As his mind cleared, a faint rhythmic cadence vibrated through him. Horses' hooves? He snapped to his feet and strode to the window. A fresh mantle of pure white snow had fallen during the night, glittering in the early morning sunlight like diamonds strewn about the landscape. Below, a team of four black horses, bodies steaming and breaths billowing from their nostrils, pulled an ebony coach to a halt. His heart kicked up a notch.

Alanna?

Thompson exited the carriage alone, glanced up at the window with a frown and a nod, and hurried inside. After a few moments of polite conversation, he asked to speak to Wolf privately.

"No need." Wolf itched to know what was important enough for Thompson to depart Boston before dawn. "Winston and Old Chinese know I'm looking for my mother's murderer."

Old Chinese signaled for tea and motioned for Winston to join them.

"The detective you hired found evidence of substantial bank transfers to London in 1843, with a solicitor acting as power of attorney." Thompson said. "However, the funds disappeared without a trace some eighteen months later. The solicitor is deceased, so that trail ended with his demise. Your father had a partner named James Grimes, with whom he had a falling-out."

An ache at the back of Wolf's neck nagged him. He dug into the taut muscles. "Go on."

"We all know sizable fortunes are being made in Boston by importing goods from China," Thompson said. "But there are those among the blue bloods of Boston who make even grander fortunes by trading both ways."

"You mean opium trade?"

Thompson nodded. "Unfortunately. Opium delivered to

China from India, and tea and goods from China back to Boston."

Wolf's gut tightened. "Are you saying my father—"

"He was a man of integrity. His falling-out with Grimes seems to have occurred because your father discovered that large sums of money had been diverted to the opium trade by Grimes and a clandestine partner."

"Do you know who?"

Thompson nodded. "Jonathan Hemenway, father to Alanna's fiancé."

"Aw, Christ." Wolf sprang to his feet and paced. "There couldn't be more than one Hemenway at the top of Boston's social ladder, by any chance?"

"Afraid not."

"What happened to Grimes?" The ache in Wolf's neck radiated upward.

"Don't know. He disappeared without a trace. Alanna doesn't know anything about your past, does she?"

"No."

"Maybe it's best to keep it that way. We wouldn't want her compromised."

Old Chinese and Winston nodded.

Wolf rubbed at his temples. "For more reasons than one, since we have no idea what the hell I'm getting into."

"Alanna came to tea yesterday and mentioned something that threw up more red flags," Thompson said. "It seems Hemenway Senior likes to punish his female servants by cutting off their hair."

"What?" Wolf's head pounded in earnest. "My mother's hair—"

"My thoughts as well. There's more. Some years back, Alanna befriended Hemenway's daughter. Apparently, Hemenway cut off her hair after he caught her with a young man who didn't fit his well-laid plans. Alanna learned of this when she sneaked into the Hemenway home to visit Miss Hemenway. Alanna reported that the daughter fled to France shortly thereafter, where she remains to this day. Alanna said she'd be shot if her mother caught her repeating the story, so Mrs. Malone must be aware of what occurred."

Wolf paced and cursed. "What are the chances I'd get mixed up with a woman who is supposed to marry into the family of my mother's killer?"

"Since we don't know if that's the case yet, rein in that temper of yours," Thompson said. "Boston isn't that large a town so we have to be very careful from this point on. With the police so corrupt, if Hemenway did have anything to do with your mother's murder, who knows who owes him favors?"

"Jeezus, this sitting out here waiting for someone else to solve things—"

"I know," Thompson interrupted. "We should get you back to Boston right away. The harbor froze seven miles out last winter, so we'd better get a man to London before the weather worsens. An Andrews Company clipper leaves for England on tomorrow's afternoon tide."

"What about Alanna?" Wolf asked.

Thompson rearranged himself in his chair. "You're going to have to steer clear of her for the time being. If we can prove Hemenway had anything to do with your mother's demise, neither one of you will have to give that fiancé of hers another thought."

Wolf's gut tightened at the idea, but he had to agree. "If someone at the top of the social hierarchy is involved, it would make sense why my visit to the police station landed me in a cell. It would also explain how someone got into the newspaper archives to do a little snipping." He wanted to get out of the barn, wanted to walk in the woods, untangle his thoughts in the cold air.

He wanted Alanna.

Thompson eyed Wolf over his cup. "I see the wheels spinning. Sneaking Alanna into a hotel room is too risky. You can lie low in my home and when the time's right, we'll figure out how the two of you can meet up, but for now, keep your distance. Besides, the holidays are upon us, and you don't need to spend them alone."

Wolf pinched the bridge of his nose. "I'm beginning to remember details about the night my mother was murdered. If I could get a look at Hemenway, maybe I'd recognize him."

Old Chinese flashed a silent message to Winston before he veiled his gaze.

Wolf caught the exchange. "What the hell was that about?"

Instead of responding, Old Chinese poured more tea.

Thompson lifted his cup to the pot's spout. "The Searses' Christmas ball next weekend is the finest the season has to offer. The Hemenways attend, as do Martha and I. We'll get you an invitation."

"What about the police recognizing me?"

Thompson shook his head. "The police commissioner may attend, but no one of a lower rank would be invited."

Again, Old Chinese eyed Winston. The air sizzled between them. "Winston will drive the carriage back so you two can mull over whatever needs discussing."

"Winston can stay with us, as well," Thompson said.

Old Chinese shook his head. "Winston practices the art of invisibility. He knows where to go so no one can find him but me."

Boston—December 5

A stalwart, sixtyish-looking gentleman with a generous display of gray side-whiskers marched boldly into the vestibule of the Sears mansion with an elegantly dressed woman on his arm.

Hemonway?

A muscle in Wolf's jaw rippled. Even his teeth hurt, he was so tense. It took everything he had to appear relaxed.

The couple paused. A much younger woman, wearing a jewel-encrusted tiara, approached with her hand tucked into the elbow of a man who wore a red sash festooned with medals across his chest. The foursome moved into the ball-room.

"The elder man is Augustus Lowell," Martha Thompson murmured in her clipped British accent. "The young woman who joined them is his niece, married to the Duke of Leaventhal."

"Let me guess," Wolf whispered, hoping to alleviate some of his tension with a little humor. "The man beside her, looking like he's all wrapped up for Christmas, is his royal what's-his-name."

Martha suppressed a grin. "I suspect you are about to become quite wicked again."

A hearty chuckle erupted from Thompson. "Has he ever stopped?"

Martha turned to her husband, her soft green eyes crinkling at the corners of an otherwise dignified face. "I don't know about you, Captain, but I am enjoying myself immensely. However, I'm afraid I shan't have much of an opportunity to enjoy our dashing *Mr. Wolf's* sly comments—not with the young ladies circling him. We haven't been here the better part of an hour and would you listen to the silk of those fashionable ball gowns rustle like dry leaves in an autumn breeze around our dear friend."

She touched Wolf's sleeve. "But, oh my, you do look delicious. Were I young and single, I would be begging for an introduction as well. Do save a waltz for me, darling?"

"Of course."

From where the three stood in the immense Greek Revival ballroom, they were afforded a full view of everyone who entered, as well as a view of the dance floor. Wolf had already commented that if the polished surface held a bit more sheen, its mirror finish could be quite an embarrassment for the ladies. They also stood near the elaborately decorated banquet tables holding enough food to serve Boston's poor for a week. It was, according to Martha, another fine place for people watching.

Wolf glanced to the entry and nearly gaped at the couple entering. "Good Lord, that has to be the homeliest woman I have ever laid eyes on. My horse's face is better-looking. Although, I do see a resemblance, come to think of it. And that gown of hers beats Mrs. Bumblebee's taste all to hell. Don't tell me one of them is another Cabot or Lowell, since the room's full of them."

Martha leaned toward him. "A little of both on her side, actually. My dear Wolf, those are the Jonathan Hemenways."

Wolf froze.

Here was the very man who'd instigated Wolf's attending the damnable ball in the first place. He recognized nothing about Hemenway. There wasn't much to set him apart from the other portly men in the room, either in dress or figure. Wolf couldn't know if Hemenway was the man he sought. Not yet, anyway. Still, the very idea sent another ripple through his jaw.

Martha moved closer to Wolf, slipped her arm into the crook of his elbow, and gave it a squeeze. Thompson stepped to the other side of him.

"I'm fine," Wolf said. "I know better than to act on impulse."

"Tell that to your face," Thompson replied. "It could use some blood running into it."

Wolf shifted his attention to Mrs. Hemenway. She had the

face of a man, with a head too large for her body, and a long, square jaw. Low, thick eyebrows slashed across a broad forehead. "Yup, looks like my horse. She has a decent nose, though."

Thompson pursed his lips together.

"It looks as though the entire social registry is here tonight," Martha commented.

Wolf didn't catch what Martha meant until he looked past the Hemenways. He wished he hadn't—the Malones were in tow. Mrs. Malone's portly frame was swathed in bright chartreuse and olive green.

Wolf groaned and turned his back on them. "No wonder those two women get along. They share the same blind dressmaker." A chill snaked down his spine. Some sixth sense told him Alanna had entered the room. He turned.

She stood at the entry, a beautiful vision in blue.

Unequivocally, painfully beautiful.

God, he'd missed her.

He was surprised by the man standing at her side. Jonathan Hemenway III was the spitting image of his mother, only taller. Wolf had been right—Mrs. Hemenway did make a good man. Odd, but on her son, the horsey features didn't look half-bad, and he didn't appear to be sniveling.

Wolf needed to turn his back. Either that or give himself away. With as much interest as he could muster, he smiled warmly at one of the single ladies waiting for an introduction.

The sapphire and diamond engagement ring that had been thrust upon Alanna this evening hung heavy on her finger—seemed to cut through her glove and right to the bone. She wanted to grind her teeth in frustration. Captain Thompson had told her to play along and not disrupt her parents' matchmaking while he worked on a plan to help her out of her predicament. He'd exuded some kind of underlying tension when he'd told her, but he'd asked her to trust him and not question his actions. The Thompsons would surely be here tonight. She hoped for a moment of his time to find out whatever she could.

She assessed the crowd—the same boring people as always, out to impress one another. Didn't they tire of the game? And what in the world did they speak of at function after function, year after year? At least the music was fine. Since this was the night of her formal engagement, she'd not have to dance but once with Jonathan; numerous well-wishers were sure to take their turns.

She caught sight of a tall, broad-shouldered stranger dressed in the same black tails as the other men in the room. Who was he? Even with his back turned and his profile un-clear, a lithe elegance in the way he moved cast him apart from the others. His hair, clubbed at his neck and shining golden under the chandeliers reminded her of Wolf, which was likely the reason she thought of him as sensuous.

He turned.

His hoop earring caught the glint of candlelight, his pro-file unmistakable.

She gasped.

Her knees weakened, and the dull energy she'd arrived with drained from her fingertips, replaced by fire and light-ning.

Jonathan's hand went over the one she'd tucked in the crook of his arm. "Are you all right?"

She hadn't realized she'd clutched his arm at the sight of Wolf. "Yes. Something must have been on the floor. . . . I nearly tripped. Thank you." She loosened her grip.

"We'll catch up with our parents later," Jonathan said. "Right now you need something to drink." He steered her to the punch bowl as if she were a filly hitched to a carriage and he the driver.

Alanna detested the way he directed everything. "I never said I was thirsty."

Jonathan sniffed. "Well, you will be in due time if I don't prevent it."

Before she could move closer to the Thompsons and Wolf, a bevy of Boston's single females intervened. It didn't take her long to conclude that she wasn't the only woman in attendance affected by Wolf's arresting charisma. The knot in her stomach tightened each time she discreetly caught sight of him—and his surrounding feminine entourage.

As the evening wore on, no one was the wiser to Alanna's chagrin. She nearly choked on her punch when one of her peers whispered in her ear and giggled over the enchanting and devilishly handsome gentleman accompanying the Thompsons—the one with the golden earring and impeccable manners.

Wolf stepped onto the floor with yet another beauty on his arm. As the other young women had, she beamed when the music ended, convinced he was enchanted by her alone. By no means did he appear bored. Alanna doubted there was an available woman left who hadn't been touched by his attention. How she wished it were she he devoted himself to, her hand he kissed, the small of her back he set his fingers against. Her skin quivered. She knew exactly what all those things felt like.

Finally, she'd had enough. "Where's Mother?"

"About ten feet behind you," Jonathan responded. "Why?"

"Fair warning," Wolf said to Thompson through closed teeth. Mrs. Malone scowled his way while Alanna whispered in her ear.

He'd watched the Malones cast worried glances over their shoulders at the Thompsons for the better part of the evening. At last, they turned and marched forward with the Hemenways in tow, a façade of interest suddenly washing over their faces. The Hemenways appeared none the wiser.

Wolf cursed. "Here comes that ill-tempered, squawking—"

"The Malones would be remiss if they did not pay their respects," Thompson said. "My wife is of noble birth, and as they are with the Hemenways, the Malones would not choose to ignore Martha. Besides, Mrs. Malone gets to wave Alanna's ring right under your nose. She'll likely count the days to the wedding, as well."

Wolf snorted and turned his back on the approaching group as if he was unaware of their existence. "Then why the hell is Malone taking a chance on speaking to me?"

"He may not like you or think you good enough for his daughter, but he knows you wouldn't do anything to cause me social embarrassment." Thompson grinned and greeted the Hemenways, the Malones, and their offspring in order of hierarchy.

With everything he had in him, Wolf ignored Alanna while the introductions began. He shook the senior Hemenway's hand. Not a sliver of recognition. The grasp of the younger Hemenway's hand aroused more emotion in Wolf. He hid his reaction to the man's cold demeanor and haughty arrogance.

He had the same severe look as his mother and the same coldness in his eyes, but he appeared much less the fool than Wolf had expected. He was nearly as tall as Wolf, and although his hair was thinning on top, he couldn't have been more than thirty-five.

At last, Wolf was forced to greet Alanna. "Good evening, Miss Malone."

Mrs. Malone lifted her daughter's hand under his nose.

"My future son-in-law has fine taste, does he not, Mr. Wolf?"

Wolf turned squarely on Mrs. Malone. *Go to hell.* "Indeed he does, madam. I was about to tell Mr. Hemenway that very thing. But then, anyone could tell by the fine choice he's made in a wife—and in the family she comes from—that his good taste should go unchallenged henceforth."

"But of course, thank you," Mrs. Malone sputtered. As had occurred aboard ship, uncertainty clouded her face at Wolf's remarks. "Mr. Hemenway simply cannot wait to take our daughter's hand. He's insisted the wedding be moved to this coming June, have you not, sir?"

Jonathan sniffed lightly. "I have." He wiped the tip of his nose with a neatly folded square of cloth, regarded Wolf with frosty arrogance, and then fell into brittle silence.

Wolf stared back, longer than was socially acceptable. So the ass was sniveling after all.

Hemenway's eyes cast a dark and unfathomable glimmer. He hadn't missed Wolf's cunning insolence.

Wolf continued on in polite fashion, dropping humorous anecdotes here and there with regard to their sailing on the same ship. Had Mrs. Malone hired someone to speak well of her in front of the Hemenways, none could have outdone Wolf.

Thompson asked Alanna to dance in celebration of her engagement. The others joined them, with Martha on Wolf's arm.

Well into the evening, Wolf found himself standing near the musicians alongside Alanna and Martha. Malone and the senior Hemenway were in the crowd discussing business with several other men, and Thompson had offered to waltz with Mrs. Malone. Where the younger Hemenway and his mother had wandered off to was anyone's guess.

Martha excused herself and turned to speak to the matriarch of the Appleton clan, the self-avowed authority on

Boston's entire family tree. In truth, she carried the history of every scandal and smoldering speculation that lay beneath the unruffled veneer of Boston society.

Wolf watched the couples whirling around the room with feigned attentiveness while out of the corner of his eye, he observed Alanna. When her mother whirled by on Thompson's arm, Alanna tossed a gratuitous smile at Mrs. Malone's ever-watchful gaze and then blew a breath of relief when she disappeared among the other couples, thanks to Thompson's deft manipulations.

"Are we meant to exchange clever little on-dits at this juncture, *Mr. Wolf*?"

Wolf's mouth tipped at one corner. "While I continue enjoying lascivious thoughts of you? I suppose so."

Mrs. Malone twirled around on Thompson's arm, a furious scowl on her face at catching sight of Wolf standing beside Alanna. "Mother has horrible taste in clothing, don't you think?"

"At least the music is good," Wolf responded.

At Alanna's soft laugh, a quiver ran through him. Standing next to her while both pretended interest in the couples moving about the dance floor grew more tedious by the second. He could stand it no longer—he turned and allowed his gaze to run the length of her voluptuous form. "But we can't say the same about your taste, can we? You look lovely."

Her cheeks pinkened. "Why, thank you, Mr. Wolf. Would you believe it was Mother who taught me about clothing?"

Wolf chuckled.

"It's true. Mother's credo was a veritable chant—the cardinal virtue of all beauty is restraint." She laughed lightly. "Can you imagine if Mother didn't restrain herself?"

The threads of Alanna's velvet voice wove through Wolf's heart. Suddenly, he realized she made his world real in a way it had never been before. A hunger gnawed at him. "You take my breath away, Alanna, darlin'."

"Oh, Wolf." Her cheeks flushed a deeper rose. She turned back to the couples whirling about, the rise and fall of her chest quickening. "Will you waltz with me? I so want to touch you."

"If I take you in my arms out there, it'll put everyone in the room on their ear. But it's either that or you must walk away from me, because I cannot keep my hands off you much longer."

She lifted her hand to his. "My thoughts exactly."

Blood raced wildly through Wolf's veins as he led her to the center of the floor and eased her into his arms. "We'll face the consequences later."

"What consequences? Tonight I am formally engaged, and everyone will think you're no different from any of the other gentlemen who've wished me well with a turn around the floor. And you certainly are a fine gentleman tonight, by the way."

She fed Wolf's aching hunger with her loving gaze. "Alanna, you're so beautiful it actually pains me to look at you."

Mrs. Appleton's eyes suddenly glittered and a narrow smile touched her thin mouth. She raised her glass to her lips and spoke to Martha. "Now there's an intriguing couple who look made for one another."

Martha followed Mrs. Appleton's gaze to a handsome, golden-haired man filled with grace and virility who fairly floated around the room with a raven-haired beauty in his arms. A shock wave passed through her, rippled the liquid in her glass.

Oh, dear Lord!

Wolf swept Alanna in graceful circles, his hand stretched nearly around her slender waist. They were close—too close. He held her as lightly as a fragile bird, yet every bit as securely and knowingly as the fire in his eyes captured and held her upturned gaze—a gaze blazing with utter and helpless adoration. It was as though a spotlight shone on the couple as they glided about, its light gleaming off his golden earring and glittering off the brilliance of the diamond and sapphire ring on her hand as it rested on his broad shoulder.

The magnetic strength of him—of the couple—shot right through Martha. Oh Lord, they looked as if they were born for one another's arms, and who wouldn't think they were ecstatically in love?

With her heart knocking against her ribs, Martha tore her eyes from Wolf and Alanna long enough to glance around the room. Everyone stared. Unspoken words hung in the air as people hushed their conversations—some so quickly they forgot to close their mouths.

The music, the other dancers, only played backdrop to the dazzling couple as they twirled about, holding one another, completely oblivious to the electrifying energy they produced.

Martha thanked God when the music ended. A low, savage growl rumbled next to her. She turned.

Malone!

Frantically, she searched through the couples exiting the dance floor, trying to head Wolf off or capture her husband's attention, whichever she could manage.

Too late.

"Take your hands off my daughter," Malone hissed. He grabbed Alanna's arm and shoved Wolf away from her. "And don't you ever look her way again, you filth, you . . . you vermin!"

Alanna gasped. "Father!"

* * *

Wolf's jaw clenched. He stared at her arm, white where her father's fingers dug deep into tender flesh. "If you want me to leave quietly, release her."

He stood, unmoving, until Malone eased his grip and the pink in Alanna's skin returned. Wolf inclined his head, backed into the crowd, and strode to one of the unlocked balcony doors lining the ballroom. The cold outside was a welcome relief from the stuffy, overcrowded atmosphere within. He set his palms on the cold granite rail, closed his eyes, and breathed deep of the icy winter air.

"God, when will this end?" Every nerve in his body screamed and his chest hurt. He hadn't wept since he was six years old. This was the first time he'd come close.

Damn it, he cared too much about Alanna.

What was the point of it all? A life with her was impossible. He had to settle his affairs and leave Boston. If he ever gave another thought to a future with her, he needed to remember this particular evening, with its crowd of smooth-talking hypocrites. Had his parents survived, would they have gathered together with these people? Would he, too, have ended up paying homage to such shallowness? How different his life would have been. Worthless thoughts, these—and ones he'd had too many times to count of late.

A quick rise and fall in the volume of noise told Wolf someone had slipped through another set of doors. He turned to look behind him.

No one.

He realized each balcony was separate and had its own private entry. Potted evergreens situated between them afforded a modicum of privacy. A snarl of muffled voices caught his attention.

Malone.

Wolf would have recognized that guttural growl anywhere. And Hemenway? Or both Hemenways? He couldn't catch much, only a few expletives, and his own name. He stood unmoving, his silhouette carved in the darkness, blending with the spruce.

Time to leave.

He eyed the street below.

Too far to jump.

He waited to make his exit until after Malone left, in order to find out whom he'd been with. But before he could leave, the door behind him swung open. He eyed the ground below him once again.

He caught her perfume, and swore under his breath. She had no idea that this mess went so much deeper than getting caught dancing with her. He kept his back to her while his grip on the railing tightened. "Alanna, get the hell away from me."

She didn't move.

"Now!"

"Wolf, please, don't. I . . . I came to apologize for my father. It was the drink talking, not him. Mother is taking him home."

"Your father doesn't have to leave on my account. I'm the one leaving."

"Mother desires him home regardless. He isn't good at handling a great deal of alcohol."

Wolf gritted his teeth. "Go back inside with your fiancé and his family."

"But it's you I want. And I know you want me. Isn't that—"

"Stop it, Alanna." He sucked in a breath, still staring into the night, still trying to control himself. He should have told her everything. He should have told her he was after Hemenway. But not now—what good would it do? Surely someone had realized she was missing and was looking for her. If anyone found them together, she'd be ruined. He had to get rid of her, for her own safety as well as his. "You have no idea what a life together would mean in the long run. It can't work between us. Hemenway is a rotten choice and you can do far better, but I'm no choice at all."

"But I could never desire anyone but you."

Pain ground into his heart like gravel beneath his heels. "It's even easier to fall in love with someone who can give you the security you need than it is to fall out of love with a vagabond once you've grown tired of his ways. I'm not sticking around here, Alanna. Once I finish with my business, you'll never see me again. Don't be a fool and jeopardize a secure future for yourself. Go back inside before someone catches you with me."

She stepped closer, her voice shaking, but holding firm in her convictions. "Don't patronize me. I *know* what I want. And I *know* what the depth of my wanting is."

It was all he could do to get the words out. "Alanna, please. Go."

"Not until you hear me out. I listened to you, now give me the same courtesy." Alanna's voice grew stronger. "Jonathan is graceless. His manner is pathetic, and commonplace. The others are just like him—cold Bostonians. How can a man give me a spit of joy when he can only speak of his work, or . . . or similar everyday things?"

"I would think a woman like you would have enough fire in her to make a man forget about his work." Wolf heaved a sigh. What he'd just said probably cut deeper into him than into her.

"Men like him want me to be the same thing my father desires me to be—an obedient wife. They aren't interested in a woman with fire in her veins. That would only complicate matters. So what is it you are telling me? That it's my duty to *obey* someone like Jonathan?"

"Ask yourself this, Alanna—have you ever given it a try?" God, but he wanted to escape. He looked to the street again. Jumping simply wasn't an option. He threw his head to the sky to fight for air. Anger and pain, and hatred of the circumstances overwhelmed him. "For the last time, get the hell away from me!"

Silence.

"Do you understand me? Back off!" His vehement words, the only way he knew to keep from desperately reaching for her, sliced through to his marrow. God, the pain.

"Wolf, look at me!" Panic sounded in her voice as she stepped forward, clutched his arm, and tried to pull him around.

With a hard jerk, he yanked his sleeve from her grip and swiped his hand across his face. "I *have* looked at you, Alanna. A thousand times. Now please—"

"Time to leave, darling." A male voice, shards of ice, rose from the shadows behind Wolf. "Come along."

Silence.

"*Now,* Alanna." Hemenway's words came low, menacing. "You'll catch your death out here."

Aw, hell! Protective urges fueled Wolf's anger. He fought the fiery impulse to take the man down. Instead, he turned toward the two and leaned casually against the balcony's rail.

Hemenway stood beside Alanna, his cold eyes unflinching, a predator before the strike.

Wolf crossed his arms over his chest. His deceiving air of conceit and smirking indifference were the only weapons he had to use in her defense. Slowly, he shook his head back and forth in ridicule and disgust at her antics.

Alanna retreated, her face set in disbelief, her fiancé's hand straining at the bend of her arm.

The man sniffed.

Sniveling little bastard. Wolf fought the urge to reach out and grab Hemenway by the throat and toss him over the rail. "Don't make a scene, Alanna. Go."

Hemenway turned and disappeared with her in tow.

Wolf waited a few minutes, and then lost himself in the

crowd while he located Thompson. "I'm getting the hell out of here. Malone and his future son-in-law are on a rampage."

"We'll get our things," Thompson replied.

"No, I'd rather you didn't. Besides, I could use the fresh air. I'll hail a cab if I get chilled. Stick it out here, and don't let on to Martha." He turned on his heel and headed for the front door.

As Wolf descended the stairs, the cold night air and a line of elegant carriages parked at the curb greeted him. His long strides sent him beyond the mansion amid golden shafts of light that shone through the windows and striped the walkway.

Silent streets insulated in a thick layer of snow refreshed Wolf's senses. Nonetheless, a vast melancholy filled him. The heavy weight in his chest that had gripped him at Malone's assault had spread outward until it filled him entirely.

Living in reality could be harsh, he thought derisively, as he wandered through Boston's cold, darkened streets toward Thompson's home. No matter how much they tried to make him feel at home, he was still only their guest. And no matter how much he desired Alanna, or she him, her future had already drawn tight around her neck, like a hangman's noose before sunrise.

She belonged here.

He didn't.

The loud crunch of his feet hitting the hard pack of snow was the only sound to break the hollow silence, touching a mournful chord in him. He trudged along the darkened streets, gazed into the occasional undraped window filled with cozy scenes of Christmas trees, candles burning brightly, fireplaces ablaze—and families.

Families.

A lost sob within his own emptiness echoed his loneliness. He hurt again, for everything he'd lost, and for the things he could not have.

A strange chill suddenly coursed through him.

He shivered, pulled up his collar and dug his hands deep into the pockets of his coat. He thrust his head to the sky to try to bring the cold air deeper into his tight chest.

The hair stood up on the back of his neck.

He stopped in his tracks, as though his feet heard it first. Silence.

He tilted his head to listen harder.

Only a shadow in the soundless night?

A flicker of coldness traced the column of his spine. He stood perfectly still.

Nothing.

He cocked his head at another angle.

Sudden suspicion.

His survival instincts were years strong—something lurked in the darkness.

Then he heard a soft thud.

Something accompanied him in the dark of the night.

Stalked him.

A long moment of silence dragged past as he inched his hand inside his coat to a knife hidden there. The cold steel of another strapped near his ankle buzzed up his leg.

A bulky form materialized out of the corner of his right eye.

Another dark shadow to his left.

For a brief, agonizing moment, chagrin melted into rapid shock as the horrible dawning came—they surrounded him.

The hair stood up at his nape again as a sinister presence slid into place behind him. A silhouette appeared directly ahead.

Dead calm, the only saving grace of his sixth sense, descended on him. As he let his instincts take over, he gave up looking for a way out. Whoever *they* were, they were out to get him, not to frighten him—and they knew the city and its warren of streets. He didn't.

His only hope for survival was to know which of them to concentrate on first—and where the first thrust of his knife should strike.

The click of a gun's hammer from behind gave him the answer. By the sound of it, the man behind him was right-handed.

With a sudden roll of his left shoulder, he turned and released the knife toward where he'd heard the snap of the hammer.

A soft grunt.

The thud of the gun hitting the frozen ground.

And then a sickening crack, wood to bone at the base of his skull, and his own grunt as a blast of hot pain exploded inside his head. He grappled for the small knife strapped to his leg.

A tangle of muscled arms seized him, held him fast to the cold ground. The nauseating stench of sweat and whiskey filled his nostrils.

A shadowed figure rose in the air above him. As if in slow motion, it seemed to float downward until it covered him in black shadow.

He heard the crisp snap of his own ribs and a raspy guffaw. A fist pummeled his face. Merciless hands dug into him, squeezed the length of his legs and body—searching. Someone snatched the chain holding his mother's earring from around his neck. Another wrenched the knife from his calf.

Pain was no longer a part of him. It was as though he'd stepped outside of his own body and hovered nearby. No longer was he a participant in the killing taking place—he was merely a detached observer to his own death.

He watched as his own knife plunged deep into a writhing, bloody form—his own. The body twitched and then lay still.

Suddenly he was back inside his body.

Wasn't he?

Another black shadow appeared from nowhere—only this one floated silently through the air above him and attacked the others. Did this one actually smell clean?

As Wolf sank into welcoming velvet darkness, the world he knew had been entirely recast. It was now peopled by inky, scattering shadows.

Chapter Fourteen

Alanna wanted to bolt out the door after Wolf. She'd be damned if he'd get away with so rudely casting her off. And with his back turned to her no less. Distancing herself from Jonathan was easy enough—when he joined a group of cronies and left her standing on the sidelines like a witless subservient, she simply wandered off. She located her mother near the refreshment table. "I'm leaving. Old Chinese can see me home in a cab."

"You'll do no such thing." A faint, humorless smile meant for any onlookers touched her mother's lips.

"Think, Mother. Since you can't talk Father into leaving, and since my engagement was announced tonight, would it do to have me trail after a man deep in his cups? Give Jonathan and his parents my regards."

Her mother's indrawn breath sounded more like a hiss. "Don't think this is the last you'll hear of what you did tonight."

"Spare me." Alanna turned to leave and then paused. "We can speak in the morning, once you've had time to justify Father's behavior. That should keep me abed most of the day." She made her way to the cloakroom, collected her fur-lined cape, and slipped outside, her focus back on finding

Wolf. Either his eyes had lied while they'd danced, or damn him, he was double-dealing on the balcony. Let him explain *that* to her face.

Blast it! Old Chinese wasn't cooling his heels in the family barouche. If he didn't show himself in five minutes, she'd steal around the corner and walk to the damn hotel by herself. Surely Wolf would have made his way to his rooms by now.

She pulled her cloak tight against the cold and surveyed her surroundings. Where the devil was Old Chinese? She spied the Thompsons heading for their carriage and hurried toward them. "Would you mind seeing me home? My parents wish to remain, and I'm a bit fatigued." She made certain to speak loudly enough that any eavesdroppers would over-hear. One never knew.

Of course they agreed, and once inside, Alanna waited until the rockaway pulled past the line of waiting carriages before she spoke. "You can let me off in front of the Tremont House Hotel."

Martha gasped.

Thompson's brows furrowed. "Why the devil a hotel?"

Alanna lifted her chin. "That's likely where I'll find Wolf. He has some explaining to do."

Martha and Thompson exchanged speaking glances. "What?"

Thompson heaved a sigh. "He's our guest."

Despite the hurt still running rampant in Alanna, her heart skipped a beat. She lifted her chin and folded her hands in her lap. "Well, then."

Thompson removed his top hat and raked his fingers through his hair. "I don't think coming home with us is such a good idea after what happened tonight."

Martha leaned forward and touched her husband's knee. "I doubt you'll convince her otherwise, Captain." She slid her other hand over a cloud of silk skirts and squeezed

Alanna's clasped fingers. "You know how willful our Alanna can be. I'll not have her ruin her beautiful gown by using other means to gain entry."

Thompson set his mouth in a grim line. They rode the rest of the way in silence.

A lone gas lamp lit the entrance beneath the porte cochère. At their entry into the home, a familiar incense touched Alanna's nostrils. Cold slid down her spine and her trained senses snapped to full alert. She backed up, pulling Martha with her. "Something's terribly wrong," she whispered.

Old Chinese stepped from the shadows. "Wolf has met with an accident."

Alanna's heart shuddered as fear replaced anger. "Where is he?"

"Upstairs. Winston sneaked him in through a rear cellar window." Old Chinese turned to Thompson. "We placed him in the room you had locked off rather than the one he'd been assigned. It's best if nosy servants aren't aware of his presence. He was attacked by several men, and my warriors are making certain all traces of what occurred have been swept away."

"Oh, my God!" Frantic, Alanna started past Old Chinese, but he grabbed her arm. "He's in no shape to be seen. Dr. Choate and my team are tending to him."

She gasped. This had to be bad. Very bad. The physician worked clandestinely with Old Chinese. Lord, he was never called into service unless things were extremely serious. She tried to shake off Old Chinese's steel grip, but he held firm. "Let go. . . . Wolf needs me."

"Alanna—" Thompson reached for her other arm.

Martha stepped forward. "She's right. If that were you, no one would stop me."

Thompson dropped his hand and nodded. "I'll come along as well. Martha, you stay—"

Martha lifted her skirts and fell into place behind the

others. "What makes you think I would cower in another room?"

When they reached the top of the stairs, Old Chinese handed a lantern to one of his students and told him to trace a lighted path to the Thompson bedchamber at the front of the house. "Make it appear as if they are retiring in case anyone is prowling around outside."

When Alanna stepped through the door, her knees buckled. Wolf's battered and bloodied body, naked except for one corner of a sheet drawn between his legs, lay deathly still on a bed centered in the room.

The once elaborate bedroom had been transformed into a brightly lit surgery. Gas lamps blazed; whale oil lamps and candles had been pressed into service and hung or set around the bed on tables or chairs. Mirrors, large and small, had been collected from other rooms and set at every imaginable angle, multiplying the light shining around the bed until the center of the room blazed as if the sun itself hovered over Wolf's unmoving form.

Heavy blankets had been tacked to the windows to prevent telltale light from escaping. A drape hung across the bedroom door, further preventing any spillage down the corridor, and keeping curious servants at bay.

Alanna made her way to the foot of the bed. Someone pressed a chair to the back of her knees. She waved off whoever it was. A ragged sob escaped her lips when Thompson slipped an arm around her shoulders.

Old Chinese was clearly in charge of the skilled team he'd trained for such an emergency. Dr. Choate responded quickly and efficiently to little more than a brief nod or a slight glance from Old Chinese.

He and the doctor cleaned the gaping wound on Wolf's right side while two students worked on the remaining lesions. They labored swiftly, using squares of white cloth saturated in a pungent-smelling liquid that wafted under Alanna's nose and stole her breath.

Winston, sitting on a chair at the foot of the bed, worked in the same meticulous and calm manner as did the others. He pierced Wolf's lower limbs with thread-thin needles that protruded from his flesh like miniature spears.

Another student stepped forward with a large bowl holding an opalescent liquid that carried the same acrid odor as the soaked cloths. Dr. Choate dipped his hands into the solution, staining it pink from Wolf's blood. And then the doctor plunged his hand into Wolf's gaping wound. Alanna gasped at the grotesque rolling about of Wolf's belly.

The doctor removed his hand from inside Wolf's flesh. "A knife lacerated his liver. We've cleaned the injury as best we can, but now he needs the natural flow of his own blood to flush the wound clean. In a moment, I'll ask Winston to remove a few needles and a good deal of bleeding will result. This is our intention, so do not be alarmed."

Why hadn't Alanna realized this? Because most of his body resembled raw meat, that was why. God, she wished this were a bad dream. An ugly thought crawled beneath her skin and snaked down her spine. Could this have been her fault—because of what happened at the ball? Jonathan's doing? Her father's?

The doctor nodded to Winston, who removed some of the needles piercing Wolf's flesh. A gush of bright red spewed onto a stack of towels tucked against his side. A scarlet halo soaking the pillow beneath his head inched wider.

Dear Lord! Alanna's hand flailed out behind her, grasping nothing but air. The chair she'd earlier refused tapped at her knees. She sank into it, close to where a composed Winston worked intently.

"You need to calm yourself," Winston said quietly.

Alanna conjured up everything Old Chinese had taught her. After a moment, her panic slipped away, replaced by an urge to connect with Wolf. With a small nod, Winston motioned for her to touch the top of Wolf's foot.

Her fingers quivered so much, she couldn't weave them through the delicate needles, and her eyes were too moist to see her way clearly. Winston reached out and gently guided her hand.

Her head snapped up. She looked from Winston, to Old Chinese, to the doctor and students. She *felt* them—every single one of them who now touched Wolf. She distinctly *felt* their life force coursing through him, keeping him alive.

In the midst of Wolf's hell, Alanna took in the quiet scene before her, her fingers still on his warm flesh. *He couldn't be in better hands.*

She had no idea how much time had passed, but when the team completed all that could be done, Old Chinese addressed Thompson. "Until we know what this is about and who is involved, we need to keep Wolf's presence a secret."

Thompson nodded. "I've already thought of that. I'll accelerate the countless Christmas activities around here—create a hectic pace so that a stream of visitors will leave the servants with little time to tend to anything other than their own frenzied duties. They won't pay any attention to how many are being fed or where each member of the family is at any given time. I must keep my youngest daughter in the dark as well."

"I'll see to her," Martha said.

Alanna fought to control her voice. "What about me?"

Old Chinese regarded her. "It's nearly dawn. You should leave now. I'll fill you in on Wolf's condition as I come and go. Except for two who will remain with me, it's time for the team to vanish, back the way we came. Winston will see you home in the way he knows how."

Alanna stood over Wolf for as long as she dared. When she gathered enough strength to leave, she was painfully aware that Old Chinese never mentioned the fact that Wolf had not regained consciousness. The thought that perhaps he never would was too painful even to consider.

Old Chinese appeared and disappeared at will, bringing reports to Alanna, who spent her days in her room, refusing to speak to her parents. On the fifth day, Old Chinese brought her back to Wolf.

Naked beneath a light blanket, his body bruised and swollen, he looked even worse than he had the night of the attack. His chest was tightly bound to hold his broken bones in place. A pillow, constructed with a hollowed-out center, held his head in place, but allowed the gash at the base of his skull to heal. Purple bruises marred his face, and his split and swollen lips sent a shaft of pain through her. He had yet to awaken.

"Oh, God, oh, God, oh, God!" A jerk of her body was the only notice Alanna had before her legs gave out from under her. She slid halfway down Old Chinese's side before he caught her.

And then the tears fell. From the very depths of her soul, they came. The utter and gripping pain drove her to incoherency.

Old Chinese swept her into his arms and carried her to a wingback chair. She curled into his lap, little different from when she'd been a small girl. She buried her head against his chest and swallowed cries that exploded in the back of her throat.

Her hair, wrenched loose from the knot at the back of her head, streamed about her face and shoulders. Gently, he tucked the tumbled locks into place. His sad eyes, unfocused and unblinking, stared out the window at the gray sky. Suddenly, he looked so very old.

When she finally collected herself, she slipped from his lap and made her way back to Wolf's bedside. "I would never have recognized him. How can we humans do such terrible things to one another?"

"Once the swelling goes down, he won't look quite so bad," Old Chinese said. "Nothing in his face is broken, and with time, perhaps the scars will fade."

Alanna reached out and touched her fingers to Wolf's hair. "Can I have him to myself for a bit?"

Once alone, she found a small space on his cheek where her lips could touch his skin. As a multitude of foreign emotions invaded her, a tear splashed down her cheek and a kind of panic set in. "It's been five days, Wolf. Wake up."

He lay before her, pale as death. She noticed a hand mirror on a table next to the bed. She knew what that mirror was for, but she couldn't bring herself to set it near his nose and mouth and look for the telltale mist of his breath against the glass. A ragged sob escaped her.

"Don't you dare leave me. Can you hear me? Don't you ever leave me!" And then her voice softened, quivered as she begged. "Please, Wolf. I would perish without you."

Chapter Fifteen

With the aid of Old Chinese, Alanna managed to sneak in to visit Wolf daily. At times the two of them put in brief public appearances wherever she was certain gossips would be, so they would inform her mother. Then she and Old Chinese would hurry to the Thompson home.

She was careful never to enter the premises without Old Chinese. He told her he wasn't certain if the house was being watched, even though Wolf was kept well hidden.

Alanna grew wearier by the day. She slept little, and the strain of Wolf's not awakening began to show.

Dr. Choate came regularly to check on his patient— nothing out of the ordinary since the doctor was Martha's cousin, and it was the holiday season, but only Alanna and Old Chinese replaced the bandages and forced the liquids down Wolf's throat. These past two days, except for assistance required to wrap his ribs, she'd tackled the burden on her own.

Dr. Choate and Old Chinese observed while she applied the last of the fresh bandages to Wolf's side. "At least I know his exact degree of healing," she murmured when she finished.

She wiped a thin film of perspiration from her brow with

the back of her hand and, glancing at the clock over the mantel, shed a weary sigh. "Time for my nap, gentlemen. Off with you."

When they left, she slid the wingback chair close to Wolf, and curled up with a chenille coverlet over her lap. Leaning her head against the chair's back, she settled in to study his swollen and bruised countenance. This was her favorite time of day with him, quiet and peaceful.

Not a flicker to his gilded lashes. Memories of the night in his room at the Hotel Tremont—when he lay healthy and vibrant on his bed, impishly tempting her into the open crook of his arm—kept her company until she dozed.

When she roused, her neck had stiffened and her hip ached. She wriggled about until she found a more comfortable seat, then let her eyes flutter open. Her blurred vision drifted across the bed, focusing as she went. Her eyes flew wide as she shot forward.

Wolf's left arm—it was in a different position!

She leaned her elbows on the bed and studied his hand as though it were a piece of fragile art come to life. Blood thundered in her ears. "You moved," she whispered.

His lashes flickered.

"Wolf!"

Then she laughed while tears spilled freely. She slid onto the bed beside him, not daring to touch him, not daring to disturb his tender body, only near enough to feel his heat meld with hers.

Alanna's velvet-soft laughter and her quiet sobbing washed through Wolf like a gentle spring rain.

An image, along with her scent, filtered through his numbed mind. An old, baronial manor house, sitting grand and majestic among tall pines grew clear in his mind.

The warmth of Alanna's body swept through him.

His mind filled with fresh images of green meadows dotted with pastured horses, rolling hills cut through with the rush of a river, silver-blue ponds, and two graceful, white swans. Her warmth, her scent invaded his senses once again.

Had he returned home?

With all the strength his mind and body could summon, he willed his hand to inch forward until it touched the heat of her soft flesh.

"Oh, God, Wolf. You're awake. Can you open your eyes? Speak to me."

He heard tears in her voice, but he could not gather the strength to speak. He managed to squeeze her hand. She gasped and her breath brushed his cheek. She was so very close to him and yet, he couldn't quite manage to open his eyes.

He tried to move, but pain pricked every part of him, and he grew pathetically weary from the effort. For now, he would sleep. But soon, very soon . . .

"It's only been three days since you awoke and already you're a holy terror of grumbles," Little Mary chirped, busy tucking the covers around Wolf as though the child had a right to. A cigar box she carried everywhere sat cockeyed on the bed, threatening to spill over with every yank of the blankets.

Wolf tried to smile through split lips and winced. Damn, that hurt. He had an inkling she'd been playing the invisible eavesdropper downstairs again. "You've been hiding behind the woodstove again, you little sneak." He also had a pretty good idea who she mimicked. "Alanna arrived, did she?"

Little Mary nodded and scrambled onto the bed with her legs dangling off the edge and her skirt twisted to her knees.

She plopped the cigar box into her lap. "She's having tea. Earl Grey. Mum's favorite."

"What's in the box?"

"Treasure."

"Buried treasure?" He winced as he tried to pull himself to a more upright position.

"No, silly. If it was buried, it wouldn't be on my lap, now would it?"

If that didn't sound like her father. Wolf winced again. "What's it for?"

"Alanna's birthday. I'm buying her a puppy. It's a secret though, so you can't say anything."

Wolf bet no one knew of her little scheme. "Will you tell me all about it if I promise not to utter a word?"

Little Mary nodded. "Miss Malone and I were playing the *if only* game. Today we played 'If only I had a puppy,' and that's when she told me she wanted a great pair of knees."

"A what?" Wolf winced again at the spread of his grin.

Little Mary heaved an exasperated sigh. "I *said* a great-pair-of-knees dog."

She rattled around in her cigar box while Wolf racked his brain. "Is that a white furry animal with a head like a bear?"

"Yes, sir."

"You mean a Great Pyrenees, Little Mary, that's what those dogs are called. Look at me and repeat after me." He said the name slowly while she studied his lips.

"That's what I said, a great pair a knees."

"So Alanna . . . Miss Malone wants a puppy. Do you know where to find one?"

Little Mary's head pumped up and down. "Papa took me to Mr. Higginson's store, and when Papa was chatting with another man, Mr. Higginson told me I could buy one of the two Great pair o . . . pyr . . . puppies he had left. It's a boy one. He's all preserved for me."

"You mean reserved. Do you have enough money for this present?"

"Uh, yes! Papa gave me a whole, whole lot of money." She opened the cigar box and set it under Wolf's nose.

His gut wrenched at the box's contents—a bunch of random buttons and a stack of worthless foreign currency. "How do you intend to bring the puppy home if it's a surprise?"

"I thought you would be pretty much better by Christmas Eve, when it's her birthday, and . . ." She shrugged and started swinging her little feet.

The idea of the oversized puppy for Alanna amused Wolf. What the hell, he should be up and around enough by then to drive a sleigh to the general store. "All right, but it's our secret."

"Done!" Little Mary scrambled off the bed, nearly dumping the contents of her cigar box. "Gotta go before Mum catches me in here."

A few minutes later, Alanna swept into the room. "Good afternoon." She grabbed his hairbrush and bent over him.

Wolf sniffed. "Ah, you've had tea. Earl Grey."

Alanna stepped back, a crimson flush flooding her cheeks. "I do apologize. I . . . I usually nap about now, but since you're awake at such odd times, I thought a little cup of tea would—"

The flush left her cheeks. Eyes narrowed, she bent to the floor and rose with one of Little Mary's worthless coins between her fingers.

Wolf laughed, and then winced, fingering his cracked lips. "Jesus, Mary, and Joseph, that hurt."

Alanna continued staring blazes at him, the coin she swept from the floor held in midair. "Tea on my breath, my eye."

"Have a sense of humor, will you?" He tried to shrug

but groaned instead. "I need a little diversion from this hellacious boredom."

She made her way to the credenza and set down the hairbrush. "What in blazes will you be like a little further down the road?"

Wolf watched the sway of her hips and lust kicked him in the loins. "If I wasn't incapacitated, you'd be in a heap of trouble about now."

She dragged the chair over to the bed and sat. A wanton grin tipped her lips. "You mean I can consider myself safe while alone with you in your bedchamber?"

Wolf managed to spread an arm out. "Come lie beside me, Alanna darlin'."

The color in her cheeks heightened. "Don't be absurd."

"What could it possibly hurt in my condition?"

Her bold stare ended with a sweep of her sooty lashes. To his surprise, she stood, gingerly climbed onto the bed, and stretched alongside him, careful not to touch his injured flesh.

"How can I hold you when you're so very far away," he murmured. "Come closer."

"I'm afraid of hurting you."

"Then inch your way over," he teased. But his eyes held hers as she followed his command. The scent of her skin, of freshly washed hair, invaded his senses. And then he caught the heat of her body. "I don't suppose you'll take your hair down for me?"

"I don't suppose I will." She nestled as close as she dared, her voice soft, receptive. With the slightest touch, she ran her finger over his cheek.

Damaged as he was, a part of his body still rose to the occasion. "Am I your knight in shining armor now, Miss Alanna Malone?"

She nodded and her finger traced a cut near his eye. "With a few dents, sir."

Warmth flowed through him. "The worst of it is that right now I want to kiss you, and I can't."

"Shh, close your eyes," she whispered. "You're wearing yourself out." She touched his lids, feather soft, forcing his eyes to close. Her fingers traced his cheek, and then slid to the golden hoop. "At least the bastards didn't tear this out of your ear."

Anger ground through him. No, they'd gotten his mother's earring, and when he was up and around, by God someone would pay. Eyes heavy, he drifted off. Thought scattered as Alanna's warmth and her sweet scent surrounded and lulled him.

When he came slowly awake, his first awareness was of the empty space beside him. He'd known she'd be gone, because the day had grown late, but her absence left him feeling hollow.

Still drugged by the impact to his skull and the pain medication he'd been given, Wolf struggled toward consciousness. The soft glow of lamplight filtered through his heavy lids. He must have slept longer than usual. The awareness of another's presence permeated his senses. He wasn't alone. His lids fluttered open.

The wingback chair, set farther back from the bed, was cast in a long ribbon of shadow. Booted feet, long, sinewy legs, and broad shoulders barely fitting the width of the chair caught Wolf's eye. He grunted in surprise when he saw who it was. "Thompson isn't particular about who he lets in, is he?"

Trevor Andrews, the other owner of the Andrews Shipping Company, sat with his chin propped in one hand. "*Merde*. You look as though you were buried deep and then dug back up as an afterthought."

Wolf moaned. "Ever the arrogant French Creole." He winced again. "I thought you sailed to China."

Trevor shook his head. "Once Celine learned my father had been ill, she insisted we change our plans. We spent two weeks trying to convince him to sell the plantation and move to England with us, but he refused so we had no choice but to leave without him. We settled in Liverpool in late October, where I'm back heading up the main offices."

"You came all this way to harass me?"

"Actually, I arrived in Boston to meet with our ship-builder about delivery of another clipper. Thought I might pay you a visit after Thompson told me what happened." Trevor stood and moved to the bed. "You have a very poor sense of timing, *mon frère*. I was in the middle of the Atlantic during your altercation. At least when I took an arrow in my back, I had the courtesy to invite you along, *Archibald Gray*."

"You've been talking to that detective, haven't you? That's my middle name, goddamn it, and if you—"

Trevor chuckled, but reached out and covered Wolf's hand with his own, his countenance shifting. "Let's not wear you out. I came to tell you that I'll do whatever needs doing to get this mess behind us."

Us? "Thanks." An odd emotion wormed its way through Wolf. The idea that people cared about what happened to him was too new to feel comfortable. He looked toward a darkened corner of the room and struggled for a deep breath, the kind that shot arrows of pain through him.

Trevor dropped his hand to his side. "It's no longer safe for you in this town." The authority in his voice told Wolf not to bother arguing. "As soon as you're able to be moved, you should return with Old Chinese to the farm. Once you're in good enough shape to travel farther, come to England. We'll work from both sides of the Atlantic to solve your mother's death. And believe me, we *will* do so."

"You don't mince words, do you? Why England?"

"Our men have been able to trace the missing funds as far as Scotland." Trevor raised a hand, signaling Wolf to lie still. "*Merde*. I hope I wasn't as unruly as you while I recovered. And don't speak. I have too much to tell you and you're already pale."

"Aw, hell," was all Wolf managed to accomplish. He must've had a double dose of something to ease the pain because his mind was muddled.

"Thompson mentioned you've recalled that as a child, you had caretakers of Scottish descent. Do you remember their names, anything about them?"

Wolf managed a small shake of his head. Trevor was right; he wore out fast.

"While you lie around healing, try to remember anything you can. The smallest scrap of information could very well be the missing piece to the puzzle."

"I'm having dreams," Wolf said. "You probably know about the ones with the smoky mirror, but now, I'm having strange dreams of a manor house that seems oddly familiar. Don't get much, just a feeling."

"Old Chinese said your dreams are coming along as he expected, so don't try to force things. Just let them happen." Trevor made his way to the fireplace. "Since you're fading on me, I need to switch subjects. This beating you were subjected to, *mon frère*, what's your gut feeling? Do you think it had any connection with your childhood and the murder? Or was it the consequence of a fiancé's wounded pride?"

"Anything about me you don't know?"

"Nothing I don't have a need to know. I'm afraid you are truly ignorant as to what the word *mon frère* can mean. When a French Creole who owes you a debt of honor calls you brother, he's telling you he is as committed to you as if you shared the same blood."

Wolf's chest tightened. Jeezus, what did he say now?

Trevor leaned an elbow on the mantel. "You saved my wife's and child's lives out there in the middle of nowhere; now it's my chance to return the favor." He smiled. "In fact, it's your *obligation* to allow a French Creole to repay his debt of honor, *mon frère.*"

Wolf was desperate to change the subject. "How's Celine?" He'd grapple with his emotions later.

"My wife is well. We're quite content." Trevor's words were simply put, but the quick fire in his eyes at the mention of his wife gave Wolf a better answer.

"And Brandon?"

"Doing well. He'll have a sibling come spring."

Wolf groaned. "Celine must not get much rest with you rutting around."

Trevor chuckled. "God gave man a most delectable way of reproducing. I've found married life has its . . . how should I say . . . constant rewards. You should try it." He returned to the chair, where he sat and stretched his legs. "Speaking of which, I've known Alanna for years."

At Wolf's disgusted sigh, Trevor laughed. "The idea of you two getting together never crossed my mind. But when I heard, I thought . . ." He lifted his fingertips to his mouth and gave them a kiss. "You two couldn't be more deserving of each other."

"Kiss my ass."

Trevor chuckled. "You grow tired, *mon frère.* It would be best if I leave, but I'll return on the morrow. I promised Celine I would be home in time for the holidays, so I won't remain in Boston but a short while and I have much to accomplish. I'll visit as frequently as possible."

A knock sounded on the door, and Thompson entered.

"Ah," Trevor said. "I was about to go looking for you. It's up to us to take care of a few things without burdening Wolf since not only is he incapacitated, he's not in the right frame of mind to make serious decisions. I know—I've been right where he is."

A look of dread shrouded Thompson's visage. "I have a bad feeling that what you learned from the detective today is somehow going to dovetail with my recent revelations."

Trevor rested an elbow on the chair's arm and set his fingertips to his temple. "Tell me about *Junior* Hemenway."

Thompson heaved a sigh. "It seems young Mr. Hemenway accompanied his future father-in-law on a recent trip to our nation's capital. The two apparently spent the better part of most evenings frequenting brothels."

"Christ," Wolf muttered. Damn, he despised being so crippled up.

"Doesn't surprise me," Trevor responded. "Malone hasn't been so faithful in other affairs, either."

"How's that?"

"He's always booked his shipping with us, right? Spills over to other lines occasionally if we're unavailable, correct?"

"Correct," Thompson replied.

"He's used other liners here when we've been at capacity, some as far away as New York, but always open and above board?"

Thompson nodded. "Always bids with us first."

"Then why has he been booking cutters out of Liverpool and Australia under a different name?"

"A partner involved?" Thompson asked.

Trevor nodded. "Junior. They're blackbirding."

Slave trading. Wolf cursed.

Thompson blew out a breath and sat in another chair. "Good God. Malone's one of the most outspoken abolitionists in New England. You're sure? Never mind. Of course you would be." His cheeks puffed, then deflated in another rush of an exhale. "Why in the world would Malone risk everything for something like slave trading?"

Trevor shrugged. "Why are some of Boston's wealthiest

running opium when they can't spend what they make running tea and household goods?"

Anger wound its way through Wolf's gut. "Any idea how long this has been going on?"

"Since last May," Trevor said. A long moment of silence sat heavy in the room. "It seems our *Monsieur* Malone has fallen into that sticky age-old trap. His reward for a lifetime of struggle sits right before him with the pending marriage of his daughter. He can smell it, but it's still just a hair's breadth beyond his reach. And I think Junior secretly wants to become independent of Senior's control. Put the two together and *voila*, diamond mines in Africa—black diamonds, that is."

"Do you think they both might be responsible for Wolf's attackers?" Thompson asked. "Alanna thinks her fiancé and her mother might be the culprits, that her mother may have fanned her fiancé's anger, naive to the deadly potential. You know what a featherbrain Mrs. Malone can be."

"Those are only some of the missing pieces," Trevor said. "But Miss Malone might be right—her mother is likely just as nervous as her husband with the culmination of their dreams in sight. Perhaps even more so now that there's no denying the attraction between Wolf and her ace in the hole."

"What about Hemenway Senior and the haircutting incident with his daughter?" Wolf asked. "The same thing was done to my mother."

Trevor shook his head. "The senior Hemenway isn't involved in his son's and Malone's mess. However, going on the assumption that he is the one who murdered your mother, and he's somehow found out who you are and believes you witnessed the act, he has more to lose than the other two with you alive."

"I had one last bit of information reported to me today," Thompson said. "It seems one of Boston's police captains hasn't been seen since the night of Wolf's attack."

Trevor frowned. "Any connection?"

Thompson nodded. "He's the same chap who detained Wolf at the precinct. The man used to work for Hemenway."

Fire and ice ran through Wolf's veins, but he was growing so weary he could do little more than grunt.

Trevor's brows furrowed. "The minute you think Wolf can be moved, make him disappear."

"I'll see to it," Thompson said. "But what about Alanna? Do you think it would be in everyone's best interests if we curb her visits?"

Wolf was drifting in and out, but the idea of not seeing her before he was transported to the farm irritated him. He groaned.

Trevor chuckled. "There's your answer, Thompson. Something tells me while Wolf has been running from any woman who wants to tie him down, he ended up running smack into one who has him tied up in knots."

Wolf struggled to get his words out. "Damn the doctor and his powders. And to hell with your cocked-up opinions."

Chapter Sixteen

Christmas Eve

The ball of white fluff asleep in Alanna's lap twisted about until he curled against her, belly-up. She buried her fingers into the puppy's deep fur and stroked his tummy. "He's so sweet, thank you."

Wolf gave a small nod. He sat before the fire, his head against the rocking chair's carved back, one long leg thrust outward, his heel controlling the slow, rhythmic movements. His thumb brushed softly along his bottom lip as he silently studied her. Dusk's deepening shadows and his half-closed lids veiled his thoughts. Her heart thumped in her chest. He'd changed recently, and the strange shift in his mood left her with a sense of discomfort.

His abrupt withdrawal had occurred right after Trevor had come to call. No longer did Wolf tease her. Ask her to brush his hair. Shave his face. Read to him. What in the world had caused him to grow so silent?

Tomorrow would be the first day she wouldn't be over to visit him. She'd been fortunate to be able to spend time with him because of the Thompsons' festivities, but Christmas Day would be too risky. Lord knew, she'd miss him. And when the celebrations were all over, what then? Gone would be the myriad social events that kept her parents too busy to bother with her whereabouts.

The prospect of returning home tonight to their shallow group of friends on this, her twenty-fourth birthday, nearly sent a rush of tears down her cheeks. Things seemed strangely out of sorts, as though something was about to change and her world would never run quite the same again.

Orange firelight flickered across Wolf's face. His lips, nearly healed and back to their soft generosity, sent waves of warmth fluttering through her belly. "What's on your mind, Wolf?"

He shrugged, but made no attempt to shift his gaze from her.

With a heavy sigh, she rose from her chair to leave. "My parents are expecting me." The rotund puppy, utterly exhausted from Little Mary's visit and her incessant pestering, gave a small grunt, rolled over, and went limp again.

Wolf stood, his movements still a bit stiff.

Alanna stood. "Oh, please, don't get up on my account." Her hand paused in midair before it touched him, and then slipped back under the dog's fat belly. She made to move past him, but his arm slid around her waist. He pulled her to him, the ball of fur in her arms their only separation. Her heart leapt to her throat, and heat rose in her cheeks. For some odd reason, she felt close to tears. What had happened to alter their easy camaraderie?

His hand disappeared into the dog's thick coat and found hers. His other hand slid from her waist to her shoulders, where he pulled her to him until her cheek rested against his chest. She caught the wild hammering of his heart. So he wasn't as calm as he pretended. Lord, she didn't want him to let go of her.

"Oh, Wolf. I shall miss you when I leave."

* * *

Wolf wanted to kiss her, but he didn't dare. He'd start something he probably couldn't stop. A ragged breath escaped his lips.

"I'll miss you, as well." He released her and walked to the far window, where he parted the drapes a mere inch and caught sight of the waiting sleigh. "Have a good Christmas."

The click of her heels against the wood floor sent lonely echoes along the hallway and down the stairs. In moments, she appeared beside the sleigh with Thompson and Old Chinese. When she disappeared from sight, he made his way back to his chair and resumed his slow rocking and staring at the firelight.

Knowing she returned to her family pained him more than he wanted anyone to know. Hell, even Old Chinese would be with her. She had been born twenty-four years ago tonight, and twenty-four years ago tomorrow his entire world had shattered. And the two events had taken place nearly across the street from one another—and not far from here. Christ! He swiped a hand over his face and wondered where he could find some good whiskey in a hurry.

"May I join you?" Martha stood at the doorway holding a silver tray laden with a cut-glass wine decanter and two crystal goblets. She stepped into the room. "Don't get up."

He did anyway. Lifting the tray from Martha's grasp, he placed it on the small table between them, then sat again. "You're welcome with or without the wine, Martha, but this looks mighty good about now."

Martha angled her chair more toward Wolf than to the fire while he filled the two glasses and pressed one into her hand. He said nothing more, only leaned his head back against the chair and studied the dancing patterns that filtered through the garnet liquid in his glass.

"Your silence has gone on for some time now," Martha said. "I think it causes Alanna pain."

A knot formed in Wolf's gut.

"Take her with you."

"What?" By the look in her eyes, she wasn't kidding. "I can hardly walk down the stairs by myself, and you suggest I take her with me? Jesus, Martha, that little sleigh ride to the wharf this morning to pick up the dog was all I could manage today."

"You're not leaving for England until spring. You'll have thoroughly healed by then. Get her out of this disaster." Martha leaned forward, her voice ardent. "Please, don't let it be too late."

"And what if I were to take her with me? After my business is finished, what then? Do I find a little thatched-roof cottage for the two of us? When this mess ends, her association with the Hemenways will terminate. She can get on with her life here in Boston or out with Old Chinese—without my interference." His damn teeth hurt again. He unclenched his jaw.

"Would you care to know what I have to say about that?"

"Do I have a choice?" A hint of surrender entered his heart. Uneasy, he shifted his gaze back to the flames and slowly rocked the chair.

"You cannot be concerned about finances, so a miserable thatched-roof cottage is of no consequence. Besides, if only half the missing funds due you are recovered, you'll be more than well set—"

"Don't go by your own experience, Martha. Your parents weren't like hers. If Alanna were involved with me, we'd spend the rest of our lives looking over our shoulders. No matter the miles between us, Malone wouldn't hesitate at a chance to turn her into a wealthy widow, which would leave Alanna miserable."

"I don't think that would happen. In the end, I suspect it's going to be quite difficult for the Malones to consider such spitefulness. They'd have too much to lose."

"Humph."

"Opium-running among Boston's merchant elite is one thing, Wolf. Most all of them do it, so there's not a one of them willing to expose the other. But slave trading by an avowed abolitionist? Well, that kind of scandal would bring great difficulties down on the Malones—perhaps even place them in harm's way."

She studied Wolf's face and frowned. "But most likely I'm not telling you anything you and Trevor haven't already discussed. I suspect Trevor's ultimate plan is to catch them red-handed, make it difficult for them to take action against you for fear of exposure. Am I right?"

He wasn't up to telling her of the latest news, that Alanna's father and Jonathan actually co-owned the brothels they'd frequented in Washington, used them to entice and persuade government officials. The maze of deceit had grown another dark corridor.

A quizzical expression flashed across Martha's features. "I apologize. I'm not trying to pressure you for information. I agree that the fewer people who know what Trevor is up to, the better. What I am saying is, I've come to the conclusion that what's holding you back is the tragic burden you've carried for the past twenty-four years. You're concerned it will haunt you the rest of your days and destroy any chance of a decent family life. If that's your worry, it doesn't have to be that way."

A tired sigh escaped Wolf's lips. "If only I could be certain."

Martha reached out and covered his hand once again, this time not letting go. "Dare to go after your dreams."

"What dreams? I've always lived like a feather in the wind, with nothing much on my mind but catching a killer one day."

"Oh, I think deep down you know what you want. You've

just never been able to acknowledge it. Now that Alanna's shown up in your life, I think your hidden dreams are trying to wiggle out of the box you locked them in long ago."

Disquieting thoughts raced through Wolf's mind. His brows furrowed. "That reminds me of an actual dream I've been having—since my little . . . misfortune occurred." He bent to refill his glass and filled hers as well.

"Is it the same one over and over?"

He nodded. "Some more detailed than others. It's a strange dream, of a grand old manor house made of gray stone—castellated, I think. Rather baronial, the kind one might think to find in the English countryside. It sits in a green valley with grazing horses and beautiful trees. There's a river out back. In front, a pond with a couple of swans."

"How do you feel when the dream is going on?"

"Good."

"How do you feel when you're in the countryside with Old Chinese?" Martha's wonderful voice, soft and clear, soothed him.

"The same. Big cities and crowded streets tend to stupefy my brain."

She smiled. "That should tell you something. But you'll know the full measure of what your dream is trying to tell you when the time is right."

He refilled the wineglasses and a long silence ensued. Martha reached into a pocket of her skirt and extracted a black velvet pouch. She handed it to Wolf.

He stopped rocking the chair and emptied the bag's contents into his hand. The chain and his mother's earring dropped into his palm, jolting him. "Jeezus, I gave that up for lost."

"One of Old Chinese's students retrieved it for you," she responded. "Old Chinese thought it fitting to return it to you this evening. I hope one day you'll trust Alanna enough to share the story behind it."

Wolf hooked the chain around his neck and slipped the earring under his shirt. "Who would've thought some twenty-four years later, I'd be sitting within spitting distance of my childhood home? Sometimes I feel like it found me, I didn't find it. I'd knock on the door and ask to look around, but who would say yes to such an insane request?"

Tears filled Martha's eyes, but her serene countenance remained. She swiped at a corner of her eye and laughed lightly. "Forgive me. I've become a bit emotional."

Wolf's insides suddenly churned. He stilled. There was something about Martha just then that distinctly reminded him of his mother. Her soft, tear-filled laughter, that was it.

Long-forgotten memories tore from their deep moorings and shot to the surface. His stomach twisted in a kaleidoscope of reeling emotions. How could he have forgotten? His mother had looked nearly the same as Martha just now—sitting by the fire when his father was away on business. Apologizing for her tears. In a similar soft voice, she'd recited wonderful stories of their life together or woven tales of incredible fantasy. He'd especially loved hearing the legends of Merlin and tales of Celtic lore.

Inexplicably, a part of him withdrew into a corner of his past. In his mind's eye, Wolf found himself looking down into a small boy's world. A similar warm blaze and a similar feminine but iron-strong woman, sat beside a child with a puff of flaxen hair. Little feet, barely stretching beyond the edge of an oversized rocker, managed a slow, steady movement of the chair. A small, wet finger found its way back and forth along small, even teeth. A mother's soft, honey-soaked voice lulled him.

Such a voice.

Such words.

Words that always made him feel secure—and loved. He'd felt life on earth was harmonious, immutable back then. Never had it occurred to him that his world would change, that his father would not always return from wherever he went, or that his mother would not always be there.

Never had it crossed his mind she could die.

"Your voice reminds me of my mother's, Martha. Except for one thing."

"What's that?"

"She had a Scottish brogue."

"You're sure? Boston is heavily populated with the Irish, but I don't know of many Scots around. The two accents do sound alike, though."

Wolf shook his head. "No mistaking the two in my mind. Hers was Scots."

With the heel of his shoe, he set his chair to rocking again. "I need to stop talking about myself. Tell me about your life after you moved to Boston." He rotated the glass of wine in his fingers and took a slow sip. He allowed Martha's silken voice to resonate through him and stir up crystal-clear memories. They rolled through him like relentless waves over both smooth and jagged boulders.

His odd dreams, his recent talking in his sleep, they were all awakenings of one kind or another, Old Chinese had said. He'd also told Wolf that he would soon begin bringing forth the ghosts of buried memories.

The pause in Martha's voice ended his musings.

He turned to her. "I'm sorry, what did you say?"

"I said, I study the origin of names, Wolf. Would you care to know what yours means?"

Every fiber in his body tensed against her offer. "I was named Wolford." He switched from staring at the dancing firelight to staring into the glass of garnet liquid. "Wolford Archibald Gray. What a ridiculous moniker to saddle someone with."

"But you were called Wolf at a young age, weren't you?"

He nodded. "For as long as I can recall. I didn't care much for Wolford from the very beginning. Or Wolfie—" Another flash of early childhood jolted him. An image of his lovely mother, all soft and sweet-smelling, tangled with the foul memory of a hand dangling limp over the edge of a bed.

Dark shadows pierced his brain and a chill skittered across his shoulders. Pain shot past the defenses he'd maintained so carefully. He squeezed his eyes shut as raw, primitive grief gripped him. "I've been lonely most of my life," he stated flatly.

His sudden, bleak confession must have startled Martha, for she left her chair and began to pace. "It's true you've spent many years alone and without ties, but that's in the past."

Wolf shrugged belligerently, but inside he knew she could be right. "Then tell me, where will I go from here once my mother's murder is resolved?"

Martha came to a halt before him. "You have the perfect woman with which to start a family. She is resilient, intelligent—"

Wolf threw his head back and sucked in his breath. "I don't know *how* to be part of a family." He rubbed at his wounded side to try to ease the contracting, stinging muscles. "Her parents despise me, and I find them disgusting. It wouldn't be fair to Alanna to put her in the middle of a mess like that. There's not a shred of hope for a decent family life with the Malones involved."

"Do you love her?" Martha's demeanor became regal, demanding the truth from her subject.

Wolf grew guarded again. Love was only a memory. "How do you suggest I handle things if it was her father who ordered me killed? Or her mother who instigated the deed?"

"Do you *love* her?"

He fought a terrible tightness in his chest. "Love isn't

some magical potion that solves all problems. The only way I could enhance Alanna's life is to stay the hell out of it."

"Like your father stayed out of yours? Aren't you tired of living like a so-called feather in the wind?" Her barbed question hooked the rest of his reserves.

His jaw clenched. He drew in a ragged breath and paused, not trusting his own voice. "It's a wonder I ever managed to make it this far in life." He swallowed an ache of defeat.

Martha reached out and smoothed the collar on his shirt. "Oh, Wolf." Her eyes filled with tears again. "Don't try to make decisions now. You're much too weak, too confused, and you've been through so very much."

Looking utterly miserable, Martha straightened her spine, dignity returning. "I warn you, whatever you do right now, *do not* throw Alanna away. Shall we have another glass of wine?"

Wolf poured as Martha went to the window and peered down at the blackened drive. "Where do you suppose the captain is all this while? It's grown quite dark, hasn't it?"

"Probably convincing the Malones to let Alanna keep the pup," Wolf said dryly. "Or trying to peel Little Mary's hands off the poor thing."

She laughed softly. "Don't you think Alanna's parents might suspect today isn't the only day their daughter has been here of late?"

Wolf shook his head. "Old Chinese is about as crafty as they come. I think her coming and going was well protected."

They both turned their heads when the brisk cadence of footsteps echoed down the hall. Thompson strode into the room with a grim set to his mouth. "You were seen at the wharf with my daughter this morning buying that dog."

Wolf jerked. "Christ!"

"What the hell were you thinking? And how did you get there and back in your condition?"

Wolf stood. "I used the enclosed sleigh you had at the

ready. No one else was in Higginson's store when I picked up the pup. I was in and out in minutes, had the sleigh back before you finished your morning paper. Who would have spotted me?"

Thompson swiped a hand over his face. "It could have been Higginson reporting your whereabouts—who knows? Spotting you isn't too difficult—you still look like someone waged a war on your face. We can't do much about the fool thing you did, but we can get you out of here, and we need to do so immediately."

Martha's hand went to her throat. "This is Christmas Eve, for heaven's sake. Can't it wait until after tomorrow?"

Thompson shook his head. "We are due in church in two hours, Martha, which is when things could get messy around here with Wolf home alone. If you value his life, we need to leave with no sign of his ever having been here."

Chapter Seventeen

January 8, 1855

"Out of my house, you wretched beast!" Alanna's mother bellowed.

At the dog's yip, Alanna halted a brushstroke midway through her hair. The ball of fur scampered down the hall, a blue slipper clutched between its teeth.

Alanna rounded the corner into her mother's bedchamber just in time to catch a flash of wide hip swathed in blue silk disappear behind the door. Alanna wedged in a foot. Grunts and scuffling sounded from both sides of the door. "Open up, Mother."

Old Chinese and Winston charged down the hall from opposite directions and halted as Alanna thrust open the door and stalked inside. She shot a glance at the two men behind her. Their mischievous looks melted into stoic resolve.

Her mother stood with her arms folded over her chest and one foot tapping on the floor. "You are in so much trouble when your father gets home, young lady."

Alanna seethed. "That is the *last* time you *ever* touch my dog."

"Then get it out of here this minute."

"You've never liked him from the minute you laid eyes on him, Mother. Is it really because he chews your slippers or wets the floor on occasion?"

Her mother's eyes narrowed. "That dog and your whining around here, and slipping over to the Thompsons' every chance you get are one and the same—and you know it."

Alanna grew suddenly tired of pretending patience while everyone else directed her life. The dog was her link to Wolf, and she'd be damned if her mother would abuse it.

The strange silence as the two women regarded one another brought Old Chinese farther into the room. Winston remained by the door.

"That despicable beast came from that *vulgar* man, and you know it."

Alanna paused for a moment and let her mother's words sink in. She could have sworn Old Chinese stiffened. "Where did you get that idea, Mother?"

"You stay away from him. You are a woman engaged to be married, and you had better act accordingly."

Alanna stared her mother down. "You did not answer my question. What makes you think the dog came from Mr. Wolf?"

Her mother threw her hands in the air in exasperation. "Enough of this nonsense. He was seen with Little Mary Thompson at Higginson's the day before your birthday. He purchased the very mongrel that wets all over my expensive carpets."

"Who saw him? You?"

"Oh, don't bother me with such nonsense." She waved Alanna off and stomped to the other side of the room. "He was seen at Higginson's looking as though he'd been rescued from the gates of Hades. Visit the Corner Bookstore for the latest gossip if you don't believe me."

A chill slithered down Alanna's spine. "And are you disappointed he didn't make it through those gates, Mother?

Did the little scheme you and Jonathan cooked up fail to get rid of him?"

Her mother whirled around. "I had nothing to do with that."

"With *what*?" Alanna's anger fueled the fire in her veins. "Tell me. What is it you had nothing to do with?"

Her mother's lips thinned. "Stay away from that no-account. You are set to marry Jonathan, and that is that. If you do anything to ruin your chances—"

"*My* chances," Alanna interrupted. "You mean *your* chances, don't you? And tell me, how might I bring ruin upon you and Father by refusing to stay away from Mr. Wolf? Loss of chastity, perhaps? Are you telling me you and Father want me pure for a man who regularly visits brothels with his future father-in-law?"

Blood drained from her mother's face.

Alanna's eyes shot wide as she came forward. "You know all about Jonathan and Father's visits to—"

"Oh, for heaven's sake. Every man does that."

"Not *every* man, Mother."

With a flip of her hand, her mother dismissed Alanna's objection. "You had better get over the notion of marrying a faithful man. Men don't love like you read about in those silly books of yours."

She wriggled a finger in front of Alanna's face. "All that border ruffian wants is the thrill of the hunt and the exhilaration of stealing your innocence." The volume of her voice rose. "Let that man near you and he'll leave you in ruins. No respectable man would have you after that gutter snipe finished with you. Why, your father would disinherit you, as well. What would you do then, go up to Lowell and work in the factories? In light of all that, does Jonathan Hemenway seem like such an ill choice, after all?"

Alanna's stomach roiled at her mother's words. "Jonathan disgusts me. You ask me to tolerate such a vile creature in order to have some grand home that a bunch of starched corsets can wander through bleating, 'oh, how wonderful for you'?"

A cruel smile tipped the corners of her mother's mouth. "I saw the way that man leered at you aboard ship. Surely even you aren't naive enough to think you are the only woman he's ever found excuse to flirt with so outrageously?"

Inwardly, Alanna shuddered at the idea.

Her mother read Alanna's thoughts precisely and shot her a wicked grin. "You wretched imbecile. Once he'd had his fill of you, you would *never* set eyes on him again. That is, unless you were to see him in the eyes of some bastard he'd settled you with."

Alanna's mind reeled as she struggled for inner balance. "You are quite right about him in one regard, Mother. No one evokes the feelings inside me that does. That's what frightens you, isn't it? Because if I were to join up with such a man, you'd lose your place at the top rung of society's ladder. Oh, what a pity, Mother. Here you've been climbing Boston's ladder of success, dragging me with you, when all the while, the blasted thing's been tilted against the wrong wall."

Her mother stood stiff. Nonetheless, her jaw twitched. "What you speak of is pure theater, pure Shakespeare."

"Oh?" Alanna's hand was on her hip now, the other still shaking the brush. "And what about bringing disgrace to the most *respected* Mr. Hemenway Senior? Why, in the good Lord's name, would you even want me connected with him?"

"What are you getting at?" Apprehension settled in her mother's plump face.

"That little story you told Mr. Wolf aboard ship about the murder when I was born? You mentioned something you've never said before in all your years of repeating that morose tale—you said the dead woman's hair had been cut off."

Her mother gasped.

"You know full well who did that terrible deed, yet you are still willing to marry me into that awful family. Aren't you afraid Mr. Hemenway will do the same to me as he did to that woman? Why, he cut off his own daughter's hair!"

"You know nothing of what you speak! You were only fourteen at the time Sarah's hair was cut off. And that was a long while after that murder took place. You can't possibly know if it was the same man."

Bile rose in Alanna's throat. "I think I do."

Her mother swung around to Old Chinese. "Get her out of here. I order you to take her to the farm at once."

Old Chinese inclined his head in deference.

She swung back to Alanna, who stood there stunned, disbelieving her good luck. "You heard me. Old Chinese is to take you with him this very minute."

Barely slowing her turn, Alanna's mother faced Old Chinese once again. "And unless her father instructs you otherwise, my daughter is to remain with you until just prior to her wedding."

With barely a blink, Old Chinese signaled Alanna to stretch out her resistance. He moved forward as Winston slipped into place in the doorway.

Alanna had to remain angry, but oh, what good fortune! She forced a scowl. "Don't think to order me from my home like I'm some kind of prisoner."

Old Chinese extended his hand toward Alanna. "It would be best for all concerned if you would come with me directly, Miss Malone."

Her mother gave a victorious nod and set her jaw. "You have lost the right to participate in your own wedding preparations." She turned to Old Chinese. "Do not, under any circumstances, return her to Boston until her father says otherwise. Do you understand?"

"As you wish, Mrs. Malone." Old Chinese grasped Alanna

by the wrist and, with a hard yank, pulled her solemnly toward the door.

Wolf stood in front of the barn's windows, watching as Winston directed the sleigh that had carried Wolf from the Thompsons' on Christmas Eve into the porte cochère of the mansion. He brought the horses to a crisp halt at the front doors.

Winston opened the carriage door and a white ball of fur, looking like a small polar bear, tumbled from the sleigh. The uncoordinated pup scrambled to its feet, then splayed all four legs on the ice as it tried to gain purchase with ungainly, oversized paws. Alanna, in a red cloak, stepped elegantly from the carriage and grasped Winston's arm, and together they watched the animal's antics. Wolf swore that even from such a distance, he could hear her throaty laughter.

A strange frustration churned in Wolf's gut. It was impossible for him to stand still, and so he swore and paced, his eyes riveted on the couple all the while. Winston gathered Alanna's luggage and headed for the main house with her by his side.

"What the hell?" Did she intend to bunk in there with thirty men? Wolf stood at the window like a wild horse tethered and straining at the bit.

His pallet still lay unmade, as it had since the day prior. It was enough that Old Chinese had left him to read the sacred esoteric books on the art of loving, but to think that all of the students received such a handbook—including Alanna—and then to watch her march into the student housing on Winston's arm? This was more than Wolf could endure.

Old Chinese trudged up the stairs, a packet of Wolf's mail in his hand. "Here are your letters and yes on both accounts."

He slapped the packet into Wolf's outstretched hand, and then shuffled to the window.

Wolf's eyes narrowed. "What 'yes on both accounts' are you talking about?"

Old Chinese rubbed his belly and peered at the manor house. "I am hungry. Unfortunately, my pork is not quite done, so they have cooked chicken, as well." He grinned, strolled to his corner of the room, and plopped down on the pallet. He lifted his favorite mug. "I'm in need of ale, if you please."

"Christ, I'd have better luck planting dragon's teeth than getting you to talk." Wolf grabbed the mug, thundered over to the keg, and gave the spigot a yank.

"The first yes is, indeed, she has decided to reside in the student housing. Since you were so reluctant to speak to her at the end of your stay at the Thompsons', she has it in her mind she would be more comfortable there. And the second yes is that she has studied the very books lying open on your bed. It is required of all my students."

"Are you telling me you will actually allow her to move in with thirty men, all of whom have read the same damn descriptions of—?"

"I have no say in the matter."

"What in God's name do you think you're doing?" Wolf roared. He watched as Winston and Alanna emerged from the main house, the dog slipping and sliding behind them. He flashed an ominous glance at Old Chinese, then looked back at the couple walking the pup. "Don't tell me she intends to room with Winston?"

Old Chinese shrugged. "I do not know. I do not care."

Wolf paced between the pallet and the window. "Has she ever stayed in there before?"

"No."

He grew more exasperated by the moment. "And Winston? You trust Winston?"

"Yes. Another ale, please."

"You trust that overgrown—" Wolf snatched the mug from the old man's hand and flipped around. "What is he, a eunuch or something?" Wolf bellowed over his shoulder while he filled the mug. In long, impatient strides, he returned to Old Chinese, staring out the window as he went. "Winston may be deaf, but he's not blind. And neither am I. He watches her all the time."

"He watches her because he feels it is his family duty," Old Chinese answered, in the same unaffected voice he would have used to give Wolf the time of day. "Winston is her brother."

"Huh?" Wolf's equilibrium rocked and his head buzzed. He made his way back to the pallet.

"Same father, different mothers," Old Chinese volunteered, sipping his ale. His obsidian eyes drilled into Wolf's depths.

"Does Alanna know?" Wolf's voice was little more than a ragged whisper.

Old Chinese shook his head and sucked foam off the draft.

"Why not?"

"Not the right time for her to know." Old Chinese's tone said, *No further questions.*

Wolf stomped back to the window. The coziness of the couple playing with the dog took on an entirely different perspective as his mind retraced his past observations.

Old Chinese sat quietly on the floor regarding Wolf and sipping contentedly. A mysterious look descended upon him like night mists floating over a slow-moving river.

"Is he about my age?" In his peripheral vision, Wolf caught three fingers held in the air. "Thirty-three?"

The old man nodded.

"Was he born in Europe then?"

Another slight nod.

"Was he born deaf?"

"No. It happened when he sickened with a high fever around the age of two. The mother was going to toss the little man aside, so I took him in."

"Jeezus!" Wolf turned to Old Chinese.

Old Chinese raised his hand. "You had no way of knowing. It pleases this old heart to know you perceived a close tie between the two. It means I have done my job."

"What about Malone?"

Old Chinese shrugged. "He didn't want the boy around, but those were my terms if I was to agree to accompany the family to America."

"He lived with you at the Malones' home?" Wolf frowned at the man's perfunctory nod. "But what of Mrs. Malone?"

The old man shrugged again. "She never asked. I raised him—took him everywhere with me. He knows no other life but this."

Wolf swiped his face in frustration. "I feel like crap." Old Chinese opened his mouth to speak, but Wolf waved him off. "Winston saved my life, and I treat him like—"

"It's called jealousy," Old Chinese responded blandly.

Wolf shot to his feet and headed to the window. "You don't know what you're talking about." He watched the couple below turn to head back toward the main house.

"You wanted to know about the *Book of Erotica*, Wolf, and why all my students are required to study it." Old Chinese spoke softly. "Even though they are, for the most part, celibate, my students will one day teach others of the sacredness of sensuous relationships. Most Westerners are ignorant of such ways."

"Then why are your students encouraged to become celibate?"

"In order to use the great passion of the sexual center for healing purposes. They are not particularly discouraged from seeking a mate."

Wolf flashed a derisive look at Old Chinese. "Does that go for you, as well?"

The older man gave a deferential nod. "As well."

Wolf went back to staring at the manor house. Desire stirred uncomfortably in every fiber of his being. His mind raced. The eroticism held within the pages of those sacred books, Alanna Malone—he could no longer separate the two. His loins ached.

He turned to Old Chinese. He should have known when he'd found the books on his pillow; the old man did nothing carelessly. "What are you going to do about her staying over there?"

"Nothing," Old Chinese responded.

Wolf stomped back to the pallet and stared daggers at Old Chinese.

Old Chinese stared back. "What is it *you* feel like doing about it?"

"Like dragging her ass back up here."

Old Chinese said nothing, only raised the mug to his lips once more.

Wolf shoved his bare feet into his boots and disappeared down the stairs.

At the slam of the door, Old Chinese scrambled to his feet and scurried to the window like an old woman gathering gossip for her next whist game. Wolf stormed over to Winston and Alanna. Stifled laughter rumbled in the old man's barrel chest as he observed Wolf's animated display of anger.

Old Chinese laughed aloud when Wolf grabbed Alanna's hand and headed back to the barn, only to halt. Backtracking, he swept the dog up in his other arm and marched forward.

Winston shot a glance upward to Old Chinese.

"Yes, yes, yes." Old Chinese clapped. "I told you this would work."

Reading his lips, Winston nodded in agreement. A wide grin settled on his face before he turned and climbed back into the sleigh.

"Mea culpa." Old Chinese chuckled as he sucked on the final draught of ale, pulled on his overcoat and headed for the stairs. He passed Alanna and Wolf along the way. Wolf's wide-eyed expression nearly made Old Chinese laugh. He didn't slow his pace as he loped down the stairs and hurried into the sleigh.

Wolf was right behind him. "Where the hell do you think you're going?"

Old Chinese nodded to Winston at the reins and snapped the door of the sleigh closed. "Back to Boston to check on a few things for you."

"What about your goddamned pork and chicken?"

"Winston packed the chicken for me; you eat the pork. Back in three days." Old Chinese tapped on the roof and the sleigh slid forward.

"Son of a bitch!" Wolf grabbed at the door, but the handle slipped from his grasp. He kicked snow at the sleigh and swore at the top of his lungs. "You can't leave Alanna here alone with me and that *Book of Erotica*. Are you daft?"

Chapter Eighteen

Alanna paced in front of the window, her focus on the woods. It was nearly dark and still, no sign of Wolf. What the devil could he be doing out there all this while? She folded her arms around her waist, as if the act would warm the chill plaguing her insides. He'd barely spoken two words to her before he'd practically dragged her to the barn and stomped off in a wild rage. And what had all that cursing at Old Chinese been about? Well, hang it all, she'd go looking for him if she had to, but she'd not walk the floor all night wondering.

Just when she was about to toss on her coat, Wolf emerged from the forest, his strides long and purposeful. She heard the door below close, and then he appeared on the stairs, his cobalt gaze fixed on her with a glimmering force she had yet to encounter.

Suddenly, she knew why he'd been out there so long. The chill inside her melted. She had a strong feeling her world was about to change. Irrevocably.

Nothing existed for her but Wolf and his slow, deliberate climb up the stairs. Flames leapt from her belly, seared the rigid tips of her breasts, and scorched the breath trapped in her lungs.

"You were a long time in the woods."

With pantherlike ease, Wolf balanced on one foot while he paused to study her. Then slowly, he rose to the next step.

"Yep." His voice, a husky rasp, washed through her like hot waves lapping the shore. She tried to swallow. Impossible.

"You must be frozen."

A sultry grin tipped a corner of his mouth. "How could I be when I've been thinking of you?"

He climbed another step. "And us."

Another step. "Naked."

Blood thundered in her ears as his lusty words sank in. Her hand splayed over her stomach, forcing her breath to her throat. "That . . . that night . . . at the Searses' party when you said you didn't want me . . ."

"I've changed my mind."

"Oh."

He approached her with those unwavering electric eyes and halted directly in front of her, so close his heat banished the cold air he'd carried in with him. His lazy grin returned as he regarded her.

She heaved in a shaky breath and exhaled. His subtle musk flowed around her like warm honey.

His own lips, lush and full, parted slightly. "I do believe it's about time you took your hair down for me, Miss Malone."

Arousal wound its way from her womb and snaked through her. Fingers trembling, she pulled the pins from her hair. They fell unheeded to the floor. She tugged at the thick coils. They gave way and tumbled about her shoulders. The sharp intake of Wolf's breath, the flaring of his nostrils, sent a dizzying current running through her veins.

His thumb traced her jawline as he backed her against the wall and braced his arms on either side of her. "I missed you."

The length of his body connected with hers. God, she didn't know if she could stand up much longer. "And I you."

A sultrier look swept over him. "What would you do if I made love to you right now?"

Oh, God. She crushed a fierce urge to close her eyes. "Right here? Against the wall?"

He chuckled. "Eventually." He nodded toward the screen fronting the bathing tub. "But at the moment, I have other things in mind."

Lord, Wolf, whatever you want! She reached up and touched the plump center of his bottom lip. The pulse at the base of his throat swelled as though his heart had risen from the depths of his chest.

His finger curled under her chin and tilted it upward. His head slanted slightly, directing his mouth over hers. He brushed his lips lightly back and forth. "I've wanted this since I first laid eyes on you."

The vapor of his words settled deep in her lungs. A slight tug of her chin, and her lips parted further. His soft, moist mouth settled fully on hers, sweeping fire through her belly. His tongue dipped in and traced the inside of her mouth. That *Book of Erotica*—it failed to cover this sweet, almost painful bliss that made her want to crawl inside his skin.

A moan filled her throat—but whose? And how had her hands found their way to his back to hold him tight against her? When had her fingers dug into him with such feverish intent?

He pulled his head back and studied her through lazy lids. "Every time you took care of me back in Boston, when you bent over me to change my bandages, to shave me, you drove me wild. I wanted to do wicked things to you. Did you know that?" He took her by the shoulders and turned her around. "I'm going to undress you now."

She pressed her forehead to the wall and bit her bottom lip to stifle a moan. Her limbs quivered as he cleverly worked the top of her dress past her shoulders. Sweeping her hair aside, he traced the curve of her neck with his mouth, and nipped softly.

"Oh, dear God!"

"You like that, do you?" He ran his tongue along her skin. "There were nights aboard ship when I couldn't sleep wondering what you tasted like. Everywhere."

For a long moment, Alanna wasn't sure her feet were on the ground. Surely, the pounding of her heart was audible. The heat of his fingers barely skimmed her shoulder, yet his touch sent another round of fireworks exploding inside her.

Her breath had been crushed from her, and Wolf must have heard it, for it seemed to draw out a feral energy in him that intensified and reverberated through her to her very marrow. She was surrounded by his scent as he pressed the length of his hot body against hers, his hard arousal searing the curve of her bottom. A delicious shudder ran through her already quaking thighs.

"Oh, Wolf, please."

He turned her around and used a knee to spread her legs. He rocked into her, pelvis to pelvis. And then he cupped her breast and worked his thumb over the nipple. His closeness, like a drug, overwhelmed her senses and sent giddy pleasure coursing through her veins.

His lashes lowered and his lips touched hers once again. He swept them ever so lightly across her mouth, the stubble of his chin rubbing against her cheek. "I need a shave, darlin'. Just the way you used to do while I was recovering."

Had she heard him right? No, she couldn't have. "You can't mean that. Right now?"

His low laughter vibrated against her mouth. "Oh, but I do." He lifted a brow. "When I lay helpless, I had wicked fantasies. Now, I intend to bring them to life." He regarded her with a curve of his mouth, his countenance filled with sensuous resolve.

"But I—" The timbre of her voice shifted downward and she ceased speaking as the possibilities dawned on her. With a slow, secret smile she yielded to him. "All right."

"First this," he murmured and pushed her dress and

crinolines from her hips until they pooled at her feet. He slipped his hand beneath her chemise and cupped her breasts.

A jolt from nipples to womb seized her. His supple fingers stroked the small erect buds jutting through the fine fabric—but then he tugged the chemise free and settled his mouth over one swollen globe. He sucked and drew his teeth over the rigid tip.

"God help me." Her head arched back, exposing her throat to his searing touch, sacrificing whatever restraint she had left to his tender mercies.

"Oh, Alanna." Gently, he swayed her back and forth, planting tender kisses over the top of her head and about the curve of her neck. He touched his lips to hers again, and undressed her completely, slowly. Tugging loose the brown belt holding the top of his gi together, he cast the tie aside, slipped the garment off him and onto her.

She looked down at herself, at her naked belly and nest of curls exposed, at her breasts and the curve of her hips hidden beneath the garment. "Another fantasy, Wolf?"

Quiet laughter rumbled through him. "Wicked as hell, aren't they?"

That lusty chuckle wound its way through her, and the secret place between her thighs wept more moisture. She raised her gaze to his bare chest—so golden and glorious. He'd worked hard on it since last she'd taken care of him, for his flat belly was strapped with new muscle, his chest broad and taut. She pressed her palm to his flesh and ran it along his rigid stomach.

A raw current of lust shot through her at the feel of his smooth skin against her hand. With trembling fingertips, she traced the jagged scar at his side. "When you were unconscious, I wanted to touch far more than your wounds. How wicked was that?"

He cocked a brow. "I would've liked that." Despite his casual words, his breath hitched.

Her fingers roved every inch of his bare, sinewy chest. "It wouldn't have been the right thing to do. To have you unaware—"

He reached up and outlined the tip of her breast. It surged and grew tauter. "Well, tonight is for nothing but pleasure, so do what you will."

Lord, but she wanted to know that part of him that was still secret to her. Slowly, her fingers traveled lower until they met the barrier of white fabric set against the proof of his hard arousal. A groan escaped his lips. He took her hand and gently guided it beneath the material.

"Oh . . . oh!" she stammered, but her fingers remained in place to circle and explore the silken, hard flesh, the smooth plump tip, slippery on the end. Liquid flames devoured her already vanquished loins. She closed her eyes and settled her full attention on his erection—skin so soft against a stiff thickness she doubted could fit inside her. Her fingers explored, sliding slowly, deliberately up and down.

He sucked in a breath and retrieved her boldly exploring hand. "That could be a very dangerous move about now." He nodded toward the gilded screens sheltering the bathing tub. "We'll be taking a bath now, darlin'."

She laughed, low and throaty. "I did a bit of my own dreaming about that tub."

He kissed the top of her head. "Did you, now?" He brushed the stubble of his chin against her cheek. "About that shave." He moved slowly backward, drawing her toward the bathing tub. "Only this time, it will be the way of my desires—my fantasies."

Sultry sensuousness filled his countenance as he set candles alight. He drew water from the pipe above the black and gold encrusted fixture into a shallow porcelain bowl. Setting it on a narrow stand, he let the steamy water continue to gush into the majestic tub.

Dragging a chair in front of her, Wolf sat down and gave her a razor and soap cup. And then he parted the gi she wore, exposing her nakedness to him. Raw desire crawled down his belly and tightened his groin. "That's right. Just how I want you."

"You can't mean to . . . why I would surely slice through your skin if . . ." And then she paused, razor in hand, a seductive smile slowly growing. "All right then," was all she said, but the way she spoke, sultry and with her entire being, caused Wolf's senses to leap up to meet hers.

Her closeness, the familiarity of her movements as she soaped Wolf's face, were poignantly reminiscent of when he was helpless even to try to touch her. But this time, damn it, he was healthy, robust, and free to allow a slow and total seduction to take place—something he'd once only dreamed of.

He reached for her creamy belly, which lay bare to his touch. She paused, the razor in midair. He leaned forward and swept his tongue in a small circle around her navel.

"Ahh," she groaned.

He grasped her hips when he felt her knees buckle. "Oh, no you don't. I intend to have my fill of you, Alanna."

"Oh, please," she murmured. "Let me have mine as well."

"Don't give in to it yet." His mouth slid down low on her belly, where the gi gaped wide.

She buried her free hand in his hair and held on. "I . . . I cannot stand much longer, Wolf. Let me sit awhile on your lap."

"Not quite yet." He drew his head back. Their eyes locked as he purposefully matched his breathing to hers. Their intimacy shifted. "Let's take our time, Alanna. Let's make the best of memories, enough to last a lifetime."

She nodded as his tongue touched the satin of her belly once again, then swept upward, circling the hard nub of her breast before his mouth settled lush and warm over the tip. Her body responded with erotic tremors, racking her at his teasing of her breast. Another soft moan escaped her lips.

Wolf pulled Alanna's head down until his mouth captured hers, demanding this time. He felt a quickening in her as her hunger invaded him. He pulled back and looked into her eyes. There was a spark of something indefinable in them, a curious, deep longing far greater than sexual desire.

Something he didn't recognize pulsed through him and left him feeling vulnerable. Too vulnerable.

"Wolf?"

He laid his cheek against her belly. This was no time to hide. They'd come too far. "You were right about what you said when you came to my hotel room in Boston." He paused a beat, uncomfortable with the sound of his voice. "I've always been afraid of the inevitable ending of a relationship."

"I would never leave you," she whispered. "That is, if *you* decide to stay."

He brushed a gentle kiss across her hip, then leaned over the tub and halted the flow of water. He didn't want to talk about such things any longer. He nodded for her to resume shaving him and swept another kiss across her mouth.

"I think you are driving me quietly insane." He reached up and wiped a fleck of shaving cream off her cheek.

She picked up the brush from the cup and soaped the side of his jaw again. "Did you have such thoughts of me back then, as well?" Her voice was honey-soft, her breath falling sweet against his cheek.

"Yes." He slid his hand up the satin of her hip, letting his thumb come to rest at the edge of the mass of dark curls at her pelvis. With a squeeze, his thumb pressed her flesh in small concentric circles.

"And that as well?" She obviously enjoyed her seductive control of him. Well, that would be temporary.

"Uh-huh." He leaned forward, his mouth replacing his thumb, his tongue tracing up her hip, nipping at firm, sleek flesh. "Getting soap all over you," he mumbled as he trailed his mouth around the side of her, traced his tongue down the tender curve of her hip, and slipped a finger inside her. "And I'm not apologizing."

A hot tide of passion hurtled Alanna past the point of return. The razor fell from her hand and clattered to the floor. In a raw, raging act of possession, she shoved his hands aside and settled astride his lap.

Wolf chuckled.

Her hair tumbled about both of them as her arms flew around his neck. His hands clamped her wrists.

He kissed the tip of her nose, sending the pit of her stomach into a strange, wild swirling as he easily regained control. He held her about her hips and bent to retrieve the razor. He set it back in her hand, but not before sucking quick and hard on a breast.

She drew in a sharp breath.

"Only the edge of my jaw to go." He kissed her neck. "Just a wee bit o' cheek, lassie," he teased in a perfect Scottish accent. "And then ye'll be free to own me soul."

His strange-sounding words echoed throughout the room and an uncomfortable pause overtook them. He grew silent and pressed his lips together, as if he struggled against some strong emotion. His sobering gaze penetrated the very depths of her and cast a shudder down her spine. His hand swept to the back of her neck, and he crushed his mouth to hers with a sudden, intense hunger that belied his outward calm.

Her senses reeled at the fierceness of his act. He eased

her back and peered deep into her eyes. Was that a flash of
pain in his?

"If I were to ask you to stay, you would never leave me?"
His voice sounded raw but resolute, as if any hesitation on
her part would send him walking away and never looking
back.

"Never," she whispered. *Because you are finally stepping
off the ends of the earth for me.*

A long pause, and then he slipped the gi from her body,
slid his hands around her, and resettled her onto his lap.
"Finish shaving me, then." With a crooked grin, his mood
shifted and he tilted his head for her.

Her hips seemed to have a mind of their own as they wan-
tonly pressed into him, searching for his hardness. Waves of
weakening fire swept through her loins. His hands at her
hips quelled her, steadied her to complete her task.

She went back to finishing her job. "I want you to explore
my body any way you like." Her silky whisper held challenge.
"I'll hold steady with the razor, I promise."

"You're not afraid?"

"No." She buried her face in the curve of his neck, and
then moved her mouth to his earlobe, catching and sliding it
between her teeth as he'd done to her. The sweet musk of
him clung to her mouth.

The back of his hand moved up to rest against the hollow
of her throat and the soft beating of her pulse. "You're so
beautiful," he murmured. His hand brushed slowly past her
breasts, then traced heated circles across her rib cage,
pausing as he went. "I can finally appreciate all the lessons
I've had in this place. I can feel you with all of my senses
heightened. It's amazing. You're amazing."

Her lips brushed slowly over his. They parted as he received her mouth. All the while, his hand traveled down to
her mound of curls, where he slid into her moist center. She

caught the quick exhale of his breath into her mouth. Her soft moan answered.

A firm hand slipped up her back as the other tenderly removed the razor from her hand. In a single movement, he lifted her from his lap, gathered her in his arms and carried her to the tub.

Gently, he lowered her through the vapors, sweeping her hair over the side as he went, letting his thumb trace her jawline as he straightened back up.

Unflinching, she watched him shed his trousers, watched the golden ripple of hard muscle stretching along his back and down his sinewy hips as he reached to the stand and retrieved a small vial of fragrant oil. He poured the lavender-scented contents over her breasts. The shiny rivulets ran off her ruched peaks and into the water.

She had never guessed a man could be capable of such tender and loving ministrations. As he slipped into the tub beside her, he cradled her in his arms and stretched his length against hers. Languidly, his fingertips spread the oil over her breasts, left them tingling wherever he went. "Beautiful."

Her body craved his touch, and her hands ached to touch his. She pressed against him, tilted her chin upward, silently seeking his mouth. "I feel as though I am about to burst," was the last thing she said before her mind disappeared altogether, and her senses took over.

He took her by the hand, invited her to discover him. Between each kiss, he whispered his longings to her. Alanna's response was one of aching consummation. She sought the pleasure points she'd read about, and marveled at his body's undisguised and fervent reactions. As she roused his passions, hers only grew stronger until her whole being flooded with desire. It was as though a golden arc of erotic pleasure connected them.

She moaned as he settled his body over hers. His knee

nudged her legs apart, and his hands stroked her back, buttocks and legs until he reached the aching core of her once again. The heat of his body coursed the length of hers as she pressed her hips against his. Searching. Urging.

He drew in a ragged breath. "Stop that. . . . Not yet."

But she grasped his hips and deftly eased herself up, edging her own heated hips inward until the part of him she'd been seeking found her aching recesses. "Yes, now. I need you. Inside me. Wolf, please."

He groaned and rolled onto his back, easing her on top of him. "Have it your way, then." His voice broke with huskiness. "I don't want to hurt you this first time."

His fiery gaze fastened to hers, tuned in to her every reaction. Sweet pleasure grasped her heart at the sight of him, and at the complete trust in him radiating within her.

"I need you, Alanna Malone," he whispered.

His words touched her to the quick. She arched her back and impaled herself. He held her still as erotic shock waves rolled through her.

"Are you all right?" he said in a voice that seemed to come from a long way off.

She nodded and slid slowly downward, until he filled her completely. He pulled her face to his chest and held her, the rest of her body floating in the heated water, like an embryo nestling in the warm fluids of life.

She lay still in his arms for a long moment, floating in the contentment of being a part of him. And then a hunger began deep within her, sending her body moving naturally in the sensuous, involuntary movement that had fostered human existence for eons.

His hand slid to her hips, gently halting her. He eased her to her side and began to pull out of her. "No," she whimpered.

"Shh," he soothed, kissing her ear, her neck, and the tips of her fingers. The water threaded pink with his exit. His hand slid down to her thighs where tenderly, he washed her clean. Then he lifted her from the tub, swept a towel over them both, and carried her to the pallet. He wiped her dry, handling her as though she were a delicate piece of porcelain.

Warm light from the fire illuminated his sultry features. She drank in his very essence, and every time his gaze captured hers, her heart thundered in response.

She reached up and traced a fingertip over his lush mouth. "Just touching you, I can't think straight," she whispered.

A small noise escaped Wolf's lips. "I'm fighting a fierce urge to act like a rutting bull." Instead, he rolled over, balancing above her. She arched into him, her legs parted, and slowly, he eased himself into her depths.

He filled her full of himself and then went still, his shoulders cast in shadow and firelight, the veins in his arms pulsating as though he strained to control himself. "Oh, God, Alanna."

She wrapped her arms around his back and raised her hips, squeezing his with her thighs. His weight shifted. He began a slow rhythmic rocking that soon set her free, until conscious thought collapsed and sensation took over. It was low at first, like a hum in her body, but then the feeling built up, spreading to every nerve until she quivered with pleasure. Pure bliss. Suddenly, with no choice but to yield, she let go of everything. Everything but him, and with instincts as her guide, she went over the edge. She cried out his name, her fingers catching his hair, her legs crossing over his, pulling him deeper into her still.

He rose up, paused inside her and peered into her eyes. "Yes," he murmured in a long exhalation and began to move again. His thrusts grew stronger, faster. "You're here. With me. All mine." She held onto him, absorbing his fierce plunges until he groaned and his hips jerked. When he finished, she would not let him roll off her. The moment was too precious.

"But I'll crush you."

"I'm resilient, remember?"

Still propped on his elbows, he smiled down at her, held the sides of her face, and kissed her forehead, her nose, her mouth. "Then gather up all your ki, darlin', because we're just getting started."

Chapter Nineteen

The bright morning sun wasn't what roused Wolf and sent his heartbeat skyrocketing; it was Alanna's bold fingers. He lay still, basking in her tactile curiosity until he could no longer pretend sleep. He lifted an eyelid a fraction. Her cloud of raven curls spread across his thighs, veiling his hard arousal. She was busy trailing little bites across his stomach, as he'd done to her so many times during the night.

"Damn it, Alanna, you've got me so hard it hurts."

A throaty laugh escaped her lips.

He touched her cheek and coaxed her to his stiffened cock. She complied, her tongue tracing a bold and lustful path down the length of his rigid flesh. He shuddered when her lips found their mark, and he groaned in sweet torment when she filled her mouth with his hardness and moved up and down. His eyes squeezed shut from the exquisite jolt and his breath escaped with a hiss. "Christ, you're a quick study."

He reached to drag her into his arms, only to knock an elbow against the open *Book of Erotica*. "What the hell are you doing with this?"

Alanna lifted her lips off his erection, tilted her head, and grinned. "I've decided to bring the book to life."

He flopped back against the pallet and grinned. "Better start from page one, then."

In one swift move, Alanna straddled his hips, her hair tumbling wildly about her shoulders. Her blue eyes flashed and sparked. "Actually, I was interested in page forty-three. I always thought that position was humanly impossible. I'm a wanton woman, aren't I?" she said, with nary a hint of ceasing her aggressive seduction. Slowly, she eased her heated, moist flesh downward over his shaft.

"Uh." He clasped the swell of her buttocks, settling her hard onto his loins. "Just don't mention it to anyone. They'll never know."

Alanna pushed her pelvis hard against his in a fierce rhythm, searching this time for quick release. Her eyes lost their focus. Kitten whimpers poured from her throat. Wolf matched her desperate tempo in exquisite harmony. As her hips began to quiver and she cried out for release, she triggered Wolf to his flash point.

Breathless, she collapsed against him, a fine mist of perspiration covering her body. "Do that again."

Wolf chuckled. "Do what? Lie here and get a free ride to heaven?" He slid his arm around her and drew her cheek to his chest. "By the way, you weren't even close to that position on page forty-three."

She laughed softly. "I'm listening to your wonderful heartbeat." Her fingers trailed along the inside of his arm and up over his shoulder, and drew circles around his still-hardened nipple. "I find it soothing. You do that for me, you know—give me sublime comfort."

At her words, a sense of belonging with someone rolled through him like a slow-moving train. He stroked his fingers through her hair, lifted a hank of it under his nose and breathed in lemon and lavender. Her parents were right—he wasn't good enough for the likes of Alanna. Never would be. What the hell was he doing with his life? When he'd returned here after having been stabbed, it had felt like coming home . . . to no home he'd ever known. And Old Chinese had asked him to stay . . . for good. This past week, the idea had been trying to take root. And then Alanna showed up. He'd missed her so goddamn bad he could taste it, but missing her didn't mean he was any good for her. His chest constricted. He ran the back of his hand along her cheek, kissed the top of her hair.

"I'd go to my death seeing to your well-being." Where in God's name had that come from?

Alanna lifted her head. A spark of something indefinable shone in her eyes. "Does that mean you won't be going back to Missouri?" When he didn't respond, she said, "I care for you, Wolf. And don't tell me what's happened between us is only a passing fancy on your part."

Wolf bent his head and tilted Alanna's. His mouth hungrily captured hers. He pulled away and peered into her eyes and then flopped back on the pallet to stare at the rafters. "You know damn well what happened when you took your hair down for me."

A beat of silence. And then she settled her cheek on his chest again. "Besides, I need your help getting rid of a fiancé. Or have you forgotten?"

"Never mind the snake. Trevor and I are working on something that'll make him slither away with barely a hiss."

Alanna was silent for a moment, her breath falling rhythmically over his skin. "I take it I'm not to ask questions— but I will whenever I want to, so consider yourself forewarned."

She gave little tugs on his chest hairs that went right to his groin. God, he couldn't leave her alone. He growled, pulled her tight against him, and gave her a hard kiss with a loud smack. "Sweet, stubborn pain in the ass, Alanna Malone." He shifted around on the pallet and rubbed at his rump. "I wonder what the hell it would feel like to make love to you in a real bed—roll you around in a feather tick so soft you'd disappear beneath me."

"Brookline," she murmured.

"Brookline?"

"Our other home. I promised my father I'd check on the new pipes he had installed last summer. We could go there."

"Your *other* home," Wolf said. "But of course." Easing her onto her back and into the curve of his arm, he ran his hand slowly over every inch of her body. "Tell me, is it a quaint little summer home, the size of this *minuscule* farm?"

"There, in my room," she said and sighed, ignoring his remarks, "you'll find a large feather bed—the likes of which you've never seen. And there, while I sink beneath you, you can do this incredible teasing and touching all you like." She ran her hand down his belly and cupped her hand over his mound of thickening male flesh and squeezed lightly. "Brookline, Wolf?"

"Aren't you sore?"

She smirked and gave a tiny shrug of her shoulders. "It's the ki and knowing how to use it." Her hand slid up and down his hardening shaft.

"Jeezus," he wheezed. "I do believe a whole new world has opened up for you."

The mansion in Brookline was far different from the farm. The horse-drawn sleigh, driven by the one student Wolf managed to talk into making the trip, halted in front of a two-story limestone structure filled with wide, airy balconies, a pitched slate roof, and long winding walkways.

Inside, other than the latest modern installation of a disgusting floral-print carpet covering every floor in its entirety, the house appeared European with its flagstone entry and high, Gothic ceilings. Here was a home in which Wolf felt instantly at ease. *Most likely a reflection of the Malones' Irish heritage—whoops, Scots-Irish.*

It was clear Alanna loved this place, a direct contradiction to her reactions whenever she made mention of the Malone home in Boston. Directing Wolf through the house like a tour guide, she took her time recounting the history of each unique piece of furniture or wall hanging. There was a sense of her here that intrigued him, from her childhood nursery, which had been left intact, to her father's library with its one wall of books belonging exclusively to her.

Along the upper gallery, near her bedroom, Alanna paused at a large, ancient-looking carved trunk. "My mother's." She flipped open the top. Colorful silk scarves filled the inside.

Wolf snorted. "So far, you've shown me everything but the Holy Grail. You don't suppose it's buried somewhere in there?"

Alanna lifted a gossamer yellow scarf from the trunk and drew it seductively over her face. "Playing with the contents of my mother's trunk was the one thing she allowed when I was young." She swept the scarf across Wolf's face, light as a breeze. "Most likely because it kept me occupied for hours on end without her having to bother with me."

"Because you were inconvenient or because she wasn't the motherly type?"

"What do you think?" Alanna withdrew an exotic turquoise and gold-threaded piece of sheer, silken fabric and tied it at her waist. "I could be whatever I chose—a mysterious harem girl, a royal princess, or the world's finest ballerina." She tossed the pieces of fluff back into the chest and closed the lid with a bang. "Too bad life isn't so simple when we become adults."

"You would've made a spectacular dancer. In fact, when I saw you climbing the mizzens aboard ship, I thought that's what your training must have been."

"Oh, I fell in love the first time I saw those lovely girls twirling around on stage. I was eight years old and left the theater dreaming of becoming a prima ballerina. But Mother said only the dregs of society danced, while the pinnacle of society observed."

Wolf rolled his eyes. "Sounds like your mother."

"She refused to let me attend the theater after that. Do you like the ballet?"

He nodded. "I do. Saw it once when a troupe came through St. Joe."

"One day I shall see the Bolshoi." Passionate defiance shadowed her features. She turned and kissed him hard.

He wrapped an arm about her shoulder, gave her a squeeze and a grin, and headed her toward her bedchamber. "I do believe you were a virgin far too long."

"What's that remark supposed to mean?"

"That it serves you quite well not to be. You are now most pleasant to be around."

"Arrogant ass."

He laughed.

Entry into her room was admission into another world— an exotic Eden. Not one vulgar rose adorned the tasteful Oriental and Persian carpets scattered over the polished, honey-colored floors. The oversized tester bed was dressed in white—white down comforters, stacks of white down pillows. A hammered brass chandelier, ancient-looking and spiked with fat white candles, looked as though it had escaped the ceiling of some old castle. Books were piled on every table and on the floor beside the chairs. The room looked lived-in, warm and inviting.

Wolf picked up a book—*The New Forest* by Horace Smith—and set it back down. "I should've known you'd live this way."

"Mother detests it."

"Of course she would." He swept Alanna into his arms and deposited her in a heap onto the feather bed. He slid alongside her and nuzzled her ear. "Alanna, darlin', don't *ever* mention that woman's name when I have an erection."

Alanna giggled and wrapped her arms around his neck.

"Wait a minute." He scrambled off the bed and headed for the door. "Don't move."

He returned with an armload of the filmy scarves and dumped them on the bed. "I've a mind to be with a harem girl tonight."

Alanna laughed lustily and stood. Holding her arms out, she waited while Wolf removed her clothing. Halfway through the process, he paused to light the candles. When he had her naked, he tied scarves to her body.

"We're getting there." He grinned and draped another across her face. "Except for jewels draping your forehead and a few bells at your ankles, you are definitely my little harem girl."

She marched over to a small wooden chest and withdrew a handful of bracelets laden with tiny bells. "From my sea travels." Barefoot, she padded back to Wolf. "Was that your stomach growling or did I hear thunder rolling?"

"I hate to tell you this, Alanna, but even though you look good enough to eat—and I mean to get there—I'm about as hungry as a bear in springtime."

"I don't cook."

He grunted. "Well, I do." He grabbed her wrist and hauled her downstairs to the kitchen, where he propped her on the worktable like a pet kitten. Then he made a fire in the wood cook stove, rooted around in the cool pantry where he found a ham, a decent enough onion, a couple of carrots, and some potatoes. Life felt pretty damn good all of a sudden. Real good.

Alanna sipped wine from a Waterford goblet and watched him prepare the food. She'd detached one side of the shimmering pink veil that had covered her face and left it to drape over her shoulder. He planned to enjoy the hell out of removing those scarves. One by one. Later.

Once he got the flames licking up just right, Wolf filled an iron skillet and set it atop the stove.

"Dear Lord!" Alanna cried. "You can't cook with the fire leaping out the top of the stove like that. Put that little round thing back on the stove and set the pan on top of it."

He grinned. "Alanna, darlin', I did all my cooking under the stars. Open flame is the only way I know, so hush. Smelling good already, huh?"

Alanna laughed and reached for more wine, but Wolf beat her to it and refilled her glass, making sure he got a couple kisses for the effort. When dinner was ready, he nodded for her to remain in place instead of moving into the dining room. "Stay there. My little harem girl deserves to be hand-fed."

As he lifted the fork to Alanna's mouth, her eyes filled with the look of wanting him once again. He groaned. "Don't you go looking at me like that or I'll never get my share. Of food."

"There are other ways to fill one's hunger," she replied, her voice throaty and filled with teasing seduction. She chewed slowly, her eyes trained boldly on his.

He held the wineglass to her lips, then to his own, pausing now and then to press his lips to hers and to nuzzle her neck. He still couldn't get enough of her. Probably never would. With an exaggerated sigh, he set the fork on the plate and trailed his fingers up the inside of her thigh, to the triangle of sheer turquoise over her lap.

Her reaction was instantaneous. Eyelids fluttered and the familiar look of passion gone wild flashed over her countenance. She raised one knee, and brushed it against his groin.

"Now see what you did." He set the wineglass down, and passed his hand over the buttons of his trousers. Brushing the scarf aside, he tipped her hips up and slid into her moist, silken warmth. His mouth covered hers, stifling her moan.

He stopped cold.

A shiver ran down his spine.

That familiar gut feeling that someone was watching them hit him dead on.

Alanna stiffened in question and looked to Wolf's eyes for silent answer. Sending her a signal not to move, he held one hand over the knife in his boot, pulled her protectively into him and shot a glance over her shoulder.

A woman stood at the doorway with a blank expression on her face.

Wolf's fingers stiffened across Alanna's back, the only indication of his having seen anything. "Who the hell are you?"

Alanna looked over her shoulder. "Oh, it's you. Go away." She turned back to Wolf, a disgusted look on her face.

But the woman stood stoic and unmoving.

Wolf managed to discreetly tend to himself with Alanna as his shield. He pulled the scarf at her waist into place and slid her from the table.

This time it was Alanna taking Wolf by the hand after pausing to tie the veil back across her face. She marched past the woman with Wolf in tow, and up the stairs to her room without uttering a word. She slammed the door with a resounding bang and locked it.

"Who the hell was that?"

"Maire Macintosh." Alanna went to the window and closed the drapes. "My nanny when I was little."

"What the devil is she doing here?"

"Most likely, she came to check the pipes for Father, since Mother sent me packing."

"Will she inform your mother?"

"No," Alanna said flatly.

"Your father?"

"No."

"She's no threat?" Puzzled, he studied her downcast eyes. "Look at me."

She raised her head and their gazes collided, hers cold. She reminded him of himself—stubborn and full of self-made boundaries.

"You don't like her much, do you?"

"No."

"Why not?"

She shrugged. "Don't know."

"Aw, come on." Wolf pivoted on his heel, his arms open, palms up. "We just got caught in an intimate act, and you're acting like Old Chinese, leaving me to plant dragon's teeth. What's the goddamn mystery here?"

"None." She slipped her arms around Wolf's neck. "I've not cared for her since as far back as I can recall, and I honestly cannot tell you why. Now, you came all the way down here for that big feather bed over there." Her words left her throat in sultry invitation. "Shouldn't we take advantage of it?"

Hunger pangs woke Wolf. His first conscious thought was that he'd only managed to swallow a couple of bites of dinner last night before discovering the voyeur. He slid from the bed, quietly eased into his trousers and shirt, and made his way to the kitchen.

When he walked in, Maire was at the sink, washing a single dish, a pan, and a few utensils. She didn't bother to turn around.

Wolf picked up an apple and a knife, and heaved himself onto the worktable. He cut a thin sliver off the fruit, balanced it on the edge of the blade, and slid the piece past his lips. While he ate slice after juicy slice, he took note of her hair and how some of the tight, black curls had managed to escape the severe bun at her nape.

The apple gone, he flipped the knife in the air and caught the handle with the tips of his fingers. "You look familiar."

"Aye," she said in a thick Scottish brogue. "Ye, as well." She turned and stared fearlessly at Wolf.

A chill swept through him. He regarded her for a long moment, and then leisurely slid off the table. He set the knife down, tossed the apple core into the trash bucket, and sauntered out of the room, back to where Alanna still slept.

He watched her slumber, his thoughts drifting back to his childhood. He'd had another nightmare last night. He could see the man in the mirror, still shrouded in fog, but less so than in previous dreams. His mind wandered to the woman downstairs. His fingers traced back and forth over his lower lip while he racked his brain as to why she seemed so familiar. The answer would come on its own, he concluded, and he left Alanna sleeping.

Making his way back downstairs, he wandered into the impressive library. Running his hand across the gold-trimmed French desk belonging to Malone, Wolf wondered what such a coarse man would do while seated at such a fine piece of furniture. He'd probably purchased it to impress others.

Curious, Wolf opened the middle drawer. It held one piece of paper—blank—and a vial of India ink—no pen. He outlined the heavy gold ornamentation on the drawer with his fingers. "Pretty expensive just to show off."

He paused. Years of investigating told him something was out of the ordinary. The drawer seemed shallower than the depth of the desk. He reached around and opened another, the top right. It held a blank ledger and two expensive quill pens. Wolf pulled the drawer open to its full length, then out entirely. It, too, hadn't anywhere near the overall depth of the desk.

"I'll be damned." He spied a set of shelves hidden the entire length of the desk inside the front. Reaching into the dark recesses, he retrieved a stack of packets, his senses throbbing.

Receipts for slaves bought and sold filled the first packet, along with a list of dates, ships, and the ships' entry points. A cold shudder ran through him. "Christ." He reached back in, feeling around for anything else before starting in on the rest of the packets.

Damn, he hated sticking his fingers into dark places. Gingerly, he traced each shelf. In the far corner, his fingertips touched something flat, not much larger than the spread of Wolf's hand and about an inch thick.

A wooden case covered in worn black velvet, perhaps some relic from the past, almost fell apart when Wolf lifted it from the desk. Carefully, he managed the frail, gold filigree clasp at its edge. An old miniature set in a gilded frame with an oval opening lay inside.

He studied the dulled image of a small boy of about three. His dark, cropped jacket was finely made, with a small white collar peeping over the neck. The matching short pants and polished shoes were of high quality as well. Short, well-manicured hair framed a face cast with the mere shadow of a haunting smile. The child stood with his hand resting against a chair's back made of ornate twisted wood.

Surprise registered.

Wolf swore he'd seen that very chair in what had been Alanna's nursery. He closed the box, stuffed it into the front of his shirt, and reached for the other packet.

Daguerreotypes. Only this time the breath wheezed from Wolf's lungs at the chilling sight. Young women in compromising positions—some obviously slaves, looking as though they were fresh from their native country, while others appeared to be dressed in costumes depicting different cultures—all with wide, frightened eyes and large hands holding them down. "Mother of God."

Bile rose in his gut. He dropped the damning pictures onto the desk as if they burned his fingers and leaned back in the chair. Were these some of the women who'd ended up in Malone's and the young Hemenway's brothels? Had Old Chinese been aware of any of this? Well, he damn well intended to find out.

Wolf swallowed an urge to vomit. He replaced the photos in the packets and shoved them inside his shirt. He slipped out of the manse to the carriage house, where the student who'd driven them over had spent the night.

"Bury these under the seat of the sleigh, or carry them with you until we get back," Wolf told him. "I don't care how you do it, just keep them out of anyone's sight, including Alanna's."

He turned to leave, and paused long enough to glance over his shoulder. "And that includes you, as well. Do not, under any circumstances, find a reason to look at them."

The student nodded in silence.

Wolf made his way to the nursery to compare the chair with that in the miniature before he returned to Alanna's room. Just as he'd thought, it was either the same one or its twin.

"Wake up." He nudged Alanna. "It's nearly noon." He kissed her ear and ran a finger down the side of her arm.

"So what?" she muttered, her eyes shut tight. She caught Wolf's fingers and drew them to her cheek.

He pulled his hand away and shook her shoulder. "I'm not up to hanging around you and Maire. Not with the way you two have your claws exposed. I'll find us some food to take along while you get dressed."

As the enclosed sleigh skated silently along the snow-packed road, Wolf stared through the window at the white landscape, still sickened by what lay in the packet beneath the seat.

"What's wrong with you?" Alanna asked.

"Nothing. I'm enjoying the scenery."

"No, you're not. You've got that distant look about you, and you're running your thumb back and forth across your bottom lip—a habit of yours when deep in thought. And you just patronized me."

Wolf pulled out of his trance and swept his arm around her. He touched his lips to her forehead. "A bad habit I picked up from years of living alone. Give me time to break it." He went back to looking out the window and thinking about what he'd found, and why the hell Maire Macintosh seemed so familiar.

He leaned his head back against the leather seat and regarded her. "Did you spend time with Winston when you were little? Old Chinese said Winston lived with him in his rooms until they both moved to the farm."

She nodded. "Winston was around before I was born. Kept safely under Old Chinese's protective wing. We studied together when I was a little older and able to spend most of my time at the farm. Even though I wasn't anywhere near his age, we grew close."

Guilt flooded Wolf at what lay hidden in the carriage. "It struck me aboard ship that you seemed rather studious yourself, and the books in your room confirm it."

She bowed her head. "The profound influence of Old Chinese."

An image of Maire Macintosh skittered from the periphery of his mind. Realization knifed through him as if a hot poker had been shoved into his brain. The dark, curly hair, the shape of her nose and mouth. So that was why she looked so damn familiar: she was Winston's mother! Did Alanna have any inkling? Was that why she was so distant with the woman who'd been her nanny?

She lifted a brow. "The strangest look came over you just then. What were you thinking?"

He turned away from her and stared out the window again. Dark thoughts clouded his brain. He decided he had some talking to do before they reached the farm.

Alanna first heard Wolf's heavy sigh before he turned her way. His eyes held a strange, faraway look, his expression grim. "It's time I told you all of what I know about myself."

She stiffened, her senses sharpening—both at his seriousness, and at his reaching under his shirt and withdrawing the mysterious golden chain and garnet earring. She stared at the crimson bauble swinging back and forth with the rocking of the sleigh.

"Do you recall when your mother spoke aboard ship of the murder of a young woman the night after you were born, and of the disappearance of her young son?"

Alanna nodded, shifting her gaze from the earring to the vivid pain in Wolf's eyes. The hairs stood up on her nape and shivers raced up and down her arms. "I've heard that sordid tale many, many times over the years. Why do you ask?"

His penetrating eyes touched her very soul. "That little boy was me."

Chapter Twenty

After making certain Alanna stayed put in the main house, Wolf turned from the barn's window. A muscle flicked alongside his clenched jaw. He shot a scowl at Old Chinese and paced once again, his breath ragged. Stopping to pause at the window again, as he'd done for the better part of an hour, he shifted from one foot to the other. Abruptly, he began his agitated pacing once again.

Old Chinese sipped on a cup of hot tea. "Shouldn't I be the one incensed because you left here when you gave your word you would not? Instead, you seem to be the one directing some rather vitriolic anger my way."

Wolf took long, furious strides to where Old Chinese stood and halted in front of him. Christ, he had to get this over with, but he had no idea where to begin.

Old Chinese settled his gaze on the garnet earring plainly visible in Wolf's earlobe.

An exasperated hiss escaped Wolf's lips. He swiped his fingers through his hair and swallowed the bile in his throat. A litany of whatever curse words he could manage to string together flew out of his mouth. "Did you know about Malone's depraved ways?" His chest heaved—he was fighting for air as if he'd run miles.

Old Chinese stood with his feet apart, hands folded across his chest. "What are you talking about?"

"What am I talking about?" Wolf snarled. He pulled the packet he'd found in Malone's desk from inside his shirt and sent the contents tumbling across the floor. Dozens of photos of young females in various stages of undress, all looking scared out of their wits, scattered across the floor. "Did you know of this?"

Old Chinese nodded. "The knowledge was one of the reasons I bargained for the right to raise his daughter."

"One of the reasons? There were more?"

"I had an ill feeling one night that all was not well in Miss Malone's nursery, so I investigated. Her father was in the final throes of seducing the nanny in front of the girl."

"How old was Alanna?" The images of her and Maire Macintosh warily eyeing one another in Brookline flashed through Wolf's mind. God, he needed a drink. He snatched up his mug and strode over to the wine barrel.

"Nearly three."

"And she was awake and taking it all in?" At Old Chinese's nod, disgust rolled through Wolf, leaving a bitter taste in his mouth. He bent and gathered up the scattered photographs and tossed them on his pallet.

Old Chinese approached and sat on the bare floor near Wolf.

"Would Alanna still remember such a thing?" Wolf asked.

"Perhaps not at the forefront of her mind, but it's there, buried deep."

"Is that why she doesn't care much for Winston's mother?"

Something flickered in Old Chinese's eyes. "What led you to believe Winston belongs to Maire?"

"The same dark, curly hair for one thing. Winston has his father's eyes, but Maire's nose and mouth. They both tilt their heads the same peculiar way when observing someone." Wolf swiped his hand over his face and pinched the bridge of his nose. "Jeezus, I'm surprised Alanna didn't figure things out a long time ago. Do you think her father snuck into the nursery before that night and she was privy to it all?"

A disconsolate demeanor settled about Old Chinese. "More than likely. Alanna may have thought the nanny guilty of wrongdoing, but in a way she was too young to grasp. She had no way of knowing Maire was essentially her father's captive, that she had nowhere else to go, especially since her son lived with me, close enough for her to visit him on occasion."

At the sadness flashing through Old Chinese's eyes, the bottom dropped out of Wolf's anger, replaced by a sense of deep hurt that expanded in him like wet ink spreading across paper.

He picked up the photos and slipped them back into the packet. "Took me a full day to figure out why Maire Macintosh looked familiar. Winston has her look, not Malone's. Why are you so defensive of a woman who was willing to throw her own child away?"

Old Chinese stared into the fire's flame. "I never said she was willing." His head lifted. He studied Wolf long and hard. "There is much you do not understand."

"Don't underestimate me." Despite sounding matter-of-fact, Wolf's gut wrenched. When had this man become like family to him? For that matter, when had Winston?

Old Chinese took a gulp of tea. "Maire was barely fifteen when Winston was born. She was little more than a child, raising a child. She was a young girl with big dreams, and very naive. By the time she'd grown wiser, it was too late for her to have a speck of freedom. Malone had taken her soul and there was no place for her to go."

"She's a Scot," Wolf said flatly. "Where did Malone acquire her?"

"Scotland." Old Chinese raised his mug to his lips.

"I thought the Malones were from Ireland."

Old Chinese shrugged. "The two countries are not far apart."

"The guy's a twisted bastard," Wolf snarled.

"Another of my many reasons for wanting to raise Alanna." Old Chinese's eyes narrowed. "Neither parent was good for her. I didn't trust either one."

"You know she's never going back to her family. I'd go to my grave first."

Old Chinese sat quietly, regarding Wolf through wizened eyes.

Wolf broke the tension when he scrambled up to retrieve a folded blanket for Old Chinese to sit on. "She's of age now, so why would you stay with a man like that?"

Old Chinese's wizened eyes glittered. "Ah," he said, slipping into his teacher role. "It is oftentimes the most powerful position—standing shoulder to shoulder beside your worst enemy. One knows the enemy's every move that way."

"Why did you choose to teach Malone so much?"

"At first, it was what I was employed to do. But a wise teacher never divulges all he knows to his enemy." The corners of Old Chinese's mouth turned up in a cynical grin. "Besides, he could not possibly grasp the higher, mystical teachings as you and Winston have. Or as his own daughter has. His mind is intelligent and conniving, but it is weak."

He returned to staring into the flames. "There is an old saying in kendo. Your enemy may cut your skin, but you should not miss the precise moment when you can cut him to the bone."

"So, you have waited patiently to confront Malone? But why has he kept you around? Why didn't he just have you done in?"

A peculiar *something* flickered over Old Chinese's countenance, only to disappear as quickly as it had come.

"Perhaps there is a part of him that is afraid of me. Or afraid of the ways I might have of divulging everything I know should I meet my demise."

A chill ran down Wolf's spine at the odd statement, which seemed to carry a vague threat. Changing the subject for a while might be wise. "You left your homeland and lived for years in an entirely different culture. That must have been difficult for you."

Old Chinese shrugged.

"What of your family? Your parents?" Wolf couldn't penetrate the deliberate blankness of the elder's eyes, so he sipped his wine and waited.

"My mother was Chinese, my father Japanese," Old Chinese finally said.

Wolf nodded toward the armory hanging on the walls. "That explains your unique appearance and this mishmash of teachings and hardware. But I thought those two cultures didn't mix with each other."

"Correct," Old Chinese answered. "My mother was of noble Chinese blood, my father a Japanese Samurai. It was the greatest insult for the Japanese Samurai to invade the country of my mother's husband and take his wife hostage. The Samurai raped her repeatedly, detained her until he was sure she carried his child, and then deposited her naked on her husband's doorstep."

Christ. Wolf downed the contents of his mug. "So, you're a bastard with nobility on both sides." No wonder Old Chinese carried himself with regal bearing.

He gave Wolf a gracious nod. "I was nearing twelve when I learned my mother's husband was not my father, so I left my mother's home and sought the Samurai out. He placed me in a school of kenseido. I became the highest-ranking and most powerful student in the temple. But one day word came to me of my father's plan to rid himself of me—"

"You mean to have you assassinated."

"As you wish," Old Chinese responded. "When I learned of this, I slipped away, to the docks of Hong Kong, where I publicly fought willing opponents and demonstrated my skills for enough coin to pay for passage out of the country. That is where I met Malone."

The wine had nearly done Wolf in, but he poured yet another mug. "Just tell me to shut the hell up if you've a mind to, but did you ever want a family? Ever hope to have one?"

"Of the kind you mean? Yes. Of the kind I now possess? That, as well."

There was a long stretch of silence before Wolf pulled the box from his shirt and opened it. "Who's that?"

Old Chinese picked up the miniature of the boy, studied it for a brief moment, then leaned over the brazier and tossed it into the fire.

Wolf jerked forward. Too late. "Why the hell did you do that?"

"Time has a way of fitting the proper pieces of a puzzle together on their own without one having to dig through a heap of cow dung to find them."

There was no going further with that particular subject, so Wolf moved on. "You have exactly two days to inform Alanna that Winston is her brother." He blinked, barely able to focus from all the wine.

"You forgot to expand your ki," Old Chinese said. "In the morning you will be rewarded with my mystery tea."

"Tell her," Wolf growled. "If you don't, I will."

"And why would you do so now?"

"Because today, I told her everything I know of my past, but not of hers." Wolf leaned over, his eyes narrowing, "I know more about her life than she does. If I withhold *any-thing* from her it could destroy the bond between us. I need

her. And I'm not about to take any chance of losing her."
He'd managed to keep his words from slurring together.

Humor touched the corners of Old Chinese's mouth. "Ah,
it is so pleasant to listen to the rarified speech of a learned
man."

"Kiss my ass," Wolf shot through his teeth. "You tell her.
Or I will. And you'd better tell her everything. Do you hear
me? *Everything.* Including what you know about that son of
a bitch of a father of hers."

"This night," Old Chinese replied. "I will tell her this
night."

After Old Chinese had revealed his shocking news to
Alanna, it was her turn to wander alone in the forest. She
kept to herself for two days, with only the dog following at
her heels. She slept in the student manse at night while her
days were spent either on a horse or sledding in a narrow,
single-person cutter drawn by a small Morgan.

The second night, she walked into the barn and sat down
to dinner, this time to the left of Wolf. When she'd completed
her meal, without a word she lay down, her head across his
lap. Entwining her fingers through his, she pulled his arm
tightly about her waist. An intense need emanated from
every part of her.

That night, the pleasure—and the passion—between her
and Wolf was explosive. Devouring.

In the morning, she awoke first. Silently, she watched
Wolf slumber, watched the purity of him. Instinctively, the
knowledge that he would always be faithful infused her.
Sudden, unexplainable tears swept her cheeks. Tears again?
Her emotions were oddly mercurial of late.

How lonely she'd been all her life. How hungry she'd
been all these years for a simple, loving touch. To be held.

To be nurtured. It was only now she realized that no one before Wolf, not her parents, and certainly not Maire Macintosh, had ever held her.

At her muffled sniff, Wolf's arm tightened protectively around her. He shifted his position and curled her into him. The comforting effect on Alanna was the opposite of Wolf's intentions—she burst into a cascade of tears.

"Alanna?" he whispered.

"Hush," she said. "And just keep doing what you're doing. It comforts me beyond words."

Two months later

In Wolf's estimation, spring couldn't have presented itself in any finer form. Leaves sprouted green and juicy from dormant branches. Daffodils shot from the ground. Purple lilacs hung in heavy masses, scenting the air with sweet perfume. Alanna and he tested the mettle of every horse in the barn. Rain pelted their faces as they raced one another across meadows and rolling hills. Each day their friendship grew, each night he found renewal by holding Alanna in his arms.

But on the fourth day of April, Thompson arrived and delivered a letter to Wolf from Trevor.

Wolf,

The detectives located the graves of your mother and father. They are at rest in a small cemetery near Dunmaglass, in the Scottish Highlands. You will find all of your answers there. By the time you read this the Serenity will have arrived in Boston Harbor. She will transport you to Liverpool, where the detectives and I await.

Godspeed,
Trevor

"What the hell are they doing in Scotland?"

"That's what you need to go find out, son," Thompson said. "We've learned everything we can from here."

"It is time," Old Chinese put in. "There will be instructions for you when you reach Trevor."

Alanna was silent, her eyes filled with tears.

"What of Alanna?" Wolf pulled her to him. A rush of misery at the thought of leaving her welled up from his toes and settled around his heart like cold lead.

"Take me along."

"You know damn well I can't."

Tears spilled over. "Please," she whispered.

His heart clenched. "I need to settle this once and for all, Alanna. Don't worry—I'll be back. There's no way in hell I'd ever let you return to your family."

"Wolf is right," Old Chinese responded. "He must go alone and put an end to all of this. And then he will come for you." He turned to Wolf. "No one will bother with her since her mother ordered her to remain here until the June wedding. I'll see to her well-being."

Alanna squeezed Wolf's hand, kissed his cheek, and swiped a tear from her eye. "I know you're both right. I'll be safe here."

Ghosts of buried memories haunted Wolf's dreams that night. He was transported to that placid pond in front of a familiar manor house, where he sat under a tree observing swans glide about while a pretty young woman watched over him. Suddenly, the dream twisted and the terrified eyes of his mother peered at him in a mirror, over the shoulder of a thick-necked, black-haired stocky man. Clear and piercing, her eyes sought the very depths of his young boy's soul. He was thrown awake in a cold sweat of despair. He did not know if he cried out. He only knew that when the mists of his foggy brain lifted, Alanna was there for him, her inquiring eyes filled with deep and abiding compassion.

His mood was somber the next morning when he stood beside the Thompson carriage and gathered Alanna in his arms to say good-bye. "I'll be back as soon as I can." He stroked her cheek with the back of his hand and wiped a tear from her eye with his knuckle. "Don't weep, darlin'. It rips my heart out."

She sniffed and laughed through her tears. "It seems I've turned into a nonstop fountain of late, and I don't know why."

Chapter Twenty-One

Liverpool, England—Mid-March

Wolf hitched a hip over the corner of the wide table in the center of Trevor's library, where papers were stacked in dated piles and maps of Scotland were strewn about. He folded his arms over his chest and worked to set aside his impatience. Trevor, a detective, and a Highland historian stood at the table, sifting through documents.

Dawson, a second detective, who'd recently arrived, sat in an armchair, a cup of coffee in one hand, a sandwich in the other. He swallowed his last bite of food and washed it down with a swig of coffee. "Turns out your father's partner was a cunning man who cozied up to your father, but secretly despised him."

A chill ran through Wolf. "He hated my father?"

Dawson nodded. "Grimes was nephew to Lord Selkirk of London, once head of the Hudson Bay Company in Canada. Their rival was the Northwest Trading Company in Montreal, owned by William MacGillivray before the two companies merged and Selkirk was dismissed. Grimes blamed William MacGillivray for the dwindling of Selkirk's wealth, which Grimes would have inherited."

"What does that have to do with my mother's murder?"

The Highland historian Trevor had hired, a Scot in his late sixties, slid a piece of paper under Wolf's nose with a drawing of a crest badge emblazoned with a stag and the word *Dunmaghlas*. "Looks like ye might be a Highlander."

Nothing registered with Wolf.

The man pushed another piece of paper under his watchful eye, this one a pen and ink drawing of a coat of arms. "Translated, the name is MacGillivray."

Lightning split Wolf's skull. He grabbed at the back of his neck and rubbed the tense cords. Why the pain when the name held no obvious connection for him? Clenching his jaw, he made his way to the window. He peered out at the courtyard, where Celine, Trevor's wife, sat on a bench before a wide cradle holding a set of twins. A nurse and a nanny sat on an adjacent bench.

"There must have been MacGillivray blood somewhere in your father's lineage," Dawson said. "Or your mother's, given your surname. Grimes was out to ruin any Mac-Gillivray he ran across. Somehow, he discovered your father was related and was the wealthiest of the remaining clan members. All evidence points to Grimes, who either exposed your mother to a murderer or did the deed himself. We know for a fact he was dealing with Hemenway Senior on the side."

Wolf felt sick. He shoved his hand through his hair. "Christ. My parents are buried on MacGillivray land because one of them was part of the clan?"

Trevor pushed papers around on the table. "Looks that way."

"But why kill my mother? That doesn't make any sense."

"That's why you need to head north," Trevor said. "Besides your parents' graves, the answers are likely there as well." He nodded toward the other detective. "Wakefield, here, could get nothing out of any of them. Once they knew he wanted information, they shunned him."

Wolf sifted through the documents on the table, asking questions. At times, his fingers tingled at the touch of one paper, trembled while he read others. "How do I find this clan?"

The historian scratched his head. "Since we know where your parents are buried, the particular clan yer looking for is up in Inverness. At Dunmaghlass."

Wolf pointed to the badge heralding the word *Dunmaghlas.* "My name is Gray. There's not a hint of Scots in the name."

The man squinted hard at Wolf. "But if I close me eyes tightlike and look through the slits, surely I pick up the MacGillivray in ye. They have the squareness to the jaw, ye know. Same as you. Carnaptious as well. Perhaps yer mother was a MacGillivray married to a Gray or suchlike."

"*Carnaptious?*" Wolf grew more irritable by the minute. "What the hell's that?"

The man chuckled and ran a hand over his side-whiskers. "Weil, the word means stubborn as an ass. A MacGillivray never has been known much for patience, either."

Trevor turned his back, but not before Wolf caught a hint of a grin flitting across his mouth. "Do you know the countryside up there?" he asked the historian.

"A wee bit."

"Would you be willing to accompany me there?"

The historian shook his head. "Count me too auld to be a bumpin' around in the wilds. But I can draw ye a map off these large ones here. Won't be no trouble finding yer way. And if ye are indeed a MacGillivray, then ye'll be verra safe amongst a clan of the Confederation."

Wolf glanced up. "Confederation?"

"The Clan Chattan." The historian drew Wolf's attention to a drawing.

When he saw the rendering of a rampant wild cat encircled in a silver strap and buckle that read *Touch Not This Cat Bot a Glove*, Wolf's head started to ache again. He went back to studying the map. "Where's this town, Dunmaglass?"

"'Tis no town, bucko. 'Tis a castle. Home of the Mac-Gillivray chief. It'll be he ye'll be a calling upon."

Between the detective's dismal report on Grimes and Hemenway, and now this man's revelations, Wolf's mood went to hell. He turned on his heel and stalked off to the garden, where Celine sat beneath a hickory tree.

He stood looking down at the four-month-old twin boys lying side by side in the cradle, a shock of black hair covering each of their heads. "How do you tell them apart?"

Celine sighed. "Honestly, I hope it gets easier as they grow."

Unceremoniously, he plopped into a wrought-iron chair, stretched out his legs, and studied Celine. *She's Trevor's other half.*

Alanna. A shaft of misery knifed through his chest. She was what he was missing.

Celine lifted a red flower to her nose and sniffed. "How do you think you'll feel if you discover that whoever you sought revenge on all this time has been dead for years?"

Something in Wolf's chest twisted. "Like I've been cheated."

"What if it is Hemenway, and not a man already dead? How would you confront him?"

"Offer him the same courtesy he extended to my mother."

"Do you honestly think you have it in your nature to snuff the life from a man in the same manner he claimed your mother's? I doubt you could live with the guilt."

"Guilt?" He threw his head back and gulped for air. "You have no idea what it's like to be a child, to watch your mother die and feel helpless to defend her. I'll likely feel remorse for the rest of my life for being too much of a coward to try and save her."

Celine reached out and laid her hand over his. "Oh, Wolf. You were a helpless six-year-old. You couldn't possibly have defended your mother against a grown man."

"Tell that to the six-year-old still living inside me."

"Oh, dear."

"I've lived with the pain of that terrible night every waking day of my life, Celine. Whatever I end up doing will finally be in defense of my mother." Wolf's throat closed up on him and his voice cracked. "I'm just a little late, that's all. Twenty-four years late."

The pale moon, so large it devoured the windows of the second-floor bedchamber, gave Wolf little solace when he awoke, drenched in the sweat of yet another nightmare. His mother's eyes, peering at him through the murky mirror, had been crystal clear this time, and filled with love. But then they looked over the shoulder of the thick-necked, stocky man whose form had grown increasingly resolute with each marauding dream. Only on this night, the oblique angle of the glass showed Wolf there was now an open door beyond the mirror. And another man, visible from the knees down, stood sentry. Although Wolf had always remembered the killer's quick trip to the door and the muffled conversation, strangely, he'd never bridged the two scenes. Until now.

He left the bed and moved to the balcony, no longer denying himself contact with the awfulness within his weary soul. As Old Chinese had suggested, during Wolf's trip across the Atlantic, he'd embraced the pain that had burdened his life. But what came each time he moved through it surprised him. In some moments, he swept past the horror, and what prevailed were the memories of his mother's smooth ivory skin, a haunting scent of cinnabar, and her soft Scottish brogue.

The recollection of his mother's last kiss, just before she'd shoved him under the bed, coalesced with the kiss Celine had planted on her sons' cheeks before they were carried off to the nursery. Tears stung his eyes. They were cold, angry tears, when what he was desperate for were warm tears. Tears of joy. What he wanted beside him this lonely night was Alanna.

Alanna.

Every cell in him pulsated with wanting her. He'd known the awful hell of having peered desperately into the eyes of a dying loved one. It had shattered his life. Lately, he was beginning to comprehend the joy of looking into the eyes of love and being swept away in its sweet world.

He sighed, long and deep, then pushed away from the rail. He returned to the bed, where he settled back, hands behind his head, and stared out the window at the clouds drifting across the moon.

Reluctantly, he surrendered to sleep and to his dreams. But this time the nocturnal images were pleasant. They were again of the great manor house. He rode in slow motion across the panorama of his dream on a fleet-footed steed. This time, the resolution of his dream remained clear, and he was able to gaze at length upon the peaceful gathering by the silver pond. He saw contentment reflected in the calm eyes of the child with the fluff of white hair—and in the eyes of his mother.

Alanna was among them this time, her hair flowing long and free in the breeze. Her hand moved slowly over her belly—a belly swollen with the burden of a child. A look of deep and enduring love shining forth from her glowing cobalt eyes shattered the impenetrable boundaries around his wary heart.

Chapter Twenty-Two

After six days alone upon the mystical Highland moors, glens, and mountains, Wolf felt strangely disconnected from himself and the life he'd left behind.

He rode Trevor's horse. His friend had insisted Wolf borrow the hardy Friesian for the difficult trek north. He worked Panther through thick patches of early morning mist, so deep in places it buried the horse's belly in swirling white froth. Every now and then, a stag sprinted into a dense thicket, startled by the mighty blue-black stallion with its curling mane tumbling to its knees. In other places, free of the Highland's misty veil, Wolf rode along in dew-kissed grass and sparkling mosses of emerald green.

As he made his way to Dunmaglass, the air, crisp and clean, filled his lungs and left him nearly light-headed. The few Highlanders he ran across, with their ageless demeanor and the glint of humor touching the corners of their eyes, sent a rare comfort to the pit of his stomach.

The sun inched over the horizon, splaying its morning rays across the rolling landscape, vaporizing the white veil swathing the green hills. When they reached the disquieting moors of Culloden, battleground of the forty-five, he eased Panther into a swifter gait. Here, the historian had told him, was where Captain Alexander MacGillivray, then chief of the Clan MacGillivray, had lost his life one cold and drizzly morning.

Alexander the Tall, as he was called, had been a blond, handsome, and well-built young chieftain who died a hero's death. Unmarried and childless at his demise, Alexander had been succeeded by his brother William. Wolf sought Alexander Lachlan MacGillivray of Dunmaglass, William's grandson and current chief of the MacGillivray Clan.

He paused Panther beside a narrow opening in the ground. A large stone adjacent to the hole was carved with the words: WELL OF THE DEAD. HERE THE CHIEF OF THE MACGILLIVRAYS FELL.

A lonesome birdcall caught Wolf's ear. He looked about the moor, at the stones among the heather. A chill ran down his spine. If it *were* true that he was indeed a MacGillivray, then he actually gazed upon a connecting link. At this point, he didn't care how long ago the Battle of Culloden had been fought; the carved stone was *something,* even if it was just a cold, gray lump of granite. He bent across his saddle and ran his fingers over the rough letters carved in the stone, half hoping the touch would stir some deep and long forgotten memory.

Nothing.

Panther let out a soft nicker. Wolf stroked the horse's neck and urged him onward. As Panther chugged along like a locomotive, Wolf took in the sights and smells more carefully. Arable land and plantation forests alternated with the Scotch firs growing along the plains. Farmers tilled the soil and planted new crops. Highland cattle—strange-looking beasts with long curved horns and furry, russet-colored hair hanging over their eyes—grazed in the meadows.

Wolf turned Panther off the road and onto another that led into a dense stand of Scotch firs. The entry to Dunmaglass.

Clearing the wooded forest, Panther picked up his pace with no encouragement from Wolf. The horse trotted through a glen, its mane flying in the breeze. As they reached the crest of a daffodil-laden knoll overlooking a valley, Wolf's jaw slackened. He jerked the reins so hard, the animal danced sideways.

The gray stone manor of Wolf's dreams sat nestled in a morning mist so thick it looked as though the whole of it sat on a fallen cloud. Two white swans floated in a silver pond flanked by tall trees. A horse the size of a dog in perspective, one of several dotting the sloping glen, raised its head and whinnied. Panther danced forward and arrogantly whinnied back. Gathering in the sight that lay before him like an apparition, Wolf held the beast in check while he caught his breath.

"Jesus God!" His heart hammered wildly. He barely squeezed his thighs and the horse lengthened its stride, broke into a smooth canter, and darted down the hill into the glen. Had he just signaled Panther forward into a self-induced dream? He moved trancelike past the pond and toward the castle.

Despite the chill in the air, perspiration flecked Wolf's brow. As he rode forward, the great manor house, with its square and toothy castellated towers cut through with the sign of the cross, loomed in front of him. His bones turned to jelly.

His nostrils flared at the scent of the Highland spring, a pure fragrance that held a faint familiarity. Breathing deeply, he tried to garner some measure of control over his wayward emotions. He halted in front of the huge double doors studded with iron, and dismounted.

Hands on hips, Wolf stood for a long while, staring upward, past the MacGillivray crest etched in stone above the door, past the cross carved above the crest and beyond, until the building seemed to sway while the clouds stood still. Gathering courage, he lifted the round iron ring attached to the door and let it clamor against the metal plate.

He waited, not wanting to knock again. The huge door

swung open. A narrow-shouldered, reed-thin woman wrapped in a thick sweater the color of porridge stood before him.

"The MacGillivray cannae see you just now," she said, but her eyes narrowed. "What be yer name?"

"Wolford Archibald Gray. People call me Wolf."

Her face paled.

"I'll see to fetching Mr. Fraser for ye. Come." She flapped her hand, waving Wolf in and glancing up at the fast-gathering clouds. "If ye hesitate, ye're likely to be surprised by a quick change in the weather."

Wolf stepped inside the large foyer with its flagstone floor and arched Gothic ceiling. He halted. Every nerve in his body tingled. The place felt familiar.

The woman urged him on. "This way if ye've a mind to warm yerself. 'Tis a good fire going in here and ye look as though ye've frozen yer blood. Or seen a ghost, so pale ye be."

She stopped abruptly in front of a fireplace so immense, Wolf could easily fit his six-foot frame inside without having to bend an inch. Burning peat, with its hauntingly familiar odor, spit flames to heat his face.

"I'll get ye Mr. Fraser, a toddy to warm ye, and someone to see to yer horse." She was off with a quick nod, her words trailing behind the click of heels against the stone floor.

Wolf perused the room. Although the place held fine furnishings, it had the look of being inhabited by a family who didn't sacrifice personal comfort for looks. Oversized, well-used leather chairs flanked the fireplace. In front of one chair stood a sturdy wooden trunk banded with metal, the corners worn away as if years of booted feet propped there had given it the right to remain, no matter its condition. Despite its formidable size, the hall held the look of a cozy family gathering place as well as one that could hold a hundred if need be.

The home of a clan chief.

Wolf rubbed his hands together while the fire warmed his face. Still, the chill refused to leave him. As did the buzzing in his brain. His gaze traveled upward, perused the rough, cut-granite wall in front of him, came to rest on the colorful coat of arms and two claymores crossed high above.

"Mr. Fraser will be honored to meet with ye." The woman's voice followed the quick cadence of her heels, but her tone held a curious lilt. As Wolf drew closer, there seemed to be a subtle difference in her appearance as well, as though a glow now hovered in her eyes.

Unsure of what lay ahead, Wolf followed behind her, taking in as much of the layout as he could, committing exits to memory.

"I'll be takin' ye to the courtyard to meet with Mr. Fraser. He's like you, he is—stays fit in the cauld air." Her words were clipped and matter of fact, but the edges held warmth.

Wolf managed a small grin.

"Ye have to like the cauld air if ye're any kind of a good Scot." She smiled back. "But I'm getting a wee auld to want to stand in it any longer than I must."

She turned left at the third doorway. Wolf caught his breath. Blood hammered in his ears. He *knew* which way to turn before she did so.

The courtyard, enclosed on three sides by the granite walls of the castle, held solid doors opening from each wall into it. A large, weathered gate leading to a field took up most of the fourth side. A fountain stood in the center, surrounded by empty clay pots. A haunting urge swept over Wolf to skip around the fountain to see how close he could manage to get to the crocks without knocking them over.

Perspiration beaded his brow. Confusion dizzied his mind as he struggled to draw air deeper into his lungs. He whipped his head around at the flash of a small, wild-haired boy disappearing to the side of the back gate.

A fiftyish-looking man with fluffy gray sideburns appeared at the gate, swung it open, and stepped inside. He stood before Wolf dressed in a red plaid kilt, white knee-length wool stockings, and a thick gray sweater. A *sgian dubh*, the same kind of small knife Alanna had had strapped to her leg while aboard ship, was tucked inside the top of his right stocking. Despite his large size and formidable carriage, the man held an air of gentleness about him.

"I'm Aiden Fraser." He gave Wolf a tilt of his head. "And the lad ye see flitting about is wee Jamie MacGillivray."

Wolf stood there, listening to the man's rich, melodious words, unable to recall the speech he'd planned. Everything seemed unreal, as though his entire life until now had been some sort of wicked devil's prank.

Aiden Fraser finally broke the silence. "I'm yer cousin. Once removed."

Fraser's words drugged Wolf like a subtle poison. He wanted to speak, but found himself thick-tongued and hoarse of voice. "You know me, then?"

"Aye, ye've the look of yer father, God rest his soul. And the look of his father, as well. A bit of yer mother around the mouth. But ye stand there and throw yer head in the air just as yer father used to do when he couldna take charge of himself, either. Yer grandfather did the same. 'Tis no mistakin' who ye be."

"And who is that?" Wolf struggled to keep the panic from his voice.

"Och, lad, ye've been through a life of hell, have ye not?" Fraser held the stem of a weed in his hand, fiddling it between his fingers.

Despite feeling as if he might crumble to his knees, Wolf stood tall and square-shouldered, jaw clenched, his gaze unwavering, determined to let things unfold on their own.

Fraser started toward the door leading back inside. "Come. I've something to show ye."

In silence, the two entered the castle again and climbed a set of stairs with a landing at the second level as wide as a room before it turned and led up yet again to another level of rooms. Wolf followed behind the dignified Highlander, no longer looking for safe exits, unable even to concentrate on the full-length portraits—kilted lairds of days past— lining the hallways.

Led to a smallish room on the third floor, Wolf poked his head inside. It took a long moment for things to register in his disoriented brain. He looked to Aiden, and then scanned the room again, his brows knitting together.

Aiden gave a nod along with a slight smile. "Go on then, inside with ye."

Stunned, Wolf stepped to the center of a room furnished with the things he'd left behind when he'd run away from school in England. Books, candles, bed—they were all there, the setting reproduced exactly as he'd left it. Even a pen lay at the ready on his desk. And the note. He'd written it to the school authorities when he was seventeen, informing them he'd not met with foul play, but had struck out on his own. God, it seemed a century ago since he'd somehow ended up in St. Joe.

"Yer grandfather had yer things brought in." Aiden's voice came soft and filled with a kind of tenderness. "'Twas his only way of keepin' ye alive in his heart."

Wolf turned from Aiden, made his way to the window, and tilted his head upward, sucking in air. "Why the hell didn't he come for me? What was my father doing in India?" He found himself dumb, wanting to speak but unable to say more, afraid he would break into sobs.

Aiden moved to stand beside Wolf. "After yer father returned to Boston to find yer mother murdered and ye hidden away in the hills outside the city, he didna collect ye fer fear someone might follow. Instead, he went to India to set up a new life fer the two of ye. That's when ye were put aboard a ship bound for Liverpool. He intended to meet ye there and secret ye away, but someone found him and he never made it out of Calcutta."

"He intended to come for me?"

"Aye, but when yer grandfather got word that yer father had been done in, and ye were next, he decided to place ye in a school where no one knew ye."

Renewed frustration bloomed in Wolf. "But why didn't he ever come? Why didn't he let me know who I was?"

"Fer yer own safety. Ye were an angry lad, and rightly so, but he figured if someone found yer father all the way in India, it wouldn't take much for them to find ye up here. And since ye had a penchant for being hot-tempered, he thought it best to wait until ye were a bit older to tell ye, so ye wouldn't give yerself away. He had someone watching over ye and reporting back to him, but then ye up and ran off. That's when we lost track of ye for all those years."

Wolf shoved his hand through his hair. "I stowed away on a ship to America and wandered." He studied Aiden. "I've got a helluva lot of questions that have haunted me through the years."

"Yer grandfather keeps his secrets, so I can't say as I have all the answers. There's plenty of time for ye to be learning everything—"

"I don't even know when my birthday is, for Christ's sake, and that's the least of what I want to know." Wolf dragged his sleeve across the corner of one eye. "Who the hell am I, Aiden?"

The man paused for a moment to study Wolf. "Ye're Alexander William Wolf MacGillivray."

Wolf spun around. "MacGillivray? What happened to Wolford Archibald Gray?" His hand swept the room and the array of schoolbooks. Fire lit his eyes. And pain. Awful, deep, and torturous pain.

Aiden winced. "If it gives ye any peace, yer parents are together in Dunlichity. 'Tis the MacGillivray cemetery. The name Wolford Archibald Gray was given to ye when ye was three. 'Twas done to protect ye, to protect the lot of ye when ye fled to Boston. But I'm sorry to say, it didna keep yer mother alive."

Wolf sat on the bed as a gush of air left his lungs. He shut his eyes and pinched the bridge of his nose. "My parents fled to Boston? Because of Grimes? I thought he found us in Boston?"

"Yer mother's body was secreted here after her death, to be with her people. Yer father died in India and was brought home to lie beside the woman he dearly loved and lost. There is a place there for ye, as well, when the time comes. But as for now, ye still have a grandfather—"

"You didn't answer me." Wolf's shoulders gave a shudder, but his eyes remained shut.

"He's not well, lad. Cannae speak no more, or walk. But he'll know ye. He's The MacGillivray."

Wolf's eyes shot wide and he stared blankly at Fraser.

"In case ye canna figure things just right yet, Wolf, ye're the next in line. Ye're to be The Mor—the MacGillivray chief, when yer grandfather makes his way to the pearly gates." He paused, giving his words time to sink in.

"Ye need time to get used to things, to adjust to all ye'll be told before ye meet him. We protect him in his auldness, just as he protected us in his vigor. I've been acting guardian of the lairdship until ye'd a mind to show yerself. But this'll be yer burden now, to keep the fine points of order and structure intact for yer kin and clan."

Wolf leaned back in a defensive gesture and shook his head slowly back and forth. He hadn't heard right. He couldn't have.

"Ye canna refuse, lad. I know Scotland isn't like it used to be, but we still need our lairds. The clan needs you."

Wolf stood, ice water running through his veins. "Take me to my parents' graves, Aiden. Now."

* * *

Alanna wandered aimlessly through her Brookline home. After asking Old Chinese's permission to check on the pipes for her father, she'd spent five days alone, in weather so dreary as to make even the most optimistic feel half dead.

Reading books meant paging through them impatiently until she flung them down in frustration. She'd dug through her father's desk, but Wolf had swept its secret compartments clean.

She missed Wolf with a vengeance, and would give anything to be held by him, to press her cheek against his chest and feel his living warmth. More and more, she was becoming a stranger to herself. The carefully cultivated self-control that gave her a sense of security and order seemed to slip away daily under her dismal circumstances.

The old steamer trunk full of scarves lay open where Alanna had casually flipped the lid in passing earlier in the day. Pausing in front of the chest, she picked up one of the scarves and buried her face in it. Memories of Wolf dressing her in them, of the lovemaking they'd shared, cleaved a path through her heart. Tears spilled from her eyes once more.

"Oh, God help me." She sat in a heap on the floor and for a long while, leaned her head against the hard wood of the trunk. Numb from weeping, she sorted through the scarves for no particular reason, pulled them out one by one, and grouped them in colors. Reaching deeper into the trunk, Alanna's hand struck a long tubelike object. She sucked in her breath as she brought the object to the surface. "My kaleidoscope! So that's why it went missing, Mother."

She held Wolf's gift to her breast, and rocked back and forth. "And just what else might you have hidden since I was here last, you wicked woman?" Setting the kaleidoscope aside, she dug through to the bottom of the trunk, haphazardly flinging the brightly colored pieces of silk onto the floor as she went.

Her hand struck another object. She pulled the flat,

narrow container from its hiding place, not recognizing its green leather covering etched in gold. Locked. "Damn you, Mother." She scrambled to her feet and fairly flew to her father's study, where she retrieved a letter opener from his desk. Working its point into the lock, she twisted until the latch gave way.

A flat piece of paper lay folded on top, part of it charred, as though someone had tried to burn it and failed. Alanna opened it, but was unable to read all of its scorched contents, only able to make out a partial birth date and the partial name of a male—Malco . . .

The Malones were listed as the boy's parents.

With trembling fingers, Alanna laid the paper aside and picked up a round brooch. She dropped it like a hot poker when she realized the tiny flowers and scrollwork woven into the lace backing were made of human hair, golden in color. Another pin, similar in design and made up of a darker color of hair, rested on the emerald velvet inside the box. Even though wearing mourning jewelry made from the hair of a deceased loved one was a popular way of showing respect, the idea repulsed Alanna, and she refused to touch them. Instead, she focused on another box, about two inches square.

She lifted the lid of the smallest box. "Oh, dear God!" Her eyes closed for a long moment while she gathered her wits about her. She could barely catch her breath as she snapped the box shut and replaced it inside the larger one. Gingerly, she lifted the breast pin she'd dropped on her father's desk, replaced it in the box as well, then picked up the birth certificate, and studied it for a long while before returning it to its resting place.

What else? Carrying the box with her, she returned to her mother's trunk and emptied all the scarves into a heap on the floor. She pressed at the corners of the empty trunk. One corner gave way. "I thought so, a false bottom."

Working the sharp point of her father's letter opener

underneath the corner, Alanna eased it up until she could slip her fingers beneath the wood, revealing a shallow compartment.

"Mother!"

With trembling fingers, she gathered the contents scattered about the bottom of the trunk. She couldn't move fast enough as, breathlessly, she placed all of her findings in a carpetbag and headed for the stables. And back to Old Chinese at the farm.

"I found this hidden in Mother's old steamer trunk at Brookline." Alanna waved the kaleidoscope in the air. "The one in the hallway with all the scarves I used to play with."

Old Chinese gave a nod. "I see."

"And this." Alanna pulled out the green leather box. "Do you know of this?"

Old Chinese shook his head. Alanna opened the box and pointed to the mourning brooches. Old Chinese looked at them and then into her eyes.

"And these." She opened the remains of the birth certificate and handed it to him. Then she emptied the carpetbag. "Who is that boy?" Her voice rose hysterically as she pointed to the miniature.

"Alanna—" Old Chinese reached a hand out to her.

She waved him off. "And this." She opened the small box and shoved it under his nose.

"Oh!" he let out. His eyelids swept shut for a brief moment before he met her gaze, his head slowly shaking back and forth. "I am so sorry you had to find this."

She snapped the box shut and pointed to the miniature. "Who is that boy?"

Old Chinese remained silent.

Alanna's panic lit to full flame. "Tell me, for God's sake! Is this a miniature of Wolf? Is he another brother like Winston?"

"Alanna."

She fell in a heap at his feet, her body racked with sobs.

He knelt in front of her and, grasping her by the shoulders, shook her. "Alanna, stop this."

She raised her head, tears streaming down her face. "Is that why Wolf and I have exactly the same kind of eyes, Old Chinese? Are his the eyes of my father, too? Oh, God forbid," she wailed.

He held her tightly by her shoulders, forcing her to look him in the eye as he demanded her answer. "What exactly are you trying to tell me?"

"I carry Wolf's child," she sobbed, disintegrating in the old man's arms. "Oh, God, I carry his child."

It was the fatherly Old Chinese who swept her up in his arms, the role of master forgotten. "Oh no, dear child, no," he murmured as he rocked her back and forth. "He is not your brother." He sighed as he tilted his weary head to stare out the window at nothing.

"You are certain?"

He reached into his pocket, withdrew a handkerchief, and stuffed it in her fist. "Quite certain. You see, Wolf does not know this, but I have known him for a very, very long time."

She lifted a finger to his chin and urged him to look into her eyes. "Tell me. I need to know everything."

Old Chinese pulled away and stood. "You must return to Boston and pack your things without your parents knowing. I'll be taking you to Wolf."

Chapter Twenty-Three

Dunmaglass—Late April

Wolf had no idea how long he'd sat beside the pond watching the swans glide about. He'd yet to meet his grandfather. He needed time to adjust to the heady sensation that he actually belonged to a large, connected family. Most of all, he wanted to be well away from the curious clansmen whose presence exposed the enormity of what a clan chief faced. Christ, he'd lived alone and lonely most of his life, and suddenly he had so many cousins he couldn't keep track of them.

He'd spent three bitter days at Dunlichity, hunched over his parents' graves. The chill wind had blown cold rain off the brim of his hat and sent rivulets of icy water down his spine. Again and again, he'd traced the names Glenda Mary and William Duncan carved in cold granite, searching for something to fill his empty soul.

No one would tell him—but he suspected Aiden Fraser knew—why his parents had fled Scotland in the first place. That secret lay with his grandfather, who could no longer speak. Wolf stood, brushed off the seat of his trousers, and headed for the castle. Putting off meeting his grandfather had grown damned uncomfortable.

When he stepped to the foot of the old man's bed, Wolf encountered a mere suggestion of the handsome and fiery-eyed Scot displayed in proud portraiture on the second-floor landing. As he gazed into his grandfather's ancient, milky blue eyes, Wolf's insides withered.

He had trouble keeping his eyes on The Mor, on his hollow cheeks, his bony fingers clawing the air in a feeble attempt to grasp the hand of his prodigal grandson. The old man's arms, once sturdy enough to swing a six-foot claymore, were now rail-thin. The flesh of his upper arms sagged against the bed linens like a turkey's loose neck. Bile rose in Wolf's throat when his grandfather moved his toothless mouth in a vain attempt to speak with a voice that had gone silent.

Anger, unexpected and profound, permeated Wolf. Damn it, he'd missed out on a life with this man as well. Despite the compassion that flowed through him with regard to his grandfather's condition, he wasn't about to forgive him, or his father, much less God, for the three having deserted him. Nor was he about to attach himself to a man with so little time left in the world.

He turned on his heel and made for his room to pack his saddlebags. He paused at the sound of footsteps. Aiden.

"Where do ye think to be off to, lad?"

The saddlebags slid off the bed and scattered Wolf's belongings on the floor. "Fuck!" Swearing seemed a safer outlet for his rage than slamming his fist into his cousin's face. "You can keep your MacGillivray chief crap, and the whole goddamn village that goes with it."

"Whether ye like it or not, 'tis what ye sought when ye went looking for yer mother's killer." Aiden said in a voice that seemed to come from a long way off.

"Bullshit!" Wolf slapped the empty saddlebags back onto the bed, stepped over the mess he'd made on the floor, and stormed to the balcony. "I'm looking for answers, not some half-dead, old crippled man who threw me to the dogs years ago." A vein throbbed wildly alongside his neck. He rubbed at it. "And I sure as hell wasn't looking for a slew of people expecting me to be some goddamned Highland shepherd herding a bunch of brainless bastards."

He caught sight of the scruffy boy who'd peeked through the back gate of the castle when he'd arrived. The six-year-old's hair blew wild in the stiff wind as he struggled toward the barn with a bleating lamb in his arms. The lamb's mother, still bloody-rumped from giving birth, waddled behind. "Christ Almighty, why doesn't someone help that kid?"

Fraser followed Wolf onto the balcony. "Have ye thought of seein' to wee Jamie yerself?"

"Go to hell." Wolf shoved a hand through his hair and turned his back to the scene below. "I want to know why my parents left the Highlands."

"Ye've got to cut me some slack, lad. Yer grandfather kept things to himself. The fewer people who knew the details the better, he said. He kept the door of this room locked. We tacksmen only knew what was in it when The Mor had his seizure and couldn't fend fer himself." Fatigue carved deep shadows beneath Aiden's eyes. "That's when I knew ye had to return one day."

Wolf stomped back into the room and paced. "I guess I never figured on having the truth come with so many strings attached." He kicked at a fallen pillow and sent it flying. "I thought things would be a helluva lot simpler."

"The only thing that comes with no strings attached, lad, is our commitment to you." Aiden's voice softened. "And that we give ye, free and clear."

Wolf didn't know what the hell to do with that remark. He turned his face to the ceiling and fought the urge to destroy everything in the room with his bare hands. "How can I be so damned confused, and at the same time feel . . . I don't know . . . comfortable here? Something I don't remember knowing since my mother died."

"Feeling the peace of something doesna mean ye won't feel the pain of it as well." Aiden hesitated a moment. "I've been keeping a few things for ye. Of yer father's. Would ye care to have a peek? Mayhap ye'll have recollections that'll awaken more memories."

At Aiden's words, Wolf's mouth went dry. He nodded. Silently, they made their way down to the second level of Dunmaglass, to the room he'd thus far avoided—one he'd been told had belonged to his parents before they'd left the Highlands.

The room faced the rear of the castle. A large accoutrement bed draped in blue tapestries was centered on a wall across from a stone fireplace that jutted to the high, bold rafters. Heavy blue velvet drapes flanked leaded-glass doors that led to a large balcony. Twin wardrobes stood at attention against opposite walls like sullen, brown sentries. There was a scent in the room that rattled him—violets and fresh air.

Aiden led Wolf to the right of the fireplace, to a door that opened into a small room stacked high with personal items. "It used to be a nursery. When ye were a wean, yer father saw to it ye were as close to yer mother as would satisfy her." Aiden swept up a length of red plaid, the same print as the one he wore. "Yer father's kilt."

He laid the bright length of wool across Wolf's forearm, then bent and raised the lid of a heavy trunk. Folded inside was his father's Highland dress, both casual and formal—a badger-skin sporran, shirts, jackets, knitted knee-length stockings, and beneath that, muted green and brown hunting plaids and several heavy knitted sweaters.

Wolf's heart thundered in his ears. A hunting rifle stood at an angle against the wall beneath a shelf holding dirks and *sgian dubhs*. An array of hunting gear hung at the ready, as if the owner might reappear momentarily.

"Would ye have them?" Aiden asked. "Yer parents would have wanted it just so."

Wolf surveyed the room again, his insides trembling. "I . . . I had no idea . . . no memory of my father like this. I only remember him as a staid businessman."

"Ye were barely three when ye left, and the mind has a queer way of rememberin' things. Perhaps using his things will help fill that big hole in yer heart."

Wolf wanted Fraser gone—and fast—before he lost control of his emotions. He turned his back on his cousin.

"Aye," Aiden said softly, and left the room.

Wolf dragged the trunk into the cavernous bedroom. Slowly, he examined each article of clothing, buried his nose in some. The lavender that kept the moths at bay had long ago replaced his father's scent, but somehow he muddled through his memories and rescued a hint of musk, fresh air, and Marseille soap. A sob hitched in his throat, but the damn tears he wished would fall to relieve his pain wouldn't come.

"Christ Almighty." He covered his eyes with the crook of his arm for a long while. He needed a drink—some good Scots whisky. He stood to leave, but at the sight of his father's things, a bit of rebellion, mixed with a whole lot of curiosity, moved through him.

He stripped naked and went about dressing himself in the inherited Highland clothing. Oddly enough, he liked the feel of the kilt, the sensation of the *sgian dubh* tucked in the top of his right stocking, the sporran hanging loose from his waist and draped low across his pelvis. Even the shoes fit. He glanced in the mirror. Damn if he didn't resemble the men in the portraits lining the staircase.

His stomach growled. Food. And whisky. That's what he needed.

He left the room and trotted down the stairs. The sun, once shining golden on one side of the manse, now thrust long purple shadows across the silver pond on the opposite side. He made his way to the kitchen, intending to make off with whatever he could carry. A woman standing in the kitchen beside Aiden knocked any notion of a stroll in the quiet wood right out of him. He stumbled to a halt.

Mrs. Guthrie, the servant who'd pulled him from under his mother's deathbed, stood before him. Except for her snow-white hair, she hadn't changed much.

All desire for food vanished.

The urge for some good whisky increased.

Mrs. Guthrie's face paled. She clutched the front panels of her sweater together. "I'd know ye anywhere, lad."

"And I'd know you too, Mrs. Guthrie," he hoarsely replied. Damn it, was his chest going to cave in altogether?

She shook her head. "Ye have the look of yer father. Like a mirror, it is."

A good swallow and he managed to settle his voice. "Except for my mother's mouth."

"Aye. But ye have more than that, lad. There's a kind of fire burning in ye that she had. Ye've turned into a fine-looking man. And not one who can verra well hide in a crowd." Her glance touched briefly on the garnet earring at Wolf's ear, then shifted back to his face. Her cheeks flushed, the only sign of having recognized the ear bob.

He didn't know quite what to say next. He took in a slow breath and let it out just as slowly. "The years have been good to you, Mrs. Guthrie."

Her mouth moved, but no words came forth. She stood there, staring at Wolf for a long moment. And then she opened her arms wide.

He went to her, just as he'd done so many times in the past. But now there was a difference—the six-year-old had disappeared, replaced by a man who towered head and shoulders above her. It was Wolf who enfolded *her* in *his* arms. She buried her face in his chest and muttered something unintelligible through muffled sobs.

Chapter Twenty-Four

Wolf thought memories of Alanna would fade with the time spent in the Highlands, but the peaceful ways at Dunmaglass only enhanced them. He imagined her everywhere, saw how easily she would fit in. The time he spent alone reminded him of life at the farm with Old Chinese. There, too, he'd lived with a vague emptiness when she was not present.

Despite spending hours in deep reflection with Mrs. Guthrie, he was no nearer to solving his mother's murder, but he'd begun to adjust to the Highlands. His anger lessened as he became familiar with his surroundings, and with the fast-growing relationship with his grandfather, one that surprised him.

Although he wasn't quite sure why, he'd begun to pop in and out of his grandfather's room at odd hours. Even though the man was mute, Wolf spoke casually to him and swore his acerbic wit was appreciated. One day, he'd caught a genuine response in The MacGillivray's eyes. That was when his visits increased.

In late afternoon, he stood at the threshold of his grandfather's room and spied Edna Fraser, Aiden's niece, asleep in the chair next to the bed. Damn it, she was neglecting her duties.

Wolf crept into the room, leaned over her, planted one

hand on each of the chair's armrests, and growled in her ear. "Do not *ever* let me catch you asleep when you're watching over The Mor."

She jerked awake with a jump and a squeal as if she'd seen the devil himself.

He stepped back.

Her eyes wide as saucers, she ran from the room without a backward glance.

Wolf took her chair and casually propped his feet on one corner of his grandfather's bed. "That oughta hold the pip in check. She's probably been driving you to Bedlam with her chatty flitting about, and you not able to tie her spry little butt down."

When his grandfather's shoulders shook, Wolf leaned over to check on him. By God, there was a grin hidden in the hollows of those cheeks! He slipped his hand over his grandfather's and gave it a squeeze. "Guess you'd have done the same back when, huh?" A whisper of a squeeze was his grandfather's response.

"Well, I'll be damned. We can communicate. Wouldn't you know it'd be over a woman?"

His grandfather squeezed again and his shoulders shook. Wolf sat back, pleased a relationship had developed, yet beset with an odd urge to weep those tears that never flowed. In moments, his grandfather slept again.

Sullen black clouds drifted over the rising moon when Wolf made his way back to Dunmaglass with a line of grouse hanging off the barrel of his rifle.

"Here ye be," he teased Mrs. Guthrie, and plopped the birds onto the table in the kitchen.

"Ye have company," she said in a dour burr and reached for his catch.

"And who might that be?"

She jerked her head toward the door leading down the

hallway. "See fer yerself, but remove yer boots or clean the mud off them."

Wolf raised a quizzical eyebrow and complied. He forced a fantasy thought of Alanna from his mind as he strode to the great room. He hesitated at the entrance when the low buzz of voices reached his ears. His pulse quickened.

First he spied Bear, the Great Pyrenees he'd given Alanna for Christmas. And then Old Chinese, sunk deep in the leather fireside chair. Wolf's pulse ran rampant. The dog saw Wolf, and whined. At the old man's silent nod, the beast jumped to its feet and galloped toward Wolf.

"You've grown." Wolf ruffled Bear's thick white coat and strode forward to where Old Chinese sat, sipping a glass of port. Aiden leaned against the mantel, a glass of whisky in hand. Wolf halted in front of Old Chinese and gave a bow of his head, student to master.

"You brought her?"

Old Chinese nodded.

Wolf poured himself a shot of whisky and made for the other chair. Changing his mind, he walked over to the fireside and stood opposite his cousin. He tried to appear his old aloof self, but impatience won out. "Ah, hell." He tossed the whisky down his throat. "Anything you brought along or have to say that can't wait 'til morning?"

Old Chinese shook his head.

"Where is she?"

"In yer room," Aiden answered.

Wolf set the whisky glass on the mantel with a dull thud and raced up the stairs.

Wolf strode through the door. "What the devil are you doing here?"

At the sight of his clamped jaw, set face, and flicker of coldness, fear scattered through Alanna like grapeshot. But then he grasped her shoulders and something powerful passed between them. She caught his familiar, musky scent.

Hot need welled in her the moment he touched her. His mouth softened as he settled his lips, cool and moist, upon hers, muffling the whimper in her throat. His fingers brushed the cape from her shoulders as his arms crossed behind her back and pulled her to him.

Her fuller, hardened breasts strained against his chest. The tight, rounded mound which had once been a flat, muscled belly also betrayed her.

He stiffened.

Holding her in place so tightly she could barely breathe, he drew his head back and gazed into her eyes, his face unreadable.

Fear rocked her soul.

He squeezed his eyes shut. She fought a tide of raw emotion so overwhelming, she could only stand there while his fingers stole along her quaking form and splayed over her belly.

When the tension in his body slackened, her held breath left her lungs. His hand traveled slowly from the bump to a ripe breast. Panicked, she gulped in more air as his hand traveled back to the swelling below her waist.

When he pulled his head back, color flooded his face. A sapphire glow glimmered in the depths of his eyes. Gently, he wiped away a stray tear from her cheek.

"Shh, shh." He kissed her wet lashes.

She gazed at him through an aqueous haze. "You don't hate me?"

His lids lowered, cloaking the mysterious flame that fired his eyes. His nostrils flared as he lifted a loose tendril of her hair to his cheek before he bowed his head and set his mouth to the contour of her neck.

"Hate you?" Wolf swept her up and carried her to the bed. He lay down beside her and cradled her in his arms.

A desperate emptiness and longing that had gathered force in her over the months coalesced with deep passion. He traced his fingertips past her shoulders, caught her hand in his, then glanced up with a slow, easy smile.

She took in the parting of his lips as if he struggled for air. He opened her palm and planted a warm kiss in its center, then touched the tip of his nose to hers with only a bare wisp of movement before he outlined her lips with small, tender kisses. "God knows how I missed you."

"Oh, Wolf, I missed you so much I thought I . . ."

"Would perish?"

She laughed.

He smiled down at her. "You should try laughing more often. It becomes you." He traced her jawline with his thumb and tilted her chin upward. His hungry mouth traced hers again, sent her universe whirling. She was drowning in him already, yet it couldn't have been five minutes since he'd walked into the room.

He reached for the raven hair lying coiled, like the twist of a rope, at her nape and set it loose. He took his time draping her curls around her shoulders. "God, you're beautiful." His hand touched her breast, caressing her.

She gasped aloud as his splayed fingers came to rest across the hard curve of her belly.

"You are insanely inviting." He planted arduous kisses about her face, her neck, the lobes of her ears until she whimpered and moved under him, trembling in ripe invitation. Her hand slid boldly below his waist, to the buttons of his trousers and to his rampant erection.

"Oh, Jesus, Alanna, don't do that!" He wrenched her hand away and held her at bay.

"Why not?" Confusion drenched her like a cold rain.

"Because, I'm not in control of myself right now." He rolled onto his back, shielded his eyes with his arm. "I didn't expect your arrival. I'm not prepared."

"Not pre . . . prepared?"

"I can't keep my hands off you, and I can't risk hurting you or the babe. Give me a minute to think."

Alanna shot up on one elbow. "It's perfectly all right. You won't harm us." She unbuttoned his shirt and kissed his chest. "I spoke with Celine. She told me it's safe enough until the final month. She also said you were afraid—"

"Jeezus." Wolf raised his head to stare down at her. "Is nothing sacred with you women? Do you discuss everything? I hope you didn't tell her—"

"About your little harem girl?" She giggled, her hand tracing directly back to where he'd just thwarted her advances.

"Christ, that, too?"

"No, silly." She began to unbutton his trousers.

Wolf chuckled and wrapped his arms around her. Grasping the round curve of her bottom, he pulled her tight, molding her to him. "Are you sure it's safe?" He bit down on the soft lobe of her ear and dragged his teeth across it.

"Positive." She tugged his shirttail free, unburdened him of the garment entirely, then plunged her hand boldly down the front of his trousers. "I'm of a mind to revisit all the marvelous places that give you pleasure." She licked his belly and caressed his shaft until he groaned and helped her dispense with the rest of his clothing.

His intense gaze locked with hers as he cupped a swollen breast and teased it with his thumb in rhythmic movements until she trembled. With a slide of his hand, he began to undress her.

"Christ," he mumbled as a tiny pearl button at the back of her dress broke loose and sprang across the bed. "One thing about women's clothing, if you've a mind to do anything, it'll be damn well changed in the time it takes to get things off." Another button popped. "To hell with it." He gave the gown a yank, buttons flying every which way. "I'll buy you a new one."

She squealed, bit into his shoulder, and held him tight as he pulled her garments off and threw them to the floor in a heap. She wrapped her legs around his hips. He pinned her back on the bed, his mouth finding hers in fiery possession. With a single thrust, he sheathed himself to the groin.

He stilled. "It's been so long. Too long," he rasped.

Her hips thrust upward in a silent message, begging for more of him. The world around her dimmed as he began a slow slide of his hips. She quivered. Her legs tightened and her heels dug into his backside, guiding him still deeper. She existed only at the point of his entry, aware only of his movements, the heat of her sheath tight around him. He was her universe now, a universe made of exquisite, exploding stars and a raw new world of hovering, electrified sensation.

Wolf's dreams were sweet as he nestled Alanna against him. But then, somewhere deep in the night they ran rampant and horrid. His mother was dead now. The stranger in the mirror had finally succeeded, nightmare after nightmare, in strangling her. And now, in dim shadow, the stranger released his hands from around her neck and stepped from the bed. The man searched for him. Wolf's heart thundered wildly in his chest as he awoke with a start, sweat soaking his brow.

He rolled onto his back and tossed the covers off with a groan.

"Wolf?" came a sleepy murmur.

"Shh, shh." He pulled her close. "You're weary from the trip. Sleep." He slid his hand across her hard belly in a move to pull her closer.

He froze.

Stark memory hit him like a bullet slamming into his chest. "Goddamn it!" He shot out of bed.

* * *

"Wolf!" Alanna scrambled after him. "What is it?"

He flung the doors to the balcony wide and was outside by the time she managed to snatch her cape from the floor and wrap it around her. She flew to his side.

He stood stiff-armed against the railing in the chill wind and stared at the full moon.

Alanna's heart hammered in her chest. Had he suffered another nightmare? Had he guessed the truth? Dear God, not before she could tell him.

"There was more than one murder that night, Alanna."

"Another?" She shivered and pulled the cape tight around her shoulders. "You're sure?" At the slow nod of his head in the moonlight, cotton plugged her throat. "And you're just now remembering?" Blood pounded in her ears.

"When I . . . after the dream, I woke up and . . . needed you."

A chill ran down her spine.

"When I slid my hand over your belly, it triggered the memory of that last night with my mother." He turned to her, touched his hand to her waist. "Jeezus, Alanna, she was heavy with child."

A moan escaped her throat as she pressed her cheek to his chest.

He slid his arms around her shoulders and pulled her close. "I remember now. She was hoping my father would be back by mid-February. In time for my sibling's birth."

Sheer panic coalesced with anguish and set Alanna's teeth chattering.

"Let me take you back to bed, darlin'. You'll catch a chill."

Tears streamed down her cheeks as she slid into bed with him. Panic etched the corners of her heart.

"What's wrong, Alanna?"

She couldn't tell him—at least not tonight. "I'm so sorry for you."

He grew still.

"Oh, God," she moaned. "I know how you hate to hear

those words." She reached up and touched her fingertips to his mouth. "But Wolf, I now know how the Guthries must have felt when they constantly repeated them. Feeble as they are, 'I'm sorry' are the only words I can find."

He kissed her forehead. "It's all right, go back to sleep."

Holding her in his arms, he smoothed her hair until she drifted off to sleep. But not much later, she awoke, alone and knowing it was his absence that stirred her. She surveyed the room in the dim firelight. His trousers were missing, but his shirt was still there, so she knew he couldn't have wandered far.

She slid from the bed and padded over to her trunk. Fumbling in the dark, she managed to find her robe and gathered it around her, then slipped barefoot into the hallway.

Old Chinese stood in the middle of the long vestibule with the Great Pyrenees by his side. He nodded to the stairwell and toward the great hall below. Bear gave a whine. Alanna tapped her thigh and the dog escorted her down the stairs.

When she spied Wolf, bare-chested and slouched in a chair before a blazing fire, her heart gave a lurch. He held a glass of whisky. His hair hung loose and his long legs were stretched in front of him. A thumb traced slowly back and forth over his bottom lip as he gazed into the leaping flames.

She sat in the chair opposite him, tucked her legs up under her robe and set about regarding him for a long while.

After a time, he turned to her, leaning against his fingers pressed to his temples. "It gives me great comfort to see you sitting there."

"I was concerned I might be intruding," she said, engulfed in his compelling gaze.

"They'll come after you."

"They?" Already she fought the dread forcing bile into her throat.

His lashes swept slowly over his eyes. "Your father. He'll

send someone for you. I'll guarantee he's pissed off with the note you left saying you intend to marry me and that you carry my child. He couldn't stomach leaving you with me—especially since this is the very month you were set to marry Hemenway."

"He wouldn't dare come after me, not under the circum . . . stances." She bit her bottom lip. "I'll never go back to Father."

She drew her robe tighter and shivered. Wolf opened his arms, reminding Alanna of the night in Boston, in his hotel room, when he'd invited her to join him on the bed.

"Come sit with me, darlin'," he whispered in a husky voice, while a slow and lazy smile tilted the corners of his mouth.

When she crawled into the warm comfort of his arms, he drew her to him and regarded her as if she were a visitor from the heavens. He caressed her with the tips of his fingers, lightly shaped the curve of her hip before his hand spread across the round curve of her belly.

"I've felt the quickening already," she said, taking great comfort in the gentle movements of his strong, masculine hand.

"Quickening?"

"The first movements. It's like a butterfly fanning its wings inside me."

A slight grin caught one corner of his mouth. "And when will you have our child?" He trailed kisses across her neck.

"Late October," she answered, breathing in his heady scent.

His eyebrow rose as he counted backward. "Hmmm, must have happened right away."

"You're not angry?"

Wolf's brows shot together. "Why would I be?"

"You said you didn't want children. You asked me if I knew how to take precautions, and I did."

He only shrugged. His hand slid under her knee and he planted a soft kiss at its crook.

Delicious.

She ran her fingers through his hair. "You look so much like the painting of Alexander MacGillivray in the upper hallway." She sighed. "And your father as well. The resemblance is remarkable."

"So I've been told." Humor danced in his eyes. "Except for my mother's mouth."

And my father's eyes. Her body gave an involuntary shudder. All pleasure drained from her.

Wolf slid his hand to her chin and forced her to look at him. "What's wrong?"

She shook her head, and leaned into him. How she wished Old Chinese had not told her the truth. Why did she have to tell Wolf everything? But it should not be Old Chinese, or Aiden, or Mrs. Guthrie who told him. In her heart of hearts, she knew it had to be her. She only hoped he wouldn't hate her in the end, because something magical, something more real than she'd ever hoped for, had built between them in the long, harrowing weeks of their separation.

"Alanna?" Wolf gave her shoulder a small shake. "What's the matter with you? If it's your father you're worried about, I won't let him take you back." His eyes searched her face. "There will be plenty of precautions taken. I'll have guards stationed around here in the morning."

Alanna heaved a sigh and leaned her head into his chest.

"We can marry tomorrow," he said.

She stiffened at his words.

"You don't care for the idea?"

"I love it," she whispered.

Wolf drew her head away from his chest. "Well then, what's wrong? Is there something I should know? If so, you'd better clear the air. Right now."

"No, Wolf." She tried to struggle free. But he held her

tightly to him. "Give me a week." Tears stung her eyes. "Please. Let's simply be with one another before we talk seriously. I . . . I want you to show me everything you know of Dunmaglass. I'd like to know what life must have been like for you when you were a child. It's important to me."

With a bend of his head, Wolf's face was so close to hers, his eyes so penetrating and demanding, it dizzied her. "Fine. But what of our wedding?"

"In a week."

"One week." He glanced across the room at the clock. "To the hour. And then you will damn well tell me what has you acting so edgy."

Alanna shifted in Wolf's lap and nestled her cheek against his chest.

"Aren't we doing things a little backward?" He slipped into his teasing voice as he stroked her hair. "If you wait too long, our child can take an active part in the wedding."

She smiled and drew an invisible cloak over her miserable feelings.

"That's better." He ruffled her hair. "You were making me worry." He settled her head against his shoulder. "You asked if I'd hate you for carrying my child. How could you possibly think I could hate you?"

You may. Alanna closed her eyes. *In one week, you just may.*

Chapter Twenty-Five

Following a long walk around the property, Wolf escorted Alanna back inside the castle through a secret passageway leading to the second-floor corridor. She felt as though she'd stepped into a fairy tale. To think he'd been born here, surrounded by an entire clan ready to love and serve him, only to end up alone most of his life. How very sad.

"I've one last thing to show you before it gets too dark." Placing a hand at the small of Alanna's back, he guided her to a door, opened it, and urged her inside. "This is a duplicate of the room I occupied at boarding school."

Books, fencing foils, trophies, and clothing, just as he'd left them when he'd struck out on his own, gave her a deeper insight into him. She picked up the fountain pen and rolled it between her fingers. Even with him standing behind her, she felt as if she were snooping. She flipped open a ledger and found a detailed list of offensive Saxon words alongside their more refined Norman counterparts scrawled in a youthful script. "What's *this*?"

A ghost of a smile touched Wolf's lips. He folded his arms over his chest and leaned against the door's frame. "That's how I learned to curse."

Heaven forbid. "And how old were you when you ciphered this?"

A glitter of the defiant rebel sparkled in his eyes. "Eleven. That's when I decided life was little more than a game, so I decided to play by the Old Saxon rules."

Dear Lord, even his cursing hadn't been happenstance. "So your shocking language was the instrument you've used to release anger in a controlled manner."

A chuckle rolled up from somewhere deep in his belly. "That's a nice way of putting it."

"There's no need for this kind of front any longer, Wolf."

He stepped fully into the room, and the look in his eye sent her whole body tingling.

"Ah, but I like using bad words." He backed her toward the narrow cot that had once served as his bed. "Especially with you spread out under me." He set her hand to the front of his trousers and against the hard length of his arousal.

Her breath caught. "Oh, Wolf. Not here."

"Why not?"

"What if someone should happen by?" Cool air hit her legs. When had he lifted her skirts? "We . . . we should go to our bedchamber."

"Oh, we'll get there, darlin'. This won't take long."

The moon, shining through the vast, starry night, spilled a path across the bedchamber floor. Alanna slumbered. Her hand atop his chest rode the rhythmic rise and fall of his breath. God, it felt good to have her next to him. He held her close and drifted off into another dream.

He was a small boy again. This time he stood beside his mother's bed, not wanting to look at her face. He knew she was dead. He heard the echoing footsteps of the murderer returning. Wolf lunged under the bed. The door opened. His heart pounded in his chest, and he fought a moan. An earring fell from his mother's ear and hit the floor with a deafening crash. He reached out to grab it, but it exploded and shattered crimson glass over him that turned into streams of fresh blood.

The intruder entered the room, and Wolf saw the familiar black hair and thick, stocky neck. The open door caught his eye, and the pant legs of the other man who stood guard. Wolf peered past his mother's dangling arm, and recognized the face of the stranger in the hallway. *Oh, God,* he moaned, disbelieving the man's identity, but unable to bring himself out of the nightmare.

Utterly terrified, he returned his focus to the murderer. The killer swirled around and stared at Wolf, his eyes glowing red and snapping with hatred.

Malone!

"Aaagh!" Wolf came awake with a horrendous explosion from his lungs. He sprang from the bed.

"Wolf!" Alanna jumped to her feet, clutching a corner of the sheet to her chest.

"Did you know it was your father who murdered my mother?" he bellowed as he yanked on his trousers and stuffed his feet into his boots.

In the silent seconds that they faced one another, she turned a sickly white, her eyes wide as an owl's. "I—"

"Goddamn it, you knew, didn't you?"

"Only recently. That's what—"

Her words slew him as if she'd plunged a knife through his heart. "Get out. Get the hell away from me."

"Dear God, Wolf. Please let me explain—" Alanna donned her robe and backed away.

"Explain? *Explain?* You should've done that a helluva long time ago." In that instant, all the horrible pain he'd locked inside himself exploded like a keg of dynamite set alight. He snatched his knife off the bedside table, let out an ugly roar, and attacked the bed as if it were every person who'd ever done him harm. Mindless with rage, he sliced through pillows, linens, and mattress. Feathers flew around the room amid a flood of cursing and Alanna's cries for help.

The door crashed open with a loud bang. Aiden rushed in with Mrs. Guthrie behind him.

"He knows!" Alanna cried. "He saw it all in a dream."

"Get her out of here," Wolf ordered between heaving breaths. "I don't want to see another Malone for as long as I live. I want Old Chinese."

Aiden grabbed Alanna by the arm and shoved her toward Mrs. Guthrie. "Take her away."

Old Chinese stepped through the door.

"You!" Wolf turned on him. "It was you outside my mother's door, you cowardly, murdering son of a bitch!"

Old Chinese stood stoic, unflinching. His obsidian eyes glittered bright at Wolf as though he could see right through him.

Wolf raised his knife.

Aiden stepped between the two. "Don't do something ye'll regret to yer death, Wolf. Ye don't know the truth of it all."

"Get out of my way." Wolf kicked at a small table and kept kicking until it splintered.

"He didn't do what ye're thinking. He's an honorable man. He was nae in cahoots with Malone, lad."

New fury caught hold of Wolf as a different kind of betrayal set in. "You know too, don't you?" His eyes flickered from Aiden to Old Chinese. Sweat trickled down the side of Wolf's face. His lungs burned and his breath came ragged in the silence. "Every goddamned one of you knew. Why the hell didn't anyone tell me? You *all knew* what I needed to find out."

Aiden stepped forward. "I know ye've been wronged, and I know ye've endured a world of suffering, but hurting him will nae bring yer mother back from the grave. She wouldna want that, and ye know it." Aiden's eyes held steady on Wolf's. "At least give yerself the grace to hear us out."

"Go on." Wolf drew in another heavy breath. His voice was flat, but his stance was still that of a ready warrior.

"Old Chinese didna go to yer house that night for a killing," Aiden said. "He went to try to prevent one."

"Well, he did a piss-poor job of it." Wolf swiped an arm over his face, his eyes fixed on Aiden's, but he was aware of everyone, including Alanna and Old Chinese. Especially those two. The liars.

His brain began to work again, and a layer of calculated ruthlessness kept him steady. "Come now, *Cousin* Aiden. You know full well Old Chinese is a trained master. I don't think he'd go somewhere with the intention of preventing a murder and then stand in the hallway jerking off while it took place."

Alanna's whimpers distracted him. He caught a glimpse of Mrs. Guthrie hovering over her.

With a sudden and terrible dawning, he realized he'd been the last to know. After all these years of wondering, it came to this—the only people he cared for knew the truth. A great, indefinable pain surged through his veins. His glance flickered to Old Chinese, to the women in the hallway, and then to Aiden. Betrayal, ultimate and complete, shattered the tender part of Wolf's heart—as well as his disciplined, reasoning mind. Cold, lethal hatred, a desire for the ultimate revenge, took charge once more.

"Alanna, get back in here," he bellowed. "I have something to say to you."

Mrs. Guthrie's panicked voice reached his ears and then silenced as Alanna walked into the room and crossed in front of Aiden, her head held high.

Currents of raw emotion flashed through Wolf like lightning through a midnight sky. "You knew damn well what you were doing, didn't you?" His gaze raked her body in loathing. "That's why you lied and said you'd taken precautions, isn't it?"

Her head barely shook back and forth in denial. "Please, Wolf. You . . . you're not being rational. I love you. I—"

"How could you do such a thing? How could you mix my mother's blood with that of her murderer in a child of mine, and then have the nerve to say you love me?" His eyes grazed her stomach. Bile filled his throat while a new kind of pain wrenched his heart.

Her body shuddered and her trembling fingers slid to her throat. "Oh, God. I didn't know until just before I sailed here." Tears filled her eyes. "I would never do anything to purposely hurt you, Wolf. I love you."

He could barely hear her for the rage pounding in his ears. "Don't you *ever* say those words to me again. Don't you even think them." He moved closer, until her heat permeated his skin.

Alanna stared mutely, tears cascading down her cheeks. Her hand slid to her belly.

"That's enough!" Aiden cut in and stepped forward.

Old Chinese grasped his arm and held him back. "It's me Wolf wants to destroy, not Alanna."

In her closeness, in the scent of her, Wolf faltered. Fresh pain washed through him. With vindictiveness, he fought its presence, or any tender feelings for her. "I should cut your heart out."

Her spine stiffened. "You just have."

"I said that's enough!" Aiden jerked away from Old Chinese's hold and dove toward Wolf, batting at the arm that held the knife. "Leave her be if you canna listen to reason. For God's sake, man!" Fire flew from Aiden's eyes as he faced Wolf. "It wasna yer mother Malone came to kill, you bloody fool. It was you!"

Saliva tinged the corners of Aiden's mouth. He punctuated the air with a finger pointed at Old Chinese. "And he was with Malone because he tried his damnedest to see that Malone didn't drag yer mother all over hell and back trying to find ye. He did not know you were hidden in the same room. He did not know how drunk Malone was, or that he'd go so far as to attack yer mother. The door was closed when Malone killed her, and he left with Old Chinese not knowing until all of Boston did."

Aiden stood aside and held Alanna by the arm, putting empty space between her and Wolf.

Old Chinese continued to stare unflinchingly into Wolf's eyes with a look that was both deep and mysterious. It was this regard that threw Wolf, for it seemed to be one of unconditional love.

"Look at him, Wolf." The pain in Aiden's voice was raw as he pleaded. "Don't think this man hasna suffered every day of his life for having missed yer hiding place. And don't think he hasn't cursed himself for missing Malone's drunkenness. That's what did it, Wolf. It was drink that sent him over the edge, because the man standing before ye already knew the intensity of Malone's hatred for ye."

"Why me?" Wolf asked, his emotions frozen.

Old Chinese moved a little closer. "Because he is not a Malone. He's a MacGillivray."

Wolf's shoulders jerked. He glanced from Old Chinese to Aiden and then to Alanna. Mrs. Guthrie was in the room, her back to the wall, her eyes closed, and hands clenched in prayer.

"Due to terrible rivalry between brothers, his family was banished to Ireland by Alexander, the chief, right before the Battle of Culloden. Malone's line would have become lairds after Alexander's demise, but they'd been ordered not to return to the Highlands to claim their due until the fourth generation—yours."

Wolf turned and stared at Alanna's blue eyes rimmed in black, so much like his own.

"That's right," Aiden said. "She's yer cousin, four times removed. Her father being yer third. Had she been a son, she would have had legal right to what is yers when yer grandfather passed. Nothing could ever have belonged to Malone under Alexander's terms, but it could have been Malone's through his son, or so he figured. He spent his life with one goal in mind—to win back his family name and place of honor in the Highlands. So when Alanna was born instead of a son, he went looking for ye."

Wolf recalled Malone's insistent words aboard ship— "I'm not Irish, I'm Scots-Irish." He could see his arrogant sneer as plain as if Malone stood before him. He shuddered.

"I know you're in pain, lad. It wouldn't be natural for ye not to be." Aiden's voice broke. "And it has to be even worse to know the truth of things, because it's not a stranger who has the ability to hurt ye worst. That terrible power is held only in the hands of those ye love."

Wolf tossed his knife aside. He stepped forward, back into Alanna's space, but his heart was a block of ice. "You shouldn't have kept this from me. Not for one minute."

"I was trying—"

He lifted his hand, silencing her. "I trusted you." He peered deep into her eyes and felt nothing but the chill running through his veins. "You were all that I honored in life, all that was best in my world, and you betrayed me."

He glanced around the room. "Go. All of you. I don't ever want to see your faces again."

Alanna walked past him, opened her trunk, and drew out a leather pouch. She handed it to Wolf. "I found these at Brookline, hidden beneath the scarves. You'll find the clippings that went missing from the library archives in here, and a small box. When I found them, I went directly to Old Chinese. He brought me to you. I have no excuse for not immediately telling you what I knew other than fear, and for that I apologize. But I swear, Wolf, I knew nothing of what my father . . . of . . . of the cause of your circumstances, before your seed was planted in me."

The isolated world Wolf had lived in most of his life closed around him once again. He stepped back from her. "Leave me."

For a long moment, Alanna's eyes searched his. And then she paled.

Old Chinese took her by the elbow and pulled her from the room. Aiden followed. Wolf turned and walked onto the balcony. He pulled the small box from the pouch, opened it, and picked up the garnet earring matching the one in his ear. "Sweet Jesus."

"Ar n-athair ata ar neamh: gu naoemchear d'ainm," Mrs. Guthrie chanted behind him. *"Thigeadh do rioghachd."*

A chill snaked along Wolf's spine.

"Deantar do thoil air an talamh, mar a nithear air neamh."

He turned. She stood with her back pressed tight to the wall, her eyes laced tightly shut. *"Tabhair dhuinn an ar fiachan, amuil mar a mhaitheas sinne d'ar luchd-fiach."*

He moved slowly forward, listening to her speak in Gaelic.

It was the Lord's Prayer.

And Wolf understood every word, for Mrs. Guthrie had uttered them constantly as she'd held him tight that wretched morning after his mother's death. *"Agus na leig am bueaireadh sinn."* Over and over, she'd prayed as she'd rocked him in the rocking chair and while Mr. Guthrie carried him rolled in a carpet to the garbage wagon. She'd still been praying when Wolf had been spirited away undetected.

"Ach saor sinn o olc," Wolf chanted along with her as he slowly moved to where she stood. *"Oir is leatsa an rioghachd agus an cumhachd agus a'ghoir gu siorruidh."*

Mrs. Guthrie opened her eyes.

"Amen," he whispered. "Now, go."

Chapter Twenty-Six

Alanna sat at one corner of the long table near a pot of tea, her eyes swollen from a night of weeping. Mrs. Guthrie sat beside her with bony fingers wrapped around a porcelain cup and with a mantle of reserve wrapped around much deeper things.

Wolf walked in. Alanna swallowed the lump in her throat. He looked worse than she felt. He walked past her and she caught a strong scent of whisky. "We need to talk, Wolf."

He paused. "I'll take complete financial responsibility for the child, but you need to leave here at once. Go back to Boston."

Good Lord! "What . . . what are you saying?"

He'd reached the door and still hadn't glanced her way. "There'll be a substantial trust set up for you to draw on. When the child is of age, he or she will have access as well."

This can't be—he can't mean what he's saying. "Look at me, Wolf. At least have enough courage to look me in the eye when you say such awful things."

He turned and regarded her, pain clearly visible on his countenance. "I told you," he said in a nasty tone. "I intend to take complete financial responsibility for the babe. But don't you, or anyone else, *ever* expect me to have to look at a child every day of my life and see the face of your murdering father while my mother lies in Dunlichity. Surely even you are wise enough to figure out that under the circumstances, it would be detrimental to have a father like me around."

"You have to let all that go, Wolf. For our child's sake— for everyone's sake." Her voice sounded as though it echoed from an empty tomb.

"I seem to recall aboard ship your father saying he enjoyed a cozy fire keeping him warm during the cold months." Contempt spilled into each of Wolf's carefully spaced words. "Do you have any inkling, Miss Malone, just how goddamn cold and wet the ground is in Dunlichity?"

"Oh, God." Fear and anger knotted Alanna's insides. This couldn't be happening.

The muscles along Wolf's jaw twitched and his eyes narrowed in lethal penetration. "Think of the child, and its well-being. Go back to Boston, where you'll both live comfortably with Old Chinese to protect you. Purchase a home of your choice and I'll pay for it so you won't have to live with your murdering father. I'm offering you and your child a lifetime of financial care. How many men would see to the needs of the grandchild of his mother's murderer?"

She'd had enough. She stood. "You . . . you . . . I need you and your money about as much as I need my father and his. The two of you . . ." Her sputtering came to an abrupt halt. Her spine straightened and she hauled in a breath. "I understand your feelings with regard to this child I carry, Wolf. I will return to Boston, and I pray that he or she carries not a hint of your looks. That way I won't have to spend each day looking at my son or daughter and be reminded of its arrogant and self-absorbed father who spent his entire life serving no one but himself."

Wolf walked out.

"Leave him be, and he'll come around," Mrs. Guthrie

said. "He's a good man, and good men take a wee bit longer to feel and say things."

"And why is that?" Alanna's chin tilted upward in defiance.

"Because it's coming from his heart," Mrs. Guthrie answered. "He thinks he's been betrayed by the lot of us and that can add length to the time of things."

The shot rang out in Wolf's nightmare at the same time the scissors Malone had used to cut his mother's hair fell out of the man's grotesquely misshapen hand and tumbled down a hole in his dream, turning end over end into the black void of eternity.

The scream, long and horrifying, woke him. But the shriek was not in the dream after all. With a shake of his head to ward off the thickness in his whisky-laden brain, Wolf sat up in bed, his knife at the ready. He shook his head again, wondering if he'd heard right.

The noise on the stairs, like that in his horrific dream of childhood, was real and sent a chill along his flesh. He scrambled from the bed, slid into his trousers and boots, and struck out for the door, grabbing the brass-handled pistol that had been his father's. He was sober now, the liquor completely drained from him. The blood-curdling scream belonged to Alanna, he was sure of it.

He pulled open the door and a cousin, Bean MacGillivray, stood before him, the butt of his pistol raised to pound on the wooden panel.

"Are ye all right, mon!" he boomed as Wolf shot into the corridor. "Bloody Christ, what the hell was that?"

"Alanna," Wolf growled, starting for an open bedroom door when William, another MacGillivray cousin, stepped out.

"Aiden's nae here."

Wolf's gaze flicked back and forth to both ends of the corridor. "Where's Alanna's room?"

Bean pointed to a door three down from Aiden's and

sprinted toward it. Yet another guard stepped from The Mor's room, armed to the hilt.

William emerged from Old Chinese's quarters. "His bed's nae been slept in."

In unison, Wolf and Bean kicked in Alanna's locked door. Old Chinese lay on the floor in a pool of blood. Bear was at his side, his head on the man's chest, his white fur crimson-soaked. The dog's huge black eyes, filled with a look more heart-wrenching than any words, looked mournfully up at Wolf.

"Mother of God!" Wolf pushed past the two men and nearly gagged at seeing the hole in Old Chinese's stomach. "Someone get a blanket." Wolf scanned the room. "Where's Alanna?"

At William's approach, the dog gave a warning growl.

"It's all right, Bear, it's all right." Wolf lifted the blood-soaked dog from Old Chinese.

Bean grabbed a blanket off Alanna's bed and handed it to Wolf. He stanched the blood pumping from Old Chinese's lower gut.

William moved to stand beside Wolf. "What's this all aboot? We've nae left our stations, and Alanna's nowhere to be found. Nor is Aiden. They couldn't have got past us."

A flicker of hope lit Wolf's insides. He remembered the secret passageways Aiden had shown him. Of course, Aiden had her in one of them. Or someone did.

Wolf jerked his head toward William. "Send someone to fetch Mrs. Guthrie."

"I'm here." Mrs. Guthrie stepped into the room.

"He's still breathing." Bewilderment clouded William's face. "And his heart's pumping steady. How can that be?"

"*Ibuki.*" After he uttered this word, which meant holding energy steady while mortally wounded, Old Chinese's eye-lids opened. "They took Alanna." His eyelids fluttered shut.

"Who took her?" Wolf shoved his hand through his hair. "Damn it, he's passed out."

Mrs. Guthrie stepped forward. "I've sent for the MacBeths of Aberchalder, who are physicians. Place the man on Alanna's bed and I'll see to him until then. Get yerselves where yer needing to be."

The three men lifted Old Chinese onto the mattress. Wolf glanced around the room and turned to Mrs. Guthrie. "You've been with The Mor for years. Do you know if there's a secret passageway in here and how to open it?"

"Aye." She moved to the fireplace and pushed on a stone. A panel slid open.

The three men rushed forward. A sheen of lit lanterns, left by whoever had made their exit, flickered yellow against dark walls, casting living shadows as the men worked their way silently through the twisted corridors.

A soft moan caught their ears. In front of them lay Aiden, in a heap alongside Alanna's cape.

"Aiden!" Wolf swept the cape from the dirt floor near the man's head. Her *sgian dubh* lay underneath, its blade tipped red with blood. "One of you see to him, the other come with me." He started down the corridor.

"Stop," Aiden called out. "Ye'll only make things worse if ye go looking for her. 'Twas the Farquhars of Cromarty who have her."

William swore.

Wolf sprinted back to Aiden, who was on his feet and rubbing at the bloody knot on his head. "They'll hide her in the Highlands and ye'll not find her. Ye may be a fine tracker in America, Wolf, but here in the Highlands, ye'd never out- smart a man who knows his own land blindfolded. Those neighboring lads aren't verra bright, and they'd do anything for coin, but it wasn't they who shot Old Chinese and hit me. It was the Boston man who lagged behind them."

A chill ran through Wolf. "What American?"

"'Twas one she spat on and called Jonathan," Aiden said. "Bloodied his leg with her *sgian dubh* when he said he was under her father's orders to return her to Boston."

Wolf kicked at the stone wall. "I'll kill the son of a bitch!"

William rested a hand on Wolf's shoulder. "Ye need to see to Old Chinese. Yer kin will find Miss Malone."

Wolf glanced at Aiden, who held a cloth to his head.

"We take care of our own," Bean said quietly. "The man needs ye."

Wolf slipped back into the room where Old Chinese lay silent on the bed, his face looking pink and serene as though he merely napped. When Wolf approached, the old man opened his eyes.

"*Ibuki*?" Wolf asked. *Please don't tell me you're dying.*

"Yes," Old Chinese answered. "I have taught you much, Wolf of the Highlands. And in the next few days I shall teach you how to leave this world with honor."

Wolf buried his face in his hands.

Farquhar of Cromarty reached down in the flickering candlelight and gently untied the scarf from around Alanna's mouth along with the ropes around her wrists and ankles that secured her to the ship's bunk. She rubbed her wrists, swung her legs over the side, and sneered at Jonathan, who stood in the shadows just outside the doorway. "Why don't you learn to use that pistol of yours? You could have injured someone back there."

"Beggin' yer pardon," Farquhar said. "Mr. Hemenway was well behind us. We didna know he brandished a firearm until we heard the shots. He's assured us they were aimed over Aiden's head to keep him at bay."

She regarded one brother and then the other. "If you had seen fit to merely knock on my door instead of barging in like a pack of barbarians, you would have seen my trunks already packed. I was returning to Boston on my own, you stupid fools."

Farquhar chewed on his lower lip. "We shouldna have taken Hemenway's coin or run off with ye. Is it yer wish to return to Boston or should we see ye safely back to Dunmaglass?"

She rubbed at her chafed wrists. "Since the ship is at the ready, I won't have to secure another. I'll need to send a note back to Old Chinese." She'd be damned if she'd write one to Wolf.

"I'll send my youngest brother back to Dunmaglass with yer message and word that you're being well cared for. If ye've a mind to, Miss Malone, could ye send along a proper note to The Mor, as well? Tell him you're in good health and it's yer desire to return to Boston with us acting as yer proper escorts."

Farquhar reached out in a vain attempt to smooth Alanna's shorn locks. She pulled away and his hand knocked the bruise on her cheek. She hissed.

"Beg yer pardon. Mr. Hemenway shouldna have done that to ye," he said softly. "'Twas nae a thing to do to any woman, let alone one he's to wed. I'm thinking we made the right choice in deciding to set sail with ye to America, since yer father made a bad choice in the man he sent to fetch ye."

Farquhar turned to the open door and called out. "Did my brother Donald talk with ye, Mr. Hemenway, about how ye treat the gentler sex?"

Donald shoved Jonathan into the shadowy cabin, his knuckles as raw as the side of Hemenway's face. "Aye," he said. "Mr. Hemenway is now of the understandin' that he'll nae touch the lass again; nor will he set foot in this cabin alone with her."

Farquhar handed a pencil and piece of paper to Alanna. "If things don't sit right with you in Boston, after we've had our chance to explain to yer father how things went bad, we'll get ye back to Dunmaglass."

With a heavy heart and confused mind, Alanna started writing.

Chapter Twenty-Seven

Three days later

Watching Old Chinese die inch by inch was hard enough on Wolf, but to leave his bedside before he took his last breath? "For God's sake, don't ask me to leave."

"Please, do as I wish," Old Chinese barely whispered. "It is time for me to remove myself from the clutches of what you call reality. You have served me well these past few days, but I must be alone when my ancestors come for me, and the time draws near. Until then, wait by the pond."

Christ. "How will I know when . . . when it's over?"

"My spirit will come to you in a way that you will know me. And then you may serve me one last time."

Wolf shuddered at the idea of what he'd agreed to do. He struggled to find words. "I . . . I don't want to lose you."

Old Chinese stretched out his hand to Wolf. He covered it with his own trembling fingers and squeezed—the squeeze wrenching his heart. A small groan tore loose from his throat, his mind and emotions saturated. He'd only this day learned Old Chinese had been the one who'd transported his mother's body to Scotland. A very small gesture, Old

Chinese had called it, for what he believed was his own grievous failure to save her.

"I failed you." His dark eyes never left Wolf's. "But I suppose every parent feels that way in the core of their being."

"You thought of me as your child?"

Old Chinese managed a small nod. "For years. Though I didn't save your mother, I could help keep you alive. So when Malone sent me looking for you, I searched relentlessly. I located you with the Guthries, but told Malone nothing. Instead, I pushed you deeper into the countryside. Then I presented myself to your father. We devised a plan to ship you to England and from there to India, where your father had gone to live three years after yer mum died. But before your arrival in Liverpool, word came that your father had died in Bombay. We couldn't risk sending you to the Highlands with Malone's spies everywhere, so you were sent to boarding school instead."

Wolf rubbed at his temples, his head throbbing at the news. "You actually knew me and my situation all those years?"

"Every move you made. It was my attempt to redeem my own soul. I lost track of you a few times." Even close to death, Old Chinese managed to look like he could get up and walk away at any moment. "Once, when you ran away from school. That wasn't in my well-laid plans. Your ending up in St. Joseph threw me. It took awhile to track you down."

"How did you find me?"

"I didn't." An enigmatic smile touched Old Chinese's mouth. "Winston did."

Wolf came out of the chair. "Winston was familiar with me, as well?"

The old man nodded. "Locating you was Winston's graduation exercise. It only took him four months."

A vague memory of an elusive watcher, one Wolf could

never nail down, crept from the recesses of his mind. So that was Winston. "Any other times?"

"When you left St. Joseph for San Francisco. But then, to my surprise, Alanna took me to you. That night in the Tremont House Hotel in Boston, if you recall."

Wolf nodded. How could he ever forget?

"Quite a surprise for me when Alanna returned from San Francisco with details of the man she'd fallen in love with while aboard ship. To think I might have lost track of you for good and here my little Alanna took me right to you. When I stepped into your hotel room and faced the man I saw last as a boy, that was one of the finest nights of my life."

Old Chinese paused to take in a couple of labored breaths before continuing. "You must forgive Alanna's father for what he did."

Wolf cursed. "My mother is in a grave, and I'm supposed to forgive her killer and dance a jig? I've listened to you and respected your teachings, but this one doesn't work for me."

"You do not have to like Malone, or be around him. But if you forgive him, he loses his hold on you."

"And never seek retribution for my mother's death? Just let him walk free?"

Old Chinese looked deep into Wolf's eyes. "He'll never be free. Cain was not imprisoned or executed for the death of Abel. He was condemned to walk endlessly over the earth, shunned and despised. It is time to release all the anger and hatred inside you and move on with your life."

Old Chinese waited quietly until Wolf returned to the bedside. "Try always to love, Wolf. And love Alanna without expecting anything in return. Love because you live, and you'll catch glimpses of yourself in ways you never expected."

"Did you want Alanna and me together?"

Old Chinese nodded. "Odd as it seems after what took place between your parents. I would like to see you together again." He paused and gathered a breath. "Only this time I'll see it from the other side."

Wolf's heart clenched in his chest. He struggled to find the right words. "It wouldn't be fair to the child to have a father who constantly sees the reflection of a murderer in his or her eyes. What pain would I cause the child? Alanna would end up hating me. So would her child." Dear God, *his child.* "I can't give either one what they need."

Old Chinese raised his feeble hand in protest. "You *can.* You must." He began to cough. "Help me to sit."

Wolf eased pillows behind Old Chinese. God, Wolf didn't know if he could take much more of this. "You speak of love between Alanna and me, but have you ever loved a woman?"

"Yes." Old Chinese opened his eyes. "Maire Macintosh and I loved one another."

"Winston's mother?"

"The very one," Old Chinese answered.

"Why did it come to an end?"

"We had to put Winston first. We feared Malone would harm the boy if he found out about us. He is jealous and selfish. Then, after Alanna came along . . ." Old Chinese's voice drifted off, leaving the thought to finish in Wolf's mind.

"Then surely you understand my concerns about being around a child who carries Malone's blood. And after everything that's happened, I don't want any part of love."

"Yes, you do," Old Chinese answered. "You're simply afraid. Afraid of being vulnerable to Alanna again, and to a child who will love you unconditionally. What if you gave your heart to them and they left you for one reason or another? Betrayal is your greatest fear. You feel betrayed by everyone, even by your mother for having died and left you. And you already feel betrayed by your child because he or she carries the blood of your mother's murderer and there isn't anything you can do about it."

Wolf's thoughts shot to the night his mother died and

merged with memories of Malone aboard ship in all his finery, and of Alanna standing before Wolf here in Scotland— lying. His despondency grew even grimmer.

"Don't, Wolf—" Old Chinese tried to speak, but he paused, unable to complete his sentence. *Go,* he mouthed, dismissing Wolf from the room.

Jesus, he was about to lose Old Chinese. "What were you going to say?" As if the question would prolong a life.

Go, Old Chinese mouthed again.

Wolf kissed the back of Old Chinese's hand, placed it gently on the bed, and stood. "Good-bye, sir." His voice broke. "I'm going to miss the hell out of you." He walked to the doorway, paused, and turned, waiting for the faint chance Old Chinese might finish what he'd been about to say. But Old Chinese only grew still and his lips stopped moving.

Wolf raised his hands in a prayerful position and bowed his head. He turned and walked out of the room, down the stairs, and out to the pond.

At his approach, the pair of swans glided away from him and to the covering of reeds at the pond's edge. Graceful and elegant, they disappeared from sight, the weeds joining together in their wake, a nut-brown curtain silently drawn.

Wolf sat with his back against a tree near the water and contemplated his final meeting with Old Chinese. No wonder he'd not defended his actions to Wolf regarding the night of the murder. No wonder he'd let Aiden do the defending—Old Chinese loved Wolf like a son. Something caught in his throat, and he swallowed hard. He reached into his jacket and retrieved the dark green box Alanna had given him along with the note she'd sent to his grandfather.

Moment by moment, the pain of waiting for Old Chinese to die found new places to lance his heart. He rested his head against the tree's trunk and struggled for breath. "Ah, hell." A glance at the second-story window to the room where Old

Chinese lay caused another pain to shoot through his chest. Damn, he hated not being there, but he'd honor Old Chinese's wishes no matter how much he himself suffered.

He opened the box and picked up the earring that matched the one he wore. He turned it until light from the gray sky glanced off its crimson face. With a resigned sigh, he set it back onto the black velvet and picked up the brooch made of human hair—from his mother's shorn locks.

A sting of rage hit his gut. An urge to throw the box and its contents into the pond rushed through him. But he couldn't move. It was as though something unearthly held him paralyzed against the tree. The same mysterious *something* that prevented him from taking even one step back to Old Chinese. In quiet desperation, he waited.

Suddenly, something split Wolf's thinking. A chill ran the length of his spine. It was as though the wind swirling around him echoed the voice of Old Chinese, speaking the very words the man had been trying to say before he'd dismissed him. "While it is a hardened heart that throws it all away, it is a soft heart that simply lets it all go."

Wolf's head snapped to the window. At that moment, he knew without doubt that for Old Chinese, human life had come to an end.

Wolf struggled with Old Chinese's linen-clad body, trying to get it atop the stacked wood he'd built as a funeral pyre.

Aiden Fraser stepped from the shadows. "How long are ye going to try to do things all on yer own?"

Wolf paused in his efforts long enough to look steadily at Aiden and speak through gritted teeth. "I told Old Chinese I'd do exactly as he wished." He wiped at his sweaty brow.

Aiden groaned. "Ye can't keep to yerself with this, lad. How long are ye going to try to live life alone afore ye figure out it does nae work that way? Ye've got to let someone into yer life sooner or later or you might as well climb on up there with the old man."

Wolf turned his face from Aiden, his insides splitting in two, his breath laboring.

"Don't be standing here all alone when ye strike the match, fer Christ Almighty."

A gush of air left Wolf's lungs, followed by a low moan. He turned his face to the sky and shut his eyes tight, felt his face turn into a grimace as he fought tears. A choked noise left his lips.

Aiden jumped forward. Wordlessly, and with tears streaking Wolf's face, they eased Old Chinese's body atop the pyre.

"Burning is a hellish way to go." Wolf wiped moisture and grime from his face with his shirtsleeve and sniffed. "Doesn't sit right with me, somehow."

"Then rest for a while 'til you're ready to carry out the man's wishes," Aiden said softly and rolled an uncut log over to where Wolf stood. They sat in the rawness of the cold air until dark. "This cremation, lad, 'tis not only his kind who wishes a suchlike funeral. 'Tis said the firing of a body leaves no bad spirits behind to wander the earth or cause trouble to the living. Feel proud of what ye can do fer yer friend."

Wolf lit the match.

A brittle snap of wood, as it caught and burst into flame, cut a pain so deep, it went clear to the marrow. The flames leapt to fire the night sky.

Silently, Wolf's fellow clansmen gathered around him, their arms held tight to their loved ones. Wolf stood with them as the flames arced high against the night sky, on a ridge not far from Dunmaglass, one that could be seen from The Mor's window. Wolf's family sent up a prayer for Old Chinese—and for Wolf.

Chapter Twenty-Eight

July

The Mor passed away one month after Old Chinese.

Bells tolled his death at the top of each hour for three days and nights. Young boys, paid sixpence apiece, fanned out far and wide to spread the word of the laird's passing. Clansmen took turns sitting day and night with the corpse in lyke wake, comforted by their *spirit refreshments*—good Scotch whisky.

The funeral for The Mor was a weeklong celebration of his life, filled with food, drink, and music. Wolf recalled little of it. His mind was too blurred by the amount of whisky it took to keep from feeling much of anything. Sleep—rare and in snatches—wreaked havoc on his numbness. Slumber was where he couldn't escape Alanna's soulful eyes staring at him in wretched sadness.

When the celebrating was over, Wolf withdrew from everyone. Even Aiden's visits grew infrequent as Wolf's self-imposed isolation stretched from days into weeks.

One lonely night after another, Wolf woke in the outline of his own sweat, his hand grasping empty air in search of his beloved. He began to exist on the castle's supply of whisky. Steadily, he grew numb to the world around him until the only sensation he experienced was that of the amber liquid swirling about in his mouth before it ran a harsh course down his throat.

At dusk, Wolf wandered into the kitchen, bleary-eyed and unshaven. Not bothering to sit, he picked up a knife, sliced at a leg of lamb, and popped the pieces into his mouth.

Mrs. Guthrie closed the pages of her book and eyed him with a stern, tight-lipped regard. "Would ye mind putting on a pot of tea?"

Wolf looked around for the teakettle. "I give up. Where the hell is it?"

"'Tis the ninth of October. Ye've lived here alone since yer grandfather passed away and ye don't even know where the bloody teakettle is?" She walked across the room, opened a cupboard, retrieved the kettle, and set it on the counter with a bang. "Ye can fill it. That is, if ye've any idea where the water is."

Wolf shot her a dangerous look.

"The day 'tis near gone and yer just now showing yer face," she grumbled. "And ye look as though ye haven't slept at all. Not that it's anything new."

He wasn't about to admit she was right. "Have you seen what it looks like out there?" He jerked his head toward the window and the wild weather hammering at the glass. "Why bother?"

"Because ye've a destiny, that's why. And 'tis nae a destiny of drinking yerself blind and not showing yerself until right before nightfall."

"Enough," Wolf growled.

"No," she snapped. "'Tis time ye took responsibility for yer position. I willna run this place any longer for ye, nor will Aiden act as guardian for the lairdship. Ye are not missing from the land, a youth, or infirm, so he doesna have the right."

Wolf slammed the kettle on the stove. "I'm not staying."

"Och, been hearing that from ye for about as long as I care to." She waved him away with her hand. "If ye were truly of a mind to go, ye'd be gone already. Yer playing insignificant doesna serve ye well. And shrinking from life and yer duties with drink doesn't make me proud of ye, either."

A rapping at the door behind Wolf's shoulder sounded like the back end of an ax being used.

"Who in God's name is that?" He opened the door with a wild jerk.

A tiny, gray-haired woman held an old cane in the air with one gnarled hand and held a basket of wet eggs in the other. A faded brown shawl over her head and shoulders acted as feeble protection against the rain. He stepped aside for her to enter, but she stood in place and shoved the ragged basket at him.

"Me roof's beggin' a fixin', sir. 'Tis taken to leakin'."

He glanced at the mound of eggs, some cracked, all unclean. "So what do these have to do with a leaky roof?"

In the dim light, Wolf caught her look of confusion. "Why they be fer ye, Laird. Fer . . . fer fixin' me roof."

Wolf heaved a sigh, grabbed the basket, and plopped the flimsy thing on the edge of the table, where it teetered. Mrs. Guthrie dashed to catch it before it fell. One egg crashed to the floor with a slimy splash.

The old lady stared at the egg. Her frail fingers trembled as she clutched the tattered shawl tighter and backed off into the cold night. "I'll be goin', then."

Wolf's heart constricted in his chest. "Damn it." He stepped into the rain after her, but when he reached her, she paused and turned at the shoulder, her eyes glistening with pride. "One day ye'll be auld and alone and nae able to see to things on yer own, sir. Mayhaps ye'll only have eggs to give, as well. What then?" She turned and disappeared into the night.

"That's enough!" Mrs. Guthrie screeched when Wolf

returned. "I'll take no more of yer rudeness and self-pity. 'Tis a pathetic thing yer doing to yerself, Wolf."

She stood and headed for the door. "Yer just like yer father, with all yer drinking and such. And the way ye deserted that poor girl. Left her as miserable as yer mother. I wash my hands of ye."

Mrs. Guthrie's words cracked through Wolf's head like a rifle shot. "What do you mean, my mother was miserable?"

She stepped back into the room. "The way ye drink, 'tis like yer father. And it'll get ye in as much trouble, as well."

"My father drank?"

"Aye, yer father drank! Enough for an entire Highland platoon. Just like ye be doing. 'Tis what caused all the trouble in the first place. 'Tis the cause of why yer mother sat in this very kitchen crying and carrying on like Alanna Malone did. They sounded just alike, they did."

Stunned, Wolf leaned against the kitchen counter for support. "What . . . what the hell are you saying?"

"Stop yer cursing in front of me," she snapped. "I'll hear no more of it!" .

Wolf made his way to a chair. Emotion, for the first time in weeks, washed through him. He looked around.

"Don't be lookin' for another drink to put in yer belly. It sickens me."

"My mother cried a great deal?" He pressed his fingers to his pounding temples.

"Do ye think she wanted to leave her people? People who were a comfortable and happy lot?" Mrs. Guthrie's eyes filled with tears. "Do ye think she wanted to hide ye away in America for them to never see yer wee face again?"

Something sacred crumbled inside Wolf. He shook his head to clear it. His father was a drunk? His mother miserable?

"Ye had no right to force the sins of Alanna's father on

her." Mrs. Guthrie reached for her cape. "Not when yer own father was about as guilty as he in the tragedy."

"Hold on." Wolf clutched Mrs. Guthrie by the shoulders. He set her in a chair and dragged another in front of her. Blood ran hot through his veins once again. "Tell me."

Mrs. Guthrie's shoulders slumped. "Yer mother didna stop her weeping 'til we were well out in the Atlantic. That was when she pulled herself together and became yer sweet mother once again. And by the way, I didna want to leave my home much, neither. But we went along, Mr. Guthrie and I, God rest his soul, to see to yer needs."

"What happened?" Wolf closed his eyes to the pain he saw in hers.

"Ye had a brother."

Wolf's eyes flew open and his heart hammered in his chest. "A brother?"

"He died of the grippe, and Mr. Malone, living in Ireland, heard of it. 'Twas when he came to the Highlands with his wife and son."

"His son?" The boy in the picture? He'd forgotten.

Mrs. Guthrie nodded. "His family was banished to Ireland by citation of the clan chief generations back and ordered not to return until yer generation. If not for that, he believed his son would've been in line for the lairdship all along instead of ye."

She sniffed and straightened her back. "When yer brother died, that placed Malcolm Malone, who was but a month older than ye, in line after yer father. Malone petitioned Lord Lyon, a close friend of yer father's, to restore his status, but the petition was refused. And so, he went back to Ireland, more bitter than ever."

Wolf opened his mouth to speak, but Mrs. Guthrie shook her head. "Shortly thereafter, Lord Lyon died, and a new heraldic authority was appointed, one unknown to yer father. Malone returned to Scotland, petitioned the new King of

Arms, and settled in Inverness to hover like a hawk. It set yer
father to drinking heavy, it did. He went to Inverness filled
with whisky and threats. Malone, drunk as well, went looking for yer father, but he had his son in tow." She shook her
head back and forth. "Only three years old and frightened
out of his wits, poor thing.

"The innkeeper put them in the street, tired of their quar-
relling and drunkenness. Yer father climbed into his buggy
cursing and threatening Malone with the horsewhip. When
Malone tried to grab the whip, the boy set to wailin' and the
horses took a fright. They reared and the lad went under
them. When it was over, Malone's only child was gone—
crushed beneath the great thundering hooves of those two
huge beasts."

"Oh, God." Wolf bent forward, elbows on knees and
hands clasped. "That's why Malone came looking for me the
night after Alanna was born—a daughter, not the son he
needed."

"Aye," she said softly. "He vowed to yer father back in
Scotland that he would find ye and throw ye under a team of
horses—an eye for an eye, he called it. Someone he'd hired
told him of yer whereabouts not a week before yer mum's
murder."

"That would've been Grimes." Wolf sat back. "If I look
so much like my father, why didn't Malone recognize me
when we traveled together aboard ship?"

"Likely because yer father was heavy bearded and
Malone had never laid eyes on him afore that night. Dark
as it was, and drunk as Malone was, 'tis easy to see how he'd
miss ye."

Wolf swiped his hand over his eyes and heaved a sigh.
"Don't you see why it wouldn't have worked with Alanna
and me?"

"I told ye, don't be accusing her of her father's sins." Mrs.
Guthrie stood, gathered her cape, and settled it over her

shoulders. "I'm tired of finding ye every morning asleep in the chair before a cold fire with an empty whisky bottle and no one but that dog lying at yer feet."

"You can't go out in this storm."

"Weil, it's a sight better out there than being in here with the likes of ye."

Late October

Wolf sat before the fire with Bear curled on the hearth, his head on his paws and brown eyes staring sadly at his master. "Don't tell me you've had enough of me, too?"

The dog's ears pitched forward.

"Humph." Wolf propped his booted feet atop an old wooden chest, hunkered down in the leather chair, and took another pull off the whisky bottle. He should have left Dunmaglass long ago. He sure as hell didn't want the burden of a lairdship. But no matter how many times he packed his saddlebags, he couldn't bring himself to ride off. Besides, where the devil would he go? St. Joseph was a distant memory, and he wasn't about to set foot in Boston again.

Alanna.

Could she be having the baby about now?

What if it was happening this very day?

Christ, he wished the pain would subside. The thought of going after her played about the periphery of his mind at all times, shot to the surface when he wasn't careful. She hated him, had said so in the note. Well, he didn't blame her—he didn't much like himself either. And for the love of God, he might look in his own child's eyes and see Malone. No, Wolf couldn't take that. What if he ended up resenting the child? He or she was better off without him.

Wolf's heart was sliced open again, spilled new blood. And here he'd thought it was empty. He took another slug of whisky and set the bottle on the table beside him. Firelight wavered through the glass and gave the contents a warm, honeyed glow. Whether it was the firelight or the amount of drink, he was having trouble focusing on it.

An echo of heavy footsteps rang out.

Who the hell could that be at this hour?

Silence.

The heavy cadence of boot heels against hard stone resumed, grew louder until the sound resonated directly in front of him and halted.

Wolf looked up into the blazing eyes of Trevor Andrews. "What the hell are you doing here?" Damn, he could barely get the words past his numb lips.

Trevor leaned over, gave Bear a pat on the head and glanced around at his surroundings. *"Merde.* Here you mocked me for having grown up on a plantation with a few emancipated slaves, and look at your roots. *Tsk. Tsk."*

"You look like hell. Who sent you?"

"No one. I came for a certain horse you never bothered to return, and to give you some information." Trevor made his way to the fireplace, picked up an andiron, and poked around at the burning log. "Do you ever wonder whatever became of Alanna? Or to the child she carried?"

A sharp pain lanced Wolf's heart. He refused to ask the obvious. "Is that what you rode all this way to say to me? Best get back on your horse."

"I spent months in hell when I thought Celine was dead," Trevor continued as if Wolf hadn't said a word. "And I never had a clue she carried my child since we both thought she was barren. Had I any inkling she might be alive or that there was a child, I would've turned Hades upside down to find her."

When Wolf said nothing, Trevor threw the andiron down with a clang against the stone. Setting his elbow on the mantel, he pinched the bridge of his nose.

Wolf curled his lip sarcastically. "Alanna will do all right. She's not out in some snow-covered teepee like Celine was. Her father agreed to deed the farm to her when the child is six months old."

Trevor turned and cocked a brow. "How do you know that?"

"She wrote back after I sent her the news about Old Chinese. In between the nasty things she called me, she said she didn't need my offer to take care of her and the child— not in such nice words, I might add."

Trevor shoved a hand through his hair and heaved an audible breath. "And how much shallow thinking and hard whisky did it take to convince yourself of that manure? How do you know she's even alive? Or that the child is alive?"

Despair cut into Wolf's gut. The thought had never crossed his mind. "Alanna is the healthiest woman I've ever met."

Despite his declaration of her well-being, a suffocating sensation tightened around Wolf's neck. He stared at the fire for a long while. The sounds of the ticking clock and the crackling fire filled the room. "Alanna didn't have any desire for me to see the child or her again. She made it clear in the note."

"Your senses are besotted along with your pickled brain." Trevor's voice turned hard with disgust. "Alanna's fine— physically fine, that is. And you have a healthy baby daughter. Born the sixth of September, with no thanks to you."

A daughter? A fist punched Wolf's gut. "Alanna wasn't due until now."

"Tell that to the babe."

Wolf gripped the arms of the chair. "How do you know?"

"Thompson takes the Boston–Liverpool run now. He showed up with the news. Soon as I heard, I rode here hell-bent for leather. Jonathan Hemenway still wants to marry her, by the way."

A new jolt ran up Wolf's spine, but he said nothing.

"Hemenway doesn't really want her, but he's in too thick with her father to refuse. Her mother's going in a different direction. She's trying to convince Alanna it would be in the child's best interest to pass it off as belonging to an unmarried female servant."

"Like Winston," Wolf muttered. "Alanna would never do that. She'll end up at the farm. I know her."

"Things change when a woman bears a child, Wolf. Even as independent as Alanna was on her own, what recourse does she have with the burden of a child? And what if Malone doesn't follow through on his agreement to deed her the farm?"

"I told her I would see to the child's financial well-being. Alanna's as well—"

"Then do it!" Trevor roared. His back to Wolf, he flattened his hands against the stones and leaned his forehead against its coolness. "They cut Alanna's hair off, Wolf."

Jeezus! Wolf swiped his hand over his face. "Shut the hell up."

"Not once, but twice," Trevor continued as though Wolf hadn't spoken. "The first time it was Jonathan when he got her aboard ship here in Scotland. The second time was only a couple of months ago, when her father had had enough of Alanna constantly declaring her love for you."

Another jolt shot through Wolf. "That's enough, goddamn it!"

Trevor tossed another log on the fire, picked up the andiron and poked around. "Maire says Alanna takes great relish in daily taunting her mother and father with that bit of news. No matter what her mother's caustic remarks are in return, Alanna seems to repeat the words like a spiritual mantra."

Throat parched, Wolf picked up the whisky bottle.

Trevor replaced the andiron and stood quietly before the fire, his back to Wolf. "What the devil are you going to do when that child of yours begins to haunt your dreams? When you begin to wonder how she's turned out, what she looks like? Or how about when she's old enough to catch Malone's eye? Do you really want that twisted man alone—"

That did it. Wolf sprang from the chair, slammed into the small of Trevor's back with his head, and butted him up against the craggy stone.

"Oof," Trevor grunted.

Wolf shoved Trevor harder against the stone, grinding his temple and cheek into the rough granite surface. "You bastard." Wolf staggered forward for another blow to Trevor's kidneys. "You baited me."

Trevor spun around and with a furious slam of his fist, sent Wolf crashing backward. He fell over the chair and landed behind it. He clutched the chair's back and managed to pull himself up. Blood ran from his nose and split lip, his eye already swelling shut. He steadied himself against the chair, swiped his sleeve across his face and, with his head bent, charged forward.

Trevor, the side of his face scraped raw and bloody, stood with fists in front of him.

Wolf halted. They stood staring at one another, both streaming scarlet. Wolf touched his cut lip. "Who the hell do you think you are, waltzing in here like God Almighty out to save my soul?"

Disbelief crept over Trevor's face. "You actually think that? *Merde*, Wolf. When you and I met, I was in no better shape than you are right now. The only difference between you and me is when I hired you to help me find Celine, I'd already decided to chase after a woman who thought she didn't want me. Now, I suggest you make the same decision and pack your bags."

"Alanna wouldn't have me." Suddenly, his words sounded false, trite even. The past was the past, damn it. He couldn't change it, but he sure as hell didn't have to let it destroy his future. Trevor had risked his life going after Celine. What the hell did Wolf have to lose by going after Alanna? And his daughter? His heart swelled. He had a daughter, and no matter whom she resembled, she would always be a part of him—and Alanna. Christ, he wanted to be in their lives. The intensity of his realization stopped his breath.

A half grin tipped Trevor's mouth. "Bring her back here, Wolf. Take on your family . . . all of it." He swept his arms wide. "Would you look at this, *mon frère*? A sixteenth-century castle big enough to house the whole of New Orleans, and land filled with sheep and leasehold tenants as far as the eye can see."

"Yeah? Well, the tenants are so well off, they pay in eggs or a leg of lamb, *mon sewer*."

Trevor picked up the bottle of whisky, and gingerly tested his jaw. "I think it best to use this on our wounds." He slapped an arm around Wolf's shoulder and headed toward the stairs. "Come. I could use a warm bed and a bath, and you look like you could use about a week's worth of sleep."

Wolf shrugged Trevor's arm off his shoulder and tested his split lip with his finger. "If that's an invitation, *mon sewer*, I agree to getting some sleep—in my own bed. The bath you can damn well take alone."

Trevor chuckled. "We'll leave in the morning. Thompson can deliver you to Boston. We've a ship waiting."

"Can't go right now," Wolf mumbled and plopped down on the top stair of the landing. "Something I have to do first."

Trevor sat beside him. "What?"

"I need to fix an old lady's leaky roof." Wolf leaned back on the landing and stared at the ceiling overhead. It spun around like a slow-moving top. He closed one eye to see if that stopped the movement. It didn't. "She's already paid me in eggs. Celine doing all right?"

Trevor balanced his elbows on his knees and rested his

chin on his fists. "Healthy and content. So are Brandon and the twins."

Wolf couldn't manage to keep his eyes open and his tongue working properly. "I believe I drank a helluva lot of whisky tonight."

Trevor groaned. "If you could manage to make it up the stairs before you fall asleep, I won't have to drag you to bed. You're no pullet, you know."

"Are you forgetting I had to haul your ass away from those braves wanting a piece of your scalp? Damn tough trying to hide your sorry-looking butt." A riot of emotion bloomed in his chest. "I have a daughter. I like females. Did you know that?"

"I suspected as much."

"They don't irritate me the way men can. Did Thompson ever say what her name was?"

"Glenda Mary," Trevor answered quietly.

Wolf smiled, but at the mention of his mother's name, a single tear slid from beneath his closed lids. "I'm going after them, Trevor—my baby girl and Alanna."

Chapter Twenty-Nine

Wolf sat back in his chair, his legs thrust out in front of him, and sipped a cup of strong coffee.

Aiden reached inside his jacket and withdrew a narrow green box edged in gold. "I have something for ye."

He opened the box and slid it across the table to Wolf. A necklace of small uniform garnet beads winked at him. At its middle hung a crimson stone encased in gold, matching the ear bob Wolf wore.

Wolf lifted the necklace from its velvet moorings, removed the earring from his ear, and set them side by side. They matched perfectly. He looked at Aiden curiously.

"'Tis yers now that ye'll be going after Alanna. They belong to every chief's wife, to be passed down the line. The Mor gave the earrings to yer mother just before she sailed away. 'Twas his way of givin' her hope that she'd return one day. He gave me the necklace fer safekeeping. Good that he did, since his belongings were ransacked before Malone left Scotland."

Wolf thought of the other earring in the box upstairs and of Malone's squat hand searching under his mother's bed so many years ago. "Why would Malone take such a risk to get his hands on this when he can well afford better?" Wolf flicked the necklace with his finger.

Aiden's eyes grew wide and he swept the garnet beads from Wolf's reach. "Dinna be so heavy-handed. They're near sacred in these parts."

"Sorry," Wolf muttered.

"'Twas Mary, Queen of Scots, who gave these to Duncan MacGillivray, seventh chief of Dunmaglass, when she rode through here on her way to Inverness. The laird hid her here. When she left, she gave him the jewels in gratitude."

Wolf picked up the ear bob. "You mean I've worn this to hell and back for the past twenty-six years and the damn thing belonged to Mary, Queen of Scots?"

Aiden nodded.

"Someone should've kicked my ass."

"I would've liked to have done that a few times."

Wolf grunted. "What of Mrs. Malone's part in all this? Obviously she knew a helluva lot, but she doesn't seem to have a killing personality."

"No," Aiden answered. "But she did have a newborn. And she was verra young. Most likely scared to death being all alone in a new country. Hard to ken what her thinking was, but I have a feelin' she was a bit like a child who closes her eyes and thinks no one can see her—hoped if she ignored what her husband did to yer mother, it would all go away."

"But why bother making a mourning brooch out of my mother's hair and then stuff it into the bottom of a trunk? Christ, that's morose."

"Mayhap she was in a bit of sorrow over the whole mess. After all, she had the thing tucked into the same box along with her dead son's brooch. Hard to understand what sort of life Malone bullied her into that made her the way she is. I met her when they were in the Highlands. She doesna have more than a wee bit o' brain inside her head."

"It's about the size of her integrity." Wolf replaced the ear bob in his lobe. "Keep the necklace until Alanna returns. It's the way my mother would've wanted it."

Aiden nodded and withdrew the box from the table.

Wolf stood. "Before I leave, I need to tell you that I can't give you any guarantee that I'll stay forever."

"'Tis enough that ye take yer rightful place," Aiden answered. "Yer great-grandfather, William, didna spend much time at Dunmaglass. Spent a good bit of it in America."

"Yep." Wolf leaned back in his chair. "Until they kicked his ass out of the country."

"Ha! The MacGillivrays have always had a few unpopular political opinions. But he made a verra good amount of money before his departure. What's left is for ye to oversee."

"And if I don't stay, will you help me out?" Wolf queried.

"I don't expect ye to live all the while in Dunmaglass—it's too isolated for ye. Even Alexander spent most of his time at the house near Inverness. But let me ask ye this. Have ye the heart to run off and leave yer people entirely? For the rest of yer remaining days?"

Wolf studied Aiden's face. A grin tilted one corner of his mouth. "Go to hell." He lifted a hand to stop Aiden's retort. "I'll quit swearing when Alanna takes me back."

A door slammed and Wolf's cousin William bounded into the room. "Are ye makin' plans to leave so soon?"

"You've been talking to Trevor," Wolf replied.

"Would ye be needin' some accompaniment, then?"

"Might be."

A broad grin settled across William's mouth. "Would ye care for a few cousins to attend ye? We've some to spare."

Wolf nodded. "I could use a few. I have a point to make."

* * *

Boston—December 12

While Thompson held the darkened ship steady in the harbor, Wolf and Winston slipped into the Malone mansion through the cellar window. From above, the soft lilt of a pianoforte sounded through the floorboards.

Winston took the lead up the basement stairs, and headed for the servants' stairway and to the second-floor bedrooms. Wolf nodded to a warrior hidden in the shadows. He was dressed in black. Only a small slit in the cloth around his eyes revealed any flesh. At every turn, Wolf spied his fellow students lurking in the darkness.

Winston pointed toward a door indicating the nursery. Wolf's heartbeat quickened. The music Alanna played wafted upward and struck a deep longing in his chest. Silently, Winston opened the door and slipped inside. Wolf followed. He paused, surprised to see Maire Macintosh standing beside the crib. He looked to Winston, and then to Maire. Had she known he was coming?

Of course, Winston would have alerted her.

She lifted the candle from the stand and held it over the crib.

Wolf moved forward, his heart pounding erratically. He bent over the crib and his breath left his lungs with a *whoosh*. At the sound, the babe's huge, angel eyes opened. She looked directly into his without as much as a flutter of her lashes. Dark curls framed her round face. She turned her head and looked at Maire for a long moment, then grinned a toothless grin and gave an enthusiastic kick.

Maire pointed to Wolf. "'Tis yer father."

Glenda Mary's gaze followed Maire's hand to the tip of its finger resting at the center of Wolf's chest. She blinked again, and stared into Wolf's eyes for a brief moment.

And then she smiled.

His heart rocked sideways. He reached out and wiped the clear drool wetting his daughter's lips. The touch sent a sobering shock through his body. "She's beautiful." He stared in awestruck silence until Winston tapped him on the shoulder.

"Take me with ye." Maire's hushed voice was steady and calm but her gaze was fraught with desperation.

He glanced to Winston. A beseeching flame was lit in his gaze, as well. Wolf nodded to Maire. "You have five minutes to get your things."

"I already have them. Alanna and Glenda's, too." Maire wrapped the baby in several lightweight woolen blankets. "Take yer daughter. I'll help Winston with her things."

As Wolf reached in and lifted Glenda from the crib, he caught the warmth of her, the sweet, powdery scent. It was as though an incandescent light suddenly lit the room—for him alone. The shadows across his heart fell away.

Winston opened the door. A cadre of warriors escorted the small group down the front stairs leading to the main rooms.

Wolf stood with his daughter in his arms, watching Alanna's stiff back as she sat at the piano, playing for her parents, who sat off to the left of the wide arched doorway, not seeing him. It took all he had to stand there—to will his body to steady itself.

Thoughts of Wolf cleaved a path through Alanna's mind. She faltered and sent a sour note into the room. She closed her eyes to collect herself. How long—how long before her memories of him stopped cutting her to the bone?

Recollections swirled in her mind's eye and coalesced with images of little Glenda. She sighed and picked up where she'd gone off. Eyes still closed, she relaxed into the music until she lost herself within the soothing rhythm. She played to the memory of Wolf—as she always did—it was the only way to remain sane.

The air shifted around her.

Alanna *felt* them first.

The music halted, her last note hanging in midair. She opened her eyes. Familiar black forms eased silently into the room. *Students from the farm! Why?* Then her senses shifted to a powerful force vibrating directly behind her.

She gasped. With her lips parted to catch her breath, she turned around.

Wolf stepped into the room.

As did other warriors behind him.

Her mother's eyes grew wide and a small gasp escaped her lips. Her father stilled at the press of a sharp blade against his throat, held by a black-gloved hand. Students silently poured in from every opening in the room, like dark quicksilver.

Wolf stood silently before Alanna. The light from the chandelier reflected off his golden hair flowing free. The red MacGillivray plaid and white ermine sporran he wore showed beneath the corners of a white blanket hanging off the bundle in his arms. A small hand appeared from the depths of the coverings and grasped at the small golden hoop shining at Wolf's earlobe.

It was his eyes, so very blue and compelling, and glittering with unearthly intensity, that did it. Her own filled to overflowing, spinning a veil. She gripped the edge of the piano bench for support.

Winston opened the front door. Six men dressed in kilts—the MacGillivray plaid—filed into the room and stood behind Wolf. He moved forward and knelt on one knee in front of Alanna. Speechless, she caught his scent and the room spun.

He settled their child on Alanna's lap between them, and

covering her hand with his, he brought both to the child's breast. He leaned close, his voice hushed but clearly audible to all in the room. "I had another recurring dream, Alanna. This one was of a bagpiper below my window wailing a funereal *pibroch*. In the nightmare, I heard wagon wheels creaking as they carried you away. I heard your terrible screams, but no matter where I searched I could not find you."

Anguish filled his eyes. "When I woke up, I drank. Rarely was there a time I was sober." His blue eyes blazed into hers. "But no matter how much whisky I downed, no matter what I did, the nightmares refused to die. I roved constantly in my dreams, searching, asking anyone I met along the way if they knew of you. In time, I realized that I was the one who was lost. I wandered endlessly, hunting for my place in the world. But one night I found it. In my dream, I was dead. I read my own gravestone. I woke up calling out for you."

Pain gripped Alanna's chest. Tears spilled down her cheeks, and the lip she'd been biting was released with a soft moan.

Wolf loosened his hand from hers and brushed her cheek. He ran his fingers through her shorn locks. His hand slipped behind her neck, and with the same tenderness of his first touch, he pulled her forward and swept his lips to hers with a whisper of a kiss.

"I love you, Alanna. And I need you. I need your forgiveness." He looked down at the child between them and then back up. "And I need our daughter. Already I've missed far too much. I want to see her take her first steps. I want to see the first snowflakes on her lashes. I want to walk with her, to pick stars from the skies for her. I want to give her—and you, the best."

He separated the covers, his face lighting spontaneously

at the sight of the child who lay asleep once again. "Isn't she beautiful?" His voice choked. "She looks just like you."

"Yes," Alanna said, her words quivering. "But since she has your mouth, then she has your mother's as well." At the sound of his soft sob, she closed her eyes from her own pain.

He pressed his lips to her temple. "If you turn me away, from you and from our daughter, I'm sure to perish."

She couldn't find her voice again. God, where was it?

Confusion swept through his gaze. "I've been a fool. Can you forgive me?"

She shook her head. It was she who needed his forgiveness.

He paled.

"No . . . no!" she cried. "I mean yes, but I . . . I mean no, you have no reason to be forgiven."

Color crept back into his face.

"What I mean is . . . is can you forgive me for those horrid letters I wrote you?"

He heaved a slow breath. "God, Alanna, I deserved every word."

She shook her head and wiped at a tear. "You were in pain, and I only added to it. I have regretted those awful words every waking moment." She pressed her forehead to his. "We MacGillivrays are a stubborn lot, aren't we?"

He kissed her hard.

"Oh, Wolf, I have never stopped loving you. Take me away from here."

Wolf drew his head back. Alanna shuddered at the deep pain in his eyes. He lifted his hands to her earlobes and gently removed the emerald studs she wore. Leaning back, he opened the sporran hanging at his waist, dropped in the studs and took out the pair of garnet earrings.

The wheeze of Malone's breath filled the room, but Wolf

ignored him as he attached the ear bobs to Alanna's lobes. "There's a necklace that goes with them, Alanna. It's back at Dunmaglass, waiting for the clan chief's wife. I'd like you to wear it when I take you to the Bolshoi next year."

"Oh, God, the Bolshoi—you remembered." She collapsed against Wolf's shoulder amid a rush of tears. He gathered their babe in his arms, helped Alanna to her feet, and escorted her to the hallway.

Her jaw dropped at the sight of Maire Macintosh, her overcoat on and a shawl in hand as Wolf placed Glenda Mary in her arms. Alanna's gaze flickered from the woman she detested to Wolf. Fury and confusion descended upon her.

"I'll not leave her behind, Alanna. There's much you still don't know and there's no time to explain. I'm not asking you to like Maire, just tolerate her until we get back to Dunmaglass, then the two of you can go your separate ways. I won't see another family split up if I can help it."

Alanna's gaze flashed from Maire to Winston, "Oh!" she blurted out when she realized Wolf's meaning. She threw her arms around Winston. "Oh, you're coming along! My dear, dear brother."

Winston slid an arm around her.

"Wait here," Wolf said. "I have some business with your father."

He turned and made his way back into the parlor. He stood in front of Malone, who sat at one end of the chesterfield opposite his wife, the warrior still holding a knife at his neck. Malone's eyes were filled with panic, and he'd shoved his hands between his legs like a naughty boy awaiting punishment.

"You didn't have to kill my mother," Wolf said quietly. "If you had left things alone, your daughter would have had the position you coveted anyway. And her daughter after that. Now my mother's blood and her murderer's are mixed in my little girl and on into eternity. The only thing to stop the mingling of our families will be someone like yourself killing off the lineage."

Malone's entire body began to tremble.

Wolf regarded the pathetic creature before him. The words of Old Chinese echoed through his head: *If you want to truly destroy an enemy, you do not kill him. Instead, you remove his power. You demean him. You destroy all that he stands for within himself.*

A sudden truth washed over Wolf like a fresh rain— Malone would never get past his anger and pride. He was stuck. He was a man of ambition living an empty life in a city filled with ambition. Nothing Malone could do, no amount of money he earned, would ever be enough to grant him a place here.

Killing Malone would only sweep Wolf back to despair. Old Chinese was right—Cain slaying Abel. Malone was a man destined to walk the earth shunned by those who had found peace.

"I'm taking your daughter and mine with me," Wolf said softly. "If you ever so much as *think* of coming after any of us, I will have these gentlemen find you. And they will see to your death. A slow, long, painful death. Do I make myself clear?"

Malone carefully nodded as the knife pressed deeper into his neck.

"Oh, yes. There are a couple of things I'm going to have to ask of you before I leave."

Malone only nodded again.

"I'm going to ask you to be a cooperative gentleman with your new employers."

Malone's brow furrowed.

"As we speak, all the brothels you own are under new management. They're in good hands with the MacGillivrays at the helm."

At Malone's small grunt, Wolf continued. "They'll make certain all the young women who wish to return to their homelands do so, and with enough funding to see to their needs. Any children sired by you or Jonathan will, of course, receive a lifelong trust. I'm sure you will be more than comfortable with that arrangement?"

Malone nodded again.

"There are a few of the MacGillivrays who would like to try their lot in America, but they don't care much for the idea of running brothels. I'm sure you'll trust their expertise in deciding which of your fine establishments can be turned into hotels and which will be sold off as empty buildings, stripped of their former occupants."

A gurgle emanated from Malone's throat.

"Oh, yes," Wolf said. "It seems Jonathan Hemenway has curiously found passage to Australia. He carries some rather unique papers out of England that indicate he is to remain there, so I'm afraid you'll have to give up your diamond mines in Africa altogether. Do I make myself clear?"

The knife pressing deeper at Malone's throat caused another quick nod of his head. A bead of blood trickled into his collar.

"One last thing, Mr. Malone. These gentlemen are going to be watching you. For the rest of your life." Wolf swept his hand around the room at the band of black-clad men. "Should you ever place another female in harm's way, these men will escort you to a certain physician who will . . . how shall we say it . . . perform a *little* operation on you."

Malone's eyes grew wide as he realized Wolf's intent. "Nnn . . . no . . . not to worry." He tried to press into the sofa, away from Wolf, but the knife at his neck held him firmly in place.

Wolf reached into his sporran. "Here, Mrs. Malone. I believe this belongs to you." He dropped the brooch made of little Malcolm Malone's hair into her hand. "Thank you for looking after my mother's things all these years." He turned and walked away, to his daughter and to Alanna.

Mrs. Malone's footsteps followed behind him. "A word, if you please, Mr. MacGillivray."

He tucked Glenda Mary in his arms and turned, surprised at her soft-spoken words.

Mrs. Malone stood before him, her head held proudly.

"What is it?"

"Take me with you."

Small gasps exploded around the room.

"Christ Almighty! You can't be serious."

Despite her brave front, her lower lip quivered. "Didn't I hear you tell my daughter you would never split up a family if you had the power to prevent it?" Her chin rose higher. "Well, Mr. MacGillivray, you now have that terrible power."

Wolf looked to Alanna and then to Winston. Their eyes were devoid of emotion, but their bodies grew rigid. He turned back to Mrs. Malone and studied her for a long moment, and then slowly, he shook his head. "I'm afraid that won't be possible, Mrs. Malone. You see, while Maire Macintosh desperately wished to mother her son, she was prevented from doing so by both you and your husband. But you—you had every opportunity to take an interest in your daughter, yet you never did. Don't you think it's a little too late to start now?"

A myriad of emotions raced through Mrs. Malone's countenance that no amount of biting her lower lip could suppress. Suddenly, her eyes shimmered. And then tears spilled down her cheeks, dripped off her chin, and splotched her deplorable pink and brown striped gown. "You are quite right, sir. I have been a wretched mother. Truth be told, I've been a spineless creature, doing as I was told for so long that I lost sight of who I was. I won't go into particulars right now, but suffice it to say that by the time I was Alanna's age, I feared to be or do anything other than what was forced upon me."

Wolf stood before her, his mind a sudden blur. He took in a fortifying breath to clear his head. "I fully intend to protect my wife and daughter, Mrs. Malone. They've been in harm's way these past months."

Abject fear replaced all other emotions running through her eyes. "Take me with you. Let me prove to you that I am more like my daughter than the misfit I have become."

His chest tightened. "Don't do this, Mrs. Malone."

"Please," she whispered, her chin quivering. "Give me six months to prove myself to Alanna and you. If I fail, send me back."

When he didn't respond, her gaze dropped to his daughter, asleep in his arms. "If you refuse, how will you ever know? What will you tell your child?"

He fought an urge to pull little Glenda tighter to him, and glanced at Alanna, at Winston, and finally, at Winston's mother. A subtle shift in the demeanor of each gave Wolf pause. Suddenly, life with Old Chinese invaded his thoughts. What would the master of all masters do? A gentle force moved through him, as if urging him on. And then he knew what to do. He turned back to Mrs. Malone. "Come along then. You have five minutes in which to gather your things."

"That won't be necessary. I don't wish to take a speck of what is in this house. Mr. Malone will see to funding me. He'd better." It was obvious she knew something they did not.

Wolf moved to where Alanna stood and whispered in her ear. "Aren't we in for one hell of an interesting life?"

Epilogue

The faint chime of a hall clock signaled the midnight hour. Wolf rolled onto his side and tucked Alanna closer to him. His senses stirred at the heat of her breath falling rhythmically against his chest.

My wife.

He turned the thought over and over in his mind. There were days he still wondered if it was all a dream.

Alanna stirred. She flipped onto her back and nudged her naked hip against his. Her breathing fell back into a steady rhythm. He stroked her hair—haloed it more than touched it. His love for her ached through his bones.

His hand traced the swell of her hip, and his body quickened.

"Mmm," she moaned sleepily and slid her hand over his growing ardor. "Lazy love, Wolf. Make soft, lazy love to me."

He brushed her hair behind her ear and whispered, "You're sure?"

Her response was a soft moan and a light squeeze around his erection.

Gently, so as not to jar her senses, he eased her legs apart. He caught his breath at her leg gliding around him. With the prowess of a jungle cat, he poised himself over her while he eased himself into her inner core. He shuddered as erotic fingers of pleasure ran over him.

He moved within her, slowly and tenderly. Her breath caught in a little moan. Tilting her pelvis, she murmured, "I love you so much, Wolf,"

At her response, he moved in deep, unhurried thrusts. The act of making love to her while she half-slumbered cast him into his own private, erotic world. The onset of her climax, accompanied by her soft whimpers, was heady perfume. But the added anticipation of the morrow, when she'd cast him a sultry smile and thank him for what she liked to call "lazy love," sent him over the edge with a shudder.

He rolled back onto his side and with Alanna held snugly in his arms, he lay awake until nearly dawn, thinking. He heard the stirrings of his daughter. Her clothing would be soaked through. If he didn't get to her soon, she'd fuss and wake Alanna. Sliding from the bed, he donned his robe and made his way to the small nursery adjacent to the bedchamber.

"Shh, shh," he whispered. Quickly, he cleaned his daughter with a soft cloth dipped in witch hazel, then changed her clothing and wrapped her in a fresh blanket. Gathering her in his arms, he sat in the rocker, and slipped his little finger into her mouth. She sucked furiously.

"Sweet heaven, you take my breath away." He brushed a kiss across her forehead. The suckling ceased and she stilled. Her mouth and tongue flattened against his finger and he knew she grinned up at him in the darkness.

"Don't you giggle," he whispered. But she did. "Shush, you'll wake your mum." She cooed softly before she went back to her sucking. Wolf leaned his head against the chair back and settled in to watch the coming dawn. A tree thumped against the nursery window. Glenda Mary's suckling grew weak and then ceased as she fell back asleep.

Strange how the sound of a tree thumping against the house used to frighten him while it soothed her. He returned Glenda to her crib and slipped out of the nursery, into his clothes and out to greet the dawn with Old Chinese.

He stuffed his hands into his pockets for warmth and leaned against the tree near the sacred funeral site, and settled in to await the sunrise.

What a day yesterday had been. His birthday. By God, he finally knew when it was, and he had damn well celebrated it. Kinsmen had gathered from a hundred miles around while pipers wailed and torches flamed. The Thompsons were there with their daughters, as were Trevor and Celine, who each held a twin, asleep through it all, while their older son, Brandon, ran circles around the pipers. Little Mary Thompson, Jamie MacGillivray, and the two dogs, Bear and Julia, chased after them in hot pursuit.

Winston held Glenda Mary, old enough to look around wide-eyed while chewing on the brim of the bonnet she'd snatched from her head. Edna Fraser clutched Winston's other arm and stared up at him in adoration.

Mrs. Malone, dressed in gaudy attire, had bustled about in nervous anticipation of the May fifteenth wedding. Except for her awful taste in clothing, which remained unchanged, she was indeed a different woman since departing Boston. She wore her dear Malcolm's brooch pinned close to her heart at all times, and her efforts to build a familial relationship with her daughter and Wolf impressed the hell out of him. She'd even begun helping Alanna and Maire Macintosh deliver baskets to the needy. Recently, he'd heard her light laughter float in from another room, something he'd never known before. Her only complaint since arriving in the Highlands had been some mutterings under her breath about screeching bagpipes rattling her nerves.

A wicked grin touched Wolf's mouth. He'd have to see to it that pipers played more often.

The wind curled around him. The pain of missing Old Chinese mixed with love for his wife and daughter caught him off guard. He closed his eyes, and hot tears tipped his lashes. Sometimes love cut so deep it caused terrible pain, or crossed paths with the joy of his present experiences.

"So this is love." He wiped his sleeve across one corner of his eye.

He felt Alanna before he saw her. Glancing up, he caught the swirl of a red cape in the breeze.

"Listening to the wind again?" She slipped into the curve of his arm and leaned her head against his chest. "What was it you heard this time?"

"That I impregnated you while you slept."

The quick smile that touched her lips told him memories of their sensuous night were not his alone. She pulled his face to hers and kissed him. "Thank you for last night, dear husband. I don't think I shall ever get tired of loving you."

He pressed his lips atop her head. "I want another child, but I'm afraid you might be harmed and it pains me. You understand, don't you? I love you so much it wounds at times."

She nodded and tightened her hold around his waist. "They say when you touch the face of God through those you love, the joy of it is so great, it is filled with equal pain."

"It's not 'they' who said it," Wolf responded. "It was Old Chinese."

The wind kicked up just then, and swept around them in small whirls—whispering secrets to them.

ACKNOWLEDGMENTS

It's amazing the amount of research that can go into a historical romance novel in order to make it right. Even after a great deal of research, a writer can end up with only one chapter, or even one paragraph pertaining to the subject. With so much of the story surrounding Alanna and Wolf taking place on an 1850s clipper, I spent weeks researching life aboard those vessels until I felt as though I had sailed on the ship myself. Researching Boston in the 1800s took another huge chunk of time out of my life. As for the McGillivray clan, well, I'm a part of it, so that wasn't so hard. However, I did use literary license in creating a few characters, such as Wolf's grandfather and cousins. Any errors in getting things right are strictly mine.

Thanks to the Lalalas, the Dashing Duchesses, and to my wonderful RWA® Hearts Through History critique partners. You were great catching my silly errors and making suggestions, but most of all, Wendy, Anne, Tess, Averil, Renee, Barbara, Joan, and Sam, your encouragement fueled the flames of my desire to get this story completed.

To my Beta readers, Nancy Linehan, Jennifer Arp and Maxim LeFleur. Your sharp eyes and excellent input helped make this a better story. And Max, I love that an intelligent young man enjoyed the story and thought other men should read it as well.

To Jill Marsal of the Marsal Lyon Literary Agency who works diligently on my behalf: I have such great respect for you.

To my very special editor Alicia Condon, and to the rest of the wonderful crew at Kensington Publishing: You are some mighty fine people who believed in this series (and in me) enough to give it your all—thanking you is not nearly enough.

Read on for a sample of *Celine*,

the first in Kathleen Bittner Roth's

When Hearts Dare series,

available now.

Steam swirled around Celine, the tension in her muscles slipping away while Marie scrubbed her skin until it glistened. Sometimes being pampered felt simply grand.

"What a beautiful day, Marie. Open the doors to the gallery so we can get more of the scent of roses from the garden instead of Zola's cooking, will you please?"

Marie flung the French doors wide. A balmy breeze floated in, rustling the lace curtains hanging at the doors' sides until they floated like the lacy wings of a butterfly. The heady fragrance of roses wafted in and mixed with the mélange of robust smells drifting in from the cookhouse.

"I love this time of year, don't you? The spring flowers are in bloom. Everything looks so clean and fresh, and with nights still cool enough to curl up in front of a cozy fire. I'm so glad to be alive. How different things are from a year ago." Celine hummed to herself.

Marie pulled a chair behind the tub and brushed Celine's thick tresses. "Your hair looked half dead those first few months with us. Like a string mop dipped in mud."

"That's because I *was* half dead."

"Now the color reminds me of rich coffee. And so shiny.

Like it's been shot through with gold. Lovely to look at. Same as you, *mam'selle*." Marie ceased her chatter and continued to brush in slow, even strokes.

Celine slipped deeper into the tub and closed her eyes, immersed in the busy sounds and smells of plantation life. A sharp clang of three bells jolted her out of her reverie. They sounded again, a signal that the captain of a sternwheeler had stopped to unload passengers.

Marie jumped. "Lordy, three bells, not two—passengers, not goods. Don't tell me Mischie Trevor got here so soon?"

The steady pounding of feet down the hallway caught both women's attention. "Trevor's home!" Lindsey shouted with a quick rap on the door. The sound of his footsteps disappeared down the stairs along with his whoops and hollers.

Celine sat up, her heart pounding. "I thought you said he wasn't due until the last steamboat?"

Marie leapt to her feet and waved the brush about as she paced. "Oh, Miss Celine, how can I ever manage to get you dressed and your hair done up before he gets to the house?"

"For heaven's sake, such a state you're working yourself into. Settle down and hand me a towel." Celine stood amidst a cascade of water, wrapped the towel around herself, and stepped from the tub. "I have no intention of greeting your *Mischie Trevor* with the others. Introductions can be made over . . ." She gave a flip of her hand. "Over his favorite gumbo and jambalaya."

She dried herself, and then held her new lavender-sprigged muslin dress to her body. Relieved wasn't an adequate word to describe what it felt like to shed the oppressive black she'd worn for the past year. "What do you think?"

Marie stood at one corner of the bed, fidgeting and watching Celine twirl naked around the room.

She ignored the maid and picked up a purple sash and matching kid slippers. "Perfect. Help me into everything, and you can be off. No need to bother with my hair until evening."

Chemise and corset in hand, Marie frowned. "You'd best not be running around here nekkid and with the balcony doors open now that Mischie Trevor's arrived."

"This corner of the house is private," Celine said while Marie helped her into her clothing. "He'd have no need to wander around the gallery outside my door, would he? Besides, as you said, *he doan bother no woman what doan want no botherin' wif.*"

Marie laughed at Celine's exaggerated impression of her and slipped into Louisiana Cajun. "Yessah, but Mischie Trevor? Well, he's got him a way what makes the ladies *want* to be bothered wif, beggin' your pardon." She gave a small curtsy, giggled, and hurried off.

Celine made her way over to the cheval mirror and scrutinized her appearance. Satisfied, she patted a light fragrance of lily of the valley behind her ears and at the hollow of her neck. Then she slipped onto the gallery and headed toward the front of the mansion in hopes of surreptitiously observing Trevor's arrival.

She made her way to the front of the gallery and stood, hidden behind one of the ponderous Doric columns surrounding the two-story mansion. The open carriage ready to transport Trevor stood some two hundred yards away in front of *La Belle Créole*, the queen of the Mississippi.

The sight of the regal two-deck paddleboat gliding past Carlton Oaks during its regular runs between New Orleans and Baton Rouge never failed to stir Celine. What wasn't decorated with ornate iron scrollwork gleamed with fresh white paint. Her elegant twin stacks rose high in the air, billowing thick, white steam into the afternoon sky, her paddles at the stern churning the dark waters around her into white froth. Fashionably turned-out passengers lined the upper deck, hoping to catch sight of the parade of ostentatious plantations up and down the river.

A man Celine assumed to be Trevor strolled down the gangplank and climbed into the carriage. She couldn't quite tell from this distance, but he appeared tall, like his father and brothers, but with dark hair like his sister, whose excited chatter from below gained cadence.

The gangplank behind him disappeared into the boat. A tender closed the gate and with three clangs of the bell, the paddles reversed, waters churned, and the sternwheeler floated gracefully upriver.

The carriage slowly approached, looming larger as the driver made his way along the shaded drive. Majestic oaks lined both sides of the narrow road, their boughs forming a vaulted corridor leading to the mansion. Celine backed away from the rail, hoping the colorful Brasilia vines clinging to the railing and column she stood behind hid the lavender of her wide skirt. Blasted hoops.

Lindsey scrambled down a tree, and ran and skipped behind the carriage, calling excited greetings. Trevor turned, situating himself with his back to the house and toward his brother. Lindsey picked up his pace.

The carriage drew closer, and Trevor turned back to the small crowd of family and servants gathered in front of the grand plantation house. Celine caught a faltering breath. Good Lord! If that wasn't the most attractive man she had ever seen.

The driver pulled to a stop in front of the gathering. Trevor swung one long, muscular leg down from the carriage and twisted to reach for his valise. The muscles in his wide shoulders rippled beneath his dark blue broadcloth jacket. In one swift motion, he lifted the bag, sprang from the carriage, and set the baggage to the ground. He ran his hand down one thigh, smoothing his tight fawn-colored breeches tucked into shiny black boots that rose to his knees.

Celine's gaze roved the length of his body in hypnotized

fascination. She stepped closer to the edge of the balcony for a better view of this enigma, who now leaned casually against the carriage as if he'd leisurely strolled in. His eyes crinkled at the corners when he smiled, and his full mouth displayed a set of even white teeth against golden skin. Dark eyes flashed merriment.

Lindsey reached his brother first. Trevor swung him easily in the air. He set the boy down and tousled his hair. Michel, the second oldest son, and Justin, gathered around Trevor. Finally Felicité, his sister, waiting on the sidelines, could stand still no longer. She pushed through the men and threw her arms around her brother.

"*Je t'aime, je t'aime,*" she cried, smothering her brother with affectionate kisses. Her dark curls bounced gaily about a petite and lovely face. "I missed you so much, *mon frère.*"

An easy grin settled about Trevor's startlingly handsome face as he held court with the family. He and Felicité shared similar features, both of them bearing a striking resemblance to the painting of their beautiful French mother hanging in the parlor.

Suddenly confused, Celine leaned into the pillar and pressed her hot cheek against the cool column. He wasn't anything like she had imagined. He was tall and wide in the shoulders like Justin, but any resemblance ended there. He had neither the Andrews hawk nose of his father and brothers, nor the hard edge about him she had anticipated. Oh, she'd expected him to be handsome enough—the men in the family were—but she'd thought he would mirror those wealthy dandies she used to sidestep at the parties she'd attended before her marriage. No matter how suave they appeared, something usually lurked beneath their façades that repelled her. She'd been curious as to why the other young ladies failed to notice, until she figured out why—

they didn't want to, not where wealth was concerned. Trevor's demeanor held not a speck of the deceitful dandy.

Felicité stood on tiptoe, one arm hooked in Trevor's, and whispered something in his ear. He chuckled deeply, lifted her at the waist, and twirled her around in circles. Her dress danced about her ankles, the hems of her petticoats fluttering.

"Put me down!" Felicité squealed merrily, not meaning a word. Trevor laughed and tossed his head back. His gaze caught Celine's. He ceased swinging his sister in midair and set her down gently, never once taking his eyes off Celine. His lips parted and he stood as if transfixed.

Her breath caught in her throat. A vague fire smoldered in her belly. What a sensual man. He carried an aura of personal magnetism so powerful, a sensation close to fright swept through her. She stood still and aloof, masking her emotions. His intense gaze seemed almost a physical touch. She held her head at a proud, haughty angle, not flinching from his bold scrutiny.

In seconds, Trevor regained his cool, casual air. A lusty grin caught at the corners of his mouth, and fire danced in his eyes as he bent ever so slightly at the waist, tipped an imaginary hat, and strode casually into the house.

Damnation! Celine hurried along the gallery back to her room.

Slamming the French doors behind her, she kicked off her slippers in a fury, sending one crashing against the door across the room, the other falling squarely in the fireplace. She sat on the cushions in the window seat, still in a frazzle over being caught spying. Her face heated at the embarrassing thought. She wrapped her arms around her legs, set her chin to knees, and stared blankly out the window, her emotions in a whirl.

Being caught lurking on the gallery wasn't all that bothered her.

Puzzlement washed through her. Why be so upset because a man returned home? An aqueous haze clouded her vision. She swiped at one corner of her eye. How in heaven's name could there be any tears left? Hadn't she cried them all out two weeks ago over Stephen's grave? Here she thought she'd healed in mind and body, but she'd only managed to fool herself into thinking so.

It suddenly dawned on her that in the year she'd lived with the Andrews family, she'd never stepped off the land but to visit the cemetery. Life at bucolic Carlton Oaks was busy, but predictable as the setting sun. And safe. Had this predictability given her a false sense of how to face the world again once she ventured beyond the plantation's borders? So, she wasn't angry at Trevor's return after all. She was frightened of venturing forward in life; that's what all the unwanted emotion was about.